Cathy Hopkins

Mates, Dates

Strictly Gorgeous

PICCADILLY PRESS • LONDON

This edition first published in Great Britain in 2010
by Piccadilly Press Ltd,
5 Castle Road, London NW1 8PR
www.piccadillypress.co.uk

Text copyright © Cathy Hopkins 2010

Previously published seperately as:
Mates, Dates and Chocolate Cheats © Cathy Hopkins, 2005
Mates, Dates and Diamond Destiny © Cathy Hopkins, 2005
Mates, Dates and Sizzling Summers © Cathy Hopkins, 2006

A catalogue record for this book is available from
the British Library.

ISBN: 978 1 84812 079 2

Printed in the UK by CPI Bookmarque, Croydon, CR0 4TD

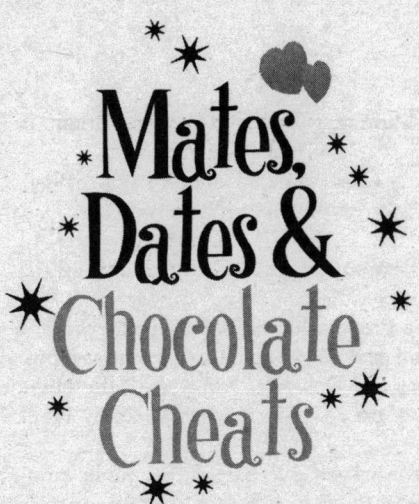

Mates, Dates & Chocolate Cheats

Cathy Hopkins

*Mates, Dates & Chocolate Cheats

PICCADILLY PRESS • LONDON

This book is dedicated to anyone who has ever tried to lose weight or isn't happy with their shape. OK. So that's just about everyone then. Thanks as always to Brenda Gardner, Jon Appleton, Melissa Patey and the team at Piccadilly Press. To Rosemary Bromley. And to Steve Lovering for his constant support, listening ear and magical ability to produce chocolate then make it disappear in seconds.

Chapter 1

The Flabmeister

'Mum,' I called down the stairs. 'My black jeans have shrunk in the wash.'

Mum appeared from the kitchen. 'Are you sure? They've never done that before.'

'Maybe you put them on too hot a wash,' I said as I went back into my room. It was the sort of thing that Mum would do without our cleaner Mrs Dawson around to do things properly. Mum might be Mrs Not-a-hair-out-of-place in her appearance and likes the house to be immaculate but domestically, she's a disaster. She's been known to turn a whole load of white washing blue or pink by mistake and she did pile all my clothes into the machine in a hurry after I got back from our school trip yesterday, so that I'd have something to wear today. It's a good job we don't have pets in this house as they'd probably have been shoved in the wash by mistake as well.

I lay back on the bed to try once again to get the zipper up on my jeans. I held my breath and pulled . . . And held my breath and pulled again . . . but no way. The zipper was not going to budge. They had definitely shrunk. Poo, I thought. And these are my favourites too. My best jeans for making me look slimmer.

Just as I was rummaging around in my wardrobe trying to find something else to wear, Mum appeared at my door.

'No luck?' she asked when she saw the discarded jeans on the floor.

I shook my head. 'Nope. Definitely shrunk.'

Mum shifted awkwardly about on her feet for a few moments. 'Um, you don't think that by any chance you might have put on a little weight while you were in Italy?' she asked.

'No way,' I said. 'With all that walking around Florence, I think I must have *lost* weight. I mean, it wasn't as though we exactly pigged out.' Except for the ice cream and pizza and pasta and . . . oh dear, better go and weigh myself, I thought as I headed for the bathroom.

I crossed my fingers and got on the scales.

'No way,' I gasped when I saw the reading. 'No *way*. They *have* to be wrong.'

Mum was hovering outside the bathroom. 'Well?' she asked.

'Scales are wrong,' I said as I passed her on my way out. 'Quite clearly nothing in this house is working properly.'

Mum smiled. 'Don't worry about it. You look fine.'

She doesn't understand. How could she when she looks like a rake and can eat as much as she likes without putting on an ounce?

'Do not,' I said. 'This is a *major* disaster.'

Back in my room, I took a long look at myself in the mirror. Back, front, sideways. Yuck. It's too horrible. Flab, flab, flabby. Mum and Dad used to call me a skinny minnie. Hah! That's a laugh. I might have been once but not any longer, I thought as I pulled in my tummy as far as it would go. The only celebrity I resemble now is Miss Piggy. Oh rat rot. I have definitely put on weight and I can't blame the mirror.

I did a quick addition in my head. OK, so I put on five pounds over Christmas and New Year. But everyone puts on a few pounds over that time and it wasn't exactly my fault – so many people bought me boxes of chocolate. It would have been impolite not to eat them. And with all the other stuff around at that time of year: pudding, mince pies, roast potatoes, turkey, stuffing . . . how can anyone not gain a little weight? But another three pounds at half-term on the school trip? How did *that* happen? Five and three. That's eight pounds. Five pounds I could just about get away with but eight? Definitely not. In Italy, we only had a tiny mirror in the hotel bathroom so I hadn't noticed the full extent of the damage but now I'm home, I can see properly. And it's serious. That's it. I'm never going out again. No way can I be seen in public looking like this. So no going out. Not until I've dropped it. No. I shall hide under the bed and starve until I'm fit to be seen again.

'Izzie,' Mum called. 'Get a move on. I'm not going to wait all day for you and we're late as it is.'

Knickers, I thought as I pulled on a pair of my old baggy jeans. Something has to change round here. And fast.

When I got to school, I waited at the gates for my mates, Nesta, TJ and Lucy. We'd all been on the school trip and I was dying to know what had happened after we'd got home last night. It had been amazing at the airport. We'd just come through the arrivals lounge when TJ spotted a boy with the most enormous bunch of roses at the end of the line of people awaiting passengers. It was Tony, Lucy's ex (and Nesta's brother). They'd had a big fall-out just before we'd left for Florence and the relationship was off but then, there he was with the flowers at the airport and he whizzed her away. It was so romantic.

I'd called Nesta for an update as soon as I got home last night and all she knew was that Tony was over at Lucy's. And we'd all called Lucy but her mobile was switched off and when we tried the landline, her brother Lal said she was busy and wasn't to be disturbed. Remind me to kill him when I see him, the rat, I thought. I bet he had his ear glued to her door all evening. He's a nosy parker and is always butting into our business especially anything to do with our love lives. Probably because he doesn't have one of his own. Anyway, by bedtime, the breaking news on the Tony and Lucy situation was they were still in 'conference'. Probably a snog conference if you asked me. But talk about suspense. It was killing me.

After a few moments, I saw Nesta's dad's BMW draw up by the bus stop. I had to smile when I saw her get out of the back. She was dressed in black with a black shawl tossed over her shoulders, her hair pulled back into a pony-tail and even though it was a dismal February day, she was still wearing the big Gucci sunglasses that she'd borrowed from her mum for the trip. With her exotic looks (half-Italian, half-Jamaican) she is stunning most of the time but today she looked every inch an Italian *Vogue* model. Typical Nesta. She likes to make an entrance, even if it's only into school assembly.

'Never forget, dahling,' she drawled in a fake Italian accent as she came to join me and took off the glasses, 'that wherever we are, we must never forget our sense of style.'

'Yeah, right,' I said as I saw her glance over my baggy outfit.

'I thought we'd decided to go mega sophisticated after Italy,' she said. 'You decided to go back to the grunge look?'

'Mum put my jeans in the wash and they shrunk and all my other stuff wasn't dry . . .'

'Rotten to be back, isn't it?' she interrupted as she leaned against the gate post and put her glasses back on.

'Tell me about it,' I said as I spotted TJ getting off the bus and waving at us.

'Hey,' she said as she came over. 'Doesn't this seem unreal? Like, straight back to the old routine. Already Italy seems like a dream.'

At least TJ was dressed normally. A week in the one of the most fashionable places in Europe and she still favoured jeans and a sweatshirt. But she looked so slim in them. Pig poo, I thought, I wonder if anyone has noticed that I have turned into the flabmeister.

Nesta wrapped her shawl tighter around herself. 'I know,' she said. 'They should have given us another week off to adjust to being back in England. It feels so much colder here.'

'So?' I asked. 'What's the gossip on Lucy and Tony? Anyone seen her yet?'

Nesta rolled her eyes. 'All I know is that Tony was over at her house all yesterday evening. He got home late and locked himself in his room and this morning, he'd already gone by the time I got up. You know what he's like, not exactly Mr Communication when it comes to spilling the beans on his love life.'

'All evening?' I asked. 'Sounds like it's back on.'

'Maybe,' said TJ. 'So I guess we'd better get ready for the roller coaster ride again.'

Tony and Lucy have been on off, on off for well over a year. The trouble usually starts when Tony starts pushing Lucy further than she wants to go in the bedroom department. That's why they split up last time because she said, no way José and he said he couldn't take it. Part of the problem is that he's eighteen and she's not even fifteen yet and she felt she wasn't ready to sleep with him. They do make a strange-looking couple really because Tony's tall and dark and Lucy is tiny (or petite as she likes to say) and looks like a blonde pixie. Just before we left for Florence, he decided that it wasn't going to work but he obviously changed his mind while we were away.

As the bell for assembly rang, there was still no sign of Lucy and although we lingered as long as we could, in the end we had to go in or else risk a detention.

In double English that morning, Lucy still hadn't shown so I reconciled myself with having to wait until break to phone her. Mr Johnson, our teacher (also fresh back from Florence) went for the easy option. Easy for him, anyway. He asked us to write an essay on 'What I Did on my Holidays'. How predictable is that after a break? I thought. Then he fell asleep.

'Frescoed out in Florence,' I wrote as my title.

After twenty minutes, I had only written four lines.

Walked a lot.

Saw a load of churches and frescos.

Ate a lot. (Oh dear, but v. enjoyable at the time. Who was it said a moment on the lips, a lifetime on the hips? I'd like to meet them so I could kill them.)

Snogged my face off. (I met this fab boy called Jay on the plane going out. He was on a school trip too and his party was staying at the same hotel as us. At first I thought it was fate bringing us together then we found out that all the schools in North London always book into the same hotel because they get a cheap package deal. Flight and room for ze 'orrible Engleesh teenagers sort of thing. Anyway, his school isn't too far from ours so . . . watch this space. I really hope to see him again.)

I rubbed out the last bit as I didn't reckon Mr Johnson would want to read about my snog fests and tried to put my mind to my essay. It's hard when you've had a week off. Like the battery in my brain had gone flat. I looked over at Nesta and TJ to see what they were up to. TJ was scribbling madly. Pff. She would be. She loved Florence and she loves history and English and all that sort of thing. She's a brainbox really. Her e-mail address is babewithbrains as she's quite a babe too, even though she doesn't think so but boys always notice her. She has lovely thick long, dark hair and a full, wide mouth that could be used to advertise collegen injections. Only hers is *au naturel*.

Nesta looked as bored as I was. She made her eyes go cross, pulled a face and flicked her rubber at me with her ruler.

'Ouch,' I cried as it hit me on the side of the head and unfortunately Mr Johnson woke up.

'Wh . . . where . . . what . . .?' he stuttered as he came out of his reverie.

He clearly hadn't quite landed either.

As soon as the bell went for break, we were out, down the corridor and I called Lucy double quick.

'Hey, skiver,' I said when I got through. 'What's happening?'

'Mum thought I still looked peaky after my food poisoning in Florence so told me to take the day off.'

'Pff,' I said. 'Lucky you. But I meant what's *happening* happening?'

'Oh . . . er . . . she said I have to drink lots of fluids . . .'

'I mean with *Tony*?'

'And rest . . .'

'Oh. Ah . . . Is someone there? You can't talk?'

'No. I mean yes. My mum's here playing Florence Nightingale. Hey, I wonder if she ever went to Florence. Florence Nightingale I mean. Then she'd have been Florence in Florence.'

'Shut up, Lucy. You are clearly delirious. Shall we come over after school?'

'Yeeesssss.'

After school, I dropped off my holiday film at the chemist's and we all headed straight over to Lucy's.

She was sitting up in bed, surrounded by glossy mags and was painting her nails turquoise blue. She looked absolutely fine. Better than fine. Rested and relaxed and she'd clearly had time to do her hair and now her nails. Huh. Some people.

'Oh thank God you're here,' she said. 'I've been so bored.'

'Well, you look all right to me,' said Nesta as she sat on the end of her bed. 'So don't expect any sympathy. You get a day off and the rest of us have had to suffer the tortures of double English and double maths, all on the same day. Life just isn't fair sometimes.'

I laughed. Nesta would make a rotten nurse.

'How are you?' asked TJ who would make a good nurse as she's always aware of others and what they're going through.

'OK, thanks,' said Lucy. 'But I did feel a bit queasy this morning. Honestly.'

'Yeah right,' said Nesta. 'So? Spill. What's going on with you and my ratfink brother?'

'Close the door,' said Lucy.

TJ quickly did as she asked and we all looked at Lucy in anticipation.

'So?' repeated Nesta.

'Nothing,' said Lucy.

'Nothing?' asked Nesta. 'What's that supposed to mean?'

'I told him I wasn't going back with him. I mean, one bunch of flowers and I'm supposed to fall at his feet. Give me a break.'

'Wow,' said TJ. 'I would have. I thought it was so romantic.'

'Yeah, but it doesn't really change things,' said Lucy.

'So why was he there?' asked TJ. '*Avec les fleurs?*'

'He said he'd done a lot of thinking while I was away and he'd realised that he'd rather be with me and not have sex than be with someone he doesn't really care about and do it.'

'Good for him,' I said. 'He really, really does like you, doesn't he?'

'And I like him,' said Lucy. 'That will never change. But I'm not going back to where we were before. I mean, get real. How long before he gets restless and starts with the wandering hands again? A month? A week?'

'A day, knowing my brother,' said Nesta. 'No, an hour.'

'Exactly,' said Lucy.

'So what now?' asked TJ.

'We move on,' said Lucy. 'Florence really helped me do that. I told him that I'm not going back.'

'How did he take it?' I asked.

Lucy grinned. 'Said he's not going to give up.'

Nesta sighed and flopped back on the bed. 'Oh, here we go again.'

'No, really,' said Lucy. 'I can be quite stubborn when I want to be. I really mean it. And anyway, he'll be going to university in September so we'd probably break up then anyway.'

'But that's ages away,' I said. 'Almost seven months.'

'So?' said Lucy. 'If we got back together, can you imagine? I'd spend seven months dreading September so I'm moving on now.'

Nesta sat up again. 'OK. Good. You move on. We all move on. A new chapter in all our books. So let's review the situation.' She looked over at me. 'Miss Foster, take a note.'

I poised myself with an imaginary pad and pen in secretary mode, ready for her plan. Nesta's big on plans and big on getting everyone to join in with them.

'OK,' said Nesta. 'Lucy. Free. Find new boy.'

'Er, not necessarily,' said Lucy.

'Miss Foster, scratch that memo,' said Nesta. 'Lucy. Free. No boy.'

'Not necessarily that, either. I want to stay open.'

Nesta sighed. 'OK. Lucy. Confused as always. Moving on. TJ. You going to see that Liam guy you met on holiday again?'

TJ shrugged. 'Nah. Don't think so. Maybe as a mate but nothing else. No chemistry.'

'OK. TJ. Free. You want a new boy?'

TJ shrugged again. 'Maybe, maybe not.'

Nesta sighed heavily. 'God, get a life, you guys. Show me some enthusiasm here. OK. Me. No boy. Love of my life left in *Italia* and he can't write English so no chance of any love letters. Not good but hey, as Lucy said, life must go on and that's precisely why I brought this issue of boys up. My philosophy is that the best way to get over one is to find a distraction. Preferably another boy.'

I laughed. Didn't take her long to recover, I thought. On the plane coming back, it was Marco this and Marco that, but then she had only pulled him on the last night so it wasn't exactly like they'd had a whole week to fall truly in love. Lucy on the other hand, had spent almost the whole week with someone – a lovely American boy called Teddy who she'd hooked up with, but then he lives on the other side of the world, so not much chance of that coming to anything while they're both at school.

'Hey, did you tell Tony about Teddy?' I asked.

'No way,' she replied. 'At least, not the whole truth. I said we met a load of boys while we were there and spent some time hanging out with them and having a laugh. He didn't seem to want details, which was a relief and as Teddy lives in the States, it's not likely to come up.'

'Yes,' said Nesta. 'We need boys who live locally.'

'So what about William, Nesta?' I asked. 'Not like you to let someone as cute as him slip away.'

Nesta grimaced. 'Luke's mate? Yes. I did consider him for a nanosecond but crossed him off the list. Friend of Luke's. Don't want to go anywhere near there again.'

TJ looked at the floor. I think she still felt uncomfortable about the 'Luke' situation. Before Christmas, he'd been going out with Nesta and then he made a play for TJ and I think she genuinely did fall in love with him and thought he was her soulmate. It all got v. complicated and almost split us up as mates, because I sided with TJ and Lucy sided with Nesta. In the end we all decided that it wasn't worth losing our friendship over a boy who couldn't be trusted. I think it left TJ feeling a bit bruised though and she doesn't like to talk about him much. Shame about William. We only met him after it was all over and he seemed really nice and clearly fancied Nesta. But I understood her reluctance to get involved with him, being Luke's friend and all.

'Izzie? What about you?' asked Nesta. 'You going to see Jay?'

'Hope so,' I said. I decided that now was the time to ask the question that I'd been wanting to ask all day. 'Hey, listen guys. I need you to tell me something and I want you to be really, *really* honest . . .'

'Sounds serious,' said Nesta.

'It is. I want you to tell me, do you think I've put on weight?'

Nesta, Lucy and TJ looked at each other.

'No,' said TJ after a moment too long. 'Not really. Well, we all did a little. So no more than the rest of us.'

'Is that a yes or a no?'

'You look great, as always,' said Lucy, ever my ally. 'Don't even think about it.'

'Well, I have to. My jeans don't fit.'

'OK . . .' said Nesta. 'Seeing as no one around here is telling the truth, yes you have put on a little weight. I noticed in Italy, actually, and didn't want to say anything but . . .'

'Nesta,' interrupted Lucy. 'You are always putting your foot in your mouth. In fact you only ever open your mouth to change feet.'

'Hey, that's not fair,' said Nesta. 'You didn't even let me finish. Yes, Izzie, you have put on a little weight but no big deal. You can carry it. You're the tallest of us all, so no biggie.'

'Hmph. I'd say it is a biggie. And I'm the biggie, to be precise. Tell me honestly, do I look fat?'

'No way,' TJ and Lucy chorused.

'Am I as big as Angela Roberts in Year Eleven?' I stood up

and stuck my stomach out for them. 'See, I look pregnant.'

'No way,' said TJ. 'That's a huge exaggeration.'

'OK, so is it my bum or my tum or my legs that look biggest?'

TJ and Nesta exchanged a look and the next thing I knew, they had pulled a pillow out from behind Lucy, wrestled me to the floor and shoved the pillow over my face.

'For heaven's sake, shut up about being fat,' said Nesta. 'Not fat, not fat, not fat. You are curvy.'

Curvy? I thought as I tried to fight them off. Curvy? That's just a polite way of saying fat. Curvy. Oh dog doo.

Suddenly I wished I hadn't asked.

I got home later to the alluring smell of garlic and onions. Mum had been doing pasta in a tuna and tomato sauce with parmesan cheese. Calorific and a half. No way could I eat that even though I was hungry. I'd hardly eaten all day. As Nesta and TJ had tucked into their sandwiches at lunch-time, I had binned mine and just eaten my apple. Then, later at Lucy's when her mum brought us up tea and cookies, I hadn't had one.

I quickly checked that Mum and Angus (my stepdad) were busy watching TV then went back to the kitchen. This is how it has to be, I thought, as I binned my supper and hid it under some newspaper so that Mum wouldn't notice. Then I made myself two ryvitas with a scraping of marmite. I have to accept that I have to suffer to be beautiful.

When I went to bed a couple of hours later, my stomach was rumbling and all I could think of was food. The song from the musical *Oliver!* began to sing in my brain, '*Food* glorious *food . . . hot bangers and mustard . . . While we're in the mood, baked apple and custard . . .*' Or something like that. Plates of steaming pasta, baked potatoes with lashings of butter, slices of toast and peanut butter, chocolate cake and blueberry muffins began to play across the screen of my mind. I am *starving*, I thought as my body seemed to rise of its own accord from the bed like a sleepwalker and make its way down the stairs and into the kitchen where it began to raid the fridge. I'll start properly tomorrow, I thought as I made myself a hot chocolate then ate my way through a huge chunk of wholemeal bread with peanut butter and damson jam, two cookies and a piece of marzipan-covered cake.

Phew, that feels better, I thought as I went back to bed full of good resolutions for the morning.

Eat, drink and be merry, for tomorrow, we may diet.

Chapter 2

Teen Talk

'Don't you keep your mobile on?' asked Nesta when I got to the school gates the next day. 'I've been trying to ring you all morning.'

Lucy and TJ were already there hanging out with her and trying to delay the moment of actually having to go in for as long as possible. Even though it was cold and drizzly, we all preferred to be outside rather than in.

'I only spoke to you last night,' I said as I rubbed my arms to try and keep warm. 'What could possibly have happened since then that can't wait?'

'Opportunity of a lifetime,' she said with a grand sweep of her hands. 'My dad told me at breakfast this morning. He was having a drink with one of his producer friends last night and he told him about a new telly programme he's launching and he wants teens to be in it. Us. We can go for it.'

'Er, slow down a moment, Nesta,' said TJ. 'One slight problem. Like we have to come to school.'

'And we're not actresses,' said Lucy.

'Not a problem. It's going to happen on a Saturday. It's going to be called *Teen Talk*, a discussion show sort of thing and they want teens in the audience to participate and a few for a panel to give their views . . .'

'Views on what?' asked Lucy.

Nesta shrugged. 'Dunno. Life. Dunno. Who cares? They want opinions, we have them and if we haven't got them, we'll get them. Anyway, he asked Dad if we'd be interested in going to the preliminary meeting on Thursday. They're seeing a whole bunch of people and are going to pick about thirty and then they'll film a pilot episode in a couple of Saturdays' time. You up for it?'

'You bet,' said Lucy.

'Not me and anyway, I can't do Saturdays,' said TJ. 'I have the magazine to do at the weekends and I'm a bit behind now after the Italy trip.'

TJ edits the school magazine, *For Real,* with Emma Ford from Year Eleven. They do a brilliant job but it's time consuming for TJ and often she can't hang out with the rest of us on a Saturday because of it.

'Oh, can't you get out of it?' asked Nesta. 'It will be so top. All of us together. A real laugh. Get Emma to do the magazine for a few weeks.'

TJ shook her head. 'I can't leave her with it. She'd kill me. Anyway, you know being on TV isn't my kind of thing. I don't mind writing opinions down but I turn into Noola the Alien Girl if I have to say much in public.'

We all laughed. We knew Noola, TJ's alter ego well. TJ, who is easily the brainiest of us all, comes out with this strange language (she calls it Outerspaceagongalese) if she's put on the spot and particularly when she meets a cute boy. It was hysterical the first time we witnessed it. It was when she met Tony and started mumbling alien speak. She could only say words like uh or nihwee or ug.

'What about you, Izzie? You in?' asked Nesta.

'Yeah, maybe.' I nodded, but in my head I'd gone into a panic. I'd read somewhere that the television camera adds ten pounds to your weight. Ten plus the five at Christmas plus the three from the Italian trip. That's eighteen pounds. Oh God. I'd look enormous. But on the other hand, I'd really love to do it. Oh hell. Maybe I'll be able to drop the weight in time for the pilot. 'What's the first meeting for exactly?' I asked.

'It's for the producers to check that we're not mad and likely to do something weird like strip naked and run in front of the cameras waving our knickers in the air . . .'

'As if,' I said. 'We'd wear them on our heads like normal people.'

Lucy and TJ laughed, but Nesta ignored what I'd said and continued.

'Then if we get selected, there's the first run-through on Saturday. If the pilot is a goer, they'll go into production in the autumn. Oh come on guys. We have to do it. It could be our first break. You never know who might be watching the show. We could be discovered and on our way to the bright lights of Hollywood.'

'Yeah, right,' I said. 'And pigs might fly.'

'No, we'll come. Won't we, Iz?' asked Lucy.

'Yeah. Sure,' I said. They usually pick a whole variety of people for audiences to represent all backgrounds and types.

I could be the token fat person.

After school, I took a detour to the local newsagent's on the way home and spent a good chunk of my pocket money on magazines. I knew exactly what I was looking for. Ones that said anything like, 'Lose ten pounds in ten easy steps' with a picture of a skinny girl holding up her old ginormous pair of trousers to show how she'd shrunk ten sizes – that kind of thing. Luckily there were loads.

I raced home, up to my bedroom and began to read.

The Atkins diet, sounds good. Good results. No carbs, only protein. Hmm. Could be difficult as I'm vegetarian. Maybe I could eat meat just for a few weeks. No. Can't. Even though I'm desperate, I still couldn't eat one of those sweet baby lambs' legs or chew my way through a cow's buttock. *Bleurghh*. Maybe I could eat just fish. That's protein. And supposed to be good for the brain. Fish for supper every night? Ohmicod. Maybe not. What else is there?

The next magazine raved on about the Hay diet. I hoped that wasn't just eating hay but no, it was all about not mixing your carbohydrates and your proteins at the same meal. That sounded more do-able and seemed like a healthy option. Tick. I'll do that. What else?

Eat Right for your Blood Type, said the next mag. Some celebrities swear by it.

'Mum,' I called down the stairs. 'What blood type am I?'

'I have no idea,' she called back. 'Red, like the rest of us. Why? Are you thinking of becoming a vampire?'

Oh, very funny. Mum's discovered she has a sense of humour. Not, I thought as I went back to my magazine and read more about that diet. Nope, sounds too complicated. You have to have a blood test to find out what kind of blood you are and I hate needles.

Bananas and milk one day, eggs and grapefruit the next. Some of the models use it when they need a quick fix. Tick. Might try that one.

The cabbage diet. Yuck. I hate cabbage. But tick. Might try that one.

No carbs after midday. Tick. Easy. I'll do that as well.

Drink at least six glasses of water a day to help eliminate toxins and keep your digestive system working well. Tick. Do that.

And low fat everything. Tick. Do that.

Hmm. But if I'm on the Atkins diet, that says I can have cheese and cream and butter. That's high fat.

Now I'm getting confused.

'Izzie,' Mum called from the kitchen. 'Supper's on the table.'

This is going to be interesting, I thought as I put my magazines aside and went down.

She'd made cheesy baked potatoes and salad. Healthy enough but . . .

'Sorry, Mum, but I can't eat that,' I said as I sat at the table.

'Why not?' asked Mum as she served out pork chops for her and Angus.

'I'm not eating carbs after midday any more,' I explained. 'And I'm on the Hay diet so I can't mix my carbohydrates and my proteins.'

Mum sighed. 'And why is that?'

I pinched a good wedge of flab on my hips and stuck my stomach out for her. 'Isn't it obvious? I'm enormous. I have to go on a diet. And the Hay diet says . . .'

Angus laughed. 'But there's nothing of you. You don't need to diet.'

He is clearly blind.

'I'll eat the salad,' I said while I tried to decide whether to have the cheese or the potato. Maybe the potato because cheese is high fat but if I'm on the Atkins, cheese would be all right. But then, if I had the potato, it's carbohydrate and I'd decided not to have carbs after midday. Oh hell, this isn't going to be easy. Maybe I'll just stick with the salad.

'Have you put dressing on the salad? Because I'm also only having low fat stuff from now on.'

Mum rolled her eyes and Angus grimaced and began to eat his meal. I think he knew what was coming, as I did. A lecture.

'Low fat products are often high in sugar and have more calories. Anyway, you do *not* need to go on a diet, Isobel,' Mum began. (I always know that she's serious when she calls me Isobel.) 'You might have a bit of puppy fat on you but you're a growing girl and it will soon –'

'Growing in *all* directions, Mum. I have to do something about it. And I'm fifteen. Way past the puppy fat stage.'

'Izzie, I have bent over backwards to get you food that you *will* eat. First it was no meat. And then it was we have to eat more healthy food. I've done that. And now you want to do the Hay diet or whatever. No. I'm not having it. Nor any other mad fad diets. You will eat sensibly and that's the end of it. A baked potato is very healthy and not going to put weight on you. Have it without the butter if you must but you *will* eat something.'

There are times when there's no point in arguing with Mum. And this was one of them. I have learned (from Nesta) that if I need to get her to agree to something, the best time to get her is when she's watching one of her favourite TV programmes and doesn't want to be disturbed. She'll agree to anything then if only to get me to shut up.

'OK,' I said as I cut a tiny piece of my potato up and put it in my mouth. 'You know best. Er . . . what's on TV tonight?'

Mum gave Angus a 'what's going on?' look but he just shrugged. He tries to stay out of our arguments.

'Why?' she asked.

'Nothing. Oh . . . talking of telly. One of Nesta's dad's mates is launching a new TV show and they want teens for the audience. He asked if we'd like to be part of it so can I go? They're selecting on Thursday and they'll do a run through on Saturday. It's a sort of discussion show thing. Very intellectual. And . . . be, er . . . great work experience.'

Mum put her knife and fork down. 'No. I don't think so.'

'Why not?'

'You've just been to Italy for a week. You're behind on your homework and need to catch up.'

I was about to object but could see that her back had stiffened and she was sitting up very straight as if primed for a fight. She was definitely in 'no' mood. Take a deep breath, I told myself. Pick your time. I took another mouthful of my potato. 'OK,' I said. 'I guess I do need to catch up on schoolwork.'

She gave me a suspicious look but I smiled back sweetly. I'll get her later when she's ensconced in the telly, I thought. Oh ja. Ve have vays of making you give in.

The skipping diet: Skipping breakfast,
skipping lunch, skipping supper.

Chapter 3

The Tummy Song

Wednesday weigh-in. Arrghhhhhh. I'd put on half a pound since Monday! How could that have happened?

Drastic measures are called for, I thought, as I had half a grapefruit and a boiled egg for breakfast, followed by two large glasses of water. Mum tried to get me to have cereal as well so I poured myself a bowl then poured it back into the packet when she was in the hall spraying posh hairspray all over her hair (which is cut into such a perfect bob that it doesn't need spray to keep it in place). I think Angus saw me as he was making himself some toast but he didn't say anything.

School was unbelievably embarrassing as halfway through PHSE, my stomach decided to sing the tummy song. Gurgle, wurgle, woggle, schlosh. And it wasn't just once. It went on *and* on. I went bright purple and tried breathing in and even holding my breath but schlosh, schlosh it went. A few girls started giggling and then a few more and even Miss Watkins began laughing in the end. And it takes a lot to get her to laugh.

'Someone's tummy is hungry,' she said finally. 'Did you miss breakfast, Izzie?'

'No, Miss,' I said as the whole class stared at me. 'Must have a bug.' A whole family of them in fact, I thought as my tummy gurgle-wurgled again.

Later, when we were changing for gym, I felt even worse. All around me, my classmates were gaily stripping off without a care in the world while I tried to change with my back turned to them all so that no one would notice that I had turned into Mrs Blobby. They were all so *skinny*. At five foot eight, I must be the tallest in our class now plus my boobs have taken on a life of their own and are expanding at twice the rate of the universe. Soon I won't be able to see my feet! And my bum. Oh, it's *too* sad. I couldn't believe it, even Candice Carter's tummy was as flat as a pancake and she's pregnant. It was the big scandal just before we left for Italy and I did feel sorry for her. She was out of her mind with worry about what her parents were going to say and what she was going to do. She'd been sleeping with her steady boyfriend for a while and she told us that they'd always used condoms but one time, the condom must have burst or leaked or whatever they do when it all goes wrong.

When she'd gone into the showers, I nudged Lucy.

'Amazing, isn't it, I look three months pregnant and Candice doesn't look as if she's having a baby at all.'

'She's not any more,' whispered Lucy. 'Apparently she lost it. Miscarriage.'

'God. How awful. Or is it?'

Lucy did a quick check to see that she wasn't coming back in. 'I think it's a relief actually. You know she wasn't ready to be a single mum. And she wants to go to college, remember?'

I did remember. We'd found her in the cloakrooms one day sobbing her heart out as she considered her options. It was a real wake-up call for everyone as although most of our year haven't slept with boys yet, we've all certainly been thinking about it. Lucy told me in Italy that seeing Candice so distraught was what made her sure that she wasn't ready to sleep with Tony. She didn't want to risk it and maybe end up going through what had happened to Candice.

At lunch, while I had my grapefruit (hmm, yummy, not), the others had sandwiches, crisps and *chocolate*. *Soooo* unfair. My mouth was watering, but I stuck to my resolve and didn't have any, even though they all told me I was mad to be on a diet and kept waving bits of chocolate in front of my nose. It's all right for them. All of them are thin with no wobbly bits at all. To distract myself from watching them wolf down their food, I pulled out my photos from the Italian trip which I'd picked up on the way to school.

We'd already looked at them first thing, then again at break but another look wouldn't hurt as the pics brought Italy (and Jay) back into sharp focus. Although the trip was over, I couldn't help but think that one part of it had come back on the plane with me. And I don't mean my memories (cue romantic violins), no, I mean the five foot ten gorgeous Indian boy by the name of Jay. He looked so good in the photos and seeing them made me want to meet up with him again as soon as possible. Unlike Florence, he wasn't far away, probably at his school in North London, maybe looking at his own photos at the same time as TJ, Nesta, Lucy and I looked at mine. Probably thinking, who's that great fairy elephant standing next to me in my pictures? I hoped not, as I think he did like me.

'They say that the camera doesn't lie but I wish sometimes it would fib a little,' I said as I looked at one particularly unflattering shot of me bending over to tie my trainers outside the Duomo. I made a mental note to rip it up or put it on the fridge as a reminder of why I had to keep to my diet.

'What do you mean?' asked Lucy.

'Duh. I look enormous.'

'No you don't,' said TJ. 'The camera just got you at a bad angle, that's all. You looked great in Italy and the boys there really liked your green eyes. Remember in the Piazza della Signoria where they kept saying *bella ochi*, beautiful eyes.'

'Yeah, because that's the only part of me that's OK at the moment. My eyes, my ear lobes and maybe my little toes. The rest of me is . . .'

'Oh for God's sake, Izzie,' Lucy interrupted. 'For the last time, you are *not* fat.'

I noticed Nesta wasn't making any comment as she flipped through the photos. Probably couldn't trust herself not to say something insulting.

'Have you heard from Jay?' she asked finally as she got to the end of the pile.

I shook my head. It would be so cool to see him again and pick up where we left off. The end of the holiday had come round so fast and then there was the flight home and being met at the airport. I hadn't thought about swapping numbers or arranging to see him again over here until it was too late. And now I wished that I had. Being with him had made the Italian trip extra special and we had got on really well. We'd talked about everything: our families, past relationships, what music we liked, fave foods, TV programmes, what we wanted to do after we'd left school, why God didn't sort out some of the mess us humans have made down here. We'd got really close.

'Well, it's only Wednesday,' said Lucy. 'Give the boy a break. You know what they're like. When a mate says she'll phone, she means probably in an hour. When a boy says he'll phone, he means sometime, maybe in a week and that's if I remember.'

'Have you heard from Teddy?' I asked.

She nodded. 'Yeah, he's e-mailed a couple of times.'

'See,' said Nesta. 'If a boy says he'll phone, if he likes you, you don't have to wait too long. I've already heard from a few boys from the trip.'

My heart sank. I knew she was right. If a boy likes you, he phones. OK, maybe not as fast as a girl would phone, but he phones.

'Actually . . . Jay didn't take my number,' I said. 'We both forgot.'

'I could get it for you,' said Nesta. 'Eddie phoned. Remember him? The one with red hair and the high forehead? He was a mate of Jay's.'

'And Liam called me,' said TJ. 'I could get it from him as well.'

'*Noooo*. Don't,' I said. If I could get Jay's number this easily, I thought, he could have got mine. So why hadn't he? I cast my mind back to the last time I'd seen him. It was at the airport and we were waiting for our luggage. It had all been such a rush with trolleys and people bashing into one another as they hauled their cases about. I remember he thanked me for a fab time in Florence and said I'd made the trip really special for him. And then Liam thought it would be funny to ride round on the carousel along with the cases and everyone started laughing when one of the security men dived on after him. Jay and Eddie darted forward to try and pull Liam off so that he didn't get into trouble and after that, everything went into a blur, like a DVD on fast forward. I spotted my case and moved in to collect it, there was a big commotion with the security guard, the boys and one of their teachers and when I looked for

Jay again, he and his mates were being escorted by their angry looking teacher towards the arrival gate. Not exactly the best time to get someone's number.

'Why not let Nesta get it for you?' asked Lucy. 'You clearly both liked each other a lot and he might be waiting to hear from you.'

I shook my head. 'I don't want to seem too keen. He could get my number if he wanted.'

'Quite right,' said Nesta. 'Treat 'em mean to keep 'em keen. That's my motto.'

Lucy laughed. 'Yeah right, it's your motto until *you're* keen and then you're as bad as the rest of us.'

Nesta chose to ignore her comment. 'But listen, Izzie,' she said, 'a bunch of the boys from the trip are meeting up in Crouch End after school. Eddie asked if I wanted to go along. Let's all go for half an hour or so. And Chris and Liam will be there . . .'

Lucy grimaced. 'No thanks. You can count me out of this one,' she said when Nesta mentioned Chris's name. He'd tried to pull her on the trip and she didn't fancy him. It all culminated in him pushing an envelope with a condom in it with a note saying, *Tonight's your lucky night* under the door for her one night. She'd filled the condom with water to make a water bomb and smashed it over his head in reply. I could understand her reluctance to meet up with him again.

'And anyway,' she continued, 'I said I'd meet Tony.'

'I thought that it was over between you,' I said. 'Remember? You're moving on?'

'We can still be friends,' said Lucy sheepishly.

Nesta rolled her eyes. 'Yeah, right,' she said.

'I know you don't believe me but it is just friends. Like – he wanted to come to the *Teen Talk* thing with us tomorrow and I told him no, I want to do some things on my own. So see, I am being independent.'

'So why are you seeing him tonight?' I asked.

'He wants to talk over his university options with me,' said Lucy. 'He's had a couple of offers but isn't sure where he wants to go. He was talking about staying here and going to one in London so that we could still be together.'

'See,' said Nesta. 'I knew it. He's wheedling his way back in.'

'He might have had offers,' I said. 'But he still has to get the results they ask for.'

'He'll get his results,' said Lucy. 'He's really clever.'

'Yeah, he is,' said Nesta. 'Just look how clever he is at getting you back. Oh Lucy, please come and help me decide which university I should go to. I think I ought to go to one near you. It's just an excuse to get you over to our flat and into his bedroom.'

'I can look after myself,' said Lucy. 'And I'm not going to let what's happening with us or not happening with us determine which university he goes to. He must go to the one that's best for him and I'm going to tell him that.'

'Huh. So you say, but don't blame me if it ends in tears,' said Nesta, and then she turned to me. 'But you should come out with TJ and me, Iz. Jay hangs out with those boys so he might be there as well. You can check out the situation without him feeling like you're closing in on him.'

'Good plan, Batgirl,' I said. If there were a bunch of us and a crowd of them, it would seem natural that I was there.

I spent the rest of the afternoon in school lost in my memories of Italy. Snogging on the Ponte Vecchio. Snogging in the courtyard at the hotel. Snogging at the back of the car park. Oh . . . and yes, all the churches and art and culture as well.

I couldn't wait for school to finish so I could see Jay. I just hoped that my stomach would have stopped gurgling by then.

The Gurgle Wurgle Song by Izzie

OK tummy, let's get this straight
We're gonna have a talk about something you'll hate
I'm cutting down the calories, gotta lose me some weight
Gonna take me some action before it's too late.

I'm going on a diet and this time it's for real
And I don't give a toss about the way you feel
You can rumble, you can grumble, you can growl,
you can gripe
You can beat out jungle rhythms all through the night
You can gurgle, you can sclurch, you can groan,
you can moan
You can mumble, you can murmur when I'm walking
my way home
You can schurgle your displeasure when I'm out with
my friends
But there's only gonna be one way that this story ends
I'm in this to win. I'm gonna be slim
I'm in this to win. I'm gonna be slim
I'm in this to win. I'm gonna be slim.

My mind's made up and my lips sealed tight
So please shut up now and give up the fight
I'm cutting down the calories, gotta lose me some weight
Gonna take me some action before it's too late.

Chapter 4

Nightmare

The evening had started out brilliantly. Nesta, TJ and I had arrived early so we'd quickly taken over the Ladies cloakroom in a café on Park Road for the necessary preparations: lip-gloss, hair brushing and a squirt of perfume. I put on a double squirt to distract myself from the gorgeous smell of baking that was permeating the café. It was making me feel ravenous.

Chris, Liam and Eddie had arrived soon after and it was a great reunion as Liam had his photos of the Italian trip as well. Mainly pictures of the boys, larking about. The ones showing Liam were particularly unflattering because someone (Chris, but Liam doesn't know that) had shaved off one of Liam's eyebrows when he was asleep one night.

After about ten minutes, the café door opened and Jay walked in.

I felt my stomach do a back flip. He looked even better than I remembered. In Italy, everything had seemed unreal and there was so much to take in – but seeing him back on our own turf, with his silky black hair and deep brown eyes, I realised he really did stand out in a crowd. He looked taken aback to see me but soon recovered and came over and gave me a big hug like he was pleased to see me. We looked at my pics (I'd taken out any offending ones) and had a laugh as we relived some of the great things we'd all got up to. After about twenty minutes, he started checking his watch and looking awkward. He suddenly stood up and said he had to go. I wondered if I'd said something to offend him. He gave no explanation as to where he was going. And he didn't ask for my number. Or give me his. I felt confused because the chemistry was definitely still there, no doubt about that.

Nesta had been in the Ladies (reapplying her lip-gloss, no doubt) when Jay left so when she came back, she looked round for him.

'Where's the Bollywood sex god?' she asked.

I shrugged and tried to look cool as I took a sip of my hot water and lemon but I noticed that Liam, Chris and Eddie exchanged uncomfortable glances. Nesta noticed it too and in her usual subtle way, plunged straight in.

'OK. What's the story?' she asked.

The boys looked at each other sheepishly and said nothing but Nesta wasn't about to give up.

'Something's going on,' she said as she grabbed Eddie's wrist and began to give him a Chinese burn. 'Spill or I kill.'

'Oww,' said Eddie. 'Get off! You're hurting me.'

'You might as well tell them,' said Liam. 'They'll find out soon enough . . .'

Nesta let go of Eddie's wrist and he gasped with relief.

'What?' she asked. 'What's the mystery?'

Eddie looked at the floor. 'Jay has a girlfriend.'

'I know,' said Nesta. 'Izzie.'

'No, another girlfriend,' said Chris. 'Tawny. He's been going out with her for almost a year now.'

TJ gasped and glanced over at me anxiously. I felt like someone had punched me in the stomach. A *girlfriend*? It couldn't be true.

Nesta looked angry. 'Where's he gone?' she asked as she stood up, rooted out a few pound coins from her pocket and tossed them on the table. 'Here. This should cover our share. Two hot chocolates and one lemon water.'

TJ and I got up to follow her out. I felt like I was in a trance. This couldn't be happening. As we got outside the café, I ran over the road to the Clocktower as I needed some time on my own.

Nesta and TJ ran after me and Nesta put her arm round me. I felt like I'd been winded. '*Girlfriend?*' I gasped as I tried to catch my breath. 'I can't believe it. He would have told me. Are you sure they meant Jay?'

'Stay cool,' whispered Nesta as we saw the boys come out of

the café and look for us. 'Don't let them see that you're upset.'

My heart was sinking as I realised the implications. 'They must have all known,' I groaned. 'This is a total nightmare. What a creep. All that time Jay and I were gazing into each other's eyes and snogging our faces off and he had a girlfriend back here. Chris, Liam and Eddie must have been having a right laugh. They all knew Jay had someone back here. And she has such a cool name. She's probably gorgeous. Oh God. I hate him. How could he have not told me? It's too awful. I feel such an idiot.'

I wanted to go home, curl up under my duvet and die.

TJ put her arm round me as well. 'I'm sure there's some explanation.'

'Like what?' I groaned. 'Like I was nothing more than a holiday fling?'

'Who knows,' said Nesta. 'But I'll find out.'

'No, please Nesta, leave it,' I said as I pulled her back. 'I just want to go home.'

The girls did their best to persuade me to let them accompany me home but I wanted to be on my own to lick my wounds in private. On the bus home, I gazed out of the window into the gloom. A cold, dark night in February. That was how I felt, cold and dark, like all the colour and sunshine had gone out of my world. I wished I hadn't been to Italy. Suddenly all the good memories of my time there seemed like a sham and I felt like binning the photos. Or burning them.

Why hadn't he told me? I kept asking myself. We'd talked so

much about our previous relationships and what we wanted. I'd told him all about my exes, not that there were many that counted. Mark, who never called when he said he would, Ben (from the band I sing with who's still a mate) and bad boy Josh who turned out to be a liar. Jay had told me about a girl called Sushila and another called Megan. Nothing about anyone called Tawny though. Nothing about a *steady* girlfriend in his life.

I'd thought I could trust him. You gullible fool, Izzie, I said to myself as I got home, let myself in and raced up the stairs. I threw myself on my bed and waited for the tears to come. But they didn't. I felt numb. And . . . *hungry*.

I went to the bathroom for a quick weigh in. I must surely have lost a few pounds after today, but no, my weight was the same as in the morning.

Now what? I thought as I went back to my room. What have I got to look forward to? Another freaking grapefruit and if I push the boat out, a piece of soggy lettuce. Maybe that's why he messed me around. I was just some fat bird he met on holiday. OK for a week but not for a steady relationship. I felt so depressed. I don't care any more, I thought as I headed for the kitchen. Need chocolate. And need it now.

Ten minutes later, Mum caught me with my hand in the cookie jar.

'I thought you were off those this week,' she said as she filled the kettle with water.

'I'm on a new diet,' I said as I pushed a chocolate chip cookie into my mouth. 'The seafood diet.'

'What? Fish?'

'No, I see food and I eat it.'

Mum laughed. 'Well, at least you haven't lost your sense of humour.'

Suddenly, I felt my eyes fill with tears and the cookie felt dry in my mouth.

'What is it, love?' Mum asked.

'Nothing,' I said. 'Just . . . I hate myself.'

Mum looked aghast. 'But why?'

'Look at me,' I groaned. 'I'm supposed to be on a diet and yet here I am stuffing my face. I'm soooo pathetic. No wonder . . .'

'No, love. No. Here, sit down. I'll make us a nice cup of tea and you can tell me all about it. What is it? No wonder what?'

I'd been about to say no wonder boys don't stay with me. How could I tell her what a fool Jay had made of me?

'Don't know . . .' I sighed. 'Just . . . why do I always pick the wrong boys? Like, do I have a sign on my forehead that reads "sucker"? I must be doing something wrong or putting out the wrong signals or maybe it's because I'm a great ugly lump and can only attract boys who mess girls' heads up.'

Mum took a deep breath. 'You're not an ugly lump, Izzie. You're a very pretty girl.'

'You have to say that. You're my mum. It comes in the contract you signed at my birth.'

I indicated the biscuit and cake wrappers on the table. 'But look at me. I don't know what's come over me this week. I wanted to lose some weight but I have *no* will-power.'

'Yes you have,' said Mum. 'What have you eaten today?'

'Before now, two grapefruit and a boiled egg.'

'Oh, Izzie,' Mum said with a sigh. 'You've just been going about losing weight the wrong way. You don't put weight on overnight, although sometimes it appears that way. It creeps on . . .'

'Tell me about it.'

'And in the same way, it's not going to come off overnight or in three days. It has to be a more long term process. You still need to eat. That's why you're here stuffing yourself. Not because you're pathetic but because you're hungry and it's perfectly natural.'

'So what can I do Mum? I really am serious about wanting to lose a bit. Half a stone, at least.'

'OK,' said Mum. 'OK. I'll help. I just want you to promise me one thing and that is that you do it slowly and sensibly with no more thoughts about crash diets. A programme of healthy eating and the weight will be off in a few months.'

A few *months*? I didn't have that kind of time to waste with the TV pilot coming up. I knew she was probably right. Eat the right kind of foods, etc., etc. but there had to be a quicker way. I still thought I needed to do something drastic at the beginning.

'And do you want to tell me why you think you attract the wrong boys?' she asked. 'What's been going on?'

I shook my head. 'Nothing,' I said. I felt tired and had done enough caring sharing for one night. Sometimes with parents, you give them an inch and they want a mile. You tell them a little about what's going on in your head and they want the whole package. I could see that Mum was settling in for a heart to heart. And what I needed was a head-to-pillow.

'Night, Mum,' I said as I got up. 'And thanks.'

Mum looked slightly bewildered. 'Anytime, Izzie. You do know that, don't you? You can talk to me about anything, anytime.'

I nodded. I knew I could. But I couldn't. Not yet. It was all too raw. Maybe later when I'd come through the other side. When I was slim and gorgeous and the boys were queuing up to date me. Maybe then.

Late night weigh-in: the same, the same, the same. Makes no sense to me. I starve, nothing changes. I stuff my face with biscuits, nothing changes.

The seafood diet: See food and you eat it.

Chapter 5

Auditions

'Quite clearly all those stupid diet magazines that say that you can lose ten pounds in a week or two are wrong,' I said to Lucy as I came out of the bathroom at her house after school the next day. I'd just been on their scales in there and my weight still hadn't shifted an ounce. And that was after four days of starvation (apart from the odd choc/cookie binge). 'The only way to lose ten pounds in a week is to chop one of your legs off.'

'I'm sure Lal will help you with that,' said Lucy as we went into her room to join Nesta and TJ. 'Just go and lie on the kitchen table and I'll get him to get the electric saw from the shed.'

I lay back on her bed and pushed my stomach out so that she

could see how bad things were. 'You don't think I'm serious do you?' I asked.

'Looking like that? No,' she replied. 'I mean, who goes round deliberately pushing their stomach out? And I've told you before, I think you're mad and I don't want to talk about it any more.'

'Ooh, get you,' I said. 'Don't want to discuss it.'

TJ lay on the floor and like me, tried to push her stomach out as far as it would go. 'See,' she said, 'anyone has a stomach if they push it out far enough.'

Nesta looked down at us with disdain from the bed. 'Much as I would like to join in the fat tum competition, we have better things to do. Come on. We have to be at the studio in Camden at six.'

I was in two minds as to whether to go, even though Mum had finally given me permission as long as I didn't fall behind with my homework. I was still worried about the camera putting another ten pounds on me and felt like I wanted to get myself in shape before I went public again. They're not filming tonight so maybe I'll just go along to check it out then back out later, I thought.

Nesta pulled a couple of outfits out of her rucksack. 'Now. The question is, what look should I go for?' she asked. 'Intellectual with a wonderbra or slut bitch with a brain?'

TJ laughed. 'Sounds like the same thing to me. Just go as you are. You're only going to be in the audience and they probably don't want anyone who attracts too much attention.'

'Ah, but you've forgotten, they're going to pick a few people for the panel.'

'In that case, Nesta,' I said, 'don't wear anything too revealing. You look good as you are and going with your chesty bits on display might give the wrong impression for the show. Are you sure you're not going to come, TJ?'

TJ shook her head. 'Nope. I am here merely in the role of slave and dresser. When you've gone, I'm going to go home, walk Mojo, then get down to some work on the magazine. Now, who needs zipping up?'

In the end, Nesta settled for a black mini, black polo neck and black knee-high boots. She looked fab. Lucy wore one of the little halter-necks she'd made herself and her black jeans. She looked fab too. I wore a baggy T-shirt and my baggy jeans as those are the only clothes that fit me at the moment. I looked like an old sack.

When we got to the studio, I instantly wished I'd made more of an effort.

'Ohmygod,' I said as I took in the crowd shivering in the cold outside the reception building at the studio where the auditions were to be held. There were some really cute boys there and most of the girls were dressed up to the nines and in skimpy outfits despite the weather. In my oversized padded jacket, gloves and scarf, I felt like a frump compared to those who were in tiny tops and miniskirts and were made up to the eye balls. It was lip-gloss city.

At six on the dot, a blonde girl in glasses opened the door and directed us all into a room where we all had to sign in, give our details and be given a number and a visitor's pass. Some people were turned away right there and then.

'Too old or too young,' said Lucy as one tiny girl who looked about eleven burst into tears as she was asked to leave.

When the remaining teens had signed in, we were ushered down a maze of corridors and into a small cosy studio that smelled of new carpets. In fact, everywhere *was* carpeted (even the walls!) and there was no natural light. It was like walking into a softly-lit cocoon and it was warm so I could take off my jacket. At the front was a stage, on the ceiling were endless wires and lights and dotted around the sides were a few cameras. It was my first time in a real studio and I felt really excited to be there. There was a buzz of anticipation in the air as everyone talked and eyed each other up.

'Eyes left, over in the corner,' said Lucy as a tall boy with dark spiky hair came in from behind the stage and began to fiddle with a microphone in the centre. He was very good looking but more than that, he had a nice face, open and friendly.

'Ding dong. Well fit,' I said as we stood in the aisle and looked for the best place to sit. 'Now *there's* a way to get over Jay. I wonder if he's attached? Oh . . . but you saw him first, Lucy.'

'All yours,' she said. 'I'm having a break from boys for a while.'

'Yeah, right,' said Nesta. 'Tony's a boy?'

'Yeah. And I told you. We're going to be friends. I said I'd hang out with him every now and then. You know, see a movie . . .'

Nesta laughed. 'I have to hand it to him. His technique is faultless.'

'What do you mean?' asked Lucy.

'I told you before. He's wheedling his way back in. I don't think you can be just friends with a boy. Not one you fancy, anyway.'

Lucy stuck her bottom lip out. 'Well I'm not going to cut him out of my life. Why should I when we still like each other?'

'See! I knew this would happen,' said Nesta. 'Your resistance is weakening day by day. Just friends! Hah. I smell trouble. It will be fine until one of you gets involved with someone else and then . . .'

'But I'm not going to get involved with someone else. Not at the moment. As I said, I'm taking a break.'

'Yeah,' said Nesta. 'Sounds like it.'

As they chatted away, I watched the boy with spiky hair working on the stage. There was something about him that was different from the majority of boys in the studio. Maybe it was because he seemed older, maybe about eighteen, whereas the other boys looked about the same age as me. That's it, I thought. That's what I need. Someone more mature. And someone tall so that I don't tower over him like I do most of the boys my age who only come up to my shoulders. Yes. I want someone who's lived a bit and had a few relationships. Maybe they'll be a bit clearer about what they want. Then I thought about Tony and Lucy. He was eighteen and had made it very clear what he wanted. Sex. At that moment, the boy on the stage looked over to where I was standing and we made eye contact. I quickly looked down. I didn't want him to notice me when I was dressed so drably. If we got picked to be in the audience for the run-through on Saturday, I would make more of an effort and turn up in something more attractive.

At the front, a group of boys were shoving each other to get seats directly in front of the stage. I made my way straight for the back row. I knew exactly where I wanted to sit, and that was nowhere near the cameras, even though I knew they weren't filming this time. Not until I was slimmer. Lucy came with me but Nesta went straight down to the stage and found a place on the front row.

After a short while, a couple of men came in and the room grew quiet. One of them looked old, at least fifty, with short grey hair and the other had a shaven head and protruding belly and looked more like a bricklayer than a TV producer. The older one looked round then took a seat at the back near me. The other one went to the microphone that Spiky-Haired Boy had set up.

'Hi,' he said. 'My name's John Maclean. And I'm one of the

producers on the show which, as you probably all know, is going to be called *Teen Talk*. So that we're all on the same page and you know what to expect, I'd like to tell you what the format is going to be. Half an hour with a break for commercials, so we'll run to about twenty-three minutes. First part, topic, nine-minute discussion, guest band. Second part, new topic, nine-minute discussion, then if we have time, we'll have the guest band again and wrap up. So you see, it's going to be tight with not a lot of time for messing around, for people who hog the microphone, for people with a chip on their shoulder or an axe to grind. If the pilot's a goer, we'll do six shows back to back in the autumn so we'll need commitment from you and permission from your parents for you to take part. Consent forms will be given out on the way out. Any questions?'

Nesta was straight in. 'What sort of topics will be up for discussion?'

'Our writers are working on that now but any suggestions from the audience will make their job easier. That's why you guys are here. To give us input.'

A pretty redhead in the second row put her hand up. 'What time will we need to be here?'

'Saturday morning, an hour before kick-off so that will be ten o'clock for you. We want everyone in their place, settled, sorted.'

'Will it be live this Saturday?' asked the redhead.

John shook his head. 'There will be cameras here but no, it will be a run-through so that we can iron out any hiccups in the early stages.'

'Do we get paid?' asked a boy at the back.

'No,' John replied. 'You won't get paid. You do it for the street cred. Right?'

A few boys from the front groaned then got up and sloped towards the door.

'Street cred?' said one. 'You must be joking.'

'Yeah. Street cred don't buy yer fags,' another called as they went out.

John watched them go with a look of indifference. 'Anyone else want to leave?'

'Have you picked the people for the panel yet?' asked a blond boy from the front.

'We'll do that this Saturday. Tonight's just a short meet. Let us meet you, let you know what will be happening. So. Any ideas for topics?'

'Is there a God?' someone called from the back.

'Terrorism,' suggested another.

'Politics.'

Ideas began flying about. After a while, John put his hand up. 'OK, good. All good ideas but what about stuff that's relevant to you as teenagers?'

'Sex,' said one of the boys at the front and everyone laughed.

'Not having sex,' said a girl behind him and everyone laughed again.

'What do girls want?' suggested another boy.

'What do *boys* want?' said a girl.

I could see that the programme was going to be great fun. I wanted to be part of it, so when we were all invited to come back on the Saturday, I decided that I didn't want to use my weight gain as an excuse to hide away. I'd miss out on what was happening. There's only one thing for it, I resolved for the umpteenth time that week. I have to lose weight so I have to be really strict with myself and no stupid weak moments where I stuff my face with chocolate or anything else.

> The only way to lose ten pounds in two weeks,
> and keep it off, is to chop off your leg.

Chapter 6

Conspiracy

Channel One: Superchef Delia concocting something delicious with raspberries, ricotta cheese and cream. Argh.

Change channels.

Channel Two: Nigella, the Domestic Goddess making ice cream out of Mars bars. Mmmmm. I felt my mouth water.

Change channels.

Channel Three: Jamie Oliver and some other celeb chef making lasagne with garlic and herbs in record time. It looked so good, I could almost smell it.

Change channels.

Channel Four: a movie. Phew . . . Safe. A movie about an Italian family. I let it run for ten minutes. Oh no, all they do in this film is eat. Pasta, pizza, tiramisu. My stomach is rumbling like crazy.

Change channels.

Channel Five: Commercials. For Maltesers. Thai food. Mexican food like Mama used to make. Cheeseburgers. Slaver, slaver. I'm so hungry, I could lick the screen. Then up comes a commercial for toothpaste. I'm so starving I could even eat some of that. All I've had today was a bowl of cereal (on Mum's insistence), and couple of rice cakes and an orange at lunchtime. No, relax, Izzie, I told myself, think about something else besides food. Another movie is starting. Must be safer than the Italian one. The credits start to roll. A French scene. A street. The title of the movie: *Chocolat*.

!!!

I give up, I thought as I flicked the TV off.

I'd popped into see Dad on my way home from the studio and while he and Anna put Tom to bed, I'd decided to watch TV. (Anna is Dad's wife, my stepmum and Tom is my stepbrother. He's four and absolutely gorgeous.) Big mistake, I thought as I flopped back on their sofa and waited for them to come down. It's hard trying not to eat. It's not the same as giving up cigarettes or alcohol (not that I do either). You need food to live and if you don't give your body any, it objects. And everywhere there are wonderful smells to tempt you. I don't think I'd ever noticed before this week how great food smells: toast wafting in the kitchen in the morning, freshly baked bread coming out of the bakery on the way to school, spices and garlic from Indian and Thai restaurants on the high street when I walked home from school. All calling, beckoning, Izzie, Izzie, eat, eat . . .

'Iz,' Anna called from the hall. 'I'm ordering takeaway. What would you like? Your usual? Veg curry, rice, chapati?'

I was tempted. Very tempted. But then I thought about the boy with spiky hair at the studio. I wanted to make a good impression and that meant getting back into my old jeans. By Saturday (which meant near starvation).

'Nothing for me,' I called back. 'I am on a diet.'

'Oh no you're not,' Dad said, grinning as he came into the living room. 'Your mum phoned. Told me all about this latest nonsense and gave me instructions that Izzie must eat. Oh ja. Or else ve make her eat.'

The world is conspiring against me, I thought. First the smells, then the TV, then my mother, then my father. It's no wonder I'm as fat as a pig.

Anna came in to join us and sat on the sofa next to me. 'What on earth are you dieting for?'

'To lose weight of course.'

'Pff,' she said. 'You don't need to do that. You're lovely as you are.'

Anna of course, like just about every female I know, is thin as a rake. At least she is now. She was a bit chubby for a while after Tom was born, but soon lost it.

'How did you lose the weight you put on when you were pregnant?' I asked in the hope that she'd reveal some great secret that I had yet to read about.

'Breast feeding, lack of sleep and a small son to chase after all day,' she replied. 'No time to think about food.'

Dad stuck his tummy out the way I had earlier this evening. 'Diet, huh? If anyone needs to go on a diet around here, it's me.'

I wasn't going to argue. He's not exactly fat. More round. Cuddly, especially round the middle although it suits him. I remember when he and Mum split up and he lost a lot of weight and looked gaunt for a while. I much prefer him this way, looking chubbier but happy.

Anna giggled and pulled her honey-coloured hair back into a scrunchy as he strutted round the room with his tummy sticking out.

'All that beer,' she said as he sat next to her and she gave his tummy a stroke.

'Beer,' he said. 'And genes. I'm prone to putting on weight if I'm not careful. So was my dad. So was my granddad. It's in the family. Genes.'

'*Noooooo,*' I groaned. What hope was there for me? Everyone always says that I take after my dad more than my mum.

'Still at least I've still got my hair,' said Dad with a grin, as he ran his fingers through his thick mane of dark hair. 'Us Foster men never were baldies. So. What's it to be, girls? Indian or Chinese?'

'Haven't you got any salad stuff or fruit or something?' I asked.

Dad grinned. 'Er . . . there might be a lemon in the fridge.'

I should have known better than to ask. He and Anna are

hopeless when it comes to stocking up on food. They might both be dead brainy (Dad works as a lecturer in English literature at a university in town and Anna is doing a PhD in medieval poetry) but they haven't a clue when it comes to eating properly. They live off takeaways. Normally I don't mind a bit, in fact I enjoy going round there for a curry night but tonight, I wanted to eat something without too many calories. What could I do to keep Mum and Dad happy but not break my diet?

'OK, I'll have a prawn curry,' I said. 'And I'll scrape the sauce off.'

'Mad.' Dad sighed as he got up to phone our order through. 'Totally bonkers.'

By the time the takeaway arrived an hour later, I thought I was going to pass out with hunger. It smelt divine. Spicy and inviting. When Dad offered me some of his spinach paneer and his naan bread, I gave in. And scrape the sauce of my prawn curry? You must be joking. I wolfed the lot and the bits of Anna's that she couldn't finish.

Hopeless, hopeless, hopeless, I told myself when Dad dropped me home later.

For a brief second, I thought about going up to the bathroom and putting my fingers down my throat. Loads of girls at our school do it. Bulimia. Kayley Morrison in our year does it. I've heard her throwing up in the cloakroom after lunch. It's weird. She eats a good lunch. I've seen her. Big sandwiches and chocolate bars. Milkshakes. Then she goes and vomits it all up. OK, she is slim but she doesn't look good. Her skin looks powdery and she looks unwell somehow. We had a health adviser come in and talk to us about it once. Apparently all the acid regenerated from your stomach rots your teeth. And I didn't fancy being slim and toothless. Not a good look in my book.

I may be desperate but I'm not *that* desperate, I thought as I went in to say hi to Mum and Angus. I shall just cut back tomorrow. If you add everything up that I've eaten so far this week, it must surely be less than I normally eat.

Upstairs, later, I decided to pick out an outfit for Saturday. There must be something that will look good, I thought as I searched through my wardrobe. A lot of my clothes are black so that's good as it's a slimming colour. But everything looked that little bit too tight. T-shirts that had fitted perfectly only months ago stretched unattractively over my boobs, and there was a welt of flab over the top of my jeans.

Maybe I won't bother going on Saturday, I thought. Maybe Mum's right and losing weight is going to be a long term thing.

My phone bleeped. It was a text message from Dad.

DIET RELIGIOUSLY, it said. EAT WHAT YOU LIKE AND PRAY THAT IT DOESN'T SHOW.

Haha. Not.

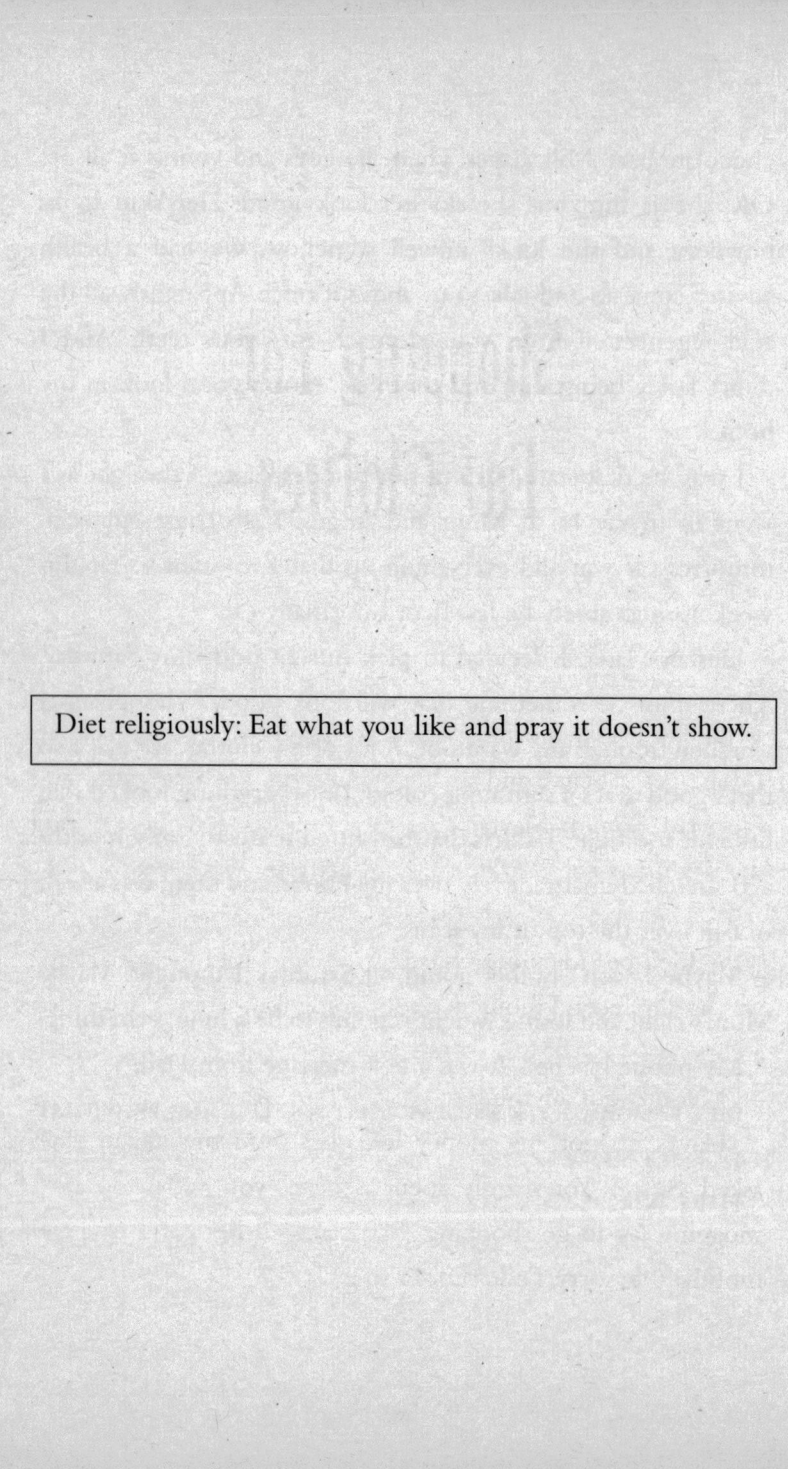

Diet religiously: Eat what you like and pray it doesn't show.

Chapter 7

Shopping For Fat Clothes

Weigh-in. Friday morning: I have dropped two pounds. Bizarre. I don't get it. Starve and nothing comes off. Eat a big curry and I lose two pounds. Maybe it was all my efforts to eat little during the day. Whatever. Two down, only six to go. V. v. happy.

'Oh, don't be ridiculous,' said Lucy when I told the girls that I was having second thoughts about going tomorrow. 'That's such a cop-out.'

'I haven't got anything to wear.'

'Have you got any money left over from the Italian trip?' asked Nesta. 'You hardly spent a bean, you were too busy snogging Jay to go shopping.' She clamped her hand over her mouth. 'Oh, sorry. Didn't mean to . . .'

'It's OK,' I said. 'You can say his name.'

'How much have you got?' asked Lucy.

I did a quick calculation in my head. With this week's pocket money and the money left over from Italy, I'd had fifty, but I'd spent some of it on slimming magazines. 'About forty pounds.'

'Right. So we go shopping after school and sort you out some new clothes,' said Lucy. 'I'll be your personal fashion adviser.'

'No. I have to lose six pounds first.'

Nesta laughed. 'Only six? Listen, girl, we're going to help you lose forty.'

The mall was heaving when we got there after school. It seemed like half the teen population of North London had had the same idea and the shops were busy, busy, busy. Outside it was wet and windy so it was good to get off the bus and into the dry where we could walk about without getting soaked and our hair wrecked.

After trawling around for the best part of an hour, I still hadn't found anything. Nesta, on the other hand, had found a gorgeous little turquoise silk camisole in Monsoon. Lucy had bought a dinky beaded handbag in Accessorize and even TJ had found something she liked, a strappy olive green T-shirt in TopShop that looked great with her brown hair and eyes.

'Why is it that when you go looking for something,' I asked, 'you never find it? And when you're not looking, you see all sorts of things?'

'Same with boys,' said Nesta. 'Go looking and all you meet are geeks. Give up and along comes Mr Right.'

'Or Mr Right Now in your case,' Lucy said, laughing.

Nesta punched her. 'Some day my prince will come.'

'That's what the girl who left a film to be developed at the photo shop said,' Lucy told us. 'Some days my prints will come.'

Nesta patted her on the head. 'Sad,' she said. 'Very sad.'

I tried all my usual shops but nothing looked right. After an hour, I was ready to give up and become a nun.

'Coffee break,' said Nesta. 'We need to regroup and re-energise.'

'Whatever,' I said. Usually I looked forward to our café breaks but today the prospect didn't hold the same allure.

'Come on,' said Nesta and led us up the escalator to the floor where all the cafés were.

'I could always make you something, Iz,' said Lucy as we stood in the queue to get served.

'By tomorrow? I don't think so.'

I felt depressed. And the last shop we'd been into had been the final straw. I had eventually seen an electric blue top that I liked and went to try it on. In the changing room, there were mirrors that showed you from every angle. Front, side and back. It was horrible. I liked the top but my usual size (twelve) was way too small. I had definitely gone up a size and the thought of being a fourteen filled me with dismay. When I'd shamefully gone out to ask for the bigger size, the snooty assistant had told me that they hadn't got it in 'the larger sizes'.

'Perhaps I should shop in one of the shops for large ladies,' I said when we'd got our drinks (chocolate milkshakes for TJ, Nesta and Lucy and tea without milk for me) and we sat down.

'Izzie, you *have* to get over this,' said Lucy. 'You are by no means a large lady. It's getting boring.'

'Pff,' I said. 'Nesta is the only one of you honest enough to say that I'm fat.'

Nesta almost spat her milkshake out. 'I never did. I *never* said fat.'

'Did.'

'Didn't.'

'Did.'

'Did *not*.'

'Rivetting conversation,' said TJ. 'Remind me to hang out with you guys again.'

Nesta ignored her. 'Did not. Did not. Did not a million times. I said that you had gained a little weight in Italy. You did. A little. But you can carry it. You're five foot eight or whatever.'

'Yeah,' said TJ. 'You're probably exactly the right weight for your height.'

'The only way I'd be the right weight for my height is if I was eight foot seven. I don't want to carry it. I want to be sylph-like. Tall and willowy. I won't be happy until I am.'

'Then you'll never be happy,' said Nesta. 'You are not a sylph-like build. Or willowy. You are, as we've said before, curvy. I really don't know what your problem is. Boys like curves.'

'Not as much as they like skinny girls,' I protested. 'Little girly girls.'

'Not what Lal and Steve say,' said Lucy. 'They say that they like girls that look female, that is, curvy. You're lucky you look the way you do.'

'You're just saying that.'

'No, I'm not,' said Nesta. 'I mean, why would you want to be Olive Oyle when you could look like Jessica Rabbit?'

'I saw this programme about body image on telly the other night,' said TJ. 'It was the top ten things that make a naked body attractive and sexy. Want to know what number one was?'

'Flat stomach,' I said.

'Nope.'

'Great boobs,' said Nesta.

'Nope,' said TJ. 'And it was something for men *and* women. Great boobs wouldn't look so great on a bloke.'

'Three nipples,' said Lucy. 'And the ability to lick your eyebrows as a party trick?'

'Yeah, right,' TJ said, laughing. 'No. It was confidence. All the experts said the same. Whatever shape or size, if you're confident, it is a million times more attractive than trying to hide your body or make excuses for some of it.'

'That's what Lal says,' said Lucy. 'He said he can't stand these girls who are always going on about the size of their bum. He said that what girls don't realise is that most boys are happy that girls have got bums, whatever the shape.'

'He would,' said Nesta. 'But it makes sense. Confidence. Yeah. Strut your stuff and if you've got it, flaunt it.'

Easier said than done, I thought. I can't imagine strutting my stuff, naked or clothed.

'So, Iz. You've got to chill,' said Nesta. 'You look great. So you've gone up a size. Big deal. We're teenagers. We're bound to be growing.'

'But not in every direction.'

'Nobody's totally happy about the way they look,' said Lucy. 'Even some of the top models hate certain aspects of their bodies.'

'Yeah. Get off this trip, Izzie. We all have hang-ups,' said Nesta. 'Like me and my stupid big feet. Size nine. I hate them. But I can't do anything about it unless I chop my toes off. And this stupid brace I have to wear. Do you think I like that? No way. Some days I think that all people see when they look at me is a metalmouth.'

'And I hate being mini me,' said Lucy. 'Don't you think I'd like to be taller? And have boobs. How do you think I feel hanging out with you three? Sometimes I think I look like I'm traipsing after my big sisters.'

'And I hate my shape,' said TJ. 'Straight, up down. No waist. At least you have a waist, Izzie.'

'And boobs,' said Lucy.

'And nice feet and great teeth,' said Nesta.

'And beautiful eyes,' said TJ. '*Bella ochi.*'

I could see I wasn't going to get any sympathy here as they all went into a mock sobbing act.

'Oh, I'm so ugly,' wailed Nesta.

'And I'm uglier,' TJ joined in.

'And *I'm* the ugliest of all,' cried Lucy.

A couple of boys went past and looked at us as though we were all barking mad and that set us off laughing.

'Seriously though, Iz,' said TJ. 'If you're really worried about having gained a few pounds, we're here to help. Aren't we guys?' She looked at Nesta and Lucy.

'Yeah. We'll give you advice,' said Lucy then grinned mischievously. 'Like want to diet? Go to the paint store – you can get thinner there.'

I laughed then punched her. 'Oh, very funny. Not.'

'And I know a great way to lose weight,' said Nesta. 'Eat naked in front of a mirror. Restaurants will almost always throw you out before you can eat too much.'

I rolled my eyes. 'You lot aren't taking me seriously.'

'We would if you had a genuine problem,' said TJ. 'But you don't, you really don't. OK, so you don't look like a stick-thin model out of a magazine but neither do they half the time. Did you know that they can airbrush them to look that way?'

'Be great if you could do that in real life,' I said. 'Someone would make a fortune.'

'It's all about dressing for your particular body shape,' said Lucy. 'I can help with that.'

'What? By advising me to cover up in a baggy top?'

'Most definitely not,' said Lucy. 'Baggy clothes can make people look bigger. You need to show off your shape, not hide it.'

'And if you want to lose a few pounds,' said TJ, 'exercise. That will burn off a few calories.'

'And in the meantime, let's talk about something more interesting,' said Nesta. 'Like that group of lads at the table over there. They've been eyeing us up since we sat down. Now, can we be bothered with them or shall we resume our shopping?'

We all did the room scan the way that Nesta had taught us, i.e.: don't look directly at boys in question, instead look around the whole room in a general sweep taking in the boys as you do. That way, you appear to be cool and not desperate and on the look out.

'No thanks,' I said when I'd done the 'sweep'. There was no one there I fancied. They looked about our age. Too young. And short.

As we finished our drinks, I made a mental note to lighten up. Even though I felt that the girls were only saying that I looked OK to make me feel better, I could see that I was in danger of becoming a real bore about being big. I resolved to be more fun in future so on the escalator going back down into the mall, I treated them to my impersonation of a cross-eyed robot.

For some reason, they all decided to join in. It was then that I spotted a boy I dated last year. Mark. I quickly darted behind a pillar at the bottom of the escalator. He was the last person I wanted to see. And he was holding hands with a girl. A willowy, thin girl wearing a tiny tank top, which revealed a midriff as flat as a pancake.

So boys prefer curvy girls do they? Yeah right. I felt more determined than ever to drop some weight. I just wouldn't go on about it any more to the girls.

Number One secret to being attractive: Confidence.

Chapter 8

Knock Out

I started my exercise regime first thing the next morning.

Up down, up down, up down. And now the other eyelid.

After I'd got out of bed, I went into my preparations for the run-through of *Teen Talk*. The girls wouldn't hear of me not going so I'd decided to be positive about it. Today, I wanted to make an impression on Studio Boy and I was determined not to let my weight problem get in the way.

I made a big effort blow-drying my hair, then ran my ceramic irons through it so that it was dead straight. Then I tried on some of the clothes in my wardrobe. First, my black jeans and I found that they were a tad looser than they had been on Monday. Hurrah. If I held my breath, I could get away with wearing them. I could wear a little camisole on top and a jacket over it. If I kept the jacket on, then no one would notice the wodge of splodge hanging over my waistband. Final touches were my amethyst earrings, purple bead choker, a slick of lip-gloss, a squirt of the Jo Malone Tuberose perfume that my stepsister Amelia had given me for my last birthday and I was ready to go.

After dressing, I went downstairs and had a piece of dry toast for breakfast (as the last thing I wanted was my stomach to start rumbling when we were in the audience). Mum was in a really good mood and happy to see me eating, if only toast. I asked her if I could join the local gym and miracle of miracles, she said it was a great idea and asked me to drop in and check out the joining fees. She said that she had been thinking about getting fitter and that her and Angus might join as well, though Angus went as white as his hair and didn't look too happy about the suggestion at all.

Nesta and Lucy were meeting up in Highgate and going on the Tube down to Camden but I had taken on board what TJ had said yesterday about exercise and decided to walk there. It was the new, upbeat, 'I can do this, I shall exercise myself thin' me. It would take about half an hour if I went at a good pace.

Big mistake.

When I set off, the sky was clear but as I reached Highgate Hill, clouds began to appear. And then more clouds. By the time I reached Kentish Town, the heavens opened and it poured down. I hadn't thought to take an umbrella so I ran as fast as I could and by the time I reached the studio, I was red in the face, my lovely straightened hair was plastered to my cheeks, my mascara had run and I was soaked through.

I was also ten minutes late and the guy on the reception had closed the entrance door.

'Please,' I mouthed to him through the glass.

I must have looked such a pathetic sight that he relented and let me in.

'Better move it,' he said. 'The others went in ages ago.'

I raced along the corridor and just as I was turning into the studio, the door opened and someone came out. Mature boy with the spiky hair and I smacked right into him.

The papers he was carrying went everywhere and as I bent down to help him retrieve them, unfortunately it was at exactly the same time that he did and our heads banged together.

'Ow,' he said, coming up fast.

'Ouch,' I said, coming up after him.

'You always make this kind of impression on first encounter?' he asked.

'Yeah,' I said as I rubbed my head. 'I like to knock people out when I meet them.'

He sniffed the air near my neck. 'Hey, you smell nice.'

I smiled. 'Jo Malone.'

He put out a hand. 'Gabriel.'

'No,' I said. 'My name's Izzie. Jo Malone is the maker of the perfume.'

'I know. Just joshing,' he said, then raised an eyebrow. 'Classy stuff. I like her scented candles.'

As we talked, I noticed that I was dripping water onto the floor.

'Oh God,' I said. 'I got caught in the rain. I must look such a mess . . .'

'Not at all.' Gabriel smiled. 'Just a bit wet that's all. Actually I . . . I noticed you the other day . . .'

'Because I was a mess then too? I felt such a frump when I got here and saw how everyone else looked.'

'No. But that's why I noticed you. Not because you looked like a frump at all. Far from it. You looked like a real person. So many of the others had put on all their clubbing clothes, like dressed to impress. I noticed you and thought, she looks like a girl you could actually have a proper conversation with.'

Wow, I thought as he opened the studio door for me. A boy who knows his perfumes, likes scented candles and makes you feel good even when you know you look like crapola.

'You'd better go in. And don't worry, they haven't got started yet.'

'Thanks,' I said as I tiptoed in.

'Catch you later,' he said.

Nesta was sitting down near the front with Lucy and they gave me a wave as an usher directed me to a seat on the back row.

Nothing much was happening yet and for the next forty minutes or so, everyone in the audience just sat about, chatted and watched as the crew set up lighting and cameras and Gabriel brought in a stool and a guitar and set up a mike in front of them. Rumour had it that the guest on the first show was going to be Alicia Prowdy, an American singer-songwriter. I couldn't wait. I loved her stuff and had one of her CDs at home.

At around eleven, just as I was about to nod off, John (the producer we'd met on Thursday) came in with Geena Parker and everyone sat up in anticipation. I'd seen Geena before on TV. She had the usual teen show presenter looks: long legs, slim, blonde, smiley face. She was one of the celebrities that I'd read about in one of my slimming magazines. She said in the article that it's part of her job to stay in shape and she has to work hard at it as TV can make you look bigger than you are. She said she jogs every day and never drinks alcohol. As she went down to the stage, I wondered if she ever splurged out on chips or chocolate or if she was always strict with herself? She began talking to four teens in the front row and asked them to take their places. Must be the panel, I thought as they made their way onto the stage. There was a tall blond boy, quite cute-looking in the King of the Elves, *Lord of the Rings* kind of way but not my type. Next to him was a pretty brunette with a pony-tail who looked very uncomfortable, next to her, a girl with short red hair and a cheeky face who looked like she might be interesting, and beside her at the end, a boy with dark hair and bushy eyebrows.

After a few preliminary instructions from John, the first discussion soon got under way. I was so busy watching what Gabriel was doing that I missed what the topic was.

'What's it about?' I asked the girl sitting next to me.

'Jealousy,' she whispered back as the noise level at the front grew.

Geena began roving the stage and the audience. Immediately I could see that she was having a hard time controlling the proceedings as people kept calling out from the audience, talking over each other, shouting, and Mr Eyebrows was the loudest of them all. He seemed to be doing his best to dominate the whole discussion.

After about five minutes, John shouted, 'Cut.'

He went on to the stage and shook his head. 'Right. This isn't working, guys,' he said. 'We have to have some order here. Geena will let you know when she wants you to speak and you lot on the panel, for heaven's sake, give each other a break. Let each other talk or no one's going to get heard.' At this point he looked at Eyebrows.

The discussion got underway again as Geena asked, 'So . . . jealousy. A green-eyed monster or a healthy emotion? Let's hear what our panel has to say.' She looked at the redhead girl to say something.

'It can be difficult if someone's flirty by nature and their partner is insecure,' she started, 'but I guess it all comes down to trust. I think . . .'

'If you're in a relationship,' Eyebrows butted in, 'why are you flirting?'

'I didn't say *I* was flirting or that I was in a relationship,' said the redhead. 'I was about to . . .'

'Jealousy sucks,' said Eyebrows. 'It's a negative emotion.'

The Elfin King on the panel began to try and say something but Eyebrows talked (or rather shouted) over him so he backed down. The redhead looked as though she wanted to sock Eyebrows and the girl with the pony-tail looked like she was going to cry. And then she did.

'Stop shouting,' she said then got up and ran off.

Geena looked bewildered for a moment then turned to the audience. 'Let's hear from our studio audience. Anyone got anything to say?'

'Cut, cut,' called John from the back. 'Cue the song.'

A few moments later, a stunning tall thin girl with long, dark hair and wearing jeans and cowboy boots got up and began to sing a country and western type ballad. It *was* Alicia Prowdy. She's one of my favourite singer-songwriters as not only do I love her voice but also her image. She's exactly how I'd like to look. I couldn't believe my luck in being there to see her and hear her sing live. The moment didn't last long though because behind me, I could hear Geena and John having a heated discussion about how best to run the show.

'This is a disaster,' whispered John. 'You have to take control. Get them to raise their hands.'

'Like in school? No way,' said Geena. 'They're teens, not kids.'

'It's not going to work otherwise . . .'

I tried to concentrate on Alicia but it was useless with them bickering behind me and just as they stopped, the song finished and John announced that we were having a break.

The noise level grew as everyone started chatting and Lucy crept up to sit with me. 'Think I'll stay back here from now on,' she said. 'I thought it was going to end up in fisticuffs down there.'

After about ten minutes, John went back down to the stage.

'We're going to try again,' he said then pointed at Nesta. 'You, second row. Want to try out for the panel?'

Nesta nodded, quickly took her place on the stage then looked to find Lucy and me at the back. We gave her the thumbs-up.

'You,' said John pointing at Eyebrows, 'thanks a lot and we'll get back to you. For the moment, could you sit at the back, and we'll give someone else a go.'

Eyebrows looked surprised and got up, but instead of going to the back, he walked out, slamming the door behind him.

John pointed at a small Harry Potter lookalike in the second row. 'You. Panel. Let's go again and try to keep it civil this time. If you want to say anything, raise your hand.'

As Harry Potter boy took his place on the stage, Geena walked back down to the front and beamed into one of the cameras. 'Welcome back to *Teen Talk*. The show where we want to hear what teens are talking. No. Can I do that again? OK. Welcome to *Teen Talk* where we listen, teens talk. Oh, bugger. I'll do that again. Welcome to *Teen Talk*. The topic for the second part of our show is faithfulness. How important is it in a relationship?'

This time the discussion proceeded more successfully with Geena making it very clear who she wanted to talk and when.

'I believe it's one hundred percent important,' said the redhead girl. 'Why be in a relationship if you're not going to stick with it?'

'Even if your partner wasn't being faithful?' asked Geena.

Nesta raised her hand and Geena indicated for her to go ahead. 'I think if he's being unfaithful, there's no point in having a relationship because the trust can't be there and that's one of the most important things.' I got the feeling she was talking about herself and Luke and TJ before Christmas.

'Good point,' said Geena. 'But sometimes you don't know when someone's being unfaithful.'

'Tell me about it,' said Nesta, rolling her eyes. Everyone laughed.

'But at our age, how can we know what we want if we don't experiment?' said Elfin King. 'And sometimes that means letting someone down.'

'Yeah, but what about loyalty? What about commitment?' asked Geena. 'In fact is there a difference?'

It was at this moment that I felt a rush of adrenaline and before I had time to think about speaking in front of so many people, I had put my hand up.

'At the back,' said Geena. 'Dark hair.'

'Um . . .' I began as all eyes turned to look at me. 'I think there's a huge difference. Loyalty is something you want to do, whereas commitment sounds like something you have to do.'

'Explain,' said Geena.

'Um . . . commitment is the word used for when people get sent to prison, you know, they get committed. Like there's no choice involved. Loyalty is different. You choose to be loyal to certain people because you care about them. And if you care about someone – whether it's a mate or a boyfriend, then you wouldn't want to hurt them by being unfaithful.'

'But what if the relationship isn't working any more and you meet someone you like better? That will hurt them. Should you tell them?' asked a boy in the row in front of me.

I waited until he had finished, then nodded. 'Absolutely. What could be worse than stringing someone along? It might hurt but I think it's better to admit when something isn't working. So what I'd say is that you have to be faithful to the truth.'

A couple of girls in the audience clapped and the discussion carried on. I hardly heard anyone for the next few minutes as I couldn't believe that I had managed to get my thoughts out.

After the run-through, Gabriel came over and sat beside me.

'Hey, you were really good,' he said. 'I liked what you said.'

'Thanks. It's weird talking in front of so many people. It's like everything goes into slow motion.'

He nodded. 'Some people totally lose it in front of a camera. People who are normally coherent go blank or freeze. You seemed completely at ease.'

I laughed. 'Not how I felt.'

'Shame it's only the run-through today as your comments would have made good TV. Still, we have to do it this way so that we can see how it looks and we can get a rough idea of who can talk and who's going to choke before we do the first show. As you can see, we have a few things to iron out but we'll get there.'

'But what about Alicia?'

'Oh, her bit will be used. She's only here this week so we had to pre-record her.'

'So what do you do here?'

'I'm on work experience from college. I'm doing media studies and want to work in TV. Producing, I think. I'm still not sure. Our tutor fixed it up so that I could work here for a few days a week. My official title is General Dogsbody.'

I laughed. 'OK, General.'

After that we got chatting and I found him really easy to talk to, like he was one of the gang and as people milled around the studio, we sat there having a laugh and making bitchy comments about what people were wearing and what they'd said. As everyone was getting ready to leave, he put his hand over mine.

'Been great to meet you, Izzie. As I said before when you tried to knock me out, I thought we'd get on the first time I saw you. In fact, you remind me of my sister.'

Sister? I thought as I got up to go. *Sister!* I really fancied him and had hoped that he felt the same way but I reminded him of his sister? Who'd want to snog their sister? I hoped that he'd ask for my number or ask if we could see each other again but he didn't. Maybe it's because I'm fat, I thought. Maybe he feels safe with me and that's why he can chat away to me. No danger of any complications. I remember when TJ went through something similar. She fancied this boy called Scott but he treated her like a confidant and said he could talk to her as she was like one of the boys. By now, the wonderful high I'd felt earlier had vanished and I felt like a deflated balloon brought down to earth after losing its air.

One of the boys. A sister. Safe. Dogs' poo, I thought as I joined the others filing out of the studio into the horrible grey afternoon.

Izzie's exercise regime:
Up down, up down.
And now the other eyelid.

Chapter 9

Temptation Alley

As it had stopped raining when we got out of the studio, we decided to go up to Camden Lock and have a cruise around the market. Nesta was over the moon at having been picked to be on the panel and she wondered why I didn't feel the same high.

'Because Gabriel thinks I'm like his sister,' I groaned as we headed up the high street and I filled them in on my conversation with him.

'His sister might be a real hottie,' said Nesta. 'He might have paid you the most wonderful compliment in the world. What is going on with you lately, Izzie? You're so down on yourself.'

'Yeah,' said Lucy. 'And you're usually Miss Positive.'

I shrugged. 'Dunno. Just . . . oh, it's just I seem to be losing all my confidence. It's gone down the plughole.'

'Why don't you do some of your affirmations?' asked Lucy. 'All that full of joy stuff you always used to chant. Remember I am full of joy, I am full of joy, I am full of joy.'

'Right. I am full of joy,' I said miserably.

Usually I'm a great believer that state of mind is often due to choice. Tell yourself that you're miserable and your mind goes OK, yeah, I am. Choose to be happy and you can be – and you can boost the feeling by making positive affirmations. But fat? I hadn't chosen that and yet it was the reason for my mood and my loss of confidence. Maybe Lucy was right. I should start doing my affirmations.

'And do one of your visualisations,' said Nesta. 'Visualise yourself the exact size you want to be, having a great time with Gabriel. Maybe it will come true.'

I knew that Nesta thought that visualisations (unless they were of racks of clothes at the mall) were baloney, and she was just trying to be supportive.

'Thanks, Nesta. I will.' I tried to imagine myself as she said but couldn't get the image right. I kept seeing myself as the Blob girl surrounded by skinny minnies.

Just as we were going over the bridge on the approach to the Lock, Lucy swerved to the left.

'Let's cross over,' she said and tried to hustle us across the road which wasn't a good idea as there was a great double decker bus coming straight at us.

'Woah, what's the hurry?' I asked as I pulled her back on to the pavement.

Lucy looked over my shoulder, then tried to drag me over the road again. She'd clearly seen someone she wanted to avoid so I looked around to see who it might be. About ten metres down the pavement, Jay was coming towards us, hand in hand, with a pretty blonde girl. She was pointing at something in a shop and he was pulling her on. And then he saw us, met my eyes and froze. He looked away and hauled the girl into the nearest shop.

'Ohmigod!' said Lucy.

'She must be the steady girlfriend,' I said. 'Tawny.'

'What? Who?' asked Nesta, who had missed the whole episode.

'Jay,' I said. 'He just went into that shop over there with his girlfriend.'

'Did he see you?'

'Oh yes. Most definitely.'

I felt sick. First Gabriel tells me I remind him of his sister and now Jay appears, as if to remind me that I was just a holiday fling. I felt a negative visualisation coming on. Primarily of meeting Jay down an alley and whacking him around the head. With a wet fish.

'Done a runner, has he?' asked Nesta. 'Let's follow him in there and see how he handles it. We could offer to show him some photos from the Italian trip, some of him snuggling up to you. Have you got any with you? Yeah. Let's see him worm his way out of that.'

She was about to race into the shop after him but I pulled her back.

'No, Nesta, leave it,' I said.

'But you can't. I think you should go after him and tell him what you think of him,' said Nesta.

'What? When Tawny's with him?'

'She needs to hear what he's like. Tell her how he was two-timing her while he was in Italy.'

I shook my head. 'No. Leave it.'

'I'll go,' said Nesta. 'What was it you were saying earlier about being faithful to the truth? Now's your chance.'

'No. I don't want to cause a scene.'

Nesta hurrumphed. 'I am *sooo* sick of boys who think they can get away with MURDER,' she said at the top of her voice causing a passing punk guy to stop and stare at her. 'He had a fab time with you and now he's back with his girlfriend having a merry old time and you've been hurt. It's not fair. You weren't to know that he was in a relationship. I could kill him.'

'Yeah, go and kill him,' muttered the punk guy before walking on.

'I am full of joy,' I chanted. 'I am full of joy, full of joy, full of joy.'

'I'm not,' said Nesta. 'I am full of anger, full of anger, full of anger.' She kicked a lamppost causing another passer by to stare at her.

'Well, I am full of wee, full of wee, full of wee,' said Lucy as she began to cross the road again. 'I need to find a Ladies.'

'Yeah, let's go to the market,' I said as I began to follow her. 'I need retail therapy.'

We walked into the indoor market which was heaving with the usual Saturday Camden crowd: goths, punks, hippies, townies, people of every nationality. Everyone was swarming around looking at the stalls selling everything under the sun: jewellery, clothes, Eastern artefacts, antiques, oils, CDs, cushions – you name it and you can probably find it at the Lock.

After mooching about there for a while, we wandered through to the back of the Lock to see what was going on in the shops under the arches and in the outdoor section.

As we headed out, the delicious aroma of spices, onions and garlic wafted towards us.

'Oh no,' I said. 'Temptation alley.'

Just outside the indoor market is a maze of corridors with stalls selling every kind of food you can imagine: Thai, Indian, Mexican, Greek, burgers, muffins, bagels.

'Come, eat,' called a pretty Thai girl from behind one stall. In front of her was an array of fabulous-looking exotic dishes.

'Mmm,' said Nesta. 'I'm starving. Fancy some noodles?'

'Or a burrito,' said Lucy looking at a Mexican stall.

'I'm going to make a run for it,' I said thinking that the faster I was away from there, the better. 'I'll see you in Cyberdog.'

And with that, I ran down the alley until I was out of the

vicinity of all the appetising smells and into another alleyway under the arches that smelt heavily of joss sticks.

'Phew, made it,' I said to myself as I had a quick look at a stall selling Indian artefacts and then went on into Cyberdog.

Cyberdog is my favourite shop in London. It's like nowhere else. When you walk in, it's as if you've entered a time capsule in a sci-fi movie. The front of the shop is an open area with a café pounding with music. Through arches at the back are the clothes rails and the assistants who look like they're extras in *Star Trek*.

I gazed in awe at one tall girl whose head was shaved at the back, with a sprout of dark hair at the top like a black tiara. She was dressed from head to toe in black with silver belts and boots and glasses. She looked like an alien princess.

The clothes were something else, too. They always are in there. Tops with the bottom seams lined with coathanger-type wire so that they stick out from your body. Stunning perspex chokers and bracelets with studs in them that look glamorous and dangerous at the same time. I spied a gorgeous black mesh top with satin ribs sewn up the front and then I saw the outfit that had my name on it. Absolutely perfect *and* it was reduced from fifty-five pounds to thirty. It was a sleeveless top and mini skirt in black pinstripe. Up the centre of the skirt was a silver zip and on the top, from the collarbone to the waist over the boobs were two more silver zips. It looked fabulous. And if I bought it I could wear them separately. I quickly took it off the rail and went to try it on.

As I was in the changing room, I heard Nesta and Lucy calling my name.

'In here,' I said and peeked round the curtain.

'Wow,' said Lucy as she pulled the curtain aside so that she could see. 'That makes you look amazing. And really slim.'

'You have to buy it,' said Nesta. 'Can you afford it?'

I looked at the price again. With the money I had left from Italy, I could easily do it and have ten pounds over.

I nodded. 'Mum's going to hate it but . . . give me a tick and we'll go to the cash desk.'

At that moment, Nesta's phone rang. A second later, she handed the phone to me in the changing room.

'Jay,' she said as her and Lucy crowded in with me so that they could listen. 'He must have got my number from Chris or Liam.'

'Is that Izzie?' asked Jay as I took the phone.

'Yes.'

'Listen. About earlier . . . I'm so sorry and I want to explain. Can you talk?'

Nesta, who had her ear pressed against my head, pulled a disapproving face.

'Yes. But I haven't got a lot to say.'

'That girl you saw me with . . .'

'Yes. Tawny. We . . . I know all about her. Your steady girlfriend. Funny how you forgot to mention her when we were in Florence.'

'I . . . I only didn't mention her because . . . well, it's over . . .'

'Oh. Didn't look that way to me.'

Lucy, who had her ear pressed to the other side of my face, gave me the thumbs-up.

'I'm just waiting for the right time to tell her,' said Jay.

Nesta feigned a yawn.

'Yeah, right,' I said.

'No, really. I still want to see you and I'm sorry that you saw us before I'd got it sorted. Can we meet up?'

'Oh. So you've told her already?'

'No . . . not exactly. But I will. I'm going to.'

'Yeah, sure,' I said again. 'Heard that one before.'

And I ended the call and gave Nesta back her phone.

She looked at me in surprise. 'That it?'

'That's it.'

'You're not going to see him?'

'No way,' I said as I picked up my new outfit and headed for the cash desk. 'I'm not stupid. Remember what you went through with Luke? No way am I going there. Someone's either involved with someone else or they're free. I don't do in-betweens.'

'That's what's so top about you, Izzie,' said Nesta. 'You're brilliant. So clear about things. Like the rest of us are all more easily taken in by a bit of smooth talk . . .'

'Speak for yourself,' said Lucy. 'Your brother's one of the smoothest talkers around and I'm resisting him.'

'For the moment,' said Nesta. 'But he's wearing you down. Anyone can see that . . .'

'Hey, give me some credit,' said Lucy. 'He's not wearing me down at all. I'm a free agent at the moment and enjoying it, but that doesn't mean to say that I can't see who I want, when I want, and that includes Tony.'

'Yeah. OK,' said Nesta, 'but before we went to Italy, you were determined that it was all over. End of story. And now, you're seeing him again. I bet Izzie's not going to start seeing Jay again as friends are you, Iz?'

I shook my head. 'No way.'

'See, you're nobody's fool. You're a wise woman. Smart about what matters.'

I could see that Lucy was starting to get annoyed. 'And are you saying that I'm not smart because I'm seeing your brother?'

'Yeah,' said Nesta.

'But it's different with us,' said Lucy. 'Tony hasn't been two-timing me. I have no reason to cut him out of my life. We still like each other. OK, so we want different things right now but that needn't stop us being mates.'

'She's right,' I said. 'Jay has behaved really badly. Tony hasn't.'

'Not yet,' said Nesta.

'Sometimes, I think that you're jealous,' said Lucy. 'Jealous that I hang out with him so much.'

Nesta shrugged. 'Whatever,' she said. 'I just wish I was as clear about things as Izzie.'

'But you are,' I said. 'You cut Luke out of your life after you'd found out that he was messing you around. So you're nobody's fool either. In fact, I think we're all pretty smart these days when it comes to boys.'

'I guess,' said Nesta. 'Yeah. OK. So I'm smart too. Just . . . all I'm saying Lucy, is be careful with Tony. I don't want to see you get hurt.'

'I will be,' said Lucy. 'And you needn't worry. I don't want to get involved with him again. I know he might be leaving in September and once he starts university, he's not going to want some girlfriend back home that he has to answer to. I'm aware of that so I'm not going to set myself up to get hurt.'

'But I thought he said he'd go to a university in London so he could be near you,' I said.

'He did,' said Lucy. 'But I also know that he applied to Oxford and if he gets an interview there and they make him an offer, it's going to be hard to resist.'

For a moment, she looked sad. She's putting on a brave face about all of this, I thought as I watched her. It must be hard keeping her feelings at bay because she knows it's inevitable that Tony will move on, no matter what he says to her about wanting to stay in London. His life is going to take him in another direction and she's trying really hard to accept that.

I gave her a hug. 'I reckon we've all got our heads well screwed on,' I said as the *Star Trek* princess assistant began to pack my outfit. 'Shame, though. I did like Jay. He was probably the best-looking boy who's ever shown an interest in me.'

'What about Gabriel? He's pretty hot,' said Nesta. 'Not my type but he's a cutie.'

'And I remind him of his sister.'

'You won't when he sees you in that new outfit,' said Nesta.

'Whatever,' said Lucy. 'But what does it matter that Jay is good looking or Gabriel? Beauty is only skin deep and anyway it's better to be beautiful on the inside. Like you Izzie.'

'Pff,' I said. 'Born inside out. Just my luck.'

Lucy laughed. 'No. It's true, Izzie. But you look beautiful on the outside too. Course you do. But one of the things we love about you is that you're clear about what you want, you take no bull from anyone and you *are* wise.'

If they knew what really went on in my head, they wouldn't say that, I thought, as I paid for my outfit and we headed back out into the market.

I suppose I can be clear and give advice sometimes, but only to others. I can't do it for myself. And so here I am, the Wise Woman of Wonga with no boyfriend. Why do I even bother about losing weight and trying to look good when Gabriel, the only boy I fancy at the moment, hasn't even taken my number and Jay, the boy I did fancy, is a two-timing waste of space?

As we strolled along, a bunch of boys cruised past. They looked like they hadn't a care in the world.

'It's not fair, is it? I said as I watched the boys saunter up to a coffee bar and order drinks.

'What's not?' asked Lucy.

'Looking good,' I said. 'It's so easy for boys. Us girls, we cleanse, we tone, we exfoliate, we moisturise, we diet, we exercise, we wax, we make up and rub lotions and potions into our bodies so that we smell sweet. We agonise over what to wear. And what do boys do. Shave and maybe whack on a bit of hair gel. Huh! That's what I say.'

'That's if they do shave,' said Nesta. 'Some of the ones I know don't even do that yet or only have to do it every other week.'

'Huh to boys,' said Lucy. 'It's true. They don't have to suffer to be beautiful at all, least not in the same way that we do.'

As the enticing aromas of temptation alley hit me on the way out, I thought, I'm sick of suffering to be beautiful. To hell with it, Lucy is right about one thing. I do know what I want and the smell is calling me to it. Izzie, Izzieeeeee . . .

Like, who needs boys when you can have burritos?

> I can resist everything except temptation
> – Oscar Wilde

Chapter 10

The X Factor

On the way home, we met up with TJ then stopped off at the gym in Muswell Hill and picked up a brochure and price list for Mum. A girl from the reception showed us around and it did look fab. It had a good sized pool, two studios offering classes in everything from dance and yoga to Pilates. The gym had all the latest equipment and best of all, there were some fit looking trainers hanging about ready to help anyone in need. I was looking forward to making exercise a part of my plan, since I didn't seem to be able to stick to any of the diets I'd tried for even twenty-four hours. Exercise was the clearly the solution, burn off the extra calories instead of starving then stuffing.

'Poor Angus,' I said as we stepped back out into the street

after our look round. 'Mum wants him to join the gym as well, so there goes his peace and quiet.'

'Don't worry,' said Nesta. 'My dad joined a gym in the new year in a fit of inspiration, but I think he thought that it was all he had to do. Join the gym and bingo, he'd be fit. I think he only ever went once.'

'I always liked your dad,' I said. 'Good man.'

'That's not the attitude,' said TJ. 'If you want to get in shape, you just have to find the type of exercise that you like doing.'

'I am in shape,' I said. 'Round is a shape. And no problem in knowing exactly what I like. Lying on the sofa, watching a good DVD, munching Maltesers.'

TJ rolled her eyes. 'I give up.'

'No. I'm just kidding. I will do it. I'm serious about the exercise thing. Honest.'

'Yeah, I may have to join as well,' said Nesta. 'Those cute instructors, hubba hubba, ding dong.'

'Me too,' said Lucy then she sighed. 'But then I suppose we'd have to exercise wouldn't we? We couldn't just go along to ogle the guys?'

I was glad that I wasn't the only one who wasn't fitness mad, like TJ. But it did seem unfair that Lucy and Nesta could avoid it and still stay slim.

'Exercise is good for you,' said TJ and did a handstand up against a wall. Unfortunately, her jacket and T-shirt slipped down exposing her bra and a boy of about eleven who was walking past almost choked on the ice cream he was eating.

'Cool,' he said when she flipped back up onto her feet. 'Do that again.'

'She's old enough to be your mother, sonny,' said Nesta.

'I like older women,' said the boy, grinning.

As we walked back up to The Broadway in Muswell Hill and the shops (trying to shake off the boy who tried to follow us in the hope that TJ would do another handstand), I couldn't help but notice that all the boys we passed did a double take when they saw Nesta. When she went into a shop to get some water, I turned to Lucy and TJ.

'Do you ever feel invisible when you're with Nesta?'

Lucy faked shock horror. 'Oh, you spoke to me? I didn't realise that I could be seen.'

'I'll take that as a yes then?'

'Double yes. It's amazing how people stare at her and never even notice that I'm here too. I could be walking along with my knickers on my head and they wouldn't look when she's around.'

'And boys only notice me when I stand upside down,' said TJ, 'and show the world my bra.'

'What are you talking about?' asked Nesta coming back out to join us.

'You,' I said. 'And the fact that you have amazing pulling power. We were just saying that we feel invisible when we're with you.'

'Rubbish. You have pulling power too.' She pointed at a group of boys sitting on the other side of the road on the wall outside Ryman's stationery shop. 'I'll prove it.'

'Prove it? How?' asked TJ.

'Come with me, my little fruitcakes,' she said as she led us across the zebra crossing and into the entrance of Sainsbury's supermarket. 'OK,' she said. 'I'll go first. I'll walk past the boys, then come back, and you have to watch how many of them check me out.'

'You don't need to bother,' I said. 'They all will.'

But she was off. And I was right. As she sauntered casually by, they stared at her appreciatively and a couple nudged each other.

A few minutes later, she was back. 'Score?'

I counted the boys. Six of them.

'Six out of six,' said Lucy.

TJ went next. This time four of the boys gave her the once-over as one seemed to be engrossed on his mobile and another was busy picking his nose.

Next was Lucy and she got the same score. Four out of four as the fifth boy was still talking on his phone and nose picker had started on his other nostril.

'OK, Iz. Your turn,' said Nesta.

I began to walk past the boys but I could see already that they were distracted by some of their mates who'd appeared from inside a café. As I approached them, only one of them checked me out. Doomed to failure, I thought. Invisible. And then I remembered a film I'd seen at Christmas with Judy Garland in it. I couldn't remember what it was called but she was after a part in a show and the producers took her out to see if she had the X factor in public. Just as Nesta was asking us do, the producers made Judy walk down a busy street and they walked behind to see if anyone had noticed her. She did her best to look smiley and sexy but no one was taking the slightest bit of notice. She began to panic. The producers started shaking their heads in disappointment at the lack of attention she was getting. Then everything changed. The camera went behind her so all you could see was her back walking away but suddenly everyone was staring at her. Head after head turned to look after her as she walked by and the producers were well impressed. The camera then went to the front so that you could see Judy walking towards you. She was making a duck face and that was the reason everyone was turning to stare. I decided to try the same tactic.

I pushed my lips out to make a beak, blew my cheeks out and made myself go cross-eyed. It worked a treat and Nose-picker nudged his mate who nudged his mate who nudged his mate and soon all the boys were staring at me with open mouths. I turned and skipped back to the girls.

'Result,' I said as I punched the air.

'See,' said Nesta. 'I *told* you that you had the X factor. All the boys were looking. So now will you stop going on about being invisible and boys not noticing you? You got top score.'

I couldn't keep it up any more and showed them what I'd

done. They all cracked up laughing and of course had to try it for themselves. As we made our way down the road, making the ugliest faces we could, everyone stared at us. It was hysterical. Of course that had to be the moment that we bumped into Mr Johnson from school.

'Oh, for God's sake, girls,' he said with a sigh as he went past. 'When are you going to grow up?'

'Just testing to see if we have the X factor, sir,' said Nesta.

'More like the Y factor,' he said. 'Why? Why? Why?'

When I got home later, my stepsister, Amelia was over visiting her dad. Angus was making tea in the kitchen and Amelia was curled up on the sofa watching TV so I went in to join her. We get on OK now but it took some time when Mum first married Angus and I found myself with two stepsisters, Amelia and Claudia, that I didn't particularly want. I was wary of them (I used to call them the wicked stepsisters) and I think that they were worried that I was going to usurp their position in their dad's heart but no chance of that – I really didn't like him for ages. I didn't give him a chance really; I even called him the lodger to help me deal with it. I thought he was boring and the girls were too good to be true, like a pair of little blonde Miss Perfects who had never done a thing wrong. Then one day Angus showed me photos of them in their punk phase. What a pair of maniacs. I almost felt sorry for Angus. We all get on great now. Almost like real family.

Amelia was watching a programme about a group of women on a weight loss trial. Just my thing so I settled in with her.

'Why are you watching this?' I asked as Amelia has always been skinny.

'I love makeover programmes,' she replied as we gazed at the telly. 'I love the before and afters. Like that woman there on the left of the screen with the short hair. She used to be massive and now look at her. Slimmed right down. She was saying that she was so unhappy before but no one realised as she used to play the joker so that everyone would like her and not realise how unhappy she was inside.'

Sounds familiar, I thought. That's just what I was doing up in Muswell Hill doing my duck faces. Playing the fool, so that no one would realise how desperate I really feel inside.

'I want to lose weight,' I said. 'But it's soooo difficult. Especially hanging out with mates who are always eating and it doesn't help having a mum who insists on meals three times a day. And I have no will-power. It's as if I have no 'stop' button when I smell or taste food. Before I can help myself, it's off the plate or out of the cupboard and in my mouth. If only someone could do my meals for me like for those women on the telly, then I wouldn't have to think about it.'

'Best way is not to even think about diets,' said Amelia. 'You have to change the way you eat. Make healthy eating part of your life.'

'I know, I *know*,' I said with a sigh. 'I've heard it all from Mum.

The sensible approach blah de blah de blah ... I've been cutting down this past week and it's felt like eternity. See, the thing is, I want to lose weight fast for a special occasion. I haven't got months to do it the sensible way.'

'So what's the big occasion? I bet there's some boy you're trying to impress isn't there?'

'Yes and no,' I said and told her a bit about Gabriel and all about *Teen Talk* and the fact that the TV puts ten pounds on you.

'Ah,' said Amelia. 'So you want a quick fix sort of thing?'

'Exactly.'

'In that case, try what I did when I wanted to shift a few pounds for my wedding. Slim shakes.'

'What are they?'

'Meal replacement drinks. You don't have to think about food at all, just have your slim shakes. They work a treat and they have all the stuff in them that you need to stay healthy.'

Brilliant, I thought. Something new to try. I had ten pounds left from my Italian trip and Mum would give me next week's pocket money tomorrow. I could easily afford them, I decided. It was way too complicated trying to work out what was low fat, high fat, protein, carb and what size portion I could or couldn't have. Anyway, I didn't have weeks left before the pilot show to do it the sensible way. This sounded perfect for a quick result. Just have a shake three times a day and then there was nothing else to think about. I knew Mum would never agree to it but I got the details from Amelia and decided to buy some the next day.

At last I had the way forward. Exercise and slim shakes. I was going to be a skinny minnie in no time.

I'm in shape. Round is a shape.

Chapter 11

Doing the Camel

'We have so many different classes on offer,' said the gym instructor when Mum went to sign us up the next day, 'I suggest that you try a few of them and see what suits you best. It's important to enjoy what you do.'

I couldn't wait. I'd try them all. I was fired up with enthusiasm, slim shakes hidden in my bag and ready to do a different class every day after school to see which suited me best. Outside, the weather was still cold but the sun was shining for the first time in weeks. At last it was March, the winter months were behind us and spring was on its way. It felt symbolic of a new start. A new me.

Monday: I went for my first session in the gym. Karl, who is a total hunk (but not my type, too er . . . bulgy in the lycra shorts department and legs like tree trunks), showed me how to use all the machines then stood there watching while I did my circuit. I was ready for a lie down after the first machine. It was called a cross trainer and, according to Karl, good for burning off calories. I thought I was going to die of a heart attack after about ten minutes. I carried on because Karl was watching and I didn't want to appear a total wimp, plus there were a couple of older guys there who had been going for ages and hadn't even broken into a sweat. After the cross trainer was the rowing machine. I gave it my all and pulled and pulled with all my might. By now, Karl was starting to annoy me as he said that if it had been a real boat, it would have sunk at the pace I was rowing. Very funny, not, I thought as I puffed and panted away.

Then there were machines for abs, machines for triceps, biceps, machines for muscles I didn't even know I had.

By the end of forty-five minutes, I realised that all these machines aren't new at all. They were used in the Middle Ages to torture people in dungeons.

'No pain, no gain,' Karl said, grinning, as I staggered out.

I decided the machines weren't for me. I'm more of the no pain, no pain school of philosophy and I had the rest of the week to find something I enjoyed and that didn't feel like punishment.

After my session, I went to treat myself to a little relaxation in the sauna. It was lovely and smelt fab because someone had put some eucalyptus oil on the burner. And then a bald old man came in and contributed his own aromatherapy. He did an SBD (silent but deadly). You've never seen a room clear so fast.

Slim shake report: two shakes, one vanilla for lunch, one chocolate for dinner. Not bad. Not great but they are drinkable. The trick, I realised, was to keep busy, busy, busy and then I didn't think about my stomach growling.

Tuesday: Pilates class. I thought the Pilates class would be good after yesterday, as when I woke up this morning, every muscle in my body was aching. TJ recommended Pilates as she said it is gentle, stretches you out and is very effective. It sounded better than the pain of the machines so I decided to give it a try and was there bright and enthusiastic at four-thirty after school.

Ten minutes later, I was on a mat on the floor gasping with agony. Olga, the teacher was clearly a sadist, as she seemed to take great pleasure in seeing others suffer.

'Breathe in, zip, breathe out,' she'd cry as we lay on our backs with our legs suspended at ninety degrees, our heads up and our arms pumping at our sides. It was so complicated. You breathe in, you breathe out, you zip (which means pulling your tummy up and in as though zipping your jeans up only with Pilates you zip your flabby tummy in). I got totally confused as I didn't know when I was supposed to move, when to breathe in, when to zip, when to breathe out and I almost passed out through lack of oxygen. Still, it's early days, I told myself. Maybe I'll get the hang of it in the end.

Shake report: only managed one today at lunch because Mum was around at breakfast and supper. Strawberry. Didn't like it so only had half and my tummy did the rumble tum song again in afternoon classes. When people started giggling, I just called out, 'It's sing along with Izzie's tum time, come along everyone, ah – one, two, three . . .'

I think some of the girls think I'm mad.

Wednesday: at school, TJ suggested I do a class at the gym that I really enjoyed, so I decided to go for one of the dance options. Salsa. Lucy came with me since you can pay to go to the dance classes without being a member of the gym. We both hoped that there would be loads of cute boys ready to groove on the dancefloor. Sadly, the only males at the class looked like they lived with their mothers which would have been OK if they were in their teens but they all looked about forty. My partner had two left feet and kept standing on my toes plus his shirt smelt like it hadn't been washed for days.

Shake report: a chocolate one at lunch-time and just for a change, hurrah, a slim a soup in the evening.

Discovered a side-effect that wasn't mentioned on the packet. Wind. Stormy weather *à la* lower regions. Awful and I was in danger of being as bad as the man in the sauna on Monday doing SBDs all over the place. Eeeww.

*　*　*

Thursday: flamenco. Fab. This time Nesta came with me after school and we stomped our feet off. The teacher was a total babe with wild, dark, curly hair and black eyes like a gypsy and his class was full of women who were all clearly in love with him. Nesta took to it straight away but I found the footwork hard to do. Toe, heel, stomp, toe, heel, stomp. Stompity, stompity, stomp. Wave your arms gracefully in the air. It was going all right until I heel, toed then stomped on the foot of the lady who was dancing next to me. Then I almost whacked another lady's eye out with my arm movements. Maybe flamenco isn't my thing, I thought as the woman rubbed her eye then looked at me like she was going to produce a dagger from under her skirt and stab me with it.

Shake report: stormy weather *à la* tum is in danger of becoming a hurricane. Good God. Amelia didn't warn me about this. I spent all day with a strange expression on my face and couldn't concentrate much in classes. Partly because I was beginning to feel light-headed through lack of proper food and partly because I had to walk round with my buttocks clenched in case my lower half let rip and blew down one of the school walls. Not my best day.

Friday: Egyptian dance. *Yes!* At last I have found where I belong. Again, the class was all women but of all ages, shapes and sizes. And by shapes, I mean round, pear shape, apple. And by size, I mean from eight to eighteen. When the teacher said, 'If you have a belly, all the better for the dance,' I knew I had found my place. I loved the music and the time whizzed by as we wibbled, wobbled, and gyrated round the studio like a bunch of psychotic hippies. I didn't check my watch once to see how much longer we had to go and felt like I could have danced for hours.

Shake report: just one at lunch-time. Banana. Am beginning to think I could be a danger to the environment. This wind business is *no* joke. Lucy asked why I'd looked so worried all week and I was way too embarrassed to tell her. I decided to catch up on homework in the library at lunch-time, partly so that I didn't have to watch my mates eat but also to protect them from any windy pops I couldn't keep in.

On the way home from the Egyptian dance class I felt energised and enthusiastic. As there was no one around, I carried on practising the camel (a move from the class). You put your arm and a foot out in front of you, take a step forward as you push your chest out, then curve back in as if pulling your tummy in, take a step back then step forward again while pushing forward with your belly so that your torso makes a sort of S-shape if seen from the side. It was hard to do gracefully so I was determined to get it right.

'Yo, move over Michael Jackson,' said a voice behind me after I'd been going for a while.

I almost jumped out of my skin. 'Who's that?' I said as I turned and came face to face with Josh, the local bad boy and one of my exes from last year.

'Where did you come from?'

'Ah. One of the great mysteries of the universe,' he replied. 'Where did I come from? Where am I going? Why am I here? Who knows?'

Same old Josh, I thought. He never could give a straight answer. He always had to be clever or evasive.

'So what were you doing?' he asked.

'Um, the camel,' I said, then thought: if he can be evasive, so can I. 'We're studying wildlife at school.'

'Wildlife, huh? Well you can study me as part of your project any time.'

I laughed. He was so flirty but I knew better than to respond. He was trouble with a capital T. My last encounter with him had led to me being out in the park in the middle of the night, throwing up all over him. A novel way to get a boy to remember you, Nesta had said at the time.

Still, it was good to see him and he accompanied me home and we chatted about what we'd been up to. I told him all about *Teen Talk* and being part of the audience.

'They're picking a panel,' I told him, 'but they'll probably pick all the skinny girls so that the show has babe appeal.'

'Why should that give the show babe appeal?'

'You know, boys like thin girls.'

'Says who?'

'Everyone knows that.'

'No way. Most boys are just grateful if a girl likes them but most of all they want to hang out with someone who is fun. Course it helps if the girl is decent-looking like you . . .'

'Like me?'

'Yeah. You but then you probably know that.'

'Nah, I'm a frump.'

Josh looked me up and down slowly and I felt myself begin to blush.

'You? A frump. No way. I've seen frump and you are the opposite end of the scale.'

By the time we got to my house, I was beginning to feel a lot better about my shape. Josh felt it was his duty to give me a lecture on what boys found attractive and skinny didn't even come into it. When we reached my gate, I could tell he wanted to come in but I didn't want to risk it. I knew Josh. He'd want to smoke in my bedroom and probably had a bottle of vodka tucked in one of his pockets. He was one of the mad mistakes from my past that I didn't want to repeat.

Chapter 12

Clenched and Crimson

'Want to come to the gym, Angus?' I asked as I put on my coat on Saturday morning.

Angus grimaced and picked up the paper that was lying on the hall mat. 'Er . . . think I'll give it a miss. Things to do.'

'You should do something. Anything. Even if it's only walking.'

'Hmph,' he said. 'Yes. Walking. I like long walks, preferably taken by people who annoy me, like you and your mother. Now off you go and leave me in peace.'

I laughed. Angus could be quite funny when he wanted to be and I did feel for him. Mum had been as gung ho about trying the gym as I had and had been doing the classes after she'd finished work. Every supper time, she'd been nagging at Angus to go with her but he wasn't very enthusiastic preferring to stay at home with a gin and tonic and watch the history channel on cable.

It had worked out well for me though, because Mum was out every evening so she hadn't been able to keep her beady eye on what I had or hadn't been eating. I'd been able to stick to my slim shakes and bin what she'd cooked for supper. I'd lost three pounds and was feeling very virtuous and pleased with myself, if not a bit achy from all the classes and a tiny bit guilty about deceiving Mum. I'd been on the shakes for five days with only the occasional meal when Mum was around and I was definitely feeling thinner.

Our yoga instructor was a small wiry girl called Angie, and she started the class with a salute to the sun – a series of postures all put together in one fluid movement. I'd practised it loads of times before at home as I have a book and a DVD showing how it's done but it felt good to be in a class and learn how to do it properly. However, as soon as I got to the part where you have to bend over, I felt my lower tummy rumble ominously. Oh hell, I thought as I squeezed my buttocks tight. Please no, please don't let me do an SBD and alienate myself from the group. Everybody would be bound to know that it was me. Luckily, as we carried on the feeling went and I began to relax and enjoy the class.

As the class progressed, we went into a shoulder stand, then Angie told us to roll further back and put our knees over our shoulders. Not the most elegant of positions as my stomach flopped forward over my trackie bottoms but everyone was in the same boat, so it didn't matter. But once again, came the feeling that a windy pop was on its way. Oh God, oh God, I thought as I clenched my buttocks again, this is just horrendous. How can you relax and breathe when the lower part of your body is about to play a trumpet fanfare? I clenched even harder determined not to let it happen. Clearly I wasn't the only one as an elderly lady in the corner of the room, let one rip. She didn't seem fazed by it at all.

'Oops,' she said, then laughed. 'Sorry, everyone.'

For a moment, I felt like I was going to get the giggles as I had an image of everyone having the same problem and that we were all lying there, pretending to be all serene and yoga-like when actually we were all clenching our buttocks for Britain.

As I lay there, clenched and crimson, I heard the studio door open, and footsteps.

'Sorry I'm so late,' a male voice said to the teacher. 'My bike got a puncture.'

I strained to turn my neck so that I could see who had come in. Oh nooooo, I thought when I saw who it was and that he was laying out his mat behind me.

'Oh hi, Izzie.' Gabriel grinned down at me. 'We meet again.'

'Umph . . . Gabriel! Hi,' I smiled back trying to act as if being red in the face, my bum in the air and knees over my shoulders was a perfectly normal position to be in when greeting someone. I lost my balance and fell over onto my side. 'Oof.'

Gabriel tried not to laugh as he knelt on his mat, lay back, went smoothly into the position and somehow managed to look handsome even when upside down.

For the rest of the class, I couldn't concentrate. I was so aware of the angles that Gabriel was seeing me from as we went through the postures: the crab, the cat, the dog, the snake and so on. It was awful. In every position, my tummy was hanging out or he was face to face with my backside. Not a great way to make a good impression, I thought. He, on the other hand, seemed to have mastered all the positions and in each one, looked graceful and serene. Rats' droppings, I thought, I'd hoped I'd found a class that I wanted to do as well as the Egyptian dance but I'm not going to be able to come here every Saturday and look a fool in front of him.

When the class was over, I was about to scarper but he caught up with me and asked if I fancied a juice in the bar at the front of the gym. I agreed because I wanted his last impression of me to be the right way up, not on the floor doing the twisted snake or demented cat or whatever the positions were called.

'Been a member long?' he asked as we collected our carrot and ginger drinks from the counter.

'Just joined,' I said. 'You?'

'Since last September,' he said. 'I come most Saturdays when there's nothing on in the TV studio.'

Poo, I thought. That's yoga out then. It was one thing doing the lion (tongue out as far as you can stick it) when there were no boys around, another thing if the boy you fancied was right next to you. At least he didn't come to Egyptian dancing.

We chatted for about half an hour and, as before, got on really well. He was into all sorts of things that I am, like aromatherapy, crystals and astrology. He'd just moved out of his parents' house into lodgings and was really enthusiastic about doing up his room and living independently for the first time. It was nice to talk to a boy about stuff like that because all the ones I know aren't remotely interested in décor or paint colours.

'So what are you up to over the weekend?' he asked as we got up to go our separate ways.

'Oh, see my mates. Homework. Maybe do another class. You?'

'Working on my room.' He reached into his gym bag and produced a piece of paper on which he scribbled an address.

'Here. That's where I live now. If you've got a moment, pop over. You can tell me what you think of my colour scheme. It's a bit of a mess still but almost ready for visitors.'

Result, I thought. Maybe the sight of my bum hanging in the air when I did the snarling caterpillar didn't put him off after all.

'I'd love to,' I said. 'And I could bring my feng shui book if you're interested.'

'Oh definitely,' he said as we went out to the pavement from where he unchained a bike from a lamppost. 'OK then, see you around and come visit.'

'Yeah.' Definitely, I thought as he gave me a wave, got on his bike and rode away.

Halfway down the road, he stopped then circled back. I tried to look cool and pretended that I hadn't actually been staring at him on his bike. He stopped at the kerb next to me.

'And hey, if your mates have time, bring them too. The more the merrier. Now I have my own place I want it to be an open house. When I lived at home with my parents, visitors were never welcome. My dad is an unsociable old codger. I really, really want my new place to be different, with people dropping in all the time.'

And off he rode again. I felt confused. Bring my mates? Why? Wouldn't he want to be alone with me? Did he fancy me or not? What was going on?

After the gym, I went over to TJ's to meet the girls. TJ's house was only a short walk from the gym but by the time I got there, I felt exhausted and faint with hunger having only had a vanilla shake and carrot juice so far that day. Lucy, TJ and Nesta were in the kitchen with croissants and hot chocolates, talking about going to the mall or Camden as TJ wanted a break because she'd been in all morning working on the school magazine.

'And Lucy needs cheering up,' said Nesta.

'Why? What's happened?' I asked.

'Nothing,' she said. 'I'm fine.'

'Tony's got his interview for Oxford,' said Nesta. 'The letter came this morning. If they make him an offer, he'd be mad not to go.'

'I know that,' said Lucy. 'I've been ready for it all along. That's why I've been trying to cool it with him. Well, that and the wandering hands . . .'

'Has he started with that again?' asked Nesta.

Lucy shook her head. 'No. He's been very well behaved but you know it was the reason we broke up before Italy.'

'Oh let's go out and meet loads of new boys,' said Nesta. 'Distractions. New love interests.'

'Yeah,' said TJ. 'First one to get a date with a new boy wins.'

Although it sounded like a fun afternoon was planned, I had no energy. I wanted to crawl up to the nearest bedroom, lie on a bed and go to sleep.

'You guys go,' I said. 'I'll just go home and vegetate, that is if I can get there. I can hardly walk after all the classes I've done this week.'

'You've been overdoing it,' said TJ. 'Three classes a week is enough to be fit. How many have you done?'

'One every day but only because I wanted to find out which ones I want to do,' I said, then went on to fill them in on seeing Gabriel again at yoga.

'He's probably just playing it cool,' said Lucy. 'Wants to get to know you better before he makes his move.'

'Maybe,' I said. 'But maybe the sight of my bum in the air put him off.'

Nesta made a disapproving face. 'Oh, for heaven's sake, Izzie, you've got a great bum. All you seem to go on about these days is how awful you look or what diet you're on. And at school, you hide in the library and then take off afterwards to the gym. We've hardly seen you this week.'

'We hung out at the flamenco class,' I objected, 'and Lucy, you came with me to salsa.'

'Not the same,' said Lucy. 'We used to spend time having a laugh in the lunch break then after school. It's like you've got so serious about all this losing weight lark. Where's the old fun Izzie?'

'Here,' I said. 'Just a bit knackerooed at the moment. And I am still fun. Remember last weekend? Discovering the X factor. That was fun.'

'I agree with TJ,' said Nesta. 'I think you're overdoing the classes. You need to chill out a bit, spend proper time with mates and eat something besides those stupid shakes.'

I looked at them sitting there. A familiar scene with mugs of steaming chocolate, croissants in hands, jam pots open, crumbs all over the table. It wasn't fair that I had to deny myself once again when they could eat and enjoy it. Food was such a bonding thing at all times of the year: cakes on birthdays, pizza and a DVD on rainy nights, toast and peanut butter when you're starving and back from school, mince pies at Christmas, Sunday lunches for catching up with family, muffins at the mall with mates. I was beginning to feel left out and even though it was only two weeks since I'd been trying to lose weight, it felt like I'd been denying myself for ever.

TJ's mum, Dr Watts, came in from the utility room where she'd been putting the washing on.

'What's all this about classes?' she asked. 'And shakes?'

'Izzie,' said TJ. 'She's joined the gym to lose weight.'

'Ah,' said Dr Watts. 'Cardiovascular exercise. That's what's best for losing weight. Anything that gets the heart pumping.'

'Just the sight of the cute instructors there does that for me,' said Nesta. 'Does that count?'

Dr Watts laughed. 'Not exactly. But what's all this about you wanting to lose weight, Izzie?'

Here we go, I thought. Mention that you want to lose weight to an adult and they all feel the need to give a lecture.

Dr Watts sat down at the table and looked at me with concern. 'Does your mum know that you're trying to lose weight?'

'Yeah. Course.'

'And how are you going about it?' she asked. 'What's this about shakes?'

I felt like I was a criminal being cross-examined. 'Er . . .'

'First she spent a week starving herself,' Lucy burst out. 'And now she's drinking only slim shakes and her stomach rumbles like mad in school and . . . well, we're worried about her.'

Oh thanks a lot, I thought. Why not tell her all my secrets while you're at it?

Dr Watts's concerned look grew. 'Oh, Izzie,' she said. 'That's not the way to go about it. On those diets, yes, some weight appears to come off quickly but a lot of it is water and the moment you start eating properly again, it all piles on again. If you deprive your body of proper food, it goes onto alert, thinking that you're starving and then burns what food you are eating slowly to compensate. Then the moment you start eating properly again, the weight goes straight back on because your system is still trying to protect you by burning up food slowly. And as for those slim shakes, you may as well eat a good nutritious meal as it would probably contain the same calories. The only way to lose weight and keep it off is to do it slowly, aim for a loss of a pound or two a week.'

'That's what Mum said,' I groaned, 'but that will take forever.'

'Well, the weight doesn't go on overnight and it's not going to come off overnight, no matter what mad fad diet you do.'

Yeah, yeah, I thought, I've heard it all before.

'A good eating plan and exercise, that's the way to do it for a permanent weight loss,' continued Dr Watts.

'But it's *so* hard . . .'

'It needn't be,' said Dr Watts. 'I always advise the people who come to me wanting to lose weight to join a club. That way, you learn about healthy eating and you have the support of a group. If you're really serious about it and your mum agrees, I could give you a note – under-sixteens need one to join a slimming club in this country.'

She got up, rooted around in a drawer and pulled out a leaflet. 'Here you are. Weight Winners. There's a class on Monday evening and it's not far from you, just at the top of East Finchley High Road.'

I pulled a face. I felt tired. Tired of the shakes. Tired of feeling tired. Tired of the windy pops. Tired of feeling left out of the good time munchie moments.

'Really,' continued Dr Watts, 'you don't have to starve to lose weight. It's just a question of eating the right foods and the weight will come right off in no time. And with the right plan, you can even have a little treat every now and again.'

I nodded. I was beginning to realise that she was right. Maybe I should try a more sensible approach. There was no way I could do another week on the slim shakes. I felt weird and light-headed and the idea of a decent meal was very tempting. 'OK,' I said. 'I'll give it a go.'

'Hurrah!' said Lucy. 'Because we want Izzie back, no matter what shape or size she is.'

Later that night, I sat down to a plate of pasta with Mum and Angus and enjoyed every minute of it. Mum was all for me joining the club when she heard that Dr Watts had given it the OK.

'As long as you do it sensibly,' she said as she watched me bolt down my food. 'You have to have balance.'

I picked up two cookies from the plate on the table and held one each hand.

'There you go. A balanced diet. A cookie in either hand.'

Angus laughed but Mum pursed her lips. 'Honestly, Izzie. I despair sometimes. It's always all or nothing with you. One minute you're eating hardly anything, the next, you eat everything that's in front of you. Why can't you find a happy medium?'

'I will. I will, at the club. Dr Watts said they teach a healthy eating plan there.'

'Well, I hope so,' said Mum. 'You've been looking peaky this week and I've been worried about you.'

'No need,' I said. 'Mad fad diets are not for me, believe me.'

After supper, I felt so much better just for having eaten. And I had a day and a half before I joined the club. A day and a half to eat all the things I would never be able to eat again, ever, for all eternity. Better make the most of it, I thought as I snuck into the kitchen later to find Mum's treat tin.

'Izzie, what are you doing?' she asked when she caught me with a fudge bar in my hand.

'New diet,' I said with a weak grin. 'I've tried the Atkins diet, this is the Fatkins diet.'

Mum looked up to heaven. 'You're mad.'

'No, I'm not.' I grinned back at her. 'I'll start properly on Monday. Promise.'

'Yeah, yeah. Heard that one before,' said Mum as she went back in to watch telly.

A balanced diet: a cookie in each hand.

Chapter 13

Starstruck

'Arghhhhhhhhhhhhhhhhhhhhhh!'

I wanted to kick something. Or someone. It was Monday morning and I'd just weighed myself. My weight was exactly the same as last Monday. *Exactly*. Urghhhhhhhhh. I felt soooo frustrated. After all that I'd been through! The wind, the stomach gurgles, the feeling like I was going to pass out. And for what? For *this*! I wanted to chuck the scales right out of the window. Dr Watts was blooming right about slim shakes. You lose some weight. Yahey. You eat again and it all goes straight back on. Bummer. Still, I guess the 'last ever in the world for all eternity' cookies on Saturday evening, slice of pizza at Ben's during band practice on Sunday, portion of chips on the way back from my guitar lesson with Lucy's dad and the final final *final* bowl of ice cream last night after I'd dropped round to Gabriel's with Lucy (he wasn't in) hadn't exactly helped. But it was no more than the others had. They just never seemed to gain an ounce. Pfff.

Breathe, I told myself, calm down. It's OK. There is hope.

New week. New start. I was going to join the Weight Winner's club tonight and learn how to drop a few pounds sensibly. I was well ready for it. I'd had enough of my own mad roller coaster ways of doing it.

After school, I went and had a swim at the gym, then made my way up the high street to find the hall where the meeting was being held.

Oh no, I thought when I got close and finished off my 'last ever in the whole of eternity and beyond and even after that' fudge bar. A load of boys I knew were sitting on a wall opposite the hall. Biff from the band was there, plus a few of his mates from Lal's school. They were laughing and smoking fags and messing about. No way could I go past them and into the slimming club. It would be all around North London in no time.

I felt so disappointed. I'd been pinning my hopes on this. I quickly called Nesta on my mobile and explained my dilemma.

'I'll be right there,' she said. 'Meet you down by the pharmacy in ten minutes and I'll distract them for you while you sneak in. I've been doing my history homework and am bored out of my mind so I need something to do.'

I hovered round a corner waiting for her and by the time she appeared, the boys had pushed off, no doubt to sit on another wall somewhere. Such is the glamorous life of teenage boys in Finchley.

'Sorry, false alarm,' I said as Nesta looked around for the boys.

'Never mind,' said Nesta. 'I'll come to the class with you.'

'You?'

'Yeah. It will be good experience in case I ever have to play someone with weight problems when I'm an actress.'

'Hardly, Nesta. I mean who would cast you as a fatty?'

Nesta rolled her eyes. 'Haven't you ever heard of padding? Costumes? Come on, let's go in.'

I didn't object as I'd been feeling nervous about going in on my own so it was nice to have some company.

Inside the hall were an assortment of women, some young, some old, some slim, some really enormous. One large lady gave Nesta a strange look as if to say, why are you here?

Nesta beamed at her and did a twirl. 'I've lost four stone so far. This plan really works if you stick to it.'

She sat down next to the lady, who was called Jean, and soon they were like old pals, swapping tips and recipes. You have a great career as a character actress ahead of you Nesta Williams, I thought as I went to register.

Our group leader was a middle-aged blonde lady called Shirley and as the meeting got going, I settled in to listen to what she had to say.

'No mad lose-a-stone-in-a-week diets here,' she said, 'because they don't work . . .'

As she went on to explain the plan, it sounded reasonable enough. All foods were listed in a booklet and each one was given a number of stars, for example: an apple, half a star; a chunk of cheddar cheese, six stars! A piece of bread, one and a half stars. A pizza, five million thousand stars. A tub of my favourite ice cream, ten thousand trillion stars. Well, a lot of stars, anyway. It was beginning to dawn on me why my weight had been fluctuating. In Florence, I must have been swallowing a whole blooming solar system every day.

'Each day you're allowed between eighteen and twenty stars depending on your start weight plus as many vegetables as you like,' continued Shirley.

'Puts a whole new meaning on being starstruck,' whispered Nesta.

'I know, I've been a celestial disaster so far,' I whispered back.

However, it sounded simple enough and what I liked was the fact that no food was excluded, it was just a question of totting up the stars and not eating too many that were star loaded.

I turned to the part of the booklet that listed chocolate. Two squares of any type = one and a half stars. Four squares = three stars. Eight squares = six stars. In most bars, there are about twelve squares so I quickly did my maths. A bar would be about nine stars. Two bars a day, eighteen stars and I'd have used up my allowance.

'So are you saying that if I wanted to use up my stars on chocolate that I could?' I asked.

'Or on wine?' asked Jean.

Shirley smiled. 'You could, in theory, but that wouldn't leave you many stars left for proper food, and you'd end up feeling depleted. Sugar is like empty food, no nutritious value. No. This plan is about learning to eat the right foods. Read the booklets and try and pick a range of foods from all the food groups: protein, carbohydrate, a little fat, lots of fresh fruit and vegetables and then you can have a little chocolate or wine as long as you allow for it in your star allowance.'

Cool, I thought. I could do this. And fruit was low in stars, vegetables were star free so I'd be able to eat plenty.

'Make sure you keep a food diary in the first week,' advised Shirley, 'so that I can see if you've got the hang of it. And *don't* weigh yourself every day. Weight fluctuates up and down in a week and a daily weigh-in won't give you an accurate reading.'

Tell me about it, I thought.

After running through the rules, Shirley got round to the task of weighing the members in. It was hilarious. If someone lost a pound or so, she rang a bell and everyone clapped. If someone hadn't lost any weight or had put on some, she'd frown and wag her finger at them and tell them to try harder next week and they'd slink away, then have a giggle at the back of the class.

It was going to be OK, I thought. They were a nice bunch of women and it wasn't embarrassing at all.

After the class, Nesta and I did a detour to the house where

Gabriel lived. It was on North Road between East Finchley and Highgate and was a huge, old Victorian place set back from the road. Judging by the number of bells in the porch, it looked like about twelve people lived there.

'Who's there?' Gabriel's voice came through the intercom after I'd rung the bell with his name on.

'Um . . . Izzie and Nesta,' I said.

He buzzed us in and we entered a brown and dingy hallway. It had paint peeling off the walls and smelled like old welly boots and boiled cabbage. We stepped over a pile of junk mail on the floor, squeezed our way past a pile of bikes, and then Gabriel appeared at the top of the stairs.

'I'm up here,' he said, beaming at us. 'Come on in.'

'We were just passing,' I replied as we made our way up.

'I'm so pleased you dropped by,' said Gabriel as he ushered us along the corridor. So am I, I thought. Poor Gabriel having to live in a dump like this, he probably needs some company to cheer him up.

He opened his door with a flourish. 'Sorry about the mess. I haven't finished yet.'

Once inside his room, another world opened up. It was like stepping into something off one of the makeover shows on telly. The place was immaculate with soft gold lighting from a couple of elegant lampshades. In the centre of the room was a huge double bed with a dark red cover folded neatly back and behind it a Japanese black lacquered screen. One wall he'd painted red like the bedcover, the others he'd done a pale cream. The whole effect looked simple and stylish.

'Wow,' said Nesta as she looked at a gold Thai statue of a goddess in the fireplace. 'I've seen these at Camden Lock. Looks great.'

Gabriel looked pleased by her reaction. 'Yeah. I got it from a stall there. So what do you think, Izzie?'

'Fab and a half,' I said as I gazed at some Japanese prints he had framed on one wall. 'But it's one room. Do you have a kitchen or bathroom tucked away somewhere?'

Gabriel grimaced. 'Ah. That's the down side of student accommodation. I have to share the kitchen and bathroom with a bunch of yobs. Um . . . I think I'll spare you that experience for now as some of them don't know the meaning of cleaning up. No. This is my oasis.'

'You've done a great job,' I said. 'I can't think what you meant by saying the place was still a mess. It looks perfect to me.'

'Still got a way to go,' said Gabriel as he pointed to few unopened boxes next to a futon with cushions at the far end of the room. 'Take a seat. I was about to make some coffee. Want some? Or juice.'

'Coffee, please,' we chorused.

'Kenyan or Columbian?'

'Oh . . . er . . . Nesta, what do we like?' I asked.

'Strong and sassy like our men,' said Nesta as she flopped down on the futon.

'You choose,' I said.

Gabriel laughed. 'Won't be a moment. Make yourself at home.'

Before he left, he quickly lit a candle and the aroma of jasmine began to fill the air. 'Just in case anyone's cooking something disgusting,' he said. 'Don't want it coming through.'

'That smells divine,' said Nesta.

'Yeah. I like nice smells, as Izzie already knows. Tuberose, Jo Malone, right?'

'Right,' I said. He'd remembered. That must mean something.

While Gabriel was out making coffee, Nesta knelt on the floor and looked at his bookshelf. 'You can tell a lot about a person by what's on his shelves,' she said.

I went to kneel next to her. There was a complete mixture. Books on interior design. Books on film and media studies. Loads of DVDs of old black and white movies. A copy of *The Wizard of Oz*. Couple of novels by people I didn't know. Photo albums. I was really tempted to have a peek but didn't dare in case he came back in.

'This guy has taste,' said Nesta as she sat back on the futon and looked around with approval.

Gabriel came back in with fresh coffee (he grinds his own beans!) and filled us in on some of the other people that lived in the house. Marcus, menopausal at twenty-three; David, love god (Nesta took note of his name for future reference); Oliver the computer geek who never went out and only ate Pot

Noodles; Jon the shy boy down from the Midlands who was over-awed by college life and a bit lonely; Jamie the hypochondriac; Eric the prankster . . .

'It sounds like half the student body of London live here,' said Nesta.

'Any girls?' I asked, trying to sound casual.

'Mary and Nicola on the top floor. They share. They're OK. At least they're clean.'

'You should write it all down,' I said when we'd stopped laughing over a story he told us about a time when Eric put chilli powder in Jamie's haemorrhoid cream. 'All these characters, it would make a great book.'

He pointed to a computer on a desk. 'Already started,' he said, grinning. 'I'm about halfway through.'

He was great company, full of enthusiasm for the media course he was on and what he wanted to do when he'd finished. And he was so interested in Nesta and me and what we wanted to do when we left school. Nesta told him all about wanting to be an actress and I told him about being in the band King Noz and wanting to be a singer-songwriter. He tried to get me to sing something but I told him I couldn't without my guitar. I liked him more and more. He didn't only look good but he was interesting and interested in others. Some boys I've known only ever talk about themselves and didn't even bother to find out what made me tick, whereas he seemed genuinely fascinated.

'So what do you think?' I asked when Nesta and I left. 'Do you think he likes me?'

'Oh yeah,' she said. 'He clearly likes you a lot.'

'So worth pursuing?'

Nesta hesitated. 'Yes. But . . .'

'But what?'

'It's like he's . . . I don't know. There's something going on with him that I can't put my finger on.'

'What?'

'Not sure . . .'

This was frustrating. Nesta was the expert on reading boys. She can usually spot a dud or a problem a mile off.

'Oh come on, Nesta . . .'

'It's nothing bad. The opposite, in fact; it's like he's too good to be true. He's like the perfect guy.'

'I thought the perfect guy was one who snogged you, then turned into a pizza,' I said, quoting the old joke.

'Pizza? Not for you any more, my dear,' said Nesta. 'Too many stars. Your perfect guy now would be one who snogged you then turned into a bowl of organic salad. *Deux* stars.'

I laughed. 'I know what you mean about Gabriel, though. He is close to perfect but I don't see why that should worry you. I knew there had to be a perfect boy out there somewhere and here he is alive and well and living around the corner.' I really hoped he asked me out when we saw him again on Saturday.

★ ★ ★

The next day, I began my food diary.

Tuesday: excellent. Eighteen stars. Cereal for brekkie, low fat sandwich at lunch, lots of fruit and vegetables, medium baked potato in the evening. Feel great. Almost normal and not so obsessed with food.

Wednesday: twenty stars, two on a bit of choc at Lucy's.

Thursday: almost got blown round at Ben's at band practice as he ordered pizza again. Pizzas are mega stars and if I'd had a piece, it would have taken me over my star ration, but it seems to be the only food that Ben knows of. Had a tiny bit so felt like I didn't miss out and counted it into my allowance. At home later, Mum had got a cake as it was Angus's birthday. I felt it would be churlish not to have any so I counted up how many stars I had left. One. So had an itsy-bitsy, tiny piece. Could have been a celestial disaster with too many stars but no, I kept it together. Feel so much better on this plan as I can eat normally. Just maybe less than I did before, like instead of having two bits of chocolate cake, I'll just have a small slice.

Friday: I am definitely feeling thinner and had a sneak weigh in to discover that I had lost two and a half pounds! Excellent. And amazing as I feel like I am eating normally, only difference is that instead of piling my plate with roast spuds, I pile it with other veg.

After doing my homework on Friday, I sat down to watch telly while I totted up my daily stars. There was a programme on about a country in Africa that had been suffering from a drought. As I sat there, I began to feel more and more guilty about how I'd been behaving over the last few weeks. I'd thought about food non-stop, what I could and couldn't eat, how I looked. Me, me, me. I'd even binned food that Mum had cooked for me, and there on the same planet as me were thousands of people with nothing to eat at all. They didn't have the luxury of wondering how they looked in clothes as they hardly had anything to wear except rags and other people's cast-offs. I felt awful. *Really* awful and I felt my eyes fill up with tears. I am the worst person in the world, bad and selfish, I thought as I watched a mother who looked like a skeleton try to feed a baby with a tummy swollen from lack of food.

Mum came in and caught me wiping my eyes.

'Izzie, what is it?'

I pointed at the television. 'All those people. They don't have enough to eat and I . . . I . . .'

'You what, love?'

'I'm such a *bad* person. All I've done for the past few weeks is moan and groan and feel sorry for myself and all the time there are people starving. It all feels so wrong.'

Mum smiled sadly. 'Isn't it supposed to be me who saying that to you? The classic parent speech, you must eat your supper, think about all the hungry people in the world . . .'

'I think you did when I was younger. It never really registered before now though.'

Mum sat on the edge of the sofa. 'I know what you mean.' She sighed. 'There's such an imbalance. It doesn't seem right does it? Sometimes when I'm at the supermarket, I watch myself and everyone else pile everything into our trolleys, especially, say, at Christmas when we all go mad and buy more than we need. We're so lucky that we have everything when others have no home or food.'

'I *hate* myself,' I said as more images of hungry families flashed across the screen. 'I've been so selfish.'

'Oh Izzie, you mustn't beat yourself up just because you were trying to lose a bit of weight. I know there are so many things that aren't right in the world but you're a fifteen-year-old girl and living in our society, you have different pressures on you. It's perfectly natural that you want to look your best.'

Duh, I thought. This is a turn around from her earlier objections to me cutting down on food.

'I wish I could do something though. What can I do?' I asked.

'You've made a start, Izzie,' said Mum. 'You've noticed. You care. Some people don't even give others a second thought.'

'I *hate* to think that people are suffering while we have it all and yet most of the time, I don't think about it for a second.'

'Yes, but suffering is relative you know. You have to remember that. It's not only people in those countries that suffer. So do people who appear to have it all. I know that yes, some people suffer for physical reasons, like having no food or clothing. But so do families over here. Different pressures, different stresses. Loneliness, loss, poverty, bad health, it happens over here too.'

I was beginning to feel really depressed. And helpless. 'But what can *I* do?'

'Oh lots, Iz, and I'm sure you will, knowing you. Start by being aware of when people are suffering for whatever the reason. Here *and* there. There's no guarantee for happiness because we live in a more affluent society; and no certainty of an easy ride for anyone, however fortunate they are or which culture they live in. Rich people who seem to have it all still experience loss, disappointment, illness, death of loved ones. Life can be a roller coaster for all of us. You have to reach out and grab the good times.'

I looked at Mum in amazement. I'd never heard her talk like that before. She was usually too busy rushing around with her job or telling me what to do. I'd never thought of her as someone who was aware of people in need.

'I guess,' I said. 'I often look at people and wonder, are you happy? What's your life like? What's your story?'

'That's a good start. Be aware. Small steps in the beginning because you are only fifteen with your whole life in front of you to do what you can. And I know it makes you sad to see this on TV but I'm glad it affects you. It means you have a heart and I'm sure in time, you'll do something about it.'

I nodded. And I would think about what I could do, then act

on it. I'd become more aware as sometimes I don't like to watch programs like the one that was on because it makes me feel so rotten but I guess that sticking my head in the sand and pretending it wasn't happening wasn't going to help much. Sometimes I hated watching the news as there seems to be so much that is wrong in the world. So many innocent people dying in wars that aren't of their making or being hungry when all that we need is here on the planet if we could redress the imbalance. It was all upside down. Why oh why can't we all live together and share our resources, I wondered and does it really matter if my bum is slightly too big when there are people on the planet who are starving?

'It's a mad, mad world,' I said.

Mum nodded. 'Isn't it? But it's also a fab, fab world. Some people make donations, others do charity events to raise money, others give their time, others their talent, others who are in a position to do so can give their name to a project and suddenly everyone wants to be a part of it just because a celebrity has become involved. Just don't be one of the people who turn their head and say not my problem.'

'I won't,' I said. 'I won't turn my head.'

Every Drop Counts
written by Izzie

Last night a hand reached out to me
Its arm withered by want and apathy
Another drought in a nameless place
Another hungry child with flies on its face
I close my eyes and avoid the news
I've seen it all before, the children always lose

Tiny fingers, tiny hands
Broken hearts in a stranger's land

Whatever I do, whatever I say,
It won't make the world spin a different way
Whatever I think, whatever I dream
Won't make this image appear less obscene
Won't do no good to sing, cry and shout
My floods of tears won't end the drought

Tiny fingers, tiny hands
Broken hearts in a stranger's land

Think again, think again
I'm too wrapped up in my pain
Gotta wake up and walk into reality
Any self doubt is just a triviality

And though my voice sounds pretty small
If we shout together, we can break down walls

Tiny fingers, tiny hands
Broken hearts in a stranger's land

Whatever we do, whatever we say
We can still make a difference, starting today
With a drop at a time, if we work as a team
We can all take a bucket down to the stream
Soon a river of compassion, a flood of joy
Will create an ocean of hope all can enjoy

Chapter 14

Pilot Show

'I wonder what's going on,' said Nesta, after we'd signed in and made our way into the studio on Saturday morning. John was running around the aisles looking as though he was going to have a heart attack. Geena was heatedly talking into a mobile phone and there was an air of panic in the place.

I on the other hand was feeling calm and more confident that I had in ages. I was wearing the pinstriped Cyberdog top with my jeans and both Lucy and TJ had told me how good I looked. Ready to be noticed this time, I thought as I spotted Gabriel at the back of the hall, and then went over to him.

'What's happening?' I asked.

'Oh, the usual disasters on a live show. Sue from the panel hasn't shown up. And our guest singer is stuck on a train somewhere north of Birmingham. Doubt if he's even going to make it.'

'Izzie can sing,' Lucy piped up behind me.

'No way. Shut up,' I said. 'And anyway, they don't want just anyone on. They want a celebrity guest.'

Gabriel studied my face. 'You up for it, Iz? I remember you telling me about your songs.'

'She's brilliant,' said Nesta. 'She could easily do it.'

'They won't want me,' I insisted. Although I'd felt ready to be noticed by Gabriel, being noticed by thousands of viewers was another matter altogether and the thought of it made me quake inside.

'Well, quite honestly, anybody would save the day at the moment,' said Gabriel before calling John over. 'Hey, John, over here. Potential guest replacement. Izzie. Singer-songwriter.'

I gave Lucy a filthy look and she gave me one back *and* stuck her tongue out at me. She pulled me aside and whispered, 'This is your chance. Show the world who you are, you idiot.'

John looked me up and down doubtfully. 'Can you really sing?'

'Yeah but . . . no, but . . . yeah, I can. I do.'

'Have you ever sung in public?'

'Loads of times,' said Nesta. 'She's in a band called King Noz. She writes her own songs too.'

I gave Nesta a swift kick.

'Ow,' she said, then rubbed her shin.

'What do you play?' asked John. 'Piano or guitar?'

'Oh . . . guitar but . . .'

'Come with me.'

I gave Nesta an 'I'll get you later' look and followed him to the back of the studio, down a corridor and into a dressing room.

'Give me five minutes,' said John and disappeared.

I took a look around. This must be how it is when you really are a celebrity guest I thought as I took in the white washed room, enormous bunch of flowers, Evian water and bowl of fruit arranged on a low coffee table.

John was back before I knew it with a guitar in hand and Gabriel not far behind him.

'OK, play,' said John.

I took the guitar and plucked a few notes. 'Give me a moment.'

'Haven't got a moment,' he said, turning to Gabriel. 'Right, we're OK for the second spot, we'll go out on the pre-recording of Alicia.' Then he turned back to me. 'Ready?'

I took a deep breath. Ready as I will ever be, I thought, and sang some of the song I'd written last night after talking to Mum about people starving in some parts of the world.

I didn't look up at John or Gabriel as I sang. I just tried to focus on getting the words right. '. . . *Tiny fingers, tiny hands, broken hearts in a stranger's land . . .*'

When I'd finished, I glanced up.

Gabriel gave me the thumbs-up and grinned. John's expression still looked harassed. He looked at what I was wearing.

'Hhm,' he said as he looked at my top. 'Nice outfit but those stripes won't work. Get her into make-up, Gabriel, and see what there is in costumes.'

And with that, he ran out.

'What did he mean?' I asked.

Gabriel beamed at me. 'You're on.'

'Oh. Wow. So why can't I wear this top?'

'Vertical lines distort like mad on camera,' said Gabriel. 'Come on. We'll find you something else. Let's get going.'

For the next half hour, I barely had time to think. Gabriel rushed me into make-up and stood and advised the make-up girl as she brushed various powders onto my face.

'Not too heavy on the eyes, keep it light but maybe a little shadow round the corners. Excellent,' said Gabriel. 'Lots of lip-gloss.'

My hair was blown even straighter than it normally is; then it was out of there, down another corridor and into a costume department where Gabriel went into hyperdrive.

'Right,' he said as he flicked through rail after rail and scoured shelf after shelf. 'I know exactly what I'm looking for. Shoe size?'

'Thirty-eight,' I said.

After a few moments, he chucked a pair of fab brown-leather cowboy boots at me. 'Get these on,' he said as he looked me up and down. 'Size?'

'Um . . . fourteen, maybe . . .'

'Never. Twelve. We'll keep the jeans you're in but I want . . .' He started flicking through the rails again. 'Ah, how about this?'

He'd picked out the most exquisite camisole. It was vintage in style, lilac crêpe silk with a tiny bit of lace around the dipped neckline and a ribbon criss cross over the boobs. 'Try it on.'

I wasn't about to strip off in front of him, especially as I had one of my faded white bras on. 'Turn round,' I said.

'Oh right, yes, course, sorry.' Gabriel turned.

I quickly stripped my black top off and slipped into the camisole.

'Done?' asked Gabriel.

'Yes but . . .'

Gabriel turned, gave me the once over then he let out a slow whistle. 'Perfect,' he said. 'That'll get them going. Perfect, perfect.'

'Can I look?'

He took my hand and pulled me back down the corridors and back into the dressing room where he stopped in front of the mirror.

I took a look.

'Ohmigod. It's too tight. My boobs! I look . . .'

'Izzie, you look great,' said Gabriel. 'Absolutely *great*. It's not tight at all. It fits like a glove. You should wear more stuff like this.'

I didn't have time to object any further as John stuck his head round the door. 'Ready? Hey Izzie, you look lovely.'

Gabriel nodded. 'Doesn't she?'

'We've just started on the first discussion then we'll go to Izzie. Get her in place.'

I grabbed the guitar and we were out of the dressing room, along another maze of corridors and led to the side of the stage where the audience discussion was going great guns.

I could hardly breathe, it was all happening so fast.

'Are you going to do the song you did in the dressing room?'

'Er yes . . . sure. If that's OK.'

'Whatever you're comfortable with,' said Gabriel then his bleeper bleeped. He checked his message. 'OK, wait for Geena to introduce you then off you go. And Izzie, remember to smile. And stand up straight. I know this may feel nerve-wracking but act confident. No one will ever know you're shaking inside.'

'Right. Smile, stand up straight,' I replied. 'Confident. Oh God.' And breathe, I told myself.

I heard Geena rounding up the discussion and then go into my intro: '. . . and now, at great expense, all the way from North London, we have our very own . . . Izzie Foster.'

Gabriel pushed me forward and I walked on to the stage and into what seemed like blinding lights. It took me a moment to adjust my eyes and see the microphone. Oh God, my knees have turned to jelly, I thought as I walked forward. Oh please, don't let me freeze. Let me get this next few minutes over with. Confident, confident. I took another deep breath, went up to the microphone and beamed a big smile.

'Hello, Camden,' I called out into the studio.

'Hello, Izzie,' the audience called back.

It was a dream come true. A moment I'd fantasised about so many times in front of the mirror at home. Just relax, I told myself. Imagine that you're at one of the gigs with Ben and King Noz. It's just another number.

'I'm going to sing you a song I wrote only last night,' I said, 'and I hope that some of you might agree with the way I feel.'

Then I went into the song. As I was singing, I tried to really feel the words. And I did feel the words as time seemed to stand still.

'. . . *Tiny fingers, tiny hands, broken hearts in a stranger's land . . .*'

When I'd finished, the place erupted. I'd done it. It was OK. I'd remembered all the lines and people were clapping, some even stomping their feet. I caught sight of Lucy and Nesta in the audience. They were jumping up and down and going ballistic.

'Cue to break,' I heard John say somewhere in the studio. I felt stunned and next thing I knew, Gabriel and Nesta were hugging me.

'Izzie, you were totally brilliant, just *brilliant*,' Nesta gushed.

'A star is born,' said Gabriel with a big smile. 'You saved the day.'

John came over and patted me on the back. 'Nice one, Izzie. Well done.'

I scanned the audience for Lucy but couldn't see her but a moment later, she was hugging me too.

'God, Izzie, I felt so proud,' she said and I swear she had tears in her eyes. 'I couldn't believe it was really you up there. You looked so confident. "Hello, Camden." Like, wow . . . You sounded like such a pro.'

I laughed. I felt brilliant. Performing in front of a live audience is the best high in the world, I thought as we made our way off the stage and back into the audience for the second half.

'And you look so good,' said Lucy. 'I couldn't have picked a better outfit for you myself.'

I hugged her back. Life was good and with the way that Gabriel had been paying me so much attention, I had a feeling that it was about to get even better.

Chapter 15

Hot or Not?

The second half of the show got off to a great start and everyone seemed to have loads to say. Gabriel told me that the phone lines had been going bonkers after my song, and people had been ringing in from all over the country to say they wanted to hear more from me. I thought my five minutes of fame was over and I was going to be able to relax in the audience and enjoy the rest of the show while I caught my breath. But no, John told me to join the panel and that they were going to pick up on a new theme for the second discussion.

When I heard what the topic was going to be, I thought it couldn't have been more relevant, as least to me anyway. The topic was: hot or not? And I soon found out that I wasn't the only one who worried about whether I was or not. It was clearly a subject close to everyone's heart – feeling inadequate or invisible to the opposite sex. Boys and girls both joined in with gusto and it was fascinating to hear the boys say, time and time again, that they didn't want a picture perfect girlfriend. They didn't want the teen queen from the magazine, they wanted normal. Fun. Confident. And curvy.

After the show, Gabriel was kept busy, clearing the stage and helping the camera crew. Lucy, Nesta and I sat at the back for a while, reliving it all; everyone seemed to be hanging about, reluctant to leave. Finally, the studio started emptying and we got up to go. I looked for Gabriel, but couldn't see him.

'Just a moment,' I said to Lucy and Nesta. 'I want to find Gabriel and say thanks.' And give him a chance to ask me out, I thought as I made my way down to the stage area to find him. I was feeling on top of the world and more confident that I had in ages. I was on a roll. How could he resist?

He didn't appear to be anywhere.

'Seen Gabriel?' I asked a cameraman.

He jerked his thumb to the door on the left that led backstage.

I followed his directions and found myself in the maze of corridors that I'd been in only half an hour earlier. I set off in the direction of the dressing room thinking that he might be in there tidying up. As I got closer, I heard his voice inside. It sounded as if he was talking on the phone so, not wanting to interrupt his call, I waited in the corridor.

'You're outside?' he said. 'You dozo, you should have bleeped me, I'd have let you in. I'll come out and get you . . . Yeah, me too, been looking forward to seeing you all day. Can't wait . . . No, it's been great. Really great, I wish you could have been here. But I'm ready for some time off. All I want to do now is spend the rest of the day with you. Maybe we could get a bite then go back to my place for a movie and chill out . . .' His voice got softer and deeper as the last sentence went on. There was no way he was talking to just a mate.

I felt a sinking feeling in the bottom of my stomach and ran back down through the corridors, out into the studio and outside to find Lucy and Nesta.

'What's the matter?' asked Lucy when she saw my face.

I scanned the crowd that was still hanging about outside. I wondered which one she was. Gabriel's girlfriend.

'Gabriel. I just heard him arranging to meet his girlfriend,' I groaned.

'How? When?' asked Nesta. 'Are you sure?'

I nodded. 'I heard him talking on the phone. And I could tell, not only by what he was saying but you know, by his tone of voice, it was all deep and smoochy . . .'

Lucy put her arm around me. 'Oh, Izzie. I'm so sorry.'

I bit my lip. I didn't want to blub in front of them. It had been such a brilliant day, the best ever and I'd really hoped that it was going to end with a date with Gabriel. Stupid, stupid, I told myself. Why do I have to go and fall for another boy who is already attached? And who had I been fooling thinking he'd feel the same way about me as I felt about him just because I'd sung a stupid song. How could he resist me? Easily.

'She's out here somewhere,' I said, as I continued looking around. There were so many girls hanging about and then I spotted one apart from the crowd sitting on a wall. She looked as though she was waiting for someone as she didn't appear to be with anyone from the show. She was tall, blonde and had cut-glass cheekbones. 'I bet it's her. No. Don't look. Behind you, Nesta. But don't stare.'

Nesta did a casual look around, scanning the area. 'Maybe,' she said. 'Could be her. She's classy-looking and we all know that Gabriel has taste.'

Yeah, I thought. Whatever made me think that he'd pick a dud like me? So I can sing. So what?

A moment later, the stage door opened and Gabriel came out. He too scanned the crowd, then saw me and came straight over.

'Izzie,' he said. 'What a day, huh? You were *so* good. You must feel brilliant after that.'

Lucy and Nesta were scowling at him and I hoped Nesta didn't butt in and say something awful. No one was to know that he was already attached and it wasn't as though we'd snogged or anything. It wasn't like it had been with Jay. Gabriel hadn't lied to me.

Gabriel put his arm round me and gave me a squeeze. 'But

listen, Izzie. Stay in touch, hey? I'd like to hear more of your songs. And you know where I live now so come over whenever you feel like it. I meant it about wanting my place to be an open house.'

I thought I heard Nesta growl as I felt my heart sink even further. Maybe he was like Jay. Another cheater.

'But what about your girlfriend?'

'*Girl*friend! What girlfriend?' he asked.

'I heard you. I . . . I wasn't eavesdropping or anything, I . . . er, came looking for you to say goodbye and you were on the phone talking to your girlfriend.'

Gabriel looked taken aback. 'When?'

'Back in the dressing room. Just now.'

Gabriel looked really puzzled then he laughed. 'Oh, God. I'm so sorry . . . I assumed that you knew . . .'

'Knew what?'

'*Boy*friend,' he said. 'I'm gay. I was talking to my boyfriend.'

Just at that moment, a stunning looking boy with short dark hair and chiselled features came over.

'Hey, Andy,' said Gabriel. 'Come and meet Iz and her mates.'

I wanted to die.

Dear
Izzie . . .

'So the singles' club meets once again,' I said. 'Will I never learn?'

'You weren't to know,' said TJ.

'*I* should have known,' said Nesta. 'The signs were all there. He was too good to be true.'

It was the following Friday and we were hanging out at TJ's, helping her with the last minute changes to the magazine. She'd been working on an article called 'Dieting Makes you Fat,' and she wanted comments from me seeing as I'm now our resident diet expert.

'I think diets make you fat because the night before you go on one, you binge as you think you can never eat anything naughty-but-nice ever again. And then after a few days or a week of denial, you get bored or hungry so you break the diet. Then you feel bad, think oh I must get back on my diet, I'll start on Monday and this time be really, really strict . . . but on Sunday, I'll have my last treat ever and the cycle starts again. If people just ate normally but less, it would work much better than all that yo-yo-ing.'

Nesta gave me the thumbs-up. 'Sounds like you've seen sense my leettle curvy chum,' she said.

I gave her the thumbs-up back. I felt that I'd found some balance in my life again and I didn't feel so bad about Gabriel any more. I'd already been over to his place in the week and we'd had a good laugh about it all and what's more, I feel like I've found a new mate. And what more could you ask for, a friend who's a boy but who has immaculate taste in everything from make-up and dress sense to décor. As Nesta had said, the perfect boy.

'Anyway, we can't be the singles' club,' said TJ, 'because Lucy's not really single are you Luce?'

Lucy blushed. 'Yes, I am.'

'So why were you snogging Tony last time you were at our flat? I saw you,' said Nesta.

Lucy squirmed in her seat. 'Oh *then*? Um . . . er . . .'

'So are you getting back with him or not?' I asked.

'I've *told* you,' she said. 'No. But that doesn't mean we can't have the occasional snog or see a movie. He agrees. Just friends. He's got his A-levels coming up so he's going to have to work really hard. He said no way is he getting involved with anyone new as the last thing he needs are distractions or complications or new girlfriends going all emotional on him. With us, it's comfortable. We can hang out. We know what to expect from each other. We give each other space. I understand he has to study. He understands that I don't want to get into a heavy involvement so there it is. Sorted. We can enjoy the last few months before he goes off to whichever university in September.'

I laughed. Some things never change. Lucy and Tony will probably be meeting up for the occasional snog or movie when they're old age pensioners.

'And hey, Iz, you needn't be single if you don't want,' said Nesta. 'I saw Chris last night and apparently Tawny dumped Jay last weekend. She saw Liam's photos of Italy and there were some of you in there so she put two and two together. Chris said that he was asking after you.'

'No thanks,' I said. 'Been there, done that. If he cheated on Tawny, how would I know he wasn't going to cheat on me? Some boys you just can't trust and I'm not going through that again.'

'Good for you, Iz,' said Lucy.

'What about you, Nesta?' I asked. 'There were so many boys on the show ogling you. Anyone you want to ogle back?'

Nesta sighed. 'Nah. I'm going through a particularly barren time with boys lately. I don't want one just for the sake of it. It's too boring. To tell you the truth, I've been enjoying being single. As Tony said, no complications. I'd rather hang out with you guys for the moment.'

Lucy mocked fainting. 'Are you ill, Nesta?'

Nesta punched her. 'No, I'm not. I just don't want to waste my time and I don't want to compromise. No, next time I date a boy, it's going to be the real thing or nothing at all.'

TJ, Lucy and I all exchanged doubtful looks.

'I give her a week,' said TJ.

'O ye of little faith,' said Nesta. 'There is more to life than boys, you know.'

'Now I *know* she's ill,' I said. 'Don't worry love, we'll take care of you. You'll be as right as rain in no time.'

'Hey how's the diet going, Iz?' asked Lucy.

'It's not a diet, it's a healthy eating plan,' I replied. 'Didn't you hear my comments for TJ's article? Dieting makes you fat.'

'Ooo, get her,' said Lucy, laughing.

'But actually I've lost three pounds already.'

I'd been back to the club and weighed in and at first I was disappointed that I hadn't lost more but then Shirley had shown us this great lump of fat. It was enormous, like a huge blob of butter.

'That's just two pounds,' she'd said.

It didn't seem so bad after that. Somehow though, my weight didn't feel like such a big issue any more. Since *Teen Talk* last Saturday, loads of people had come up to me from school and even a few boys in the street who had seen the show. All of them had complimented me on my performance and no one had said I'd looked like a great fairy elephant.

I was feeling a lot better about things. I know that having the perfect body is not what it's all about and I know that no one's ever happy; if not with their legs, it's their tum or their hair or their bum. You can't let it ruin your life. Not that that is going to stop me going to my Weight Winners class. I want to continue because I want to get back into my old clothes, but now I feel that I'm doing it for me – to feel good, not to fit in with what I think some boy wants. And the plan does seem to work, even though it sometimes feels like I'm eating a lot. Already, my clothes feel looser and the outfit from Cyberdog looks fantastic. I'm looking forward to going out partying in it and not feeling like I have to hide myself away at home, my life on hold, waiting until I'm skinny. I've learned some valuable stuff about food – mainly that I don't have to starve myself to lose weight. Learning to eat the right foods is the way, whereas starvation is just a waste of time.

Just as I was getting ready to leave TJ's, my phone rang.

'Hi, Izzie, it's Gabriel. I'm at the studio. Can you come over?'

'Sure,' I said. 'I'm with the girls. Shall we all come?'

'Yeah, sure. I've got something to show you.'

'What?'

'Aha, you'll see.'

He wouldn't tell me any more than that, so we set off, wondering what he wanted.

When we arrived at the studio, we waited in the reception area while the girl behind the desk let him know that we were there. He came out a few minutes later. He was carrying a large envelope.

'So what's the big mystery?' I asked.

Gabriel grinned and beckoned us to sit on one of the sofas by a coffee table where he produced a wad of letters from the envelope. 'Thought you might like to see some of these,' he said.

I sat next to him on the sofa and TJ, Nesta and Lucy crowded round to look.

'Ohmigod,' said Nesta. 'They're fan letters.'

Gabriel grinned again. 'They've been filtering in all week. Looks like you're a hit, Izzie Foster.'

TJ, Lucy and Nesta all took a small pile each, sat down and we began to read.

'*Dear Iz,*' read Lucy, '*I think you are the most beautiful girl in the world and what a voice . . .*'

'*Dear Ms Foster,*' read Nesta, '*I wonder if you would do me the honour of accompanying me on a date. I enclose a picture . . .*' She had a quick look at the enclosed photo. 'Eeew, I don't think so.'

I took the photo from her. The man in it was old enough to be my father, no – my stepfather, as Angus is older than Dad.

'*Dear Izzie,*' read TJ. '*I love you, will you marry me?*'

It was amazing. Letter after letter. My first fan mail. I would treasure it forever.

'*Dear Iz,*' read Nesta. 'Oh . . . no, you don't want to read this one. A bit rude, but I think the gist of it is that he fancies you.'

Gabriel took the letter off her. 'You always get the odd nutter in there but wow, Izzie. How do these make you feel?'

I beamed out at them all. 'Pretty darned blooming amazing,' I said.

'I think that means good,' said Lucy. 'And we don't ever, ever want to hear again that you think you are a great fat ugly lump.'

'You won't,' I said. 'I promise.'

And I meant it.

Mates, Dates & Diamond Destiny

Cathy Hopkins

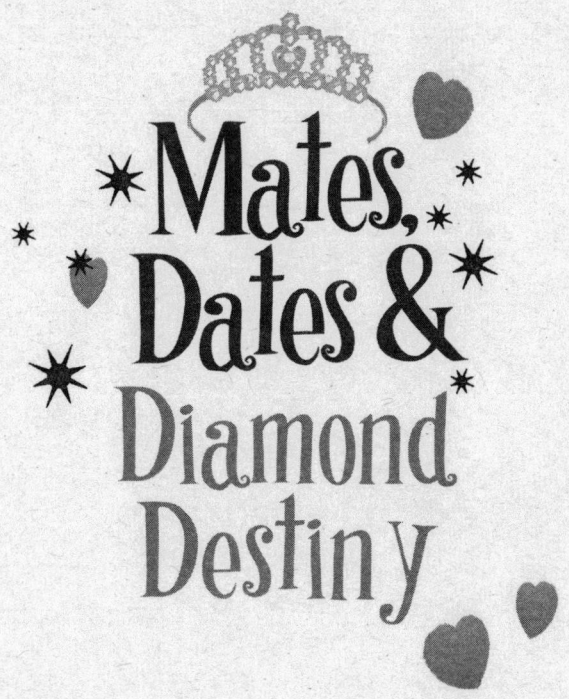

Mates, Dates & Diamond Destiny

PICCADILLY PRESS • LONDON

Thanks to Brenda Gardner, Yasemin Uçar, Jon Appleton,
Melissa Patey and the rest of the team of fabsters at Piccadilly.
To Rosemary Bromley at Juvenilia. To Steve Lovering for his
constant support and help on all aspects of the book and
for being such a good pal.

Chapter 1

Smug Slug

'I bet you can't do it,' said Tony.

'How much?' I asked.

'A pound every time you mention one,' he said.

'Done,' I said. 'Prepare to hand over all your pocket money.'

'Pfff,' smirked Tony. 'It's going to be like taking candy from a baby.'

I was sitting with my brother Tony in the Costa coffee bar in Highgate waiting for my mates on Saturday morning. We'd got into an argument and he'd bet me that I couldn't last a day without talking about boys. Thankfully Izzie, Lucy and TJ arrived soon after so I didn't push his face into his plate of panini and tomato, something I was very tempted to do.

'Are you two fighting again?' asked Izzie as she slid in next to me while Lucy and TJ sat on either side of Tony. 'We could feel the vibes from back here when we were getting our drinks at the counter.'

'He said that I had nothing going on in my head apart from boys, boys and boys,' I said. 'Blooming cheek.'

Izzie, Lucy and TJ exchanged looks as if to say that they agreed with Tony.

'Hey come on, guys,' I said. 'Give me a break. I know I'm not Einstein but . . .'

'But Tony's right, Nesta,' said Izzie. 'You are our current boy expert of North London, England . . .'

'The world, the universe, etc.,' TJ finished.

'Yeah,' said Lucy, '*and* you did put boys down as one of your hobbies on that questionnaire we had to do for Miss Watkins in PSHE.'

Tony was grinning like a smug slug. I don't know why some people find him attractive when he is clearly an annoying pain in the butt. I suppose he is the standard tall, dark and handsome but beauty's only skin deep and on the inside lurks his true self, which is a repulsive reptile. Sadly I am the only person who can see this, which is one of the many reasons that I am so misunderstood.

'OK,' I said, as I stirred the last remnants of my hot chocolate, 'so yes, maybe boys do occupy a small part of my mind but I'm a fifteen-year-old girl, get real. I just can't believe his cheek in insinuating that's *all* that's going on.'

'You're right,' said Tony. 'Sometimes you think of handbags or pointy shoes.'

I lifted my hand to punch him but Izzie caught my wrist.

'He doesn't mean it, Nesta,' she said. 'He's winding you up. Now kiss and make up. You two children have got to learn to play nicely.'

'No way,' said Tony as I stuck my tongue out at him.

'I wouldn't worry,' said Lucy. 'My brothers say far worse things to me.'

'Well, you would say that,' I said. 'You always stick up for Tony.'

'I do not.'

'Do.'

Tony put his arm round Lucy and gave her a squeeze and she smiled up at him. Sadly she can't see his true nature, no matter how many times I've warned her. She only sees love god. It's very sad, although no one's too sure what's going on with them lately. Are they an item or not? Some weeks they are, some weeks they're 'just good friends'. At the moment, they're 'just good friends'. Good friends who snog a lot, if you ask me.

'I do *not*,' Lucy insisted. 'I stick up for whoever I feel needs sticking up for at the time.'

I pushed out my bottom lip in the hope that she could see that I needed sticking up for. I felt betrayed by her lack of support. And Izzie and TJ hadn't exactly come forward to my defence either. Grrr, but I'm feeling cross with everyone today, I thought, as I ate the last piece of my chocolate pastry. Must be my hormones. My period started this morning and that always makes me feel cranky and prone to axe-murdering anyone who comes within five yards. I've tried taking painkillers for it but for me, chocolate seems to be the only thing that offers any relief.

So far, I'd had Coco Pops, two hot chocolates and the pastry but I still felt out of sorts. And no doubt all the sugar would result in me getting an almighty great spot on my forehead or chin. Sometimes it sucks being a girl.

'OK then, Lucy,' I said, 'it's the Easter hols in a couple of weeks. What if in the holidays, Tony and I were taken ill with the same kidney disease and the only thing that could save us was you donating one of yours, which one of us would you give it to?'

Lucy started laughing. 'But you're not dying of kidney disease. And neither is Tony.'

'Hypothetically.'

'Stupid question,' said Lucy.

'OK, your last Rolo then. Who would you give your last Rolo to?'

'Um. I'd give you half each.'

Typical Lucy. She'll never take sides with anyone if she can help it.

'So what did you mean when you said that your brothers used to say worse things to you, Luce?' asked TJ.

Lucy blushed. 'They used to call me Nancy No-tits.'

I sighed heavily. I knew what they were trying to do. They were trying to change the subject, divert Tony and me from annoying each other. Huh. My mates: Lucy the joker, always trying to smooth things over with a laugh. TJ the diplomat, always trying to ensure that we're all communicating. And Izzie the mystic, feeling our vibes before we've felt them ourselves. I wouldn't know a vibe if it was served up deep fried with chips and peas. Izzie's always thinking deep thoughts about the universe, life, God and stuff. That's not me at all. Waste of time, I think. Who knows why we are here or what for? We might as well just get on with it and have as nice a time as we can. That's my philosophy. Sometimes I wonder where I fit in with the three of them, especially when they start having their 'deep' conversations.

Not that I can't talk or don't have anything to say for myself. In fact I often talk too much. I'm a stick-my-foot-in-it with my big mouth type person. At least everyone knows where they stand with me, though. What you see is what you get. Simple and uncomplicated. I don't think that makes me an airhead. Those are the other things Tony calls me: Big-mouth and Airhead. Not very flattering. Oh God. Maybe they all hang out with me out of pity. Their good deed for the week. Or maybe, my mum and dad have paid them to be my friends. God it's sad when actually I'm quite a nice person deep inside. At least *I* think I am.

'What's going on in your head, Nesta?' asked Izzie. 'You look miles away.'

'Um . . .' I wasn't sure myself. Sometimes I think some really insane thoughts I wouldn't want to share with anyone. Normally I can be really cool and in control but these days, when I've got my period, I turn into someone who is likely to cry at the drop of a hat or kill someone for saying something annoying, and God only knows what madness might come out of my mouth if I'm not careful. I put on my best 'deep thinker' look so that hopefully Izzie wouldn't spot that I'd turned into psycho girl.

'Oh you know, just thinking . . . about life and stuff,' I replied. 'So what other names did your brothers call you, Luce?'

Lucy blushed. 'Squirt. Short-arse. At least Tony has never called you a name like that.'

Tony was looking so smarmy and pleased with himself that I decided to blow his cover. 'No? So what about Airhead? Maggot brain? Nappy bucket? Slimeball? Droopy drawers . . .? The list goes on and *on*.'

'That was when you were little,' said Tony. 'All I said this time was you think about boys a lot. All the time in fact . . .'

'As usual, no one realises that actually I think really deep thoughts,' I objected, 'and there is a hell of a lot that goes on in my head besides boys.'

'So prove it,' said Tony. 'As I said before your mates arrived, I bet you can't do it.'

'Do what? Bet her what?' asked Lucy.

'My dingbat of a brother has bet me that I can't go a day without mentioning boys. And I have accepted the challenge. You guys can be my witnesses.'

'Yeah, but it's not just a general wager,' said Tony. 'It's specific. She has to give me a pound each time she mentions a boy, boys in plural or in fact any reference to boys at all.'

'Just Nesta?' asked Lucy. 'The rest of us can talk about boys?'

Tony narrowed his eyes and peered at Lucy in what I can only suppose he thought was an attractive manner. I thought it made him look like he was about to fall asleep. 'OK. These are the rules. Izzie and TJ can mention boys as much as they like. Nesta can't or if she does, she has to pay up. For you Lucy, it's different. For you, there is only one boy on the planet. And that is me.'

Lucy punched him playfully, laughed and gazed into his eyes. Really. Those two are vomitous when they're together. It's enough to bring up your breakfast.

'So what's on the agenda?' asked Tony. 'What are you girls going to do today? Isn't Saturday the day for you all to be TV stars?'

He was referring to the TV pilot that Izzie, Lucy and I were in last weekend. It was for a show called *Teen Talk*, a discussion programme about issues that affect teenagers.

'That was just the pilot. The series isn't due to start until September or October,' said Izzie.

'And was there any talent there?' asked Tony with a sly look.

There had been lots of boys there and I was about to jump in and give him the details when I saw TJ shaking her head at me.

'Didn't notice,' I said. 'And don't think that you can trick me into talking about the forbidden subject, *mon frère stupide*. We may be related but quite clearly one of us is far superior in the brain department.'

After that it was war. Tony did everything he could to get me to mention boys or refer to them in some way but I can be a good match for him if I want and I wasn't going to give in easily. After a while, the lady behind the counter at the front of the café started giving us a 'you've outstayed the allotted time to drink one drink in here so if you're going to stay, buy something else' look. It was time to go or else we'd end up frittering all our pocket money away on hot chocolates.

'OK, So, top five interests?' asked Tony as the lady from behind the counter came over to clear our table. 'Izzie?'

'Astrology, music, aromatherapy, witchcraft and boys,' said Izzie. 'And chocolate.'

'That's six,' said Tony, 'but I'll let you have it. TJ?'

'Er . . . reading, boys, music, movies, sport.'

'Lucy?' asked Tony.

Lucy gave him a coy look. 'Boys, definitely . . . er, fashion, movies, travel . . . although I haven't done a lot yet, it is going to be one of my major interests and . . . cooking.'

'Cooking!' said Izzie. 'Since when have you been into cooking?'

'Since those two gorgeous Italian guys got their own TV show,' she replied. 'Oh yes, cooking is well up there on the list.'

'I can cook,' said Tony. 'And I'm Italian. I told you that you didn't need to look anywhere else. So . . . what about you, Nesta?'

All eyes turned to me. I knew that by leaving me to last that he was trying to lull me into a false sense of security and that I'd blab out . . . boys. But I wasn't going to fall into his stupid little trap.

'Quantum physics, history, particularly the period between 1824 and 1828 in . . . er . . . Russia. So that's two. Um. The science of amoeba reproduction. Egyptian hieroglyphics, period between 4 and 5 BC and finally . . . b – b – bo – botulism, the study of infected sausages.'

Lucy, Izzie and TJ cracked up and even Tony almost laughed. As we were messing around, I noticed a boy with ginger hair and glasses come into the café with a collection tin. It looked like he was asking the manager for permission to take it round, and a moment later, he started going from table to table asking for money. We were sitting at my favourite table at the back so we were out of his way. We always sit there because it gives us the best view of who's coming in the door and as Costa is a café much frequented by the boys from Highgate School, it's a good vantage point for surveying the talent.

I nudged Izzie to look at the boy. Most of the customers waved him away. 'That charity collector isn't having much luck is he?' I said being careful not to say the word 'boy'.

'I feel sorry for him,' said Izzie. 'It takes a lot of nerve to go round people you don't know asking for money.'

'I feel sorry for the customers in here,' I said. 'All they want is to have a cup of something on a Saturday morning in peace and someone's bothering them to give away their money.'

'Don't be so tight, Nesta,' said Izzie in what I thought was an unnecessarily cross manner. 'They only have to give some loose change, and it's probably for a good cause.'

'Probably for a good cause,' I mimicked. 'I bet his mum has made him do it anyway . . .' I was about to continue and object that I wasn't being tight, when Lucy elbowed me in the ribs.

'Ohmigod. Eyes right,' she said. 'Door. Look who's just come in.'

I turned to see who she was talking about and my stomach tightened. It was William, a boy I'd met just before Christmas last year. He was a friend of Luke de Biasi's (otherwise known as love rat extraordinaire). For a while I had considered getting serious with Luke (i.e. going out longer than three weeks). But then he got into TJ as well (behind my back) and she thought he was The One. She fell for him really badly. It was an awkward time for all of us and got really complicated with no one knowing who had said what to who. It almost split us up as mates as Lucy took sides with me and Izzie took sides with TJ. In the end, we all realised that it wasn't worth losing our friendship over a boy who told lies. I met William after it was all over with Luke. A cutenik by anyone's standards. I remember wishing that I'd met him before Luke. But I didn't. Bad timing. And he's still Luke's mate as far as I know. So strictly out of bounds as far as I'm concerned. Shame.

I quickly turned away so that he didn't catch me staring but not before I'd noticed that he seemed to be looking for someone. I sat up straight, flicked my hair back and put my chin down so that if he saw us, he'd get my best angle. When I looked over at him a few moments later, he seemed not to have noticed us at all as he was heading for the boy with the collection tin. And then I saw that William had a similar tin and after exchanging a few words with the ginger-haired boy, was heading for the back area of the café. As he did the rounds of the tables, all the girls on the various tables perked up and within seconds, he had them reaching for their purses. He did look good, in fact I remember TJ saying that he could be Orlando Bloom's younger brother. I'd say a cross between Johnny Depp and Orlando. Same great cheekbones and he'd grown his hair since I'd last seen him and now it was on his shoulders, giving him that Victorian poet look that I'm into these days.

'I can't believe the effect that boy is having on the females in here,' I said. 'It's pathetic.'

'Pound,' said Tony.

'What for? Why?'

'You said "boy". You can't believe the effect that boy . . .'

'Oh for heaven's sake, Tony. Get a grip. I wasn't exactly talking about *boy* boys, I was merely commenting on the effect that William was having on the girls in here.'

'Another pound.'

'Why? I didn't say boy then.'

'You said William,' said Tony. 'That's a boy's name.'

'Now that's being *stupid*,' I said. 'I've got to be able to say people's names. I don't know what's the matter with you today.'

Tony looked shocked. '*Me?* *You've* been in a weird mood all morning. You've argued with every single thing I've said.' Suddenly he slapped his forehead. 'Oh . . . I know. Should have guessed. Have you got your period?'

A wave of fury went through me and this time I really was ready to sock him. I *hate* boys who assume that just because you're a bit off with them that it's because it's that time of the month. Even if it's true.

At that moment, William appeared at our table, smiled a hundred watt smile and held out his tin.

'Collecting for the . . .' And then he *finally* noticed me. He narrowed his eyes in a manner not unlike the way that Tony had for Lucy only five minutes ago, only when William did it, it made me want to slide to the floor, wrap myself around his ankles and say, 'Take me, I'm yours.' He said, 'We've met before, haven't we?'

I was about to be all cool and say that I didn't remember when Izzie piped up.

'End of autumn term show last year,' she said. 'The mayor's project about London.'

William turned to TJ. 'Yeah course, you were on the history team with my sister Olivia and my mate Luke.'

'Umf, niwih,' said TJ. Poor TJ. She was looking at the floor as though she wished it would swallow her up. She never said much about the Luke affair once it was over but I got the feeling that it affected her more than she let on. Izzie told me that she genuinely thought that Luke was her soul mate and that up until she'd met him, she thought soul mates were a load of rubbish. She needed rescuing from William's spotlight gaze.

'Yes, how is Luke?' I asked tossing my hair back and almost hitting Izzie in the eye. (That's another thing that happens when I have a period. I get clumsy and my co-ordination goes to pieces.)

'Good. Great. Shall I tell him you asked after him?'

'As *if*,' I said with as much disdain as I could muster. I hadn't meant to ask after Luke. It had slipped out before I could help it, when I saw TJ looking uncomfortable.

'What's your name again?' asked William.

Unbelievable, I thought. He hasn't even remembered my name and to think that I spent two nights having major snogging fantasies featuring him when I was falling asleep.

'Eleanor,' I said.

William looked puzzled. And so did Tony, Izzie, Lucy and TJ.

'Eleanor? Hmm. Strange I didn't remember that as Eleanor's

my sister's name as well. OK. So *Eleanor* . . . I'll tell Luke that I saw you, but that you made it clear that you weren't asking after him.' His tone of voice suggested that he was laughing at me in some way.

'Your sister's not called Eleanor,' I said.

'Er . . . *my* sister. *I* ought to know.'

'Ah, but you just said you remembered TJ from the project she did with your sister *Olivia*. You can't catch me out.'

William looked at me as if I was really dim. 'Duh. I wasn't trying to catch you out. Why would I want to do that? It is possible to have two sisters, you know. Sometimes people even have three! Olivia's my younger sister. Eleanor, my older.'

I felt a complete idiot. Of course it was possible that he had more than one sister. 'OK,' I said. 'No need to be sarcastic, William . . . oh . . . or whatever your name is . . . I don't really remember . . .'

'It *is* William,' he said as he smiled his hundred watt smile again. 'How *nice* that you remembered.'

Oh God. Now I look *so* uncool. I'd let him know that I'd remembered his name when he'd forgotten mine. And I'd asked after ratfink Luke! Why? Why? Why? Now it sounds like I'm still interested in him. I'm acting like I'm brain-dead. And I think I may be going to blush which is something I *don't* do! Oh why did I say my name was Eleanor? What is *wrong* with me?

And then the worst possible thing that could ever happen, happened. Mary O'Connor, one of our classmates, walked past on her way to the Ladies.

'Hi guys,' she said, coming over to our table. Then she turned to me. 'Hey, Nesta, remind me on Monday. You left your passionfruit and mango body lotion in the showers after gym yesterday. I put it in my locker for you.'

'Oh um, thanks, Mary.' I glanced up at William who looked highly amused; in fact, he looked like he was going to burst out laughing.

'Nesta. *Nesta!* That's it. Now I remember. So, have you changed your name or something or is Eleanor like a nickname?'

'Eleanor?' asked Mary. 'Who's Eleanor?'

Now I knew I was definitely blushing. No doubt about it.

'I . . . I . . .' Stupid, stupid me. *Why* had I lied about my name? It always backfires on me when I lie. Stupid, stupid.

Lucy and Izzie both spoke up at the same time.

'Nesta is her second name,' said Lucy.

'Eleanor is her stage name,' said Izzie.

'Right,' said William. 'Second name. Stage name. So what should I call you?'

I'd had enough of feeling like a prize idiot. I got up and stood directly in front of him. Nice eyes, I couldn't help but notice. Brown with thick black lashes. But still with a look of high amusement that was *very* annoying.

'*You* can call me . . . sir,' I said and turned back to the others. 'And now I'm going to the Ladies.'

'Shouldn't that be the Gents, if you're a sir?' said William with a smirk as he began to move on.

'Thank God he's cleared off,' I said turning back to my mates as he went to the next table. 'Some boys are just so full of themselves . . .'

'Pound,' said Tony.

I didn't care any more. 'Boys, boys, boys. A trillion times. I've said it. So there. What are you going to do? Sue me?'

Izzie chuckled and looked after William who turned and gave me a quick glance up and down. 'Me thinks a leetle spark of fancying going on there,' she said.

'Yeah,' said TJ. 'Eeelectricity. You like him, don't you?'

'No way. I do *not*,' I said. 'I did when we met last year but not now. I can tell exactly what type he is. He's the kind that thinks he's God's gift.'

Lucy nodded. 'She definitely likes him.'

'Eeewww!' I said. 'As *if*.'

What's the difference between a girl with
PMS and a rottweiler?
Lip-gloss.

Chapter 2

PMS

'I'm so short,' groaned Lucy as she gazed at her reflection in the mirror in the Ladies at the back of Costa. 'I hate standing next to you guys in the mirror as then I see how tiny I really am.'

'Small but perfectly formed, oh little one,' said Izzie. 'Unlike me. I'm so freaking enorm—?' She was about to go on but Lucy reached up and clamped her hand over her mouth. We'd all told Izzie in no uncertain terms that if she went on about being fat that we would have to kill her. Izzie isn't fat. She's got a great figure. Curvy. But like so many people, she wants to be a stick insect.

'And I'm so ugly,' said TJ as she wet the front of her hair from one of the taps and tried to flatten it down. 'My hair is crazy today. I look as pale as a potato and I've got a spot on the end of the nose. No boy is going to look at me ever again.'

They're bonkers, because all of them are very pretty in different ways. Lucy is blonde with blue eyes and although she is small, like Kylie, she's in proportion. She's been looking great lately and is letting her hair grow after having it short and spiky for ages. Now it's down to her shoulders again and looks really good. Izzie's hair is also to her shoulders but is chestnut and cut in layers. When the light catches it, it has the most amazing glossy conker shine. She also has beautiful eyes. Green and dreamy. She says she got them from her Irish ancestors. (I say in that case, she ought to give them back to them as they might be missing them.) And TJ is a total babe even though she seems oblivious to the fact. Her best feature is her mouth, wide and full plus she has lovely brown eyes and fabulous long, dark hair halfway down her back, which she often wears in a plait (unless we're out pulling boys when she leaves it loose).

I gazed at myself in contrast to them. Coffee-coloured skin because my mum is Jamaican and my dad Italian, long black hair, brown eyes. My mates tell me that I'm the best-looking girl in the school, which is very sweet of them, and I guess I can make myself look halfway decent when I try as long as I don't open my mouth. Last October, I had to have a brace put in and although I try my best to be positive about it, I can't wait until it comes out and I can smile properly at people again without looking like Hannibal Lecter with that wired contraption over his jaw in *Silence of the Lambs*.

I applied my lip-gloss. 'I am gorgeous. I am gorgeous. I am gorgeous,' I said to my reflection.

The others burst out laughing.

'And *sooooo* modest,' said Izzie.

'No. Nothing to do with being modest. How many times do I have to tell you? It's to do with confidence. It's the first thing they teach at model school. Learn to love yourself. Walk tall . . .'

'Yeah right,' Lucy interrupted. 'If only. Not easy to do at five foot one and it doesn't help having mates who are all at least five foot seven.'

'And growing in all directions,' said Izzie before anyone could pounce on her. 'I don't know what I'm going to do in the summer hols. Mum wants a beach holiday but I know what will happen when I get in the sea and the whales see me. They'll all start singing "We Are Family".'

Lucy and TJ cracked up laughing.

'Good one,' said Lucy. 'Must add that to my joke collection.'

'If you think you look crapola,' I said, 'everyone will pick up on it. You of all people should know that, Izzie. You're always going on about positive thinking and I honestly thought you were getting better lately and not being so down on yourself.'

'I am,' said Izzie. 'Sort of. I'm learning to accept myself . . .'

'That's not enough,' I said. 'Come on! After me – all together, a one, a two, a one, two, three. I am gorgeous.'

We all lined up, looked at ourselves in the mirror and chanted. 'I am gorgeous. I am gorgeous. I am gorgeous.'

Izzie and TJ started pulling monster faces at themselves as they chanted and unfortunately one of the customers from the café came in and saw us. She scurried into the nearest cubicle, looking as if she thought that we were mad. She might not be wrong.

'Positive thinking,' I said as she disappeared behind the door and we all burst out laughing.

★ ★ ★

I love Saturdays. It's my favourite day. And I love spending it with my mates having a good laugh and not thinking about anything remotely serious like homework or school and even though I've got stomach cramps today, I'm not going to let that get in the way one bit. It's a funny thing with periods. I remember that before mine came, I really wanted it to happen. Thought it would make me a grown up. Hah! The novelty soon wore off when I experienced what came with it. PMS, headaches, mood swings, cramps. One month, Lucy, Izzie, TJ and I all got our periods at the same time. We laughed about it after but at the time, everyone was majorly oversensitive and tetchy and we almost fell out.

Once we'd done our hair and retouched our make-up, we said goodbye to Tony, who was going off to meet some of his mates and then we were ready to set off down to Camden Lock. It's one of our favourite hang-outs as the shops there are really cool and there are stalls selling everything from bangles and beads to herbal highs. One of Lal's mates apparently bought some mushrooms from a dodgy-looking character down there by the canal last week and was as sick as a dog after taking too many. He ended up having his stomach pumped in Casualty.

TJ went into the newsagent's to buy some chewing gum while the rest of us waited at the bus stop.

'I bet he's only doing it to meet girls,' I said as I buttoned up my jacket to keep out the chilly wind that had blown up whilst we were inside the café.

'Who? What?' asked Lucy.

'That William boy . . .'

'I knew you liked him,' said Lucy.

'Pound,' said Izzie.

'A pound? Whose side are you on?' I asked.

'You said boy,' said Izzie.

'You're supposed to be my mate, not Tony's, so forget about that stupid bet, will you?'

'But we promised to be witnesses,' said Izzie.

I wrapped my arm around her neck and pulled back slightly. 'And I promise that I will kill you if you don't forget it. Understand, *amigo*?'

'Understand,' spluttered Izzie. 'So what were you saying?'

'William. I reckon he only does that collecting money for charity to pull girls.'

'No,' said Izzie. 'I disagree. He's too good looking. He wouldn't need to pull a stunt like that to get a girl.'

'Looks don't necessarily ensure you pull,' I said. 'You have to meet people too and it helps if you have a ready-made opener. He's on to a winner there, I reckon. Yes. Very clever indeed. I should put it on my list of pulling techniques after get yourself a dog.'

'A dog?' asked Lucy.

'Yeah. Look at all the attention we get when we take Ben and Jerry out. Or Mojo.'

Lucy laughed. 'We get attention all right when they've put their noses somewhere they shouldn't be.'

'Dogs are a ready-made introduction,' I said, 'whether they're well-behaved or not. It's the same with collecting for charity. It gives you an excuse to approach cute boys that you might otherwise be shy of.'

'But you're not shy,' said Lucy.

'I am sometimes,' I said.

Lucy looked at Izzie as if to say she didn't believe it one bit.

TJ came out of the shop. 'What have I missed?'

'Nesta saying that she thought William did his charity work as a way of meeting girls,' said Izzie.

'No way,' said TJ. 'No one could be that calculating, could they?'

Izzie and Lucy looked accusingly at me.

'What?' I said. '*What?*'

'*You're* that calculating,' said Izzie. 'You're thinking of doing it as a way of meeting boys.'

'And what's wrong with that, Miss High and Mighty?' I asked. 'You can do good *and* meet people at the same time. And what's wrong with being calculating about meeting boys? Sometimes you have to have a plan. Life is what you make it. And if you do charity, people automatically think you're a good person, so that's a bonus as well.'

TJ looked shocked and shook her head. 'I'm not sure about that,' she said. 'It sounds cold. Like you're using people to make yourself look better.'

'No way,' I objected. 'No way am I a user.'

'Yeah. But don't you think your intentions are supposed to be more sincere?' asked Lucy.

I had a feeling that they were ganging up on me again. I was being cast in a bad light and all because I tried to think up good ways to meet boys. It was so unfair — actually, they should be grateful that I'm so creative in my boy-meeting technique!

'I *am* sincere,' I said. 'I just like meeting boys and this seems like a good way. Two birds with one stone sort of thing.'

'That's true,' said Izzie. 'I guess whatever the reasons someone does charity work, it's better to do something than nothing. In fact, I've been thinking about doing something myself lately . . .'

'Like what?' asked Lucy.

'Dunno. Still thinking about it.'

'We're only fifteen,' I said. 'What can we do?'

'Don't know. But I want to do something. I was watching this programme recently about a country in Africa where they don't have enough to eat; it was really heartbreaking. There were children dying of malnutrition. It made me feel really bad because I'd been so obsessed with food, you know with all the mad diets I was trying. I'd even binned some of Mum's suppers. Suddenly it felt wrong as here on the same planet are people who have nothing.'

'Is that why you wrote that song about people going hungry?' asked Lucy.

Izzie nodded. Izzie wants to be a singer–songwriter when she is older. She plays guitar and writes her own lyrics and sometimes sings with a local band called King Noz. She wrote this great song a few weeks ago about the state of the world and she even got to sing it on the *Teen Talk* pilot when one of the guest singers got stuck on a train and didn't show up.

'I know what you mean,' said TJ. 'It doesn't seem right, does it? I mean, all the resources are there, it's just out of balance. Some countries have too much and some too little.'

'Yeah,' said Lucy. 'Why can't we share out a little more?'

We sat on the wall by the bus stop and talked about some of the problems in the world. Then we were silent for a few minutes while we thought about what a mess the world is in many ways. When I glanced at everyone's faces, they were really gloomy, like it was the end of life as we know it. I hadn't seen Lucy look so miserable since her favourite band, the VIPs, broke up.

'Oh come on, guys,' I said. 'It's Saturday! Time off. Lighten up. Let's talk about something else.'

'Why?' asked Izzie. 'Sometimes I want to talk about stuff like this. It bothers me. I think about it a lot and I think part of the reason that there is such a problem in the world is that people keep ignoring it or pretend it's not happening.'

'But it's making you depressed,' I said. 'Look at your faces. We didn't make everything go wrong so there's no point in going over and over it and getting frustrated. Oh, the state of the world, people are dying, starving . . . oh oh oh . . .'

'Well, they are,' said Lucy. 'I think Izzie's right. I don't think we should ignore it.'

'Yeah,' said TJ. 'I saw a programme last week that really made me sad as well. It was about an orphanage. The children were amazingly brave as most of them had nothing and no one.'

Cue gloomy faces again. Oh God, I want to shoot myself, I thought. The atmosphere was starting to get *really* heavy so I decided to try and lighten it.

'I've got a solution,' I said.

Three faces looked at me eagerly.

'Don't watch the miserable programmes. Watch comedies instead.'

'*Nesta!*' said Lucy. 'Sometimes I think you have *no* feelings.'

'It's not that.' I sighed. 'It's not that I don't care. It's . . . Oh, for heaven's sake, can we just change the subject? I'm starting to feel so miserable. Starving people. Lonely children. There are *other* things happening on the planet, you know.'

Izzie and Lucy were looking at me as if people starving in the world was *my* fault just because I didn't want to talk about it. And TJ was looking at all of us as if trying to work out what she could do to make it all better. What *is* going on today? I asked myself. What had started off as a fun day was turning into grey broody day with everyone touchy and in a weird mood. Even the weather was starting to look ominous with the sky turning greyer and threatening rain. I decided to try again to make them laugh.

'We're all dooooooooomed,' I said in a spooky voice, then mock-strangled myself. I thought it was quite funny but no one else seemed to.

'I don't think we should joke about these things,' said TJ. 'It is serious.'

'OK then,' I said. 'I'll go and do some charity work. I shall try and save the world. Will *that* make you happy and shut you up?'

'You have to want to do it,' said Lucy. 'No point in doing it to prove a point.'

'Yeah. And you just said you only want to do it to meet boys,' said Izzie. 'Maybe Tony was right. Maybe that *is* all that is going on in your head.'

That hurt, and inwardly I winced. What on earth had happened in the last ten minutes? It was like suddenly I was the bad guy and I hadn't even *done* anything. I was simply trying to get them to lighten up. I find it difficult when people start going on about the problems in the world.

What good does it do talking about it over and over? Mum and Dad do it a lot but that's partly because they both work in the media and have to keep up with world events. Mum is a news presenter on cable and Dad makes films and documentaries. They watch a lot of news discussion programmes, and I can see that the subject matter often makes them miserable too.

Usually these programmes show a couple of politicians and a couple of journalists, giving their high and mighty opinions. One jibber jabbers on from one angle, then the other jabber jibbers from the other. Jibber jabber. Jabber jibber. Then they start trying to blame each other for whatever has happened, then a load of people all with different solutions to fix the problem get going, and then *they* all argue and get heated and upset and nothing gets solved. But somehow they all go away feeling better about it because they've *talked* about it. Programmes like that give me an almighty headache. And in the meantime, there are still people starving, dying, homeless or being bombed when they only want to go about their daily lives as normal. By now, I was starting to get depressed myself.

I'd had enough. If Lucy, Izzie and TJ wanted to hang about all day talking about the sorry state of the planet they could, but I wasn't going to do it with them. Plus my stomach cramps weren't getting any better. The idea of going home to my duvet, a bar of chocolate and a hot water bottle was beginning to appeal.

When the bus finally came up the High Street and drew up

at the stop, I waited until Lucy, Izzie and TJ had got on, then stepped back.

'See you later,' I said from the pavement. 'I'm going home.'

The bus driver shut the doors and started off down the road with Lucy, Izzie and TJ staring out of the window at me, concerned and surprised.

As I made my way down the hill to our flat, the skies finally broke and it began to rain. As I hurried along, my mobile rang. I knew it would be the girls but I didn't want to talk to them. Not yet. So I let it go on to voice mail. I felt my eyes well up with tears as I went over what they'd said to me. It wasn't fair. I'm not a bad person. I do care about the state of the world. I *do.* I care that there are lonely people at Christmas and sick people with no one to visit them in hospital and old people with no heating and wars that take away people's homes and disasters that kill loved ones and dolphins that get caught in tuna nets and puppies that no one wants . . .

It was like a dam burst inside me and everything that's wrong in the world seemed to hit me with full force.

I had to sit down in a bus shelter for a while and have a good cry while I waited for the storm to blow over. Luckily there was no one around so I was able to let rip.

Got no feelings, huh, Lucy Lovering?

Don't care, huh, Izzie Foster?

Can't ever be serious, huh, TJ Watts?

Well *look* at me now, I thought as salty tears dripped down my cheeks and onto my chin. What a shame they can't see me this upset. Yeah. If they saw me now they'd see just what a serious, sincere, caring, feeling person I really am.

Out of the corner of my eye, I saw a group of cute looking boys coming down the hill so I quickly pulled myself together. It was one thing wanting my mates to see what a caring sharing person I really am, but boys can get put off by any display of intense emotion, especially when they don't know you that well.

Plus crying makes your eyes puffy. Not a good look in my book.

What does PMS really stand for?

Psychotic Mood Swings

Pardon My Sobbing

Pass My Sweatpants

Permanent Munching Spree

Puffy Mid Section

Pass Me the Shotgun

Pimples May Surface

People Make me Sick

Chapter 3

Charity Muggers

'Nesta, the girls are here,' Mum called from the front door later that afternoon.

A moment later, Izzie, Lucy and TJ trooped in to our living room where I was curled up under my duvet on the sofa watching *Breakfast at Tiffany's*, starring Audrey Hepburn.

'We're soooo sorry about earlier,' said TJ, flopping herself down at the other end of the sofa.

Lucy knelt on the floor and put her hands together as if in prayer. 'Yeah,' she said. 'Sorry, sorry, sorry. We were mean, nasty friends and we were horrid and you didn't deserve it. All you were trying to do was get us to lighten up.'

Izzie held up a carrier bag. 'We bring peace offerings,' she said and started pulling things out of it. 'The home PMS kit. Every girl should have one. Numero one. V. important. Chocolate.' She handed me a Snickers bar.

'Number two, the ultimate feel-good movie,' said TJ, reaching into the bag and producing a DVD. '*It's a Wonderful Life*. We know it's one of your favourites so we dropped back to Lucy's to pick it up from her mum's collection of oldies but goldies – and I know it's supposed to be a Christmas film and it's almost Easter, but who cares?'

'Yeah,' said Izzie and she began singing. '*We wish you a Merry Easter, we wish you a Merry Easter, we wish you a Merry Easter and a Happy New spring, summer, autumn, winter and . . . New Yeeeeeear.*'

I shook my head. 'Mad,' I said. 'Beyond help.'

Lucy put her hand in the bag. 'And I brought you this as well,' she said as she produced what looked like a little bag covered in flowery material. 'It's a wheat bag. Dad's just bought a load of them for his shop. Supposed to be brilliant. It's got all sorts of healing herbs in it and you put it in the microwave for a few minutes. It heats up like a hot water bottle and smells fab. I'll go and do it.'

And off she went to the kitchen.

'And we also got you some aromatherapy oils,' said Izzie. 'Ginger. Camomile. Ylang ylang. All good for period pains. I'll go and make a compress in the bathroom. Back in a mo.'

And off *she* disappeared.

'Wow,' I said. 'What's come over you lot?'

TJ started gently massaging my feet under the duvet. 'It was when we got on the bus and saw you standing there on the pavement. You looked so sad and we got talking about it in Camden, and Izzie said that it's all very well being concerned about people suffering in far away countries but you have to be aware of people on our doorstep. She thought that we'd upset you and you were probably having a bad period so we decided to come over and make it better.'

'So what you're saying is that *I'm* a charity case?'

TJ grinned. 'Exactly. And a head case. But we won't go into that at the moment.'

I grinned back at her. I was so glad they'd come to see me and didn't hate me after all.

A few minutes later, I was settled back on the sofa watching the movie. I had the wheat bag on my back, a warm scented compress on my tummy, TJ massaging my feet while Lucy and Izzie sat on the floor and handed me pieces of Snickers bar. Heaven. Happy, happy, happy.

Over the following week, even though my sanity returned, I felt like the whole world was conspiring against me. Everywhere I went I was accosted by people collecting for this charity, for that charity, for the homeless, the sick, the blind, the handicapped, the deaf, the abused, the hungry, the rainforest, for the dolphins, old donkeys, almost-extinct monkeys, dog homes, cat homes . . . The charity muggers were everywhere: hovering on the High Street, outside the supermarket, inside the supermarket, in pub doorways, on the pavement outside school. Waiting to pounce. It's not that I hadn't noticed them before. Of course I had and sometimes I gave some spare change, sometimes I didn't. Sometimes I just wanted to go down to the High Street and not be bothered by them. And that's just how it was when I gave money, if I'm honest. A way of not being bothered. I gave them money to leave me alone. Mostly I didn't even notice what they were collecting for or who they represented – at least not until now.

'Maybe the universe is trying to tell you something,' said Izzie on Tuesday evening after a man collecting for the homeless had accosted me outside Marks and Spencer in Muswell Hill.

'Like what?' I asked.

'Only you can know that,' she said in her Mystic Iz voice, which is deep and mysterious . . . and very annoying as often I don't have a clue what she's on about.

There was no let-up at home either. Just when I thought it was safe to think about something different, appeals came flying through the letterbox reminding me once again that out there people needed help. Letters asking for sponsorship for a child here, a child there. Charity Christmas cards on sale even though it was only March. Single mothers with no money, children without parents, old people without company, children without schools, villages without water . . . The list seemed endless, and I was starting to get seriously depressed about it. Images of the homeless and hungry were beginning to haunt me at night.

Even the telly was no escape. I was just settling down to the soaps on Wednesday night when the ads came on and it started all over again. People in need were sandwiched in between the commercials encouraging viewers to buy, buy, buy or eat, eat, eat. What a mad, mad, mad world, I thought.

'Mum,' I said when she came in to sit down and join me in

watching telly, 'do you think I'm an ignorant person?'

'Oh yes,' said Mum with a solemn expression. She curled up in the armchair next to the fireplace. She put her glass of wine on the bookshelf next to it. '*Really* ignorant.' I knew she didn't mean it because she couldn't keep a straight face and burst out laughing. 'Why do you ask?

'Been thinking. I mean, do you think I'm selfish and only think about myself?'

Mum took a sip of her wine. 'You're a *teenager*,' she said. 'Comes with the territory. All teenagers are self obsessed know-it-all horrors . . .'

'Wow. Don't hold back, Mum,' I said. 'Say what you really mean!'

'Only kidding. No, Nesta. I don't think you're selfish or ignorant. I think you're lovely. Why are you asking?'

'Just . . . well, lately it's like I've noticed – you know – all the people in the world who need help. And up until this week I haven't even given them a second thought, which is why I thought that maybe I'm ignorant. Selfish. I mean, how could I have not noticed before? I've been living in a bubble, blind to the needs of people around me . . .'

'I wouldn't go that far, love . . .'

'Izzie said that maybe the universe is trying to tell me something. That I've begun to notice for a reason.'

'A reason? Like fate or destiny?'

'Yeah. Maybe it's my fate.'

'OoooKaaaaay,' said Mum. 'And what do you think your fate might be?'

'Not entirely sure yet, but I think it's that I need to do something. Find a cause. I haven't got one. Have you got one?'

'Yes. I sponsor a child in India and I give to vari–'

'See! *See!* You give. You have a cause and I didn't even know. Seems everyone has been doing good all around me and I've been the only one in the middle of it all doing nothing but thinking of myself. Oh *God*. I must be the worst person on the planet. That's why I think I'm so ignorant!'

'You're not ignorant. You're only fifteen . . .'

'I need a cause. My own thing.'

'OK. No problem. Any ideas?'

'No. Not sure yet but one thing is for certain and that is that I can *never* be the same again. No. My eyes have been opened. I have to change. Make amends. I *have* to do what I can to change the world.'

Mum took a large gulp of her wine and looked anxious.

'Right,' she said.

At that moment, Dad came in to join us.

'What are you two talking about?' he said as he sat on the sofa with me.

'Nesta's going to change the world,' said Mum.

'Oh,' said Dad, then he chuckled. 'God help us.'

DIY feel better kit for period pains and mood swings

Chocolate

Feel-good DVDs (*It's a Wonderful Life* is our current fave)

Wheat bag or hot water bottle

Comfy jim-jams

Aromatherapy oils for a compress or a bath:
ylang ylang, ginger, camomile.
To make a compress is really simple, just put some
hot water in a bowl, add 4-6 drops of the oils and
swish them around. Soak a flannel in the scented water then
apply to the achey part.

For an aromatherapy bath: add 4-6 drops of the essential oil
to the bath water when it's running, then swish it around
so that the oils don't remain in one part (they can sting in
such a concentrated form).

Mates to make you laugh when feeling glum.

Chapter 4

Good
Works

'What on earth is going on?' asked Tony the following evening as he stepped over the pile of bin bags that I'd put in the hallway.

'Stuff for the charity shop,' I said. 'I've been doing a clear out. You should do the same since you have loads of stuff you don't need.'

It was only a start but the idea had come to me in maths that afternoon. I'd been racking my brains to try and come up with some way that I could start my good works and it came to me as Mr Hall was droning on about some boring maths equation. I could give away all the stuff I don't use to charity. That was it. Obvious!

I raced home to get started and once I'd begun, it seemed that just about everything I had wasn't really needed. Mum would be delighted as I have the reputation as the hoarder of the family. Usually I can't bear to let anything go. But not today.

I'd pulled out everything from the top of my wardrobe, from my chests of drawers, under my bed. There was all sorts or rubbish stored away in boxes and bags: all my Barbies, My Little Pony dolls, my princess doll, teddy bears, fluffy rabbits, DVDs, CDs, books, bits of jewellery, clothes I'd only worn once. Shameful, I told myself as I hurled it all into bags. It's about time I did this.

Tony had a peek in one of the bags. 'But there are loads of good CDs in here. Surely you're not giving these away?'

'Oh yes I am. I don't need them. I have too many things.'

'Are you on *drugs*?' asked Tony as he continued to sift through the CDs I was chucking out. 'You never give anything away and these are all your favourite CDs. And – I bought you this one last Christmas and . . . here's the one Lucy got you. Hey, you can't get rid of these. They were presents.'

'I don't need them. I don't need most of the things I have. From now on, I'm going to live a much simpler life.'

Tony looked at me as if I had lost my mind. 'Excuse me, but you are Nesta Williams, aren't you?' he asked. 'Or have you been possessed by an alien who's eaten your brain?'

Mum came in the front door and, like Tony had done, almost tripped over the bags.

'What's all this?' she asked as she took her jacket off and put her keys on the hall table.

'Nesta's giving away all her worldly goods and going to be a nun,' said Tony. 'But can I keep the CDs? She won't need them in the nunnery and she has a few I haven't got.'

'No way,' I said. 'They're not for you. They're for the needy.'

'Don't be mad. The charity shops will sell them for ten pence each. Tell you what. I'll give you a fiver for all of them and you can give that to the charity of your choice.'

'What? Er . . . OK, as long as I can still listen to them when I want.'

Tony rolled his eyes and Mum started having a root through the bags. She didn't look very happy with what she found in there. She picked out a jumper that she bought me a few months ago. 'Why are you getting rid of this? It's almost new.' She continued sifting and saw that I had put the contents of most of my wardrobe in. 'Nesta, take this stuff back to your room this instant. This is ridiculous. You're giving all your clothes away. What are you going to wear?'

'Sackcloth and ashes,' said Tony. 'Our Nesta's seen the light and has become a freaking saint.'

'Go on, laugh. I might have expected that from you,' I said. 'When have you ever done anything for anyone else?'

'Now enough of that, Nesta,' said Mum. 'Haven't you ever heard the expression "charity begins at home" and you having a go at your brother isn't very charitable.'

Tony stuck his tongue out at me from behind Mum's back so I made a rude hand sign back at him.

'And that certainly isn't very nice,' said Mum.

'But he started it. . .'

'Oh for heaven's sake, both of you, grow up.'

'I was only trying to do something good,' I said, 'and it's taken me ages to get all this bagged up.'

'Too bad,' said Mum. 'There are some almost new things in

these bags and you're not giving them away until we've been through it all together so that I can see what you want to get rid of. Now, tidy up this mess before your dad gets home and take all these bags back to your room.'

Tony made a smug face at me and luckily this time Mum saw him.

'And you can help her, Tony.'

'But . . .' he started.

'NOW!' said Mum.

At supper that night, I tried out my next good idea to help the poor by suggesting to my family that we cut down on our grocery bills and donate money spent on unnecessary items and treats to charity. It didn't go down too well.

'Get lost, Nesta. If you want to go without then you can, but don't bring in the rest of us,' said Tony.

'Yeah, but I read that five pounds could feed a child for a whole month in some countries.'

Tony rolled his eyes and helped himself to some ice cream.

'Like that ice cream,' I said. 'Do you really need it?'

'*Muuuum*,' groaned Tony. 'Tell her to get off my case will you?'

'Nesta,' Mum started. 'Don't you think you're being a little excessive?'

'A *little* excessive?' said Tony. 'Understatement!'

'Go on then stuff your face. Go on. Ignore all the millions of starving people . . .'

Tony got up from the table and went to the door taking the

ice cream with him. 'I'm not sitting here listening to this . . .'

'Why? The truth makes you uncomfortable does it?'

'Nesta, lose the Mother Teresa routine or go and live somewhere else,' said Tony. 'Get real. First, you go on at me about not giving all my stuff away and now I can't eat in peace. Trying to make me feel bad, telling me what everything cost and what could be done with the money. What do you want me to do? Starve? Then will you be happy?'

'No. Not starve, but maybe we don't need to consume as much as we do. We're a society of consumers. That's why there's the imbalance . . .'

Tony sighed heavily. 'What is with you? Up until last week you were Queen of the Consumers and proud of it. In fact if I remember rightly, your motto was "when the going gets tough, the tough go shopping". You weren't exactly thinking of the poor and hungry when you bought those silver snakeskin heels or that little top from Morgan were you? And now, just because some boy you fancy collects for charity, you think you have to do the same, no doubt so that you can impress him next time you see him.'

'That is soooo not true. And I don't fancy him!'

'Who?'

'William Lewis.'

'Ah,' smirked Tony, 'but you knew exactly who I was talking about, didn't you?'

Mum and Dad didn't say anything. They just looked at each other and Mum raised an eyebrow.

Sometimes I hate Tony. Now Mum and Dad think I'm only

worried about the state of the world because of some boy. Like I don't have a mind of my own.

'Are you going to finish that?' asked Mum, looking at the bowl of ice cream she'd put out for me.

I dipped my spoon in. Butter pecan. It did taste good. And it wasn't exactly as though I could put a tub of ice cream in an envelope and post it to a poor country. Maybe I'll have to think of another way of donating money, I thought as I finished the bowl. It didn't seem that it was going to come out of the housekeeping.

After school the next day, I took the one bag of stuff that Mum was allowing me to give away up to Muswell Hill. It was a lovely evening and after all the rain and chilly winds we'd had recently, at last I could feel spring in the air. I stood by the zebra crossing and wondered which charity shop to give it to: the one for cats, for cancer, for old people or for the hungry in Africa? Oh God. It's impossible to make a decision like that. I put my bag on the pavement and tried to make up my mind which was going to be *my* charity.

Maybe I could persuade Izzie, Lucy and TJ to give some of their old things away too, then we could divide our stuff between them. Yes, that would solve the problem and nobody would get left out. I popped into Sainsbury's and asked if I could have a couple of carrier bags, then sat on the kerb and sorted my things into two bags.

Unfortunately a group of lads passed by as I was dividing my stuff up.

'You look kind of young to be a bag lady,' one of them called over. 'Come with us and we'll give you a good meal and somewhere warm to sleep!'

'Yes. We've got a big fat sausage and a bed for you,' called another as his mates sniggered behind him.

Sad, I thought as I ignored them and continued dividing my clothes up. Some boys really don't have a clue. As if I'm going to respond to a chat-up line as stupid as that. We've got a big fat sausage for you? Duh. How pathetic can you get?

When I'd finished sorting, I took one of the bags to the nearest charity shop and gave it to the lady behind the counter.

She gave me a really sweet smile. 'Thanks so much dear,' she said. 'We do appreciate it.'

I left feeling really good and walked out to the Broadway where there were the usual posse of collectors hovering outside the shops by the zebra crossing. I found my purse and instead of trying to avoid eye contact as I usually do, I walked up to them and gave them some spare change. Outside Ryman's, I gave fifty pence to a man who was collecting for the disabled. And by Marks and Spencer, I put the last of my change into a homeless man's cap. By the time I had reached the bank at the roundabout where I was meeting Izzie, TJ and Lucy, I was beginning to feel positively saintly as everyone I gave money to beamed at me as though I was the only person who had donated anything that day.

'Hey guys,' I said to the girls who were already waiting for me.

'Why are you carrying your charity shop stuff?' asked TJ.

'I thought you were up here giving it away.'

'I gave half of it away,' I explained then quickly asked if they would have a clear out too so that all the shops would get something.

'Yeah, that's a good idea,' said Izzie. 'Plus all the books on Feng Shui say that it's really good to clear out any clutter.'

'But you have to decide where to take it,' I said.

'All of them need stuff,' said Lucy.

'Yeah. And that's the problem,' I said. 'I need to decide which is my charity. And seeing as I intend to be a celebrity when I grow up, it's probably a good idea to decide it now . . .'

'Why's that?' asked Lucy. 'What's being a celebrity got to do with it?'

'Obvious,' I said. 'You must have seen celebs when they're on TV raising money. It's never a general thing, like, "Oh just give the money to whoever needs it." Oh no, they all seem to have a particular cause in mind.'

'Like Bob Geldof with Band Aid,' said TJ. 'That was after he saw a programme about the plight of Ethiopia.'

'Yeah, that was brilliant,' said Izzie and put her hand on her heart. 'Sir Bob. Respect.'

'Yeah. See. He knew what his cause was. And maybe that's part of growing up,' I said. 'Part of discovering who you are. Just as you are identified by the car you drive, the clothes you wear, the drink you drink, you ought to have your own personal charity as well.'

'There's an article about Star Axford in my last *Vogue*,' said Lucy.

'God, I love her,' said Izzie. 'She's so beautiful. And so glamorous. And her dad is Zac Axford.'

'Who's he?' I asked.

'Zac Axford? Big rock and roller. He was huge in the Eighties. My dad has all his old albums. The family are mega loaded. They always appear on those England's richest people lists that are sometimes in magazines. Star's mum was a model too. The whole family sounds fab!'

'So what has this got to do with charity?' I asked.

'Apparently Star gives away ten percent of her earnings to charities,' said Lucy.

'Exactly,' I said. 'See, all the cool celebs do it.'

Izzie rolled her eyes. 'But you make it sound like having the right handbag or trainers,' she said. 'Like a designer charity. The latest accessory to make you look good.'

As usual my good intentions are being taken the wrong way, I thought.

'No. I didn't mean it like that,' I objected. 'Just I want to . . . oh never mind. I just think it's brilliant giving to charity. Makes you feel good.'

'So does a muffin and a hot chocolate,' said Lucy. 'Let's go to Costa. I'm starving.'

'Yeah,' chorused Izzie and TJ.

'Oh . . . but I've no money left,' I said as I realised that I'd given all my pocket money away.

Izzie nudged Lucy. 'Looks like we have our own charity case here. Don't worry. We'll pay for you.'

'You don't need to do that,' I said.

'Why? Too proud to accept our donation?' teased Lucy. 'As you said, it's great to give and sometimes being on the receiving end can be hard. Humbling.'

'Yes, but no, but . . .?'

'Yeah,' said TJ. 'We can't have something and let you just sit there and watch. No, come on, we'll club together.'

'No, I meant you don't need to do that, because maybe you should give the money for the hot chocolate to charity like I did,' I said. 'You don't really need it and the few pounds you'd spend in the café, you could give to a good cause.'

TJ, Lucy and Izzie looked at each other and then at me.

'Oh hell.' Lucy sighed. 'I'm confused now. I feel bad. I *do* want a hot chocolate. I was looking forward to it but I also think I ought to give my money away like you did, Nesta and I'll feel like I'm selfish or something if I don't. Oh stinkbombs . . . Why did you have to go and bring all this up? It's made things really complicated.'

'I know what you mean,' said TJ. 'Now I feel like I'm a bad person too. I feel rotten because I don't want to give my pocket money away. I don't get much and to tell the truth, if I gave what I do have away, I'd only be doing it because now I feel guilty and I don't want you to think badly of me.'

'Hhm,' said Izzie. 'Something's weird about this. The vibe isn't right any more and I'm with TJ, Nesta, I feel guilty too. We all do, so we wouldn't be able to enjoy getting a hot chocolate any more. You know what, guys? Suddenly I don't feel like hanging out. I think I'll go home. Think about it. See you all later.' And off she went towards the bus stop.

'Me too,' said TJ. 'I think I'll go and take Mojo for a walk.' And she went to join Izzie.

I turned to look at Lucy who shifted about on her feet and stared at the pavement.

'Me too,' said Lucy. 'Sorry, Nesta. Dunno why, but suddenly I feel *really* depressed.' She dug her hand into her jeans pocket and handed me two pounds. 'Here. That's all I have. Give it to whatever cause you want. Catch you later.'

Off she went, and I could tell by the way she hunched her shoulders as she walked away that she was fed up.

And so I was left standing on my own and the rosy glow I'd experienced earlier had completely disappeared. I give up, I thought. Do nothing and everyone thinks I don't care. Do what I can and everyone gets depressed and hates me. I can't win. I don't know how Sir Bob Geldof did it when he got all those pop stars to give their time and money. He must have been very persuasive or put it differently as I'm sure no one had a go at him for making them feel guilty. I don't know. Maybe I'll go and have a cappuccino. Oops. Can't. No pocket money left and it would be wrong to use Lucy's money. As I watched Izzie and TJ get on the bus that would take them towards Finchley, I felt totally confused. Trying to do good is clearly not as easy as it first appears, I thought as I walked back up the Broadway and gave Lucy's coins to the man collecting for the disabled. He beamed a thank you back at me but this time, it didn't make me feel so good.

£5 a month will help two children at a school
in Ethiopia complete their education.
£10 can pay for three text books for school
children in Zambia.
£20 can feed three children who have lost their
parents to AIDS in Malawi for a month.
£50 can pay a trainee teacher's salary in Kenya for a month.

Chapter 5

Bin bag
Hell

Lucy called a couple of hours after I got home.

'Is that Saint Nesta?' she asked when I picked up the phone. 'Feeder of the hungry, healer of the sick, benefactor of the poor?'

Phew, I thought. She can't be that mad at me if she's making jokes.

'It is,' I said. 'And pray, what dost thou want, oh sinner?'

'I may have the solution.'

'Solution to what?'

'Your sudden need to get involved in charity. I was telling Mum and Dad about what happened in Muswell Hill and Dad had an idea. You know his shop is next door to one of the charity shops?'

'Yeah.'

'Well, he says that they're often looking for volunteers there.

Mrs Owen, the lady that runs it, was looking for people to help tomorrow as she's been let down by a couple of her usuals.'

'Tomorrow? Wow. That would be cool. Working in a shop.'

'No. Not working in the shop. You're not old enough to work out the front. She wants people in the back to sort through the donations for a jumble sale in Kilburn on Sunday. She said that they're desperate for people to go through the bags and see what's there, what's to be chucked and what can go to jumble.'

'I could do that,' I said. 'You do mean tomorrow?'

'Yeah.'

'All day?'

'Yeah. Until four. I was telling Mum and Dad about you wanting to do something and giving away your pocket money and they both said that at our age, we're probably better off giving our time and energy. What shall I tell Dad, so he can let Mrs Owen know?'

'That I'll be there,' I said. 'What time?'

'Nine-thirty.'

'Right.' Nine-thirty on a Saturday. Bummer. I'd have to get up early but I'd do it. Lucy's parents were right. Using my time did seem like a better idea than giving away all my pocket money and losing my friends over it.

'And Nesta . . .'

'Yeah?'

'I'll do it with you, because even though you were an almighty pain before, laying such a guilt trip on us all, I would actually like to do something as well.'

'Top. It will be a laugh.'

'And Izzie wants to come too.'

'Izzie? Is she still mad with me?'

'Nah,' said Lucy. 'She looked up your horoscope. Some planet's square with another one or something. You'll have to ask her but she said the stars explained why you've been a bit over the top lately.'

'Good. Thank you stars. I hate it when you're all cross with me. How's TJ?' I asked. I knew that they'd all have been texting or e-mailing about me behind my back.

'TJ has footie practice in the afternoon and has to work on the school mag with Emma in the morning. But she's cool about you, although she said she did still feel a bit confused and not sure what's she's supposed to do to help the world. Said she's going to think about it, and on the one hand, she feels guilty that she has so much, like a home and a bed and food and clothes, but on the other hand, really glad she does. I guess we all have to find our way round this – although my mum came out with one of her quotes that kind of made sense.'

'What was that?' I asked. Lucy's mum works as a counsellor and collects great quotes and sayings that she can use in her work to make a point or cheer someone up. Some of them are really inspiring.

'I was telling her that in the face of all the trouble in the world I feel helpless. Like I'm too small to do anything and I don't mean my height.'

'Yeah. I know what you mean. It's like, where do you start?'

'Anyway,' Lucy continued. 'Mum said that there's a saying that goes something like, anyone who thinks that they're too small to make a difference should try sharing a bed with a mosquito.'

'Hah right! Cool. Yeah. Let's bzzz, baby.'

Lucy, Izzie and I were at the charity shop on the dot of nine-thirty the next day. A little old lady with white hair who was wearing bright pink lipstick let us in and introduced herself as Mrs Owen. She led us through to the back where there was a small room, stuffed wall to wall and floor to ceiling with black bin bags.

'Some of this has been here for months without anyone looking at it,' she said as she indicated the bags. 'We haven't enough volunteers, so it's just been left. Anyway, see what you can find. Put it into piles of books, games, toys, bric-à-brac and clothes and so on, then box them. Someone's coming to collect some of it later on. Keep the really good or designer clothes for the shop, medium good clothes for the jumble, and the rubbish can be chucked out.'

'Right, will do,' said Izzie.

'And one of you can make some tea for the shop workers,' said Mrs Owen. 'Doris and Lilian will be in shortly.'

'Is it possible to open a window somewhere?' I asked. 'It's very hot in here.' I had put a fleece on when I got dressed as it was chilly then, but already the day was warming up. I hadn't thought to wear anything underneath so that I could strip off later. Of course, Izzie and Lucy both had brains and had thin crop tops on underneath their jackets.

'Sorry, love,' said Mrs Owen. 'It's because of the boiler next door and it's always on for the water. It does tend to heat up in here and there's no window or door to let any air in. Nothing we can do, I'm afraid. See if you can find an old T-shirt you can put on in one of the bags. In fact, you don't want to ruin your nice jeans either so if you find an old pair of trousers or shorts, just slip them on as well.'

'Thanks,' I said. 'I might do that.'

Lucy went out to the small kitchen to be shown tea duties while Izzie and I took a bag each and began sorting. I looked for something I could change into while I worked. It made sense to get out of my normal clothes.

Mrs Owen had been right – the bags had been there for ages and some at the back were covered in dust. 'Poo-eeee,' said Izzie, holding her nose after she'd opened the first bag. 'This one stinks.' She pulled out the clothes in it and they were filthy. Whoever had donated them clearly hadn't washed them before handing them in, and the room began to smell of stale sweat. Ucky. No way was I going to wear any of these clothes, not even for doing the sorting.

Lucy took tea through to the shop and then brought us a mug each. 'The *girls* have arrived,' said Lucy indicating the shop where there were now three white-haired old ladies behind the counter. 'They're discussing Lilian's recent varicose vein operation so I didn't hang around. Oh, and she said we should take lunch at twelve-thirty.'

Izzie pulled her mobile out of her back pocket. 'I'll let TJ know. She said she'd come and meet us on our break.'

I scraped my hair back into a scrunchie so that it didn't get in my way and started to sift through the clothes. First we threw the contents of a few of bags into the middle of the floor and began to look through. Not a clean T-shirt in sight, only old shirts and horrible looking jumpers. Then Lucy opened a new bag and pulled out a piece of fabric and held it up.

'Here,' she said with an evil grin. 'This will do for you to wear.'

It was an old-fashioned-looking orange sundress with purple polka dots and a sailor collar. The sort of dress that normally I wouldn't be seen dead in, but at least it was clean and with no sleeves, it was the lightest thing we'd seen so far. No one was going to see us; it would do fine. So I took my clothes off and wriggled into it while Lucy and Izzie cracked up laughing.

'Well, it's *different*,' said Lucy as I modelled the dress for them and did a twirl. 'Sort of Minnie Mouse style.'

'Oh, who cares,' I said. 'It's like an oven in here. I'd have died if I'd kept my fleece on.'

I did feel better in just the dress and we got stuck into the task at hand with gusto. It was really hard work sorting everything into boxes to be taken away for the jumble sale, and by twelve o'clock my back was beginning to ache. Plus it got hotter and hotter until it was like a sauna in there. I felt like I was dripping sweat. None of us could believe some of the stuff that people had handed in. Paint-stained, mud-marked, worn through, with holes in, reeking of stale cigarette smoke. Only occasionally was there a bag with pristine clean clothes and they of course went straight on to the 'shop' pile.

'I think I'm going to pass out,' said Lucy after one particularly stinky bag. 'This is bin bag hell. Why don't people just chuck this stuff instead of bringing it here and wasting people's time?'

'Yeah, whose mad idea was this?' asked Izzie as she leaned back and stretched her arms above her head. 'Maybe donating your pocket money isn't such a bad idea after all, Nesta. I think I'd rather have given someone a couple of quid if only I could have stayed in bed this morning.'

'I know, I know. Sorry,' I said as I wiped my forehead with the back of my arm. 'God, it's so hot in here. Good job there's no one to see us looking such a sweaty mess.'

I piled what seemed like the hundredth bag on to the floor and we began to sift through a treasure trove of stuff from the Sixties and Seventies. There were some hideous white plastic hoop earrings, lime green and yellow striped tights, an orange mini skirt, a pink Afro wig and a pair of turquoise and maroon platform boots.

'Be great for a fancy-dress party,' said Lucy.

I shook my head. 'Anyone would look like a complete eejit in that get up,' I said. 'I mean, a party is a party and whatever the theme, you still want to look halfway decent. In that outfit, you'd never pull anyone.'

'It's twelve-thirty,' Mrs Owen called from the shop. 'Take half an hour, girls.'

'Phew,' said Izzie as she headed for the door. 'Let's get out of here!'

Lucy didn't need much prompting either and followed her straight out. I was about to change back into my jeans and fleece but I felt so sweaty that I didn't want to wear anything so warm until I'd cooled down a bit. It would be OK to pop out in the dress for a short time. It looked like the day had turned into lovely sunshine outside.

TJ was waiting for us by the flower bed outside Ryman's. She looked so cool in her jeans and a white tank top.

'Hey, guys,' she said, then burst out laughing when she saw me. 'Hmm, a new look, I see.'

'Yeah. Like it?' I asked as I gave her a twirl. 'Polka dot and orange is the new black.'

'How's it going in there?' she asked.

Lucy pulled a grim face. 'Not great. Like a prison sentence in fact. *Not* a lot of fun.'

'We all got hard labour,' said Izzie, 'but we're hoping to get time off for good behaviour.'

I felt bad since they wouldn't have been there if it hadn't been for me making them feel guilty. And, if I was honest, I wasn't exactly enjoying myself either, even though I kept telling myself that it was all for a worthy cause.

'What have you been up to?' asked Izzie. 'Magazine stuff?'

'Yeah. Actually, I've had a great morning,' TJ replied. 'I had a long hard think about all this charity lark last night. I'd felt confused after . . . well . . . you know . . .'

'After I'd made you all feel guilty,' I said.

TJ smiled. 'I'm sure you didn't mean to. But anyway I decided, I can write. Maybe I can write something that will get people thinking or raise awareness or something. I talked it over with Emma and she agreed. A series of articles on various aspects of charity would be great for the magazine, plus it will give the different causes some exposure.'

'What a brilliant idea,' said Lucy. 'So what are you going to do first?'

'Something to draw the readers in. I reckon if we went in with a heavy article about the state of the world – you know, all gloom and doom and making people feel bad – it might turn people off,' she said. I swear Izzie gave me a meaningful look at this point. I smiled back at her like I didn't know what she was on about (though I knew exactly).

'I suggested we start with a guide to the charity shops in North London,' TJ continued. 'That's where I've just been. Some of them are amazing. The ones in St John's Wood are mega! Five-star stuff. The people who live there are so rich, their throw outs have to be seen to be believed. Prada. Chanel. Dolce and Gabbana. Honest. In a charity shop! You'd have loved it, Nesta. And you too, Lucy. All those great designer clothes going so cheap. And I got a couple of books and CDs that I wanted for almost nothing.'

'Sounds like you've had a better morning than us. Need anyone to do any more research?' asked Izzie.

'Sure,' said TJ. 'We need someone to do North Finchley and Hampstead to see what's there. So far, seems St John's Wood is the biz for fashion, Muswell Hill for books, East Finchley for bric-à-brac.'

I couldn't help feeling a stab of envy. She's a clever girl, is TJ, and sometimes I feel a bit jealous of her. Looks and brains. She has the whole package. I wished I'd thought of something like that instead of breaking my back sorting through smelly clothes and making my friends suffer with me. Suddenly I had an idea.

I didn't want TJ to think we'd had a bad time when she'd been having a great time so I decided to pop back into the shop for a minute.

Once in there, I grabbed the pair of striped yellow and lime green tights and pulled them on. I looked around for some more mad things to wear and spotted the Afro wig, a pink ostrich feather boa and a pair of swimming goggles. I quickly put them on, then made a quick dash to the little toilet area to see what I looked like. I couldn't help but laugh when I saw my reflection in the mirror above the tiny sink. I looked truly awful. Like someone with the worse possible taste ever.

A moment later, I stepped back out into the street and my outfit had exactly the right effect. Lucy, TJ and Izzie creased up laughing when they saw me.

'You're a closet Nancy No-taste,' said Lucy. 'I always knew you would come out one day.'

I went into a dance routine like Mike Myers in the movie, *Austin Powers*, and the girls continued laughing and a few passers-by looked at me as if I was bonkers. See TJ, I thought, you're not the only one having fun doing charity work. After a few moments, Izzie began to shake her head and twitch her mouth. Cool, I thought, she's getting into it as well, and I began to shake my head and twitch as well as I revved up the manic dancing.

'No, *noooo*,' grimaced Izzie, twitching her mouth more than ever.

I began to strut up and down the pavement like a model who's had too much caffeine. 'Yeah, baby, yeah. Hey, Izzie. Love and peace. Like yeah, baby, yeaaah . . .'

Lucy had joined in the twitching with Izzie by now and was also making strange faces.

'St John's Wood may be good for the more expensive designs,' I said in a high pitched squeaky voice, 'but we all know that Muswell Hill is the most brilliant place for those individual little fashions that you won't find anywhere else.'

'Yeah, *right*,' drawled a familiar voice behind me.

I spun around and almost knocked William Lewis over.

'I was trying to warn you,' said Izzie as William looked me up and down with that infuriatingly amused look of his.

'Yeah,' he said with a wicked grin. 'Individual is the word but not so much Coco Chanel as Coco the Clown. Ever thought of getting some fashion advice from an expert?'

Fashion advice? Me? Queen of style? Hurumph. Luckily Izzie, TJ and Lucy pulled me back towards the shop before I could sock him in the mouth.

If you think you're too small to have an impact,
try going to bed with a mosquito.
Anita Roddick

Chapter 6

Jumble

The cheek of him! Who does he think he is?' I asked after I'd changed back into my normal clothes in the tiny cloakroom in the shop. 'And anyway, he looks like *he* could do with some fashion advice. Those jeans are *so* yesterday. And a Busted T shirt. Give me a break. Positively prehistoric.'

'You really do fancy him, don't you?' said Lucy with a smirk.

'For the millionth time I DO NOT fancy William Lewis.'

Izzie began smirking as well. Both of them were standing in front of me smirking like smirky things competing in a smirking contest. It was sooooooo annoying.

'Oh,' continued Lucy. 'So you won't want to know that it was him who came to collect the jumble.'

'Don't worry,' added Izzie. 'He's gone. He took it while you were in the Ladies changing out of your wig. He said to see he hoped to see you there.'

'Where?'

'At the jumble sale,' said Lucy. 'Keep up!'

'And did he say that he wanted to see me or us there?'

'What does it matter if you don't fancy him?' asked Izzie.

'It doesn't. I'm just asking.'

'He said he hoped he'd see *you*,' said Lucy. 'I reckon you're in with a chance there.'

'Like I care,' I said.

'What is it with him?' asked Izzie. 'Usually you'd be right in there. Cute boy to be conquered. He's sooooo your type, so what's the problem?'

'No problem. Just he's *not* my type. Honest, I really, really, really don't fancy him,' I said. 'He thinks he's so cool. And with that look of his, like he's always laughing at some private joke.'

'I like him,' said Lucy. 'He seems on the level to me.'

'Like as in fancy?'

Lucy shook her head. 'Like as in like.'

'She's still too wrapped up in your brother to fancy anyone else,' said Izzie.

'Pfff. Him,' I said, then sighed. 'One day you'll come to your senses. At least we can only hope that you will. What do you think of William, Izzie?'

'Yeah, he's OK . . .' she started.

'Actually, I don't care. I think he thinks a lot of himself. He's a smart-arse.'

'Hmmm,' said Lucy with a grin. 'That's what he said about you too.'

'He did?'

'Yeah. Just now when you were changing,' said Izzie.

'What a cheek!'

'He said it in a nice way. Like it was a good thing,' said Lucy.

'How did he say it? Say it *exactly* how he said it,' I insisted.

'He said, she's a bit of a smart-arse your mate isn't she?' said Lucy. 'And he said it with a knowing smirk, like he knew *your* type and found you entertaining. I think he thought your manic dancing was quite funny too.'

'God, he annoys me. I really hate him.'

Lucy and Izzie exchanged knowing looks.

'Yeah, sure,' said Izzie. 'You hate him.'

Lucy started laughing as though Izzie had said something really funny. Both of them are clearly demented. They exchanged glances and Izzie raised an eyebrow

'So are you going to go?' asked Lucy.

'Might,' I said. 'In fact, Mrs Owen did mention that they need volunteers tomorrow as well so yeah, I might go along to the jumble sale just to show him how I can look when I want to make an effort. When I'm not dressed as a cartoon character. Not because I fancy him or anything, because I don't, but because I don't like people telling me I need fashion advice when they don't really know me.'

Lucy and Izzie exchanged dubious glances as if to say that they didn't believe a word of it.

On Sunday morning, I spent a good hour trying to find the perfect outfit to wear to the jumble sale. It was a difficult decision and I was glad that Mum had made me keep some of the clothes I was about to chuck out or else I'd have had nothing to choose from. Usually I'm so good at those 'what to wear to where?' type quizzes in magazines. The ones that show you five outfits and five occasions and you have to match the outfit to the occasion. I get it right every time but a jumble sale wasn't an occasion that had ever come up. What should one wear? I didn't want to look too scruffy because I wanted to show William that I could look good, but then I didn't want to look like I'd tried too hard either. He might think I was trying to impress him. Casual but stylish, that's what I need, I decided. Something that looked like I'd thrown it on without thinking, but actually showed off all my best features to their best advantage.

I know, I thought as I scanned the shelves in my wardrobe. My retro lilac cardi, my scuffed bootleg jeans and my lilac Converse Allstar sneakers. A pink tie-dye camisole underneath and the zipper on my cardi pulled just low enough to see the lace on it and that should do the trick. Bit of make up. Not too much. Squirt of Mum's Ô de Lancome as it's light but feminine and he should be falling at my feet any time soon. Not that I want him to, that is, or, I do want him to, but only so that I can tell him that I don't want him to. Hmm, I thought. Sometimes I sound mixed up. But I'm not.

I met the girls at the church hall in Kilburn where the jumble sale was taking place and it seemed a shame that we were going to be indoors again as already it was warm and looked like it was going to be a lovely clear spring day. TJ was with us this time as she wanted to be a volunteer as well. She was looking very good with her hair loose and a bit of make-up on which is unusual for TJ, who often doesn't bother.

'If there are cute boys like William getting involved, I want to be a part of it,' she said after we'd been let in and Mrs Owen had given us instructions about how to lay out the stuff to be sold on the long tables lining the sides of the hall.

'Why? Do you fancy him?' I asked as casually as I could, as I began to pull bags out from under our allotted table on the right-hand side of the hall.

'Oh God no,' she said putting her hand on her heart. 'Scout's honour. On the Holy Bible. Truly, I'd say if I did. No. He's all yours, Nesta. There's no spark there between us. Honest. Not like . . .'

'Oh not you too, TJ. I *don't* fancy him.'

'Izzie and Lucy said you did.'

Lucy gave me a big smile from the front of the table from where she had begun arranging all the clothes by colour. I glared back at her.

'Well, I don't,' I insisted. 'I was just asking if *you* fancied him.'

'Well, I don't either.'

'Neither do I.'

'Yeah, but I'm telling the truth,' she said, smirking. She had obviously been taking smirking lessons from the current champions, Izzie and Lucy.

'Oh for heaven's sake. I DO NOT FANCY WILLIAM LEWIS!'

Izzie's face registered horror and Lucy began the twitching thing that she was doing yesterday. I spun round to see that

William had just walked in the door. He was carrying an enormous box of junk and he looked straight over to where we were and gave us a brief nod. He wasn't smiling as much as usual and I wasn't sure if he had heard what I'd said or not.

Huh, be like that, I thought as I watched him put down his box then head out again without even coming over to say hi. I know *his* type exactly. Charming when they want something then cool as ice when they don't. Not that I care either way.

The next few hours flew by. From the moment the doors opened to the public at ten o'clock, we were kept really busy. Lucy was in her element and set herself up as a style guru giving fashion advice to loads of the people who came to our table.

'Oh no,' she said to one grey haired lady who had picked up a burgundy coloured cardigan. 'Not your colour. I've got one just perfect for you tucked away, let me get it.'

Soon there were more people round our table than anyone's, all asking Lucy for advice. Not to be left out, Izzie began auctioning some stuff off. It was a riot as she held up a skirt.

'Ladies, ladies, bargain of the week,' she called into the room. 'A Jaeger skirt. Yes, the genuine article in perfect condition. None of your fake stuff here, only the best designer gear. What am I bid? We're starting at fifty pence. Does anyone raise me? Ah yes, sixty pence in the corner . . .'

We were a good team and the money started coming in fast. Before I knew it, it was twelve o'clock. I'd been so distracted with the auction that I hadn't noticed the girl sitting behind the table on the opposite side of the hall who was watching us with a smile on her face. She had white blond hair tied back, showing a stunningly pretty face. And she looked familiar. A few minutes later, the hall door opened and William went over to her and handed her a bottle of juice.

Huh, I thought. I knew there'd be a girl involved. I looked around for Lucy so I could tell her and saw her heading towards the cloakroom at the back of the hall. As TJ and Izzie were still busy with the auction which was proving a great success, I followed Lucy. I needed to tell someone that I'd been right about William.

'I *knew* it,' I said as I burst into the cloakroom.

'Knew what?' asked Lucy from the sink where she had started washing her hands.

'William's out there with a girl. I told you so. He isn't Mr Super Do Gooder. He's doing volunteer work to be with this girl. And she's *very* pretty.'

'So what's wrong with that?' asked Lucy. 'You heard TJ saying part of the reason she's here is to meet cute boys like William. But not William. I don't think she fancies him. Between you and me, I think part of her thought that Luke might be here. I don't think she ever really got over him, you know . . .'

'Oh who cares about Luke. It's William I'm talking about . . .'

'But you don't care about him,' said Lucy. 'Earlier you announced to the whole hall that you don't fancy him? Or *do* you? And anyway, what's wrong with doing some charity work to be with someone? You don't have to be a saint to do it. I'm sure people get involved for all sorts of reasons. As long as the work gets done, that's what counts in the end.'

'I guess,' I said and went back to the door and half opened it ready to go back into the hall. 'It's just – he could have found a better way to impress her.'

'Who?' asked Lucy.

'William Lewis. God, Lucy, anyone would think that you're not listening. There's just something about him that I don't trust.'

'Maybe that's because he's a friend of Luke's and you know that you can't trust him after what happened last year.'

'Maybe,' I said. 'I don't know what it is about him but somehow . . . he *annoys* me. And if he only got involved with this volunteer lark to impress that girl then I think he's sad.'

'Maybe *she* got involved to be with him,' said Lucy.

'Maybe,' I said. 'Anyway, whatever. He's annoying so I'm not going to give him even another moment's thought.'

I opened the door properly to go back into the hall and who was standing in the corridor waiting to come into the cloakroom. William freaking Lewis.

'Oh God, *you* again,' I blurted before I could stop myself. It seemed that every time I turned round lately he was there.

'Well pardon *me* for breathing,' he said.

'This is the Ladies,' I said.

'I think you'll find that it's the Anybody's,' he said. 'There's only one so it's the Ladies *and* the Gents.'

'Oh. Right. Whatever. How long were you standing there?'

William leant slightly towards me and I caught the scent of his aftershave. It was nice. Light and citrus. 'Long enough,' he said, 'to know that I am annoying.'

Oh God, I thought. I've really blown my cool now. He

overhears me twice in one day. Talk about unlucky.

'Right. Sorry. Got to go. Previous engagement,' I said as I made a dash back into the hall.

Buggero, buggera, buggerat, I thought as I made my way back to the table. I felt all mixed up. But why? What was going on with me? Did I secretly fancy William a bit? So secretly that not even I knew about it? No. That's mad. But then I am mad. And I'd be mad not to fancy him as he has got gorgeous eyes and he smells nice. Maybe we'd just got off to the wrong start. Anyway, it's too late. He's got a girlfriend. And she's gorgeous even though she looks slightly older than him. Do I mind? Nah. Yeah. Maybe. Oh I don't know. I'll think about it later. In the meantime, I have things to do. Bric-à-brac to sell. God, I wish I could scream but then people really would think I was barmy.

'Need more stuff out?' I asked when I got back to the others.

Izzie nodded. 'There are loads more boxes under the table. Be great if you could get some of it out. Thanks. You could hand it up to me.'

I knelt on the floor and swivelled myself under the table and began to pull out the contents of the boxes and hand them to Izzie. It was nice to be down there and out of the way for a while. I think I'm better off not being let out in public at the moment, I thought as I surveyed the room from my strange vantage point. All I could see of people were their lower legs and shoes. Five minutes later, a pair of jeans and trainers appeared on the other side of the table. And a wheelchair. William's legs, I thought. I recognise the trainers. I tugged the hem of Izzie's jeans and shook my head so that she'd know not to let him know that I was under there.

It wasn't much use as a moment later, William's face appeared under the table as he bent down.

'Hiding from anyone I know?' he asked.

'I wasn't hiding,' I said curtly as I crawled out and stood up. I was about to say something cutting but buttoned it when I saw that he was with the pretty girl from the other side of the hall and she was in the wheelchair. 'And certainly not from . . .'

'Eleanor,' said William to the girl before I could finish, 'I'd like you to meet – er, what was your name again?' And he gave me an infuriating smile.

'Nesta,' I said to the girl. 'Hi.'

'And we're Izzie, Lucy and TJ,' chorused the others from the other end of the table.

I looked at William. Same high cheekbones, fine features. The penny dropped. Eleanor. Oh!

'William's sister?' I asked.

Eleanor nodded. 'Yep. That's me.'

'But you . . . you look familiar,' I said. 'Have we met before?'

'Before this you mean?' asked Eleanor indicating the wheelchair she was in.

'Um, yes, no. I meant before today.'

'Don't think so,' said Eleanor.

'She might have seen you on stage,' said William.

'That's it,' Izzie interrupted. 'You're Eleanor Lewis. I saw you at Jackson's Lane. You were totally brilliant. Remember, Nesta? *The Snow Queen*?'

'God, yeah. You were amazing.' It had been a Christmas performance of the ballet and Eleanor had danced the main role. I remembered her because not only was she stunningly pretty but her dancing had something special. I remembered thinking that she had the X factor and the write-ups in the local paper had thought the same, some even comparing her to Sylvie Guillem, who I think is the best dancer in the whole world. Eleanor was in the press for a while and then suddenly seemed to disappear.

'What happened?' I asked, presuming that she'd broken a leg or sprained an ankle while dancing or something.

'Nesta,' said Lucy. 'Maybe it's private. Excuse our friend, Eleanor. We call her Big Mouth.'

'S'OK,' said Eleanor. 'She can ask. I got cancer.'

'You *what*?' I think my jaw dropped open. She just came out with it in such a matter of fact way, like she was telling us she had a sore throat or a sprained wrist.

'Cancer. In the bones,' she said and she looked at me straight in the eyes as if to see if I was going to look away.

'God, how awful,' I said looking straight back at her. 'Are you going to be all right? Can it be treated?'

The others looked surprised but I really wanted to know.

Eleanor shook her head. 'No. They've done what they can. Nothing left to try.'

'But that's so unfair . . .' I blurted.

She shrugged and looked up at her brother. 'Tell me about it. Yeah, but at least I can get my brother to do anything for me now, huh, Will?'

William nodded. 'Just about.'

'One of the good things about everyone knowing that you're going to die is that no one can refuse you anything. Now when I go shopping, I can have whatever I want . . .'

'You're going to *die*?' I asked and turned to William. I had a feeling that I was reacting in completely the wrong way but I was so shocked. I couldn't help it.

William put his hand on Eleanor's shoulder and smiled at her but I saw the pain in his eyes.

'Yeah. Bummer, huh?' said Eleanor. 'Still, so are we all. It's just I know that my time's coming a bit before most.'

'I'm *so* sorry,' I said. 'And I hope I didn't offend you, just I've never met anyone with cancer before and they don't teach us the "how to deal with a person who's got cancer" lesson at school.'

'Hey Nesta, don't worry,' she said. 'Actually I like the fact that you came out and asked what you wanted to know. Some people, even those I thought were my friends, cross the road when they see me now. Can't deal with it. Hah. How do they think *I* feel? So it's refreshing when someone comes out with the questions that I know they're dying to ask . . . Dying to ask — there's a funny one.'

Just at that moment, William was called away by one of the ladies running the sale.

'Won't be long,' he said to Eleanor then turned to me. 'Keep an eye on her, will you?'

'Sure,' I said.

Eleanor looked at her wheelchair and held up her hands in

exasperation. 'Like there's anything I could get up to in this thing. Give me a break, Will, I'm fine.'

'Is there anything I can do?' I asked when he'd gone.

Eleanor looked at me then over at her brother. Then her expression took on the same amused look that I'd seen on William's face sometimes

'Yeah,' she said. 'Cheer my misery of a brother up. He's been a pain in the ass for months now. Anyone would think it was him that was ill.'

'What! *Me? Him?* I . . . er, I don't think he likes me very much.'

'I wouldn't be so sure,' said Eleanor.

'No. I am sure.'

Eleanor shrugged. 'Well you did ask what you could do. I saw him watching you before and I . . . well I just have an instinct that you two would get along.'

'Pff. Doubt it but OK. OK. I'll try,' I said.

'Cool,' said Eleanor. 'Just don't let him know I asked you will you?'

Izzie, TJ and Lucy gave me the thumbs up from the other end of the table from where they'd all been listening to every word.

Cheer William up. Now *that* was going to be a challenge.

Chapter 7

William

'So now we know why he got involved in doing all this kind of thing,' said TJ after William and Eleanor had gone.

The morning rush had faded and the hall had grown quiet. I felt all mixed up inside and judging by the looks on the other's faces, the general mood was gloom. I was beginning to wish that I'd never got involved in doing volunteer work. It stirred up too many weird feelings and made me think about stuff I wasn't sure I wanted to. Illness, death. I felt so helpless.

'I just can't believe it,' said Izzie. 'Eleanor Lewis. She's so beautiful . . .'

'Beautiful people get ill too,' said Lucy.

'But to know that you're going to die so young, I can't imagine it,' I said.

'It seems so unfair. She had such a brilliant future,' said Izzie.

'So does anyone who gets ill at her age,' said TJ. 'She's what? Seventeen, eighteen?'

'Just turned nineteen,' said Mrs Owen who had been quietly

sitting at one end of the table listening. 'She's been through a lot that one. She's a brave girl.'

'Do you know the family?' I asked

Mrs Owen nodded. 'I've known William, Olivia and Eleanor all their lives. I live on the same street and used to babysit them when they were young.'

'So what's going to happen to her?' I asked. 'I mean, how long has she got?'

'A year. Maybe two,' replied Mrs Owen. 'You can never tell. Sometimes it's very quick and sometimes people outlive all expectations.'

Poor, poor Eleanor, I thought. Poor, poor William. Poor Olivia. And their mum and dad. What must his parents be going through? I wondered.

'This is what this is all about,' said Mrs Owen, indicating the hall with a sweep of her hands. 'These jumble sales, the shop. All the money goes to help the younger people with terminal cancer.'

'Help them how?' I asked. 'Eleanor said that there was no more anyone could do.'

'We can make them as comfortable as possible when they have to go through their treatment and . . . and at the end. All the proceeds of this sale will go to the Lotus Hospice.'

'Is that like a special hospital?' asked Lucy.

Mrs Owen nodded. 'It certainly has all the equipment needed there and the drugs for pain relief like a hospital but it's more than that. We try to make it as much like home as possible so that in their last weeks or days, they don't feel like they're in a hospital ward. They can get the care and medical attention they need but they can also have their family around them should they wish, eat together, spend time together. That's the aim. A small wing with a kitchen, a living area and spare beds so that family or friends can stay over and they can bring in all their things — books, posters, whatever, and make it their own for their time there. William's been a star and so has Olivia. Both of them have worked harder than anyone to raise funds because although we have one living area like that, we need another — sometimes more than one family has a need for the place at the same time. It can be so hard for family members to stand by and know that there's nothing that they can do to save their loved one. At least with this, William can feel he is doing something.'

And I'd accused him of doing it to pull girls. And he'd probably heard. He must think that I am the worst person in the world.

'There's nothing else for it,' I said turning to Lucy. 'I have to apologise to William.'

Lucy nodded. 'I think you should. And you have to cheer him up. Eleanor said so.'

'Do you know if William will be back today?' I asked Mrs Owen.

'Later,' she replied. 'He's gone to drop Eleanor home and then he'll be back.'

Right, I thought. Apologise and commence Mission Cheer Up William. How in the world was I going to do that? I had no idea. I tried to put myself in his shoes and imagine that it was Tony who was ill, or one of my mates. I don't think I could bear it, I thought as my eyes filled with tears at the very idea of anything happening to any of them.

Mrs Owen noticed my long face. 'Hey come on, Nesta. No use in you getting all gloomy. It doesn't help. My old dad always used to say that the birds of doom may fly overhead but there's no need to let them nest in your hair. He was right. So. You know what you can do? Be happy. Enjoy your life to the best of your ability.'

'It's weird. Why are some people so well and have everything whilst others have such a hard time?'

'Big question,' said Mrs Owen. 'Which is exactly why you should enjoy your life while you *are* well. All of it. Including all the trivialities of life. Be glad that you can.'

I nodded back at her, and attempted a smile.

Then the afternoon bargain hunters appeared through the doors, including one face that was very familiar. It was Miss Watkins, our PSHE teacher. No surprise there, I thought as she began to sift through one of the tables by the door. She always looks as if she dressed from the jumble in mismatched outfits that don't really suit her. She's a funny old bird. Strict as hell when she wants to be, but supportive and kind when she sees someone making an effort. Shame she doesn't make an effort with her appearance. She has that wiry grey hair that seems to have a life of its own but I'm sure could look halfway decent if she had it blow dried. And she wears really old-fashioned glasses that make her look permanently shocked.

'Oh well done, girls,' she said coming over after she'd had a good browse round. 'So good to see some of our pupils here. How's it going?'

'Good,' said Lucy.

'Yes, in fact Lucy's set herself up as a style queen,' I interrupted. 'She could recommend a whole new image for you if you like.'

Lucy looked at me as if she'd like to kill me but I thought it was a brilliant idea.

'New image? Me? Oh no, I'm quite happy,' said Miss Watkins, causing Lucy to sigh with relief. Wacko Watkins has never been her favourite teacher.

'And we were just saying that we thought that our school should do some fundraising,' said TJ.

Miss Watkins chortled. 'What planet are you on, Theresa Watts?' she asked. 'We do. Of course we do.'

'No, we mean for charities,' continued Lucy. 'We know we do loads of fundraising for the school . . .'

'But we *do*,' Miss Watkins repeated. 'And this is one of the main charities we support.'

'Really?' said Izzie. 'How come we never knew about it?'

Miss Watkins gave us all her 'how stupid can you get look' (a look that she has clearly perfected through the years). 'How come you never knew about it? Hmm. Maybe you weren't listening. People often only hear what they want to hear. But oh yes, we do fundraising. Not that we couldn't do a lot more. The meeting is on Monday nights after school. You're all very welcome as we could do with some fresh blood.'

Lucy, Izzie, TJ and I looked at each other then we all nodded.

'We're in,' said TJ.

'Excellent,' said Miss Watkins. 'Now. What bargains have you got to show me?'

William came back at about two-thirty just as all the volunteers were beginning to pack up. He came straight over to me and pulled me to one side.

'Thanks for . . . before, with Eleanor,' he said. 'She said she really appreciated being talked to like a normal human being for change. It really is true what she said before – about people not knowing how to deal with her so they avoid her or the subject of her illness. They talk about anything else but what's happening.'

'But it must be so hard,' I replied, 'for you too. If there's anything I can do or if you want to talk . . .'

William's expression grew hard for a moment. 'Eleanor may want to talk, but not me. No. Last thing I want,' he said. 'What good would that do? Like there's anything you could say to make it better.'

He looked so intense and I remembered that I was supposed to be cheering him up. I quickly scanned my brain for something I could say to help.

'I could try and say something to make you laugh . . .'

'Don't bother.'

'Look. I'm really really sorry about . . . um, whatever I said before. About you being . . . um annoying and stuff . . .'

'Doesn't matter,' said William. 'I probably am.'

He looked so sad as he stood there. Like a little boy who

was desperately trying to be brave. He needed distracting. And fast.

'Er . . . OK,' I said and pointed to the back of the church hall. 'See that screen over there?'

'Yeah.'

'Come behind it with me and I'll snog you.'

William burst out laughing.

'See,' I said. 'I told you I could make you laugh.'

The amused look that had been annoying me so much lately appeared back on his face. 'Ah . . . but did you mean it?' he asked.

Time for a little practice flirting, I thought and glanced back at him in a coy way. 'Why? Do you want me to have meant it?'

'Depends. Do you want me to take you up on it?'

I looked at his mouth. It was a very nice mouth, wide with a bottom lip that plumped out in the middle like a tiny soft cushion. I glanced up into his eyes and a shiver of anticipation went through me. For a moment, it was as if we were locked together. Suddenly he grabbed my hand. We quickly walked over behind the screen where we were out of sight and he pulled me close to him and kissed me. Properly. Like, not a peck. I mean, *properly*. Then we pulled apart and both burst out laughing.

'Better than talking,' he said, grinning.

'Right,' I said. 'Yes. Good.' I felt weak at the knees from the kiss. I hadn't imagined for a moment that he would take me up on my offer. I'd said it to make him laugh. His response had taken me unexpectedly and on the kissing scale, he was a ten out of ten.

He gazed into my eyes and I felt myself turning to jelly. He pulled me close again and once more, we kissed. I could have stayed there forever if we hadn't heard Izzie and Lucy sniggering a short distance away. I opened my eyes.

They were doing that smirking thing again.

> The birds of doom may fly overhead
> but there's no need to let them nest in your hair.

Chapter 8

Fundraising

'Oh no. Look who's in there,' I groaned as I looked through the window of the prefab where the fundraising meeting was being held after school on Monday. I could see four prefects from Year Eleven waiting for the meeting to begin. Doreen Kennard, Blair Thorpe, Charlotte Miller and Sandra Collins.

'Who?' asked Lucy.

'Dopey Doreen and her sad bossy mates.'

'Don't be so cruel, Nesta,' said Lucy. 'You wouldn't like it if someone said that about you.'

'Yeah, but I didn't come up with that name. Everyone calls them that,' I said. 'They are so boring. Remember when Blair gave that talk in assembly last year? I can't even remember what it was about. I was asleep after five minutes.'

'It was about drugs,' said Izzie.

'None of which could possibly be as potent as her speaking voice,' I said. 'One of the most powerful tranquillisers I've ever come across.'

TJ and Izzie laughed but Lucy punched my arm.

'Come on. Let's do a runner now,' I said. 'We'll find another way to do something . . . like donating our organs when we're dead.'

'*Nesta*,' groaned Lucy. 'Gross.'

'Well, they're no use to you when you're six foot under are they? I mean, I know I'm Queen of Squeam now I'm alive but when I'm dead, anyone can have anything. Like if any of you girls want a kidney or whatever, please feel free.'

'Wow, thanks Nesta,' said TJ. 'I'd love a kidney. I could have it bottled and put on the mantelpiece as a reminder of you.'

'And I'll have your eyeballs,' said Izzie, laughing. 'I could have them made into earrings.'

Lucy put her fingers in her ears. '*Stop* it. You're all *disgusting*.'

'Oops. Too late to do a runner,' said Izzie suddenly putting a straight face on. 'Here comes Wacko.'

I turned to see Miss Watkins approaching. She was wearing a long, navy-coloured cardigan that she'd bought at the sale yesterday and her face lit up when she saw us.

'Well done, girls,' she said. 'I was hoping you lot would turn up. Come on then, let's get inside.'

Five minutes later, the meeting was underway and Miss Watkins asked Boring Blair to fill us 'new girls' in on forthcoming events.

I had a hard time not falling asleep again much as I tried to concentrate on what Blair was saying. It was something about the tone of her voice. Or lack of tone. She spoke every word on the same level. She wouldn't last five seconds on the radio.

I tried to focus once more and told myself that Blair's lack of delivery didn't matter as everyone knows she wants to be a marine biologist when she leaves school. Poor fish. The fishermen won't need nets. They can just send Blair underwater and ask her to say something and the fish will all surrender in droves. In fact maybe she is perfect for the job of fundraiser – she could hypnotise people into giving their money away. I almost laughed as an image of thousands of people walking down the road like sleepwalkers and handing over thousands of pounds to Blair played through my mind. 'Sleep sleep, hand over your cash,' she said in my fantasy.

'Nesta,' said Miss Watkins. 'What are you smiling at?'

'Smiling? Me? Oh. Yes, Miss. Just thinking about fundraising ideas.'

'Want to share those thoughts? That's what the meeting is all about. Sharing ideas.'

'Er no, Miss. Thank you. Not yet. Thank you.'

Somehow I didn't think my fantasy of Blair as Queen of the Zombies was an idea that would go down that well in the present company. Doreen, Blair and their mates are a peculiar lot. Although people call them the Dopey Doreens, actually they are all dead clever. They're not exactly pretty girls but they're not unattractive either. Somewhere in the middle and all of them look like they go to very expensive hairdressers, in fact Charlotte has the glossiest auburn hair I've ever seen even though it is a little thin. Doreen's small and brunette. Charlotte tall and skinny. Blair is tall with a mane of blond hair. And Sandra's medium-sized with wild, curly, dark hair. So pretty normal in the main. The thing about them is that they're . . . what is it? I thought as I searched my mind for the right word.

They're always up for awards for this and that. Mainly to do with science. Clever? No. Responsible? That's partly the word, as they have always been the prefect type. No. I know the word. Adult. It's like they somehow skipped childhood and adolescence and went straight into being grown up. Maybe they were even *born* grown up. I could feel myself smiling again as I imagined them in a play school reading books whilst around them other kids played with toys.

'Nesta, *Nesta*,' said Miss Watkins. 'You're daydreaming again. Come on. Join in. That's why you're here.'

'OK. So how much has been raised so far?' I asked.

'Two hundred and fifty pounds,' said Blair looking pleased with herself.

'And how much is needed to build the new wing at the Lotus Hospice?' I asked.

'Well, that's among other things,' said Sandra. 'We support a number of charities.'

'Yes, but we agreed that the hospice would be our focus for the first half of the year,' said Miss Watkins. 'They have a target that they are trying to reach and all the schools in this area did promise that we would make them our priority until the sum has been raised.'

'And the sum is?' I asked.

'Another fifty thousand pounds is needed,' said Miss Watkins. 'And they were hoping to get it by the beginning of May so the building could commence later on in the month.'

Doreen laughed. 'Unlikely,' she said.

'Not possible,' said Charlotte.

'Thanks to some very generous benefactors, four hundred thousand has been raised by various organisations so far,' said Miss Watkins, 'but all those sources have now been exhausted, so it's down to creativity and hard graft from now on. Just to make that last amount needed.'

The Dopey Doreens were all shaking their heads.

'But why not?' I asked.

Sandra gave me a very snooty look. 'Have you actually done any fundraising?' she asked.

'Yes,' I answered. So I'd only done yesterday's jumble sale, but she didn't need to know that.

'Then you'll know exactly how hard it is to extract money out of people,' Sandra continued. 'At least, enough to make a difference.'

'And you wouldn't believe how many people pitch up like you lot, full of enthusiasm, only to drop out a few weeks later when they realise what hard work it is,' said Blair and the others nodded along with her.

'Doesn't need to be hard work,' I blurted. 'Well, OK, maybe a bit of graft but I don't see why it can't be enjoyable as well.' I was thinking of the auction we'd had yesterday and what a laugh that had been for all of us. Volunteers and buyers.

'Yeah right,' drawled Doreen in a tired way. 'Just what we need. Another naïve idealist.'

'Now come on,' said Miss Watkins. 'You don't want to put off our new arrivals on their first night.'

Doreen gave her a look back which said, that's exactly what I want to do. I got a feeling that this fundraising thing was their little club and they didn't want outsiders in. It was no wonder others had dropped out so quickly. When faced with this lot, I thought, who could blame them? But I wasn't about to do a runner. I like a challenge and I don't like people insinuating that I can't do something. Huh, I thought. I'd show them who was a naïve idealist or not.

'OK then,' I said. 'So what's on the agenda? More jumble sales? Raffles? What?'

'The big event in the calendar year is the dance on May 7th,' said Miss Watkins. 'How's that going Blair?'

'Well, we've got the venue,' said Blair.

'Which is where?' asked TJ.

'It's a hall in East Finchley at the end of the High Road . . .'

'Oh, I know it,' said Izzie, then pulled a disapproving face. 'It's where I . . . er . . . It's a bit dark and stuffy in there.'

I knew the hall too. It was where Izzie went to a slimming club called Weight Winners but she obviously didn't want the others knowing how she knew the place.

'So you find somewhere on no budget,' challenged Charlotte. 'We can brighten it up on the night with a few balloons.'

Izzie caught my eye. I knew she thinking the same thing that I was: Sounds like the party of the century. Not.

'And how are the ticket sales going?' asked Miss Watkins.

At this question, Blair looked down at the floor, faintly embarrassed. 'Ah. Not brilliant so far . . .'

'How many?' asked Miss Watkins.

'Twenty-five. Sorry. I . . . Look, we've got time yet.'

'Five weeks,' said Miss Watkins. 'Five weeks and we need to

sell at least five hundred. The hall will easily take that number, and even more at a push.'

'Have you advertised it?' asked TJ. 'I could put it in the school magazine for a start. I certainly didn't know that there was going to be any event in May, and if people don't know about it, no one's going to buy tickets.'

'Yeah. Have you got any posters out there?' asked Izzie.

Charlotte pulled a pile of posters out of her bag and held them up. They were black and white and showed little sense of design, in fact they looked like newspaper cuttings.

'I've put these up in a few of the libraries,' she said.

For girls with brains, this lot aren't that bright, I thought – but then it was always the same in every year: the ones who did well academically weren't always the most sussed when it came to street cred or doing anything commercial.

After looking at the posters, I glanced over at Lucy and pulled a 'God they're awful face'.

Unfortunately Blair saw me. 'OK then, let's see you lot do better,' she said. 'Charlotte spent ages doing those. Honestly Miss Watkins. Do we have to work with this lot from Year Ten?'

Miss Watkins' eyes were twinkling as if she was secretly enjoying what was going on. 'Team effort, girls,' she said. 'Team effort. Now have you new girls got any suggestions that you'd like to throw into the pot?'

I nodded. I was sure that Lucy, Izzie, TJ and I could raise more than two hundred and fifty pounds if we put our heads together. Sir Bob raised millions for Ethiopia in one night, so what was fifty thousand?

'Give us a few days,' I said. 'We'll come up with some ideas.'

'Well, don't do anything stupid,' said Doreen. 'And make sure that you consult us before starting. We're experienced and know what we're doing.'

'Which is why you raised the grand sum of two hundred and fifty quid,' I said as Lucy, Izzie and TJ gasped in horror.

Doreen looked as if she'd like to thump me and Blair, Sandra and Charlotte scowled at all of us with undisguised disdain. Now I knew that we had definitely stamped on their territory. Not that Miss Watkins seemed bothered by any of the animosity taking place in front of her. She was still smiling away as if at some private joke. Well tough to the lot of you, I thought as I met Doreen's glare in an eyeball to eyeball staring contest. You're not getting rid of us this easily.

Doreen looked away and murmured, 'So childish.'

I didn't care what she thought. I'd made up my mind that I wanted to do something for the Lotus Hospice and she wasn't going to get in the way. It was because of something that TJ had said. It was at the jumble sale and made things click into place for me. She'd said, 'I suppose for most people, people in need are all so far away and it doesn't seem real. The people are anonymous but then when something affects someone close to you and you put a face and a family to a tragedy or disaster, then it all becomes so real.'

I nodded. That's was how I felt now having met Eleanor. She was real and I couldn't help but feel that it might have been me in her place or someone that I knew. The Lotus Hospice was my chosen charity now and I meant to give it my best.

Diamond Destiny

'We need a good theme for the dance,' said Lucy in the lunch break at school the next day.

'Yeah,' I agreed. 'It definitely needs something. I couldn't believe those posters. *A dance. The first Saturday in May.* Like, so what? How dull is that? Wouldn't attract me to go. It has to be like an event. Something you feel you can't miss out on. A happening type of happening.'

'Exactly,' said Lucy. 'Which is why we need a theme.'

'But what?' asked TJ.

'Don't know,' said Lucy. 'But we need to give people an excuse to dress up. I think people like that, least I know I do.'

'Yeah, speak for yourself,' said TJ. 'I'm happy in my jeans and T-shirt. How about we do a barn dance sort of thing.'

'Not glam enough. Who wants to dance about with a bit of straw stuck between their teeth?' said Izzie.

'Sounds OK to me,' said TJ.

'You have much to learn about being cool my dumb little chum,' I said.

'So what can our theme be?' asked Izzie. 'All in red, all in gold, all in silver?'

'Cowboys and Indians. Vicars and tarts. Hollywood,' suggested Lucy.

'I think we should write down an A–Z of themes,' said TJ. 'Be useful for when one of us throws a party in the future, as well as for the dance. Plus, it would be great to put in the mag as a feature. In fact, it would be cool to do a whole section on parties.'

We spent the next fifteen minutes trying to think up themes and although some of them were really good, none of them felt right for the dance.

'Some people hate dressing up,' I said. 'And it might put them off coming if they think they've got to hire a fancy dress costume. No. All in silver or all in white or something like that is more do-able and won't cost a lot but . . . I don't know. As Izzie said, it just needs to be more glam, I think.'

'I know,' said Lucy. 'As I said, a chance to dress up, that's it. A chance to put on your bling and strut your stuff. How about something like the Bling Ball?'

'Yeah, great idea,' said Izzie. 'But not sure about the name. Sounds a bit downmarket. We need to sell a lot of tickets to fill the place and get some atmosphere going.'

'But even if we sell a load of tickets,' said TJ, 'at only eight quid each, we still need to do something else to raise fifty thousand. I had a look on the Net last night and found a few sites with some really good ideas.'

'And I've had a few ideas,' said Lucy.

'Me too,' said Izzie.

'So let's hear them,' I said. 'Let's brainstorm.' I'd heard my dad use this term a million times when sitting round the table at home working on film ideas with his various producers.

We spent the next half hour writing down everything we could come up with for Miss Watkins and the Dopey Doreens. Soon we had a good list with suggestions from the insane to the sensible.

'So what have we got so far chairperson?' I asked TJ as she had been the one writing everything down.

TJ began to read from her list: 'Sponsored skydiving . . .'

'Bit risky,' said Izzie. 'Although we could suggest our teachers do it. Bet we'd raise a fortune!'

'Sponsored walks or marathons − bit more sensible,' continued TJ, 'raffles, home services, cleaning, mowing lawns, taking care of pets . . .'

'Oh, add car washing,' said Lucy. 'That wouldn't be hard to do.'

'And if you offer to do it naked apart from a daffodil up your bum, you could charge double,' I said.

'Oh get serious, Nesta,' said Izzie. 'Not a daffodil. No. I see Lucy with a tulip.'

TJ ignored Izzie and I and continued with the list. 'A swim-a-thon. A games night. Candle-making. Competitions like guess the age of a teacher, guess the number of coins in a jar. Face painting.'

'I've got a brilliant one,' I interrupted as an idea flashed into my head. 'A calendar. Your brother could shoot it Lucy. We could be like the women in that movie *Calendar Girls*.'

'What, as in naked? Miss Watkins would never allow it,' Lucy replied.

'She can be in it as well . . .'

'*Eeeewww*,' chorused TJ, Lucy and Izzie.

'In fact, all the teachers could be in it,' I said. 'Imagine Mr Johnson as Mr November lying over the desk . . .'

Lucy and Izzie cracked up.

'*Double* eeeewwww,' said TJ. 'You really are fixated on people being naked to raise money. But I'll put it down on the list and we can finalise things later. So, what else can we do – hopefully with our clothes on? Sports tournaments – that would give us a good chance to get loads of boys involved. Art sale. Gardening. Dog-walking – oh, got that one already. Recipe books with people's faves in. Quiz nights. Carrying groceries for people. Spelling competitions. Book sales. A football goal shoot-out . . .'

'How about a crèche for mothers who can never go shopping?' asked Izzie. 'We look after their kids for a couple of hours.'

'I'll put it on the list,' said TJ scribbling it down.

'And how about a kiss for a pound,' suggested Lucy.

'But you never know who might pay up to snog,' I said. 'You might end up kissing someone you don't like.'

Izzie got a cheeky look on her face. 'Oh you mean like you and William on Sunday?'

'I did that because Eleanor asked me to,' I said.

'She asked you to cheer him up,' said Lucy. 'Not stick your tongue down his throat.'

Of course we'd already discussed the William situation. As soon as he'd gone on Sunday, in fact. The girls had been gobsmacked to find us in an Oscar award–winning smooch at the back of the hall. My excuse to them was that it was my way of apologising and that I hadn't changed my mind about the way I felt about him. None of them bought it, and they all regard me with suspicion whenever I mention him so I decided to come clean and admit that maybe I do like him a little. Or maybe a lot as after the jumble sale I couldn't stop replaying the moment he'd grabbed me and pulled me towards him. It was *so* Rhett Butler and Scarlet in *Gone With the Wind*.

'I'm making up my mind about him,' I said.

'Looks like it's already made up to me,' said Lucy.

'Exactly,' said Izzie and TJ.

'No . . .'

'Why are you holding back with him?' asked Izzie. 'It's so clear that you like him.'

I had to admit I'd been asking that question myself and the answer was beginning to dawn on me. It was fear. Fear of being rejected. Fear of being hurt. Everyone always thinks I'm the confident one. The one who knows about boys but actually my track record isn't as brilliant as I make out. My last boyfriend Luke turned out to be two-timing me with one of my best friends and God knows how many others I don't know about. And before him, there was Simon and he dumped me. Not because he didn't like me any more but because he was going to

University in Scotland and didn't want to do the long distance thing. Still, it hurt. And then along comes William. Prince Cutenik himself but I don't want to open myself up to get hurt again. I want to be sure before I get involved again. Plus the fact that I haven't been practising what I preach. I always tell the girls, don't be too easy, play hard to get a bit. I didn't with Simon, I fell into his lap, literally as we met on a train and it lurched and there I was in his arms. And with Luke, we met and were soon an item. No, I wanted to take things with William a lot, *lot* slower.

A moment later, my mobile rang and I moved off to answer it. It was William. I went into the corridor outside the dining hall to talk to him without the others listening in and making stupid faces at me when they realised who it was.

'Oh, hi,' I said trying to sound as cool as I could. I still wasn't sure what to make of what had happened on Sunday. The kissing session had been very enjoyable (*very*) and for a few moments had completely swept me off my feet but then later, after he'd gone, that was when I began to worry that it had all happened too fast. I mean, we hadn't even been out on a date and already we'd done the lip lock. And in public. He might think I was way too easy and I didn't want that. Plus there was still the fact that he was a mate of Luke's so was he to be trusted? I felt I needed to back off a bit and just cheer him up as his sister had asked. Bake him a cake or something equally innocent.

'Hi yourself,' he said.

'So what can I do for you?' I asked.

'Yes. About Sunday . . .'

'Yes,' I said. 'Sorry. Don't know what came over me. Sorry. Won't happen again.'

'Oh,' he said and in that one word I could hear that he was disappointed. 'I was hoping that maybe we could get together for a repeat performance some time.'

'Yes. Well – about that . . .'

'What?'

I decided to take the plunge and tell him what was bothering me. 'See. Thing is William . . . you know I went out with Luke for a while?'

'Yes.'

'It makes things complicated.'

'Why? You're not going out with him any more.'

'True, but . . .'

'It's OK, Nesta. I get it. Never mind.'

'No. I don't think you do. Listen. Just he . . . um . . . it turned out I couldn't trust him.'

I heard William chuckle at the other end of the phone. 'Yeah. He does have a bit of a reputation.'

'And you're his mate.'

There was a silence for a few moments and I think the penny dropped. 'Ah. So you think that I might be the same?'

'Yes. How do I know that you're not?'

'You don't,' he said.

'Which makes it difficult.'

'So try me.'

I was beginning to feel that I was being a bit unfair on him and hearing his voice again made me remember how toe-curling the kiss had felt. It would be a shame to let it all go by just because his mate was a rat.

'So, what do you reckon?' William persisted. 'Want to go out sometime? I can probably fit you in between all my other lovers.'

'Yeah, very funny. Actually I was wondering if I could fit *you* in between all my other lovers.'

'Maybe it's just not destined to be,' said William in a sad voice but I had a feeling that he was joshing. 'But then we have seen each other twice over the last week after not seeing each other for months. Maybe it's destiny bringing us together.'

'Ah yes, destiny. Sometimes you can't fight it,' I said in an actressy-type voice.

'And by the way, Eleanor said hi. She liked meeting you.'

'I liked meeting her.' I didn't want to ask any more about her as he had made it clear on Sunday that he didn't want to talk about the situation and if there's one thing I know about boys, it's that you can't push them to open up if they don't want to.

'Good. I'm glad you like her. She's a diamond,' said William.

A light bulb flashed on in my head. 'That's it! Destiny. Diamond. Diamond destiny.'

'Pardon?'

I quickly filled him in on the fundraising events (or lack of them) at our school and how we were holding a dance in May and were looking for a name or theme for it. 'Don't you see,' I finished. 'The Diamond Destiny Dance. Everyone can come glammed up to the eyeballs.'

'Yeah. Sounds good . . . but in the meantime, what about us?

I'm away for the Easter holidays. Spain, it's been booked for ages but what about before that? I wondered if we could . . . you know? What do you think?'

'Ah . . . yes. Um. A definite maybe.'

'A definite maybe?'

'Yeah. But you have to pass my test sometime.'

William laughed again. 'You're kidding?'

'Nope.' I wasn't going to fall back into his arms just because he was such a great kisser or because his sister was ill. No. It was time to play hard to get. Or at least, a bit.

'So what is this test?' he asked.

'I'll e-mail it to you while you're away. Give me your e-mail address.'

'It's easy: w.lewis@fastmail.com.'

I jotted it down.

'And yours?' he asked.

'Nestahotbabe@retro.co.uk.'

'Cool,' he said.

'And in the meantime, what's your favourite cake?' I asked.

'*Cake?* What has cake got to do with anything? Is that the test? If I say the right cake you'll go out with me?'

'No. That's not the test. Just tell me your favourite cake.'

'Coffee and walnut.'

'Right. Thanks. I might bake you one.'

'You're a strange girl, Nesta Williams.'

'You ain't seen nothing yet, babe,' I said.

I could hear him laughing softly at the other end of the phone. It was going to be fun carrying out Eleanor's request.

'I've agreed to do your test when I get it,' he said. 'So will you agree to go out with me before we leave for Spain.'

'When are you leaving?'

'Saturday morning. So how about Friday evening?'

'Um.' Take it slow this time, said a voice in my head.

'OK,' said the voice that came out of my mouth.

An A–Z of Party Themes

A: African, Aztec, animals, *Alice in Wonderland*, Adam and Eve, Arabian Nights.

B: Beatniks, black and white, *Beauty and the Beast*, all in blue, beggars and knights, bad taste, blonde bombshells.

C: Cops and robbers, cowboys and Indians, Chinese, cartoon characters, come as you were (in a past life).

D: Devils and angels, doctors and nurses, Dickens characters, diamonds (wear all your bling).

E: Egyptian, Elizabethan, Edwardian.

F: Fairies and goblins, fat, *The Flintstones*, flowers or fruit, fave fictional character

G: Gods and goddesses, gangsters and molls, glamour, ghosts, gender swap (boys as girls and girls as boys), Goth, *Grease* (come as a character from the movie) or Greece (dressed in the national dress).

H: Hollywood (dress for the Oscars), Hawaiian, horror, hats, heroes and heroines, Harry Potter, hippies.

I: Idols, Indian.

J: Japanese.

K: Knights and damsels in distress.

L: Legends, lords and ladies

M: Marx brothers, Mexican, monsters, masks, milkmaids and farmers.

N: Nuns and priests

O: Oriental, orange

P: Pyjamas, all in purple, police men and women, Pre-Raphaelite, punk.

Q: Queens and kings.

R: Rock stars, Fifties rock and roll, all in red, Renaissance, Romans and Britons.

S: Sci-fi, *Star Trek*, all in silver, school uniforms, Shakespearean characters, superheroes.

T: Thunderbirds, toga, Twenties, teddy boys and girls, toddlers and teddies, toys.

U: Uniforms.

V: Vicars and tarts, Victorian.

W: Walt Disney characters, whore or holy, all in white, witches and warlocks.

Z: Zzzzzzz . . . attend in your night wear.

If you don't have a lot of money to spend on costumes, the simpler the theme, the easier it is, e.g. all in blue, pyjamas, gender swap or everyone wearing a hat.

Try and find a music track appropriate for the theme, e.g. Egyptian music if going for an Egyptian theme, music from the 1920s if going for the Roaring Twenties theme.

Chapter 10

Do-Good Disasters

Miss Watkins loved our fundraising suggestions. She gave us the go-ahead for just about everything but the sponsored sky diving and plans went straight into top gear.

'I knew you girls would breathe some fresh air into it all,' she said with a smile after we'd read our list out our list in the afternoon break. 'Now. No time to lose. Nesta, you can start by making an appeal for volunteers tomorrow and the rest of you, organise who's doing what and when and report back to me regularly. We have five weeks, three of which are in the Easter holidays so let's see if we can get some things organised to happen then.'

At assembly the next morning, I felt nervous when Mrs Allen, our headmistress, introduced me after she had made the usual announcements. Usually I don't mind performing in public, like if I'm in a play or something because then I'm not being me. I'm in disguise as some character. But this time I was going to speak as Nesta Williams and part of me was dreading it. I looked out at the sea of faces and took a deep breath.

'Good morning, everyone,' I started.

'Good morning,' everyone said back and I almost got the giggles as they all looked so serious. I had to resist the urge to do something stupid like tap dance or do my gangster rapper impersonation.

I took another breath, told myself to get it together, then continued. 'Imagine one of your family was dying or ill or homeless or lonely,' I read from the speech I had prepared last night. 'How would you feel? Yeah. Rotten. Most of us don't even think about such things. It's not happening to us so who cares? We're OK. Most of our families are OK. We have homes. We have food to eat, clothes to wear. Our health is good. But loads of people on the planet don't have our advantages.

'All I'm asking for is a bit of your time. Maybe an hour or two a week for the next few weeks in the holidays and you can make a difference. We're aiming to raise fifty thousand pounds to donate to a local hospice. It's a place where terminally ill teenagers go to spend their last weeks and the aim of the people who run the hospice is to make the place as much like home for them as possible. We're the lucky ones. Hopefully we all have years ahead of us to pursue careers, to travel, to fall in love, er . . . particularly to fall in love. The people who end up in hospices like the one we want to help won't have those chances. Please don't turn away this chance to do something . . .'

I was about to wind up as Mum had advised me that the

most important rule of public speaking is KISS (keep it short, stupid) but when I looked out at the faces in the hall looking back at me, I wanted to be sure that they understood what I was saying.

'Just look around you,' I continued. 'Who knows where illness is going to strike. It could be one of the people standing in the hall with us today. It could be you. It *is* someone I met recently and only last year, she was standing in assembly like we are today and she was healthy and happy with a great future. Now she knows she hasn't got long to live. The people who run the hospice want to make those last weeks as comfortable as possible. A place where their friends and family can be with them. That's all anyone can do.

'I'm not going to go on and on at you as I think those of you who want to hear and do something don't need it repeated. We've got some fab activities planned to make money over the Easter holidays. We need volunteers for everything from selling raffle tickets to walking dogs. So, if you want to be involved, don't walk away, sign up at the back after assembly. And anyone who wants to buy tickets for the Diamond Destiny Dance on May 7th, then please get them from the back. It's going to be the event of the decade. Please help. Make your destiny a diamond one. Um. Yeah. Rock on.'

The response was phenomenal and we got loads of people signing up from all years and even Doreen and her pals looked pleased with the way things were going.

We didn't have long to get everything sorted before we broke up so Izzie, TJ, Lucy and I spent every spare moment getting contact details from volunteers, so that we could give them all something to do in the holidays. It wasn't too difficult to co-ordinate a timetable of events, allocate people to each one and we were off fundraising. Even Tony and Lucy's brothers, Lal and Steve, and their mates wanted to be involved in some way.

'This is going to be the best time ever,' I said as I walked out of school with TJ on the last day of term. At last it was the Easter holidays and I had a date with William in a couple of hours' time. It felt good to know that I'd be able to tell him that we were going to do something positive to help. I was confident that we'd reach the target and more.

I got home and went to have a bath before changing into my seduction outfit for the evening. I'd arranged to meet William in Crouch End and go for a cappuccino and then a walk. His mum wanted him back at a reasonable hour because they were taking an early morning flight. I heard the phone go when I was in the bath but thought nothing of it.

A few moments later, Mum knocked on the door. 'Nesta,' she said. 'That was William Lewis. He said he's sorry but he can't make it tonight.'

I was about to get out of the bath. 'Does he want to speak to me?'

'No, love,' said Mum. 'He's gone. I asked if he wanted a word with you and he asked if I'd pass the message on.'

'Does he want me to call him?'

Mum was quiet. I got the answer without her having to say anything. I lay back in the bath and submerged my head in the water. I soooo wished I hadn't agreed to go out with him.

When I got out of the bath, I went to see if he'd tried to e-mail me. But nothing. I felt cold inside. Dumped before we'd even had a date. Well stuff you, William Lewis, I thought. I'm not going to even let this minor blip affect me in the slightest. I am going to throw myself into all the fundraising activities we have planned and not give you another thought. We're going to raise a million and when you come back from Spain, you can forget any chance you thought you were in with. This girl is moving on.

My first job was going to be a breeze. Mum had told all the neighbours about the fundraising scheme and one of them, Mrs Matthews, had asked if I'd check in on her house while she was away visiting her daughter for a couple of days. Easy peasy money. Twenty quid to look after her budgies and water a few plants.

'Now you make sure you talk to Charlie in particular,' said Mrs Matthews after she'd gone over the instructions for the fiftieth time. 'He's the one at the back, see?' She pointed to a bright blue budgie at the back of the cage.

'Oh, I will,' I assured her.

Mrs Matthews' eyes filled with tears. 'He's special, is Charlie. He was a gift from my late husband and – you make sure you look after him well. He likes it if you talk to him.'

No problem, I thought as I waved her off. Bit of water, bit of bird seed, bit of a chat. What could possibly go wrong?

All went well on the Saturday and Sunday and then Lucy and I turned up on Monday afternoon to find that Charlie was lying at the bottom of his cage with his little legs in the air.

'Ohmigod,' I said when I saw him.

Lucy gave the bird a gentle poke. It didn't move. 'This parrot is dead,' she declared.

'It's not a parrot. It's a budgie.'

'Whatever. It's dead.'

'Nooooooo, it can't be,' I cried. 'What am I going to do?'

'It wasn't your fault,' said Lucy. 'You did everything you were asked.'

'Should I try mouth to mouth?' I asked. 'Take it to the vets?'

Lucy shook her head. 'It's dead, Nesta. Not breathing. Look, just explain what happened. There was nothing you could do. It was just Charlie's time, that's all.'

'Maybe but I know she'll blame me. She's bound to. And Charlie is her favourite. Oh God.' I felt completely freaked out as I imagined Mrs Matthews coming back and finding her dead bird.

'Look,' said Lucy, 'we have to stay calm. Don't panic. Here's what we do. We'll buy another one. I bet I know exactly where they got it from as there's only one place that sells them round here. The pet shop in Muswell Hill. Mum gets squirrel nuts for Lal in there.'

'Squirrel nuts for Lal? Now I know your family is mad.'

'No. *He* doesn't eat them. He likes to feed the squirrels in the garden. You know what he's like about animals. He feeds the fox, the squirrels, the birds. It's a regular wildlife park in our back garden. So come on . . . let's go. Last time I was in the shop, they had a whole wall of birds. What time will Mrs Matthews be back?'

I checked my watch. 'Nine this evening.'

'And it's almost five now,' said Lucy. 'We just have time.'

We raced down to the pet shop as fast as we could. The shop keeper was just locking up and shook his head when I knocked on the door.

'Please,' I mouthed through the door but he just carried on locking up. I got down on my knees on the pavement and prayed to him and this time, he did take notice. He laughed and opened the door.

'All right then. So what is it you need so desperately?'

'A budgie.'

'And that can't wait until morning?'

I shook my head. 'Absolutely one hundred percent urgent.'

The shop keeper sighed. 'Always the same with you kids. Want it now and then three weeks later, you've lost interest.'

'No. No, I promise,' I said. 'It's not like that.'

The shop keeper relented. 'Come on in then. They're round the back. Let me know which one you want and be quick about it.'

Lucy and I ran through and quickly scanned the cages.

There were cages of finches and budgies all tweeting sweetly away.

'Perfect,' cried Lucy as she spied the last cage. In there was a budgie the exact same colour as Charlie. It was so perfect in fact, it looked like his twin.

'How much are they?' I asked.

'Twenty quid,' said the shopkeeper. 'Made your minds up have you?'

We nodded and soon were paying for the bird and hotfooting it back to Mrs Matthews where we replaced the dead bird with the live one. Lucy wrapped the real Charlie up in tissue and took him away with her to give him a proper burial in their back garden.

For the next couple of days, I was on tenterhooks waiting for Mrs Matthews' to notice the difference and call to complain, but she didn't. It was on the Friday night that she called me over when she saw me passing her house.

'Er, how's Charlie?' I asked as casually as I could.

'Extraordinary,' said Mrs Matthews, smiling. 'All this time I thought Charlie was a boy but I must have been wrong?'

'Oh. Why's that?' I asked.

'He laid an egg yesterday,' she said. 'I think my Charlie is a Charlotte.'

For a moment, I thought she might have rumbled me but no, she seemed to genuinely think that she'd mistaken Charlie's sex when he was first given to her. Ah well, I thought. Although I hadn't made a penny at least I still had a happy customer.

Lal and his mates were confident that they would make some fast money by offering to hand wash cars and set off on the Saturday in the sunshine with buckets and cloths in hand. In the meantime, TJ and I set off to do a stint of dog walking. Six dogs that belonged to various neighbours – I took three, TJ took three. At five quid for each dog, I thought, it should be no problem and we'd make our first bit of profit.

At twelve o'clock, Lal called us to say that they still hadn't got one job.

'We're in Shakespeare Gardens and have checked the whole area. Cleanest cars in the country,' he said. 'This calls for new tactics.'

TJ and I were doing the circuit at Cherry Tree Woods and were barely keeping up with the dogs who insisted on dragging us along for all they were worth. 'Tactics? And they are?' I asked as I pulled on the leads.

'We're going to dirty the cars up,' said Lal. 'Then they'll have to employ us.'

'*No*, Lal. That's a *mad* idea. No, please don't . . .' I pleaded into the phone but it was no use, he'd hung up.

'What's up?' asked TJ when she saw my face.

'We have to find the boys,' I said. 'Lal and his mates can't get any customers for the car wash. They're going to try dirtying them up.'

'Oh *nooooooo*,' cried TJ. 'We have to stop them. Really bad idea. There's been a spate of kids vandalising cars round where they've gone. I read about it in the local rag. People might think it's Lal and his mates. Do you know exactly what road he's on?'

I nodded. 'Shakespeare Gardens.'

I tried calling Lal's phone but the little rat wasn't answering. We both looked at the dogs who were almost chewing off their leads in their eagerness to finish their walk.

'You go. I'll stay here with the dogs,' she said.

'You sure you can handle six?'

She looked at the dogs and nodded. 'Just get back here fast.'

I legged it as fast as I could out of the park, up the alleyway and ten minutes later, I spotted the boys running down Springcroft Avenue. They were being chased by a very irate bald man. I quickly ducked down into the nearest garden and hid behind a rhododendron bush. It looked like they could outrun the man and I didn't want him to spot me and think I was with them. Unluckily, the owner of the house whose garden I was in saw me through her front window. A moment later, she had opened her door and was coming at me with a broom.

'Out, out,' she said. 'I'll have the police on you.'

'No. I'm sorry. I was – I'm not dangerous. I'm not a burglar or a vandal anything!'

'That's what they all say,' she said as she brandished her broom in my face. 'Get out of my garden.'

I decided to give up on the boys and ran back to Cherry Tree Woods. Poor TJ was almost having a heart attack by the time I got back there. She'd tied five of the dogs to a park bench from where they were all barking their objections at being kept on their leads and doing their best to drag the bench along behind them. TJ was chasing after Bonzo, a border collie, who had escaped his lead. He was causing havoc running after all the other dogs and their owners like it was a game. The dog walkers weren't at all pleased at their dogs being harassed and one of them told us in no uncertain terms to control our animal.

We tried everything but no matter what we did, he wouldn't come back. We called him. I tried throwing sticks and he ran for them but wouldn't bring them back.

'I know what will work,' said TJ after what felt like an

eternity of us running around like lunatics. 'Food. Go and buy a hamburger or hot dog, anything with meat in it and he'll soon come back.'

I raced to the nearest café on the High Street, back to the park and sure enough, it worked a treat. Bonzo was soon back on his lead. The others however were howling louder than ever having seen that one of their group got food and they didn't.

TJ looked at me and I nodded. Back I went to the café, returning with a big bag of burgers. The dogs wolfed them gratefully in seconds but at least they were quiet after that.

'Remember what I said about dog walking being a great way of meeting boys? A good pulling tactic?' I asked.

TJ laughed. 'Only people that got pulled were us. In every direction by the dogs!'

We returned the dogs to their owners but once again, our profit had been eaten into. Literally.

In the evening after the dog walking disaster, I turned on my computer and checked my e-mails for the first time that week. There was one from William, sent from an Internet café a couple of days ago.

Dear Nesta,
I am so sorry for last Friday. It's been a hellish time. Eleanor's consultant wanted to check her over before we flew to Spain which is why I couldn't make our date as she wanted me to go with her. He wasn't too happy about the results of her

blood tests and she really freaked as she'd been looking forward to this trip for months. Dad insisted that Olivia and I went out to Spain as planned and Mum stayed with Eleanor who was allowed to join us on Monday. It's been a roller coaster since then. She seemed fine when she arrived and then went under and at first we thought we'd have to fly her back and well, I don't want to go on. She's OK now but as I said, it's an up and down ride. It makes her so unhappy when she can't do the things that she had planned. Anyway, that was the reason I couldn't make it on Friday. Sorry and I hope to meet up sometime when I'm back. I haven't got my computer out here and am using an Internet café but you could text me back if you're still speaking to me. William.

I read the e-mail about ten times. That will teach me, I thought. I'd totally assumed that he'd let me down for all the wrong reasons. Assume. Dad always says: the first three letters of the word assume are ass. And I'd been an almighty one. I texted him back.

STL SPEKNG 2 U. DONG TONS OF FUNDRAYSG. GONG GUD. GONNA RAISE £££££££££££ 4 HOSPICE.

I hoped that would cheer him up.

And in the meantime, there were all those £££££ to raise. Izzie and her friend Ben (from the band she sings with) signed up to do gardening in the second week but they only lasted an hour as Ben had got a bit over enthusiastic with the shears and cut back someone's prize rose thinking that it was dead. Both of them were banned from the area and the man whose garden it was threatened to let all the neighbours know if Ben didn't pay for a replacement. Cost a fortune as it was a rare type of rose.

Once again, out went any profits.

For a while it looked as though Lucy was on a winner in the first week as she managed to get a load of people to donate bottles of spirits and she talked others (including Izzie) into giving away their Easter eggs. Whisky, vodka, gin, brandy and chocolate. She sold a load of raffle tickets and at last, it seemed that we might be in profit. Sadly, she had stored the bottles of donated spirits at her house and Lal and his mates decided to try them all out and replace what they drank with water. A trick that he'd managed to get away with before but when the raffle was drawn and the bottles were given away as prizes, the winners complained. They could tell that the bottles had been watered down and demanded compensation. Lucy tried pleading that it was for charity but was told in no uncertain terms that in that case she should be more professional about it. Lucy got her dad to replace the watered down bottles with the real stuff which meant that once again, the profit kitty was emptied but this time not for long. Lucy's mum found out what the boys had done and insisted that they pay up for what they had done out of their pocket money.

And the Easter eggs? The daft muffin left them in a bag by a radiator and they all melted. (Lucy daren't tell Izzie.)

★ ★ ★

In other parts of North London, other activities were taking place, and Mrs Owen was delighted with that fact that we'd managed to set up a rota of volunteers to help at the charity shop at weekends for the rest of the year.

Sadly, the candle-making sessions, led by Izzie, were a complete and utter disaster as the end results looked more like misshapen potatoes than candles. And her team had invested their pocket money to buy everything needed like wax and moulds and when they didn't sell, Izzie had to fork out to replenish their funds.

Candice Carter had volunteered to organise a sponsored fast and reported back to us that it was very popular. Apparently about twenty girls signed up for it but Candice finally admitted that most of them didn't actually have sponsors. They thought that it was an ace way to lose weight quickly. One of the girls fainted one lunchtime and confessed all to her mum who let the other parents know what was going on and they put a stop to it. So that was the end of that. Profit nil.

The swim-a-thon on the last Saturday of the holidays was going great, until Steve got cramp and had to be rescued by the life guard. And I got my period and got a different kind of cramp. Poor Steve could hardly walk when he got out the baths so called a cab to take him home and he dropped me off on the way. He paid for the cab with the small amount of sponsorship money he'd raised and offered to pay it back but it was only a couple of pounds.

'Hardly going to make much difference,' said TJ sadly as she

288

did the accounts. 'But we've still got almost two weeks . . .'

TJ, Izzie and I nodded back at her and tried to look hopeful but I knew that inside they were feeling like I did. Desperate.

Things didn't improve.

Last on our list of fundraising activities to try was face painting and we held a session for kids in the car park outside the local supermarket. Once again, it was a fine clear day for April and a couple of girls from Year Eleven at school, Izzie and I set ourselves up and charged a pound for each face that we painted. It was going great with happy toddlers running about looking like bunnies and lions and clowns. And then one little girl had an allergic reaction to the paint and her face swelled up. Although we cleaned her up as fast as we could and it looked like no lasting damage had been done, her mother went crazy and threatened to sue the school. We did the grown-up, responsible thing and packed up our stuff and ran for it.

At least one idea was a success. TJ and Lucy had got the local nursery to donate some fabulous plants to sell at the jumble sale on the last Sunday of the holidays and they sold out before lunchtime. Phew.

Also at the jumble sale, we raised a small sum of money by asking people to guess how many coins there were in a jar. It was all going well until an old lady guessed correctly and we had to hand the lot over to her. TJ tried to persuade her to donate her winnings to charity but she was having none of it and told TJ to get lost in a rather colourful manner.

Next was the 'guess Miss Watkins's age' competition. TJ took a Polaroid of her and it was great fun going round the hall with sheets of paper where people could put down their guesses. No one got it right and most had added on about ten years to her real age. We were in profit at the end of the competition but Miss Watkins was well miffed at the age that people estimated her as and said she's going to go on one of those make-over programmes where they lift everything!

At the end of the sale, we added up everything that had come in over the past weeks from all the various activities. It came to just under a thousand pounds. I couldn't believe it.

'I thought we'd make so much more.' I sighed as I looked at the figures. 'After three weeks of pretty much solid fundraising, we have ended up with enough to buy the hospice a few plants, but forget the new wing.'

'And I even donated my Easter eggs,' said Izzie.

Lucy looked at the floor sheepishly. 'Yeah, there were so many things going on,' she said as she scanned the accounts. 'But hey listen, there's almost a grand here. It's better than nothing.'

I nodded. But I was fast beginning to realise that the dopey Doreen's were right. Raising serious amounts money wasn't that easy after all.

Good ideas for raising money for charity:

Sponsored walks/runs/swim-a-thons.
Raffle tickets for a good prize
(make sure the prize is donated so that you don't have to
fork out for it from your profits).
Auction any of the better items donated in jumble.
Home services: cleaning, gardening, taking care of pets
while people are away, car washing, carrying groceries.
Plant sale arranged with local nursery.
Games or quiz night.
Candle-making.
Charity ball.
Guess the age of your teacher.
Guess the number of coins in a jar.
Calendar sale.
Sport's tournament (good chance to get boys involved).
Recipe books – including teachers faves etc.
Spelling competition.
Shootout (football goals).
Book sale.
Cake sale.
Kiss-o-gram.
Invite a guest speaker to the school and sell tickets.
Face painting (be careful to use hypo-allergenic products).
Art sale. Best of some Year's work.

Chapter 11

Star

'The good news is that King Noz have agreed to play for free at the DDD, Diamond Destiny Dance,' Izzie announced as we sat round the table at her house after the jumble sale to go over plans for the next couple of weeks.

'The bad news is that we're back to school tomorrow and we still have forty nine thousand pounds to raise,' I said. 'And still only a third of the tickets sold.'

'Do the dopey Doreens know about our unspectacular start?' asked Lucy.

'Nope. And nor does Miss Watkins. I told her it was all going brilliantly. And if anyone tells them otherwise, I will have to kill them,' I replied. 'I couldn't bear to hear them saying, I told you so. No. Come on! We've got almost two weeks left. We will raise the money. We will.'

'Right,' said Izzie.

'Right,' said Lucy.

'Right,' said TJ.

Not one of them looked like they meant it. And if I was really honest I was beginning to have doubts myself. But I couldn't let that happen. It would mean letting Eleanor down. It would mean letting the hospice down. And it would mean letting William down. We'd been texting regularly since his e-mail from the Internet café and he seemed genuinely touched that we were bothering to try and raise the money. He'd also asked when I was going to put him through his 'test'.

Lucy must have picked up on my thoughts as she looked over at me and asked: 'Heard anything from your lover boy lately?'

'Yeah. He texts me every other day or so. I think we're becoming mates.'

'Only mates?' asked Izzie. 'Are you still being cautious because he's Luke's friend and you don't know if you can trust him?'

I shook my head. 'No. I think he's on the level, not like Luke at all so the fact that they know each other isn't a problem . . .'

'Then why just mates?' asked Izzie. 'I mean is that all you want after that snog at the jumble sale? To be *mates*?'

TJ laughed. 'Ah, but there are mates and mates aren't there? I mean there are mates like, say, Lucy and Tony . . .'

Lucy blushed. 'Well, we are.'

'Mates who snog a lot,' said Izzie.

'Yeah,' said TJ. 'And there are mates who you just hang out and have a laugh with but wouldn't dream of locking lips with. So what kind are you and William going to be?'

'Um . . . not sure,' I said. I wasn't sure. After our first kiss, I knew that I wanted to be a lot more than mates but didn't know if he felt the same. It had been great texting him while he'd been away but I knew that he'd got back yesterday and part of me had hoped that he'd get in touch straight away and maybe even come over but I hadn't heard anything. I'd purposely not texted or called him so that he wouldn't think that I had been counting the days until his return. Even though I had. And I was beginning to realise that anything might have happened with Eleanor. She might have taken a turn for the worse.

Or maybe William was simply feeling low and not in the mood for talking. People often are when they come back from holidays and have to get back into their routines. Maybe he was feeling down because Spain might have been Eleanor's last holiday. I had no idea what was going on in his head. Maybe he wasn't that interested in me and the snog at the jumble sale had just been a one-off. 'I did say to him that I'd e-mail him a questionnaire . . .'

Izzie laughed. 'Questionnaire? Like you fill in when you want a job?'

'Yeah. To see if he is worthy of my attention.'

'Cool,' said Lucy.

'Anyway, with all the activities lately, I haven't had time to work it out, so I need you guys to help me.'

'Find out what star sign he is,' said Izzie. 'Put that as question number one then we can find out if you're compatible or not. Some star signs are much flirtier than others.'

'Like which?' asked TJ.

'Libras are the biggest flirts. Gemini's not far behind,' replied

Izzie. 'And Leo's are pretty bad too.'

'Nothing wrong with being a flirt,' I said as I wrote down Izzie's question as number one.

'I'd ask him what his idea of a perfect first date is,' said TJ. 'I think you can tell a lot about a boy by how he treats you the first time he takes you out.'

'True,' I said and wrote that down as number two.

At the end of the hour, we had ten good questions which Izzie typed into her computer.

'Have you got his e-mail address?' she asked.

I nodded. I knew it off by heart. 'w.lewis@fastmail.com.'

She typed it in.

'Oh God,' I said as we heard the ping that told us that the e-mail had gone. 'No going back now. I hope he doesn't take it the wrong way or anything. Or think I'm being too serious about it.'

'Doubt it,' said Izzie. 'Anyway, I think all boys we meet from now on should be asked those questions before any of us go out with them.'

'And it's too late to worry now,' said Lucy.

'What if he replies?' asked Izzie. 'Are you going to go on a date with him?'

'Yes. Sure. Eleanor asked me to cheer him up.'

'Yeah but what about you?' asked Lucy. 'How do you feel about him?'

'I haven't seen him for weeks,' I said. 'So. . . I don't know. I'll see how I feel when he gets in touch.'

That's *if* he gets in touch, I thought.

★ ★ ★

We went over the plans for the following week again and it was obvious that even if everything went without any more disasters, the likelihood of us raising all the money that was needed was pretty well impossible. For William or not, I thought, I do want this to work.

'It's not too late,' I said. 'What we need is something brilliant to bring in the crowds. So let's think. We've got King Noz for the show?'

Izzie nodded. 'And a good disco. A mate of Ben's, DJ Diggie said he'd do it for nothing.'

'Cool,' said Lucy. 'He's supposed to be really good. Some people will pay the price of the ticket just to see him.'

An idea began to form in my head. 'I know. I know what we need. Not so much a dance as an event. Not so much an event as a show . . .'

'Meaning?' asked TJ.

'What Lucy said. People will come to see DJ Diggie. So let's give them some *more* things to come and see.'

'Like what?' asked Izzie.

I had a sudden flash of inspiration. 'I know! What about combining the dance with a fashion show?'

Lucy nodded. 'Go on . . .'

'You could make up some new designs, Lucy,' I said. 'Plus, we could use some of the ones you've already made.'

'And we could ask DJ Diggie to put some sounds to a catwalk show,' I said.

'Yeah,' said TJ. 'We could ask some of the local clothes shops if they'd like to contribute. It could be good advertising for them.'

'But we need something else,' I said. 'Something to really draw in the crowds.'

'Such as?' asked Izzie.

'Such as – a supermodel,' I said.

'Yeah, right,' said Izzie. 'Like a supermodel is going to come to some backwater dance to model clothes – no offence, Lucy – made by a schoolgirl when she could be modelling Chanel? Get real, Nesta. These girls are used to modelling Gucci, Armani, Prada. They model in Milan, Paris, New York. Didn't one of them say she didn't get out of bed for less than ten thousand pounds? So why would one of them want to come to a hall in East Finchley?'

'Because we are going to ask them,' I said.

'But who? How?' asked TJ.

'Lucy. What was the name of that model you read about in *Vogue*?' I asked. 'The one who does charity work?'

'Star. Star Axford,' said Lucy.

'And didn't you say that she lives in London?' I asked.

'Yeah. Notting Hill, the article said.'

'I am going to find her and beg her to come to our dance and what's more, I'm going to ask her to model some of Lucy's clothes. She's bound to say yes – she sounded so nice from the article you read about her, Luce. How could she refuse such a good cause?'

'Excellent idea,' said Izzie.

'Worth a try but how do we find her?' asked TJ.

'How do you find anyone?' I said. 'Um. I'll ask my dad.'

Questionnaire for Boys

1) What is your star sign?
2) What is your idea of a perfect date?
3) Your girlfriend is out of town for a weekend and the school hot babe makes a play for you. Do you:
   a) Let her seduce you. What your girlfriend doesn't know won't hurt her?
   b) Reject her advances. You would never be unfaithful to your girlfriend?
4) Your best friend is a love rat and cheats on his girlfriends do you:
   a) Stay out of it and mind your own business?
   b) Tell the girls what is going on?
5) How many girlfriends have you had?
6) Are you still a virgin?
7) Describe your ideal woman?
8) What turns you off a girl?
9) What's your favourite chat-up line?
10) What is the best way to break up with someone?
   a) By text?
   b) Get your friend to do it for you?
   c) By phone?
   d) In person?

Chapter 12

Blagging It

'Models Five,' said a lady's voice. 'How can I help you?'

Dad had been brilliant when I told him about my idea to get Star Axford on board. He'd made a couple of phone calls and soon came back to me with the number of Star's model agency.

'I . . . Hello. I . . . I need to get in touch with Star Axford,' I said as I gave the girls the thumbs up on Monday after school.

'Who may I say is calling?'

'Nesta Williams.'

'From where?'

'Er . . . From North London.'

'No, I mean from which company?'

'No company. It's a private call.'

'Are you a friend?'

'No.'

'Are you family?'

'No.'

'Can I ask what it's regarding?'

'I have to ask her something.'

'I'm afraid Miss Axford's agent isn't here at the moment but I can pass on any messages. Would you like to leave a message?'

'No, I mean yes, please,' I said, then I left my number.

That was Monday after school. I tried again on Tuesday and told the lady that it was urgent. She promised to pass the message on. Wednesday still no reply from them. And no reply from William.

'It's not going to happen this way,' I said to Tony as we had breakfast together on Thursday.

'Let me try,' he said.

'Like Star'd speak to you,' I said.

Tony raised an eyebrow at me. 'Just give me the phone and prepare to watch the Master.'

He went through the same routine. No result.

'Ha,' I said. 'Big Head. Not as easy as it seems is it?'

'Give me the phone again,' he said. 'Winners never quit and quitters never win. Only losers give up.'

Once again I passed him the portable, he dialled and my jaw dropped open in amazement as he went into an Oscar winning performance.

'*Ciao. Si.* Thees is Antonio Costello. I phoning from *Vogue* Milano. I needa to be in touch with a Star Axford,' he said in a thick Italian accent (which isn't too hard for him as Dad's Italian). '*Si. No.* No need leave message. We have shoot next week. I need to know, is she on location out of the country or is she there in England at the moment? I fly there next week. If she no available, I find someone else. No problem. *Si*. Thank you. Oh? She at Olympia? Today? Oh *si*, *si*. Of course. I knew. I forget. And she there next week? Thank you, thank you. I ring you back immediately.' He put the phone down and grinned. 'She's doing a show at Olympia.'

'Wow. You really are the Master,' I said. I was impressed. I think even I would have been taken in by his act.

'So get on the Net. Look up what the show is at Olympia and get the details. Find the times and get down there,' said Tony.

A quick look on the Olympia website told us that there was a three day show on this week. Today was the first day and there were two shows: one at two o'clock and another at four. There was no way I could make the early one because of school but I might make the end of the four o'clock one if I left as soon as we got out.

As soon as the girls heard that I was off to Olympia, they insisted on accompanying me. Sadly, it seemed that everything was conspiring against us. Mr Johnson was still giving out our English assignment way after the bell at the end of class so in the end, Izzie stuck her hand up and said, 'Look sir, normally we don't mind staying behind but we have urgent work to do this evening.'

Mr Johnson looked at her wearily. 'Oh, something you don't want to miss on the telly, Miss Foster?'

'No, sir. We have charity work to do,' said Izzie in as important voice as she could muster. 'We have to go and enlist the services of a celebrity guest.'

Mr Johnson didn't look as if he believed a word of it but he relented. 'Oh very well, then. Go on. I've had enough of you all for one day anyway.'

Izzie, Lucy, TJ and I got up and ran for it. Raced to the bus, raced to the Tube and all was going well until it decided to stop at Camden.

'All change,' said a voice over the tannoy. 'This train will terminate here.'

'Oh no,' I said. 'We're never going to make it and the four o'clock is the last show.'

We got off the Tube and it seemed an eternity before the empty one moved off and another one arrived and at last we were on our way again. A quick change at Embankment onto the District line, *another* change at Earl's Court and at last we were at Olympia.

We ran to the entrance where a security guard asked to see our tickets.

'Tickets? Oh God,' I said. 'I didn't think. Tickets.' I'd been so focused on getting there, I hadn't thought about getting in. 'How much are they?'

'Fifteen pounds each but that was for the whole event. You've missed most of today. Not worth it for the last ten minutes,' said the guard.

We each found our purses and looked to see how much money we had between us. I had a fiver, Izzie had three pounds, Lucy one pound fifty and TJ only fifty pence. Not even enough to get one of us in.

'We could always do a Florence,' said Lucy with a grin,

referring to the time when we were on our school trip in Italy and we got stranded with no money so we tried busking.

'No way and no time,' I said as I racked my brain for what to do next. It felt so frustrating that Star was only a stone's throw away and yet I couldn't get near her.

'No, don't do a Florence,' said Izzie. 'Do a Tony.'

I'd told the girls how Tony had got the information from the model agency this morning and like me, they had been well impressed.

'Yeah,' said Lucy. 'If he could blag his way into finding out where Star was by pretending to be a photographer, you could blag your way in by pretending to be a model.'

'Yeah,' said TJ. 'People are always saying that you could be one if you wanted to be. Go for it.'

'Yeah but . . .'

'Come on, Nesta,' said Izzie. 'Now's the time to find out if what people said was for real.'

'I ca–' I was about to say I can't but in the same breathe, I decided I could. What had I to lose? But I had to act quickly before I lost my nerve. I pulled the girls away from the steps and round a corner out of sight of the main entrance and security people.

'I need to tart up a bit,' I said. 'Lucy. Lip-gloss.'

Lucy handed me some lip-gloss which I quickly applied.

'Izzie, hair brush.'

Izzie quickly brushed my hair.

'TJ, eye make-up.'

'Haven't got any.'

'Don't worry, I have some,' said Lucy handing me a wand of mascara and a stick of soft grey liner to smudge around my eyes.

Two minutes later, I was ready but as I went to go back round the corner, I felt my stomach turn over with nerves. 'Oh God, I can't do it,' I said.

'Why not?' asked Lucy.

'I'm shy.'

'Too bad,' said Izzie. 'This is important!'

'Yeah, we've come this far,' said Lucy. 'You can do it. I know you can.'

'Pretend that you're a character in a movie,' said Izzie. 'That usually helps you be brave.'

'Right,' I said. 'Who?'

'Er . . .' Izzie replied. 'Er . . . Um. Braveheart? James Bond?'

'They're men!' I said.

'OK. Uma Thurman in *Kill Bill*,' said Lucy. 'I haven't seen it but my brothers said she was a spectacular heroine.'

'I *have* seen it,' I said. 'And it's probably not the best role model for this situation as she kills just about everyone who crosses her path. I'm going to try and find Star not kung fu the security guards and then wipe out the audience in a blood bath on my way to her.'

'*Climb every mountain*,' Lucy began to sing in a really awful warbly voice. '*Follow every stream . . .*'

'And I am *not* going to pretend that I am Julie Andrews in *The Sound of Music*,' I said. 'She was a nun not a potential model.'

'Julia Roberts in *Pretty Woman*,' said TJ.

Izzie looked at her watch. 'We're running out of time, guys . . .'

'OK. So think of *why* you're doing it,' urged TJ. 'Try and remember that and you might find that it helps overcome your shyness.'

I nodded. 'Yes. Course. I can do it. I will. Now you girls go and distract the guard we were talking to earlier while I try to get in.'

The girls did as they were told and soon had the guard's attention. I flew up the steps behind them as if I was in a terrible hurry.

A lady to the left of the main door waved me over to her. 'Where are you going, miss?' she asked.

I decided to do a Tony after all. '*Scusi*,' I said with an Italian accent. 'Excuse. I here for show. My train late. I so sorry. Which way for model's from Models Five? They going to keeel me.'

The lady didn't even blink. She opened the door for me and pointed down a corridor. 'Better hop it, love. It's down there but you'd better hurry. Show's almost over.'

'*Grazie, grazie*,' I said as I flew in and down in the direction she'd pointed.

Once inside I could hear loud throbbing music coming from behind wide doors. I quickly headed for the music and found myself inside a vast auditorium. Silver laser lights were swirling round the walls and it was hard to see properly in the dim light. My eyes soon grew accustomed to the dark and I could see the catwalk and stage spotlighted in the centre of the hall. It looked like a fun show as I got closer and stood behind the seating area. Models in silver and blue shiny outfits and enormous rubber platform boots danced and strutted down the aisle in time to a funky soundtrack that was pumping through ginormous speakers on either side of the stage. What a shame Lucy didn't get in as well, I thought, as she would have loved this.

I made my way as close as I could and stood watching at the back. In front of me, I could see the back of heads of rows and rows of people all intent on watching the show.

I bent down to ask a lady sitting in front of me. 'How much longer?' I asked.

'Almost finished,' she whispered. 'Now shhhhhh.'

A couple more models bounced and bumped along the catwalk but there was no sign of Star. I hoped she hadn't been in the earlier show and then left. All of a sudden, all the lights went out. The hall was silent. And then out of the speakers blasted a funky version of the wedding march. Spotlights hit the stage and there she was. Star Axford.

She looked totally amazing in what looked like a wedding outfit for a character out of *Star Trek*. It was in ankle-length, figure-hugging, shiny silver silk fabric, with a train flowing out like a waterfall at the back. On her arms she was wearing long silver gloves. Round her head she was wearing a silver mesh veil and a space-age tiara, with what looked like three crescent moons and a star attached. Everyone cheered as she floated up and down in front of them. Moments later, a bald man with a pink goatee beard appeared and the crowd went mad again. All the models who had appeared earlier came out to join the man and Star and the cheers grew louder.

Now's the time to get backstage, I thought as I edged my way closer and closer to the stage. Luckily, everyone was so intent on watching the catwalk that no one noticed me slip behind the vast black curtain and into the models' dressing area.

'Who are you?' said an unfriendly voice behind me.

I turned to see a severe-looking lady all in black staring at me suspiciously. Blag it Nesta, blag it. It's all for a good cause.

'I Carla's seester,' I said getting back into my Italian persona. 'She out there. She say meet her back here.'

The woman looked me up and down with a bored expression and she must have decided that I didn't look like trouble, as she turned away and lit a cigarette.

After several encores, the models began to drift back into the dressing area. Bottles of champagnes started popping and glasses were filled. This is sooo glamorous, I thought, as I watched everyone, and for a moment, I was so caught up in it all that I almost forgot why I was there.

I quickly scanned the girls for a sign of Star and spotted her on the far side of the room. She was changing out of the wedding dress and into jeans and a T-shirt. I made my way over to her and watched for a second as she sat at a dressing table and began to wipe off her make-up. She really was pretty. A perfect pixie face with fabulous high cheek bones, beautiful silver blue eyes and short blond hair that was spiked up for the show. I could see exactly why the designer had picked her for his collection. She looked like an alien princess. I wondered what was the best moment to talk to her as I didn't want to disturb her routine. I waited until it looked as if she had almost finished, then I crept a bit closer.

'Er . . . Star . . .'

'Yes?' she replied as she turned round.

'I'm Nesta Williams. Can I have a quick word?'

Star looked around the room. 'Are you from a magazine?'

'No. Nothing like that. I came to ask you an enormous favour.'

For a moment Star's expression grew weary, but she didn't say anything.

'I . . . that is we . . . at our school we're doing a fundraising event for a hospice for the terminally ill. And I wondered . . .'

'Nesta, I think it's lovely. And I wish you every success but I don't carry my diary with me and you really need to talk to my agent as he deals with this kind of thing.'

'Oh, but it won't take a moment. Can you come to a dance a week on Saturday? We're doing a fashion show as well and . . .'

By this time, a security lady had noticed me and was making her way over. 'This girl bothering you, Star?' she asked.

Star shook her head. 'No. Not bothering exactly . . .'

'So will you come?' I asked.

Star stood up and picked up her bag from the dressing table. 'I have to go now Nesta and I'm sorry. I get at least a hundred requests like this every week. That's why I have to let my agent deal with them.' She slipped her hand into her bag and pulled out a card. 'Here's the number for his direct line. You can call him and see how the next few weeks are fixed but usually we book charity events months ahead.'

For a moment she hesitated, sighed and gently touched my arm. Then she was gone.

Winners never quit and quitters never win.

Chapter 13

Singing in
the Rain

'There are other celebs,' said Lucy on the Tube home from Olympia.

'Yeah,' said Izzie. 'We don't need her. We have clothes, we have a venue, we have models to show the clothes.'

'And Mrs Owen said we can have a free rein in the charity shop on Saturday to look for anything for the show,' said TJ. 'She said she's already got a couple of bags of designer gear to give us.'

'And Lucy's been working late every night,' said Izzie. 'Haven't you Luce? She's got some hot little numbers ready to go.'

Lucy nodded. 'And Steve has been putting together a great soundtrack for the models to show the clothes to. He's been really enjoying it, I think. And he's offered to take photos on the night.'

I smiled weakly. I could see that they were doing their best to be positive but I knew that behind it all, they felt as disappointed as I did. 'But we still need to sell more tickets and we've only got one week left. I'd hoped Star coming would have boosted the sales.'

Lucy put her hand over one of mine. 'You tried, Nesta. That's all anyone can do.'

It was true. I had tried. I'd got my mobile out and phoned the number on the card that Star had given me as soon as I'd left the hall. A brisk sounding man answered and after I'd made my request, he had laughed and said that Star was booked up with events for the next year. 'Give us a bit of notice next time, love,' he said in a sarcastic tone before hanging up.

For the rest of the journey, we all sat in silence, lost in our thoughts. I kept thinking of what Tony had said this morning. Only losers give up.

'There must be a way,' I said to the girls when I reached my stop at Highgate and got up to get off the Tube.

'Yeah,' Izzie said, nodding. 'Speak later. We'll think of something.'

As I walked up the hill outside the station and made my way back to our flat, I passed a house where the occupants were doing some decorating. It was a funny sight because, through a window, I could see a father plastering paste onto wallpaper on a table and two of his kids were ready with the next piece from a roll to hand to him. They were struggling to keep the roll open and it kept curling back up, taking them with it.

When I got home, I went straight to my computer to see if William had responded to my questionnaire. My chest tightened when I saw that there was a message from him in the inbox. I was just about to open it when my mobile rang. It was Lucy.

'Star Axford's on TV,' she said. 'Channel Four news.'

I quickly flicked my set on and sure enough there was Star. The interviewer was asking her about her life as a supermodel.

'I suppose it's the high life and limos everywhere for you, is it?'

Star shook her head. 'Actually, no. I don't believe in waste when I have a perfectly good pair of legs. And here in London we have a great Tube system. I usually get the Tube to work and back. It's often far quicker than being stuck in traffic.'

'But don't you get recognised?'

Star laughed. 'I don't look like I do on the front covers when I've taken all the make-up off,' she said. 'So no, I don't often get recognised.'

Huh, I thought to myself. All that trouble to get into Olympia and I could have just waited by the Tube station for her!

I flicked off the telly and was about to go back to the computer when an idea flashed through my head. I quickly dialled Lucy.

'Did you see Star?' she asked.

'Yeah. I did. And I think we ought to go and try her again,' I said.

'Again? But why? Why do you think she would change her mind?'

'I'll tell you tomorrow my little munchkin. I have a plan that I think might just work.'

After I'd hung up, I went back to my computer, took a deep breath and opened William's e-mail.

There was no dear Nesta or anything. Just the questionnaire returned with his answers. Oh dear, I thought as I began to read his replies.

```
1) What is your star sign?
The Starbucks coffee sign. They do a mean coffee
and walnut muffin.


2) What is your idea of a perfect date?
23rd January 1893.


3) Your girlfriend is out of town for a weekend
   and the school hot babe makes a play for you.
   Do you:
   a) Let her seduce you. What your girlfriend
      doesn't know won't hurt her?
   b) Reject her advances. You would never be
      unfaithful to your girlfriend?
I haven't got a girlfriend at the moment. Can you
help?


4) Your best friend is a love rat and cheats on
   his girlfriends do you:
```

    a) Stay out of it and mind your own business?
    b) Tell the girls what is going on?
I haven't got a best friend. I have lots of
friends. But no girlfriend. Can you help?

5) How many girlfriends have you had?
803, if you count my past life as a rabbit.

6) Are you still a virgin?
Not if you count my past life as a rabbit.

7) Describe your ideal woman?
My mum. Ahhh . . .

8) What turns you off a girl?
Girls with one eyebrow and three sets of nipples.
Yuk.

9) What's your favourite chat-up line?
I have a questionnaire I'd like you to do before
I'll go out with you. A very nice girl used this
line on me recently.

10) What is the best way to break up with someone?
    a) By text?
    b) Get your friend to do it for you?
    c) By phone?
    d) In person?
By carrier pigeon.

His replies made me laugh out loud and all the doubts I'd had over the holidays melted away. He *was* interested in me. Part of me felt like phoning him and setting up a date right there and then but I remembered my resolve to listen to my own advice and take it slow this time.

Instead I e-mailed him:

`Mr Lewis. You did not take your test at all seriously. You will get detention. To be taken with Nesta Williams.`

He e-mailed back later that evening:

`Sorry I wasn't in touch before. Been back and forth to hospice with Eleanor. Long story but she's stable again. So when for my punishment? Soon I hope.`

I e-mailed back:

`L8R. Will be in touch. Probably weekend as first have a V. important mission.`

The next day, I got up early and went into school in time to catch Mrs Allen before school assembly. Luckily she was in her office and I asked if I could make another appeal for volunteers at assembly.

'Well, I have to admire your tenacity, Nesta,' she said after she'd heard me out. 'Why not? Give it a go.'

Ten minutes later, I was up on stage and once more looking out on that same sea of faces but this time I didn't have the giggles.

'Hi,' I said. 'Me again. Nesta, that is. As you know we're trying to raise funds for a hospice for the terminally ill, a place where their families can also stay so that the patients are not on their own all the time. It's not going great and I won't embarrass myself by telling you the paltry amount raised so far. But we still have another week to go until the dance – I hope you've already got your tickets. It's going to be a great night.

'The Diamond Destiny Dance will now also include a fashion show, and I've been trying to get a supermodel to come and join us. But first we need to get her to notice us. She told me that she gets a hundred requests a week like mine, so I thought, how about if she gets a request that she can't ignore? What I'm asking is that as many people as possible turn up at the Tube at Olympia tomorrow.

'The plan is that we line the area from the Tube to the hall. I'll be there with my mates with rolls of wallpaper and glue. All you have to bring is a letter asking if Star will come to the dance. Make the letters as bright as you can. Stick stars all over them. We'll stick the letter to the wallpaper and make a long roll of invites. That's all. Simple. And no one can say we didn't try. So that's it. Olympia Tube station. Four-thirty-ish tomorrow. Thank you and good night. I mean, good morning.'

'Nice one,' said TJ after I'd got down from the stage and made my way over to them. 'Good plan.'

'Absurd,' said Doreen coming up behind us. 'Invites on wallpaper. That's so tacky. No one will show. You wait and see.'

'I take it that you won't be coming then?' I asked.

Doreen gave me a look as if to say, 'Are you mad?'

I didn't care. It was worth a try.

On Saturday morning, Mum took me to Homebase and we bought rolls and rolls of plain wallpaper which Mum insisted on paying for as her contribution to the cause.

'That should be enough,' she said as we paid at the till. 'How many people are you expecting?'

'Um, seven so far,' I said. 'TJ, Lucy, Izzie and I. Tony said he'd come and so did Lucy's brothers, so that's Steve and Lal.'

'Lal?' asked Mum. 'Didn't you say that he was a liability?'

'He wants to make up for drinking all the booze,' I replied. 'Lucy said that she'd make sure he behaves. And Ben told Izzie that he'd come and he might bring a few guys from the band. It's a start.'

'I think it's marvellous what you're doing,' said Mum. 'Now let's get back because I have to get to work this afternoon.'

At three o'clock I met Izzie, TJ and Lucy at the Tube where they were waiting with Lal, Steve, Tony, Ben and Baz. Soon we were in place at Olympia ready to catch Star at the end of the show.

Izzie pulled her jacket tight round her, looked up at the sky and frowned. 'It's looking a bit like rain,' she said. 'I'm glad I brought my brolly.'

'No, no, it can't,' I said. 'Please, God. No rain.'

Ben began to do a mad Native American–type dance but

instead of going round in a circle, he danced backwards.

'What on earth are you doing?' asked Izzie.

'You've heard of the rain dance,' he replied. 'This is the no-rain dance.'

We'd all cracked up and did it with him and miracle of miracle, it did seem to dry up a bit. I like Ben. He's not my type – but he is cute with his stuck in the Sixties John Lennon look. It's a shame he and Izzie didn't work out because they are good together but then they've stayed friends which is more than I've managed to do with my ex-boyfriends. I might be friends with Simon if he wasn't up in Scotland but Luke, I haven't even seen him since before Christmas and he doesn't live far away. As we continued waiting outside Olympia, I wondered if William had said anything about us to him and how he'd feel if he knew that one of his friends was going to date one of his exes.

'Four o'clock,' said Lucy as she looked around the meeting place. 'Still no one here.'

'Four o'clock and one minute,' said TJ a minute later.

'Four o'clock and two minutes,' said Izzie a minute after that.

'Shut up, will you,' I said. 'For God's sake, chill. We said for people to meet here at four-thirty, there's loads of time yet.' But inside, I was worried that Doreen had been right and no one else was going to turn up and we'd be a small pathetic group holding our letters and our wallpaper up for no one to see.

'Come on,' said Lucy. 'Let's get organised, at least.' And she went into overdrive rolling out the wallpaper and sticking the sheets of paper with our individual invites onto it.

We had all written on different coloured paper so even though there weren't many letters yet, the display at least looked colourful – and Izzie had stuck bright blue stars all over hers. We held it up to see how long it was so far and it stretched out about four feet. I'd imagined that there would be hundreds of us, all holding up the wallpaper stretched out to fill the space between the Tube station and the entrance.

A Tube train rattled into the station and a number of people got off. I strained to see if there was anyone there from school but there only seemed to be a few commuters going the other way.

Another Tube. Still no one from school.

Another Tube. Still no one. And it was twenty past four.

Another Tube. And . . .

'Hey, there's Sara Jenkins and her mates from Year Nine,' said Lucy as she waved like a lunatic at them and they came to join us. A few minutes later, another group from Year Ten arrived. Then another lot. Then another. Then Candice Carter and all her mates. Before long most of our class had shown up. Lal looked as happy as a pig in muck when he realised how many girls were turning up and he quickly made himself useful pasting letters, unrolling more wallpaper and flirting for all he was worth. Steve took photos, as TJ said it would be a great shot for the school magazine and would show Doreen that she was wrong.

By four-forty, there was a fantastic crowd. We were all ready. We were all lined up, letters in place but where were the people from inside Olympia?

'Go and check,' I said to Tony. 'Maybe the show's running late today because it's the last night.'

Tony had just set off up towards the hall when the doors opened and crowds started flowing out.

'Ah, here they come,' I said. 'I reckon the models will follow in about ten or fifteen minutes. Keep your eyes peeled for Star everyone.'

The crowd coming out of Olympia were curious about the group of teenagers hanging about outside holding up an enormous roll of wallpaper and most of them stopped to either read the letters or ask what was going on.

'Can I take a photo?' asked an American man as he held up a camera.

'Go ahead,' I said, and after he'd taken his photo, he handed me twenty pounds.

'For your cause, ma'am,' he said. 'Good luck and have a nice evening.'

'Thank you,' I said.

And then a few others followed his lead and asked if they could make donations. Before long, I'd collected fifty pounds.

Slowly the crowd dispersed and the Tube carried most of them away. Only a few people were still drifting out of the hall.

'Do you know if Star Axford has left yet?' I asked one pretty young girl who looked like she might have been a model.

'Don't think so,' she said as she held her bag up over her head as it was beginning to drizzle.

'Oh God,' I said as I looked up at the sky then down the line of people. 'OK gang, everyone with a brolly stand next to someone without one and try and keep the paper dry.'

Luckily most of the girls from our school had brought umbrellas and up they went so that we could protect our wall of letters. Oh please come soon Star, I thought as the rain got heavier, please, or else there's only going to be a soggy mess for you to look at.

A few seconds later, a white van came whizzing round the corner, pulled up and a man and a woman got out. The man was carrying a camera and the other was a blonde lady I recognised as Monisha Harris. She worked as a roving reporter for the same cable station as Mum. I'd met her last summer when she came to our flat for one of the barbecues Mum likes to throw from time to time for her work colleagues. I nudged Izzie.

'Must have come to film the last show,' I said. 'Bit late.'

'They're coming over here,' said Izzie as the cameraman strode over in our direction.

'Where's Nesta Williams?' asked Monisha and someone pointed to me.

She walked over to me. 'Hi, Nesta. So what's all this about?' she asked as the man pointed the camera at me. 'Your mum sent us down here. Said there was a story for the early evening London news.'

Good old Mum, I thought. She must have mentioned that we were down here when she went in to do her shift.

'We're here to ask Star Axford to come to our school dance,' I said looking into the camera. 'It's in aid of the Lotus Hospice, North London, and we're trying to raise fifty 'thousand pounds so that they can build a new wing.'

Monisha asked me a few more questions and let me explain a little about the cause and then went down the line filming some of the letters.

It was then that Star came out.

'There she is,' said TJ pointing then waving. 'Star. *Star*. Over here.'

Star looked over at the line of people staring at her and waving and looked bemused. Monisha and the cameraman raced over to her and said something that I couldn't hear and then the skies really did open and the rain began to pour. The camera man held up his jacket for Star so that she didn't get wet and escorted her and Monisha back up the steps to the hall where they all disappeared.

'*Noooo*,' I cried. 'Hey Star, *Star*.'

We were all yelling. 'Star. STAR. *Staaaaaaaaarrrrr.*'

But she'd gone and we hadn't had a chance to show her our letters or make our request.

And by now it was pouring down.

'So much for your no-rain dance,' I said to Ben.

'Sorry,' he said with a shrug.

Everyone did the best that they could to stop the paper getting wet but the rain was coming down at an angle and it was hard to protect it. The ink began to run. The paper grew soft. Some of it disintegrated, turned to mush and tore. Soon all that was left was a coloured streak on the pavement and we were all getting wetter by the minute.

Tony looked at me, shrugged then began singing the song

from the movie, *Singing in the Rain* and dancing around like Gene Kelly. Ben joined in and then Steve and Lal who were soon followed by some of the girls. After a few minutes, loads of people were dancing, singing, getting soaked and having a great old time. Up on the steps of Olympia, I could see the cameraman laughing as he filmed it all.

I looked around at half our school splashing about in puddles with their hair plastered flat with rain.

'Well, that was a disaster,' I said as I let my umbrella go and joined in the mad rain dance.

Chapter 14

Result

'Quick, quick, Tony, Nesta,' called Dad when we got home later that evening. 'You're on the local news.'

We raced into the living room to watch and there on the screen, in all our glory were about a hundred very wet teenagers singing and dancing outside Olympia. It looked like pandemonium but luckily the cameraman and Monisha Harris had grasped what we were trying to do.

'Ohmigod! It's me!' I gasped when suddenly I appeared on the screen explaining what it was all about.

After a few lines from me, it was cut to the line of paper before the sog set in with a voice-over from Monisha explaining why we were all there.

And then there she was with Star back inside Olympia.

'And so the big question is, Miss Axford, will you be accepting the invitation to this Diamond Destiny Dance?' asked Monisha.

I held my breath as I waited to hear Star's answer.

'I have a brother and sister about the age of everyone who

turned up this afternoon,' she said. 'I got to thinking, what if it was them out there asking me to go to their dance. So, Monisha, the answer is yes, I will be going.'

Tony and I threw cushions up into the air.

'Hurrah!' I cried. 'It worked.'

I raced to my room to get on the phone and make sure the others had seen it as well. And I couldn't resist calling William to tell him the good news.

'Yeah. I saw you,' he said. 'I was about to call you. You looked great. And the last shot of you all dancing in the rain made me laugh out loud.'

'Thanks,' I said. I felt as high as a kite. 'So you can tell Eleanor mission almost accomplished.'

'Mission accomplished? What mission?'

'Made you laugh. Cheered you up.' Oh God, *ohGod-ohGodohGodddd* I thought as I heard the words come out of my mouth and I realised it was too late to take them back.

'What do you mean?' William asked.

'Mean? Oh. Yeah. Nothing, really. Talking my usual rubbish. Just I'm glad I made you laugh. Er . . . we can celebrate at the weekend. If you . . . I mean, do you still . . .?' It was coming out all wrong and it wasn't helped by the ominous silence at the other end. 'William, are you still there?'

'Yes. I'm still here.'

'So do you still want to meet up at the weekend?'

'Doubt it. Eleanor's not good at the moment. You said something about her. Mission accomplished? What's she got to do with this?'

'Eleanor? Nothing. Not really. Me blabbing. Sorry. I don't know what I'm talking about. Stupid.'

'I'll ask her to tell me. And she will.'

I wanted the floor to open up and swallow me. Why had I opened my big stupid mouth? Stupid Stupid. 'No, please don't. Look, it's nothing. Not really. OK. Look. Just she said you'd been a bit down and that I should cheer you up. You know, she was looking after you like you look after her.'

More silence.

'So you . . . everything . . . it's all been because Eleanor asked you?' asked William finally.

'*Nooooo*. Course not. I *wanted* to. I've enjoyed . . . the . . . the contact we've had. Everything.'

'OK,' said William and the tone of his voice was cool. 'Let's get one thing clear and that is, I'm OK. I don't *need* cheering up. I am not a saddo who you need to feel sorry for just because my sister is ill. I can look after myself.'

'Oh, please don't tell Eleanor that I told you. She asked me not to tell you. I . . . I think she only wanted you to be OK.'

'I won't say anything,' he said. 'Bye then.'

And then he hung up.

I felt numb as I sat back on my bed. Hell, I thought. If only I could wipe out the last few minutes. Skip back. Delete. I felt so frustrated. I wanted to kick myself or the wall or something.

'Arrghhhhhhhhhhhhhhhhhhhhhhhhhhhhh,' I yelled and punched my pillows with all my might.

Mum came running down the corridor and rushed in.

'What's the matter? I heard you yell?' she asked as she looked around. 'Are you all right?'

'I am the most *stupid* idiot in the world and I should have my mouth taped up.'

'Why? What's happened?'

I turned over and faced the wall. 'Nothing,' I said.

Mum sighed. 'Nothing?'

I turned back to her, nodded and acted out zipping my lips. 'I've already said too much.'

'Oh, Nesta . . .'

I unzipped my lips. 'Sorry. Shouldn't have yelled. Moment of madness. Passed now. Need to be alone.'

Mum rolled her eyes. 'OK . . . but you know I'm here if you need me?'

I nodded again. Inwardly I vowed not to tell anyone about what I'd just said to William. It was so stupid and I didn't want to hear the inevitable reactions. Oh noooo. Nesta, you *didn't*? You *idiot*, etc. etc. I didn't want the looks that I knew they'd give me and each other – as if to say, oh well, that's what we've come to expect from Big Mouth Nesta. She's always putting her foot in it. Never stops to think before she speaks. She's so insensitive.

And it was true but this time, *this* time, I'd really blown it.

Tickets started to sell.

Donations started to come in.

By the following Wednesday, we had sold almost five hundred of the tickets and were having to have another batch printed. There was even talk that we might have to put a marquee in the car park next to the hall where the dance was being held to cope with the overflow of people.

After school on Wednesday, I met up with the girls at Banner's café in Crouch End to have a quick run-through the plans for Saturday night. We got a table at the back in one of the booths that feels as if you're a private compartment in an old-fashioned train.

'Music,' I said as I went through my list.

'Check,' said Izzie. 'Ben's got it sorted with the band. DJ Diggie will be there early to set up his system and Steve has done a fab soundtrack for the fashion show. His friend Mark will work the sound system while Steve takes photos out front and I think another friend is going to video it all.'

'Excellent job, Izzie. You've done brilliantly getting all that organised. Clothes?'

'Check,' said Lucy. 'We have some fabulous things for Star to choose from. And the local dry cleaners cleaned all the donations from the charity shops free of charge, so that's brillopad.'

'You guys have been so great. All of you,' I said as I could see how hard they'd all worked and I thought that they deserved to be told so. My mum is always saying, give credit where it's due so I try to do that. 'Other models?'

'*Other* models? Besides Star, you mean?' asked TJ.

'Er . . . yeah, no . . .'

'Yes, I have a list here,' said Lucy.

I felt awkward for a moment as I assumed that they'd automatically want me to be one of the models but Lucy hadn't mentioned it. My disappointment must have shown on my face as Izzie picked up on it immediately.

'Oh!' she said. 'Nesta. Did you want to model?'

'Not necessarily but – hey, yeah. Why not? I mean, I'm not being big-headed or anything but you know, people are always saying I could have been one and I did blag my way into Olympia pretending that I was one and no one asked any questions and . . .' I felt myself trailing off because it felt weird explaining myself to my best friends. I'd have thought that they would have taken it as read.

'It's not that,' said Izzie. 'Of course you'd be a fantastic model. And so would Lucy and TJ. But there's so much other stuff to do and we thought that – well, you've done so much. Organised so much. We didn't think you'd want to model as *well*.'

But that will be the best bit, I thought. I'd had visions of myself looking fab and coming down the catwalk with Star and everyone would be saying, Hey, that's Nesta Williams. She's the one behind all this you know and some of it might get back to William and when he heard how hard I'd worked, he wouldn't hate me as much as I was sure he did. But then . . . if I wasn't wanted . . .

'I have a list of about thirty people who want to model,' said Lucy. 'I thought it would be great to get as many as possible up there.'

'And we thought, let's not go for the obvious models,' said Izzie. 'Let's let everyone have a go. Short, plump, whatever. Show that you don't have to be tall and skinny to look good. With the right hair, make-up and clothes everyone can look great. And real girls are more "in" this year anyway, aren't they?'

'Yeah,' said Lucy. 'It would be a good message to have girls who looked like girls and not beanpoles who starve themselves.'

I'd been voted out and I wasn't sure how I felt about it. It was to have been my moment of glory and I already had an outfit that Lucy made for me last year picked out. I decided not to let on that I was peeved about it and then see if later, I could talk them into letting me do it.

'OK. Cool. Funds?' I asked trying to act as if I wasn't bothered at all.

'Check,' said TJ. 'We're doing well. We've sold five hundred tickets. At eight pounds each, that's four thousand and with other bits that will come in on the night, it will be closer to five thousand.'

'Is that all?' I groaned. 'After all my effort, we're still nowhere near the goal.'

Izzie looked surprised. 'Your effort?'

'Er . . . our effort,' corrected Lucy.

'Yeah. Course, I mean . . . our effort,' I stuttered. 'That's what I meant. You know it was.' And then I thought I'd gone out of my way to thank everyone for their efforts but no one had acknowledged my contribution at all. 'Although it was my idea to get Star.'

'Yeah, but it was a joint effort in the end,' said Izzie.

'Yeah, but it was my mum who sent the camera crew,' I said.

'So what? Lucy's been up late every night this week sewing,' said Izzie. 'And TJ's been holding quiz nights and all sorts of sports activities to raise money. And half the school have been involved in one way or other. It doesn't all revolve around you.'

'I know that and I said I thought you'd all been totally brill but . . .'

'Hold on a mo,' said TJ. 'Look, it doesn't matter who did what. Come on, you guys, let's not fall out. It's not about us or anyone else taking the glory.'

We all agreed. I decided that we must be tired with the late nights but I could see Lucy and Izzie giving me strange looks and the atmosphere had soured. It wasn't fair. I wasn't trying to take all the credit, not exactly. I just didn't think that anyone had appreciated how hard I'd worked too.

When the others got up to go, I hung back.

'Are you coming?' asked Izzie.

'Nah. Got a few more notes to make,' I said. 'Last minute things, you know.'

'Suit yourself,' said Lucy and left with Izzie and TJ.

They hate me. I could tell. They were going to go out to the bus stop and talk about me and how I wanted to take all the credit and how I was self-obsessed. But I wasn't. Well, only a bit. I felt peeved. It had all been my idea and if it hadn't been for me, maybe there would still only have been ten tickets sold for the stupid dance. It wouldn't hurt anyone to acknowledge that an incy wincy bit.

As I sat there feeling sorry for myself, I saw TJ come back in. 'You all right, Nesta?' she asked, as she took a seat opposite.

'Yeah.'

'Mind if I stay for a while too,' she said as she pulled out a note pad. 'I got a few things to go over.'

'Whatever.'

'You're mad with us,' she said. 'I can tell. Why?'

'No, I'm not. I'm fine.'

'Liar. You've gone all serious and intense. Come on. Spill. You know the saying, friends listen to what you say but best friends listen to what you don't say. Well. I'm one of your best friends and there's something that you're not saying.'

'Nah, nothing. Just feel a bit weird. It's probably something hormonal.'

'Is your period due?'

'No, but you know me, if I've not got PMT, I've got actual period pain or post-period pain or mid-period pain or pre-PMT or pre-pre-PMT.'

TJ smiled and began to sing, '*Sometime's it's hard to be a woman . . .*'

'Tell me about it,' I said. 'Nah. Just a bit tired, I guess.'

'And that's all?' asked TJ. 'Nothing else bothering you?'

'No. Yeah. Just . . . well . . . I'm not trying to take the credit or anything but sometimes I think that you guys misunderstand me. You don't get me. I'm only trying to do my best and it's not good enough.'

TJ listened patiently as I rambled on and on and finally admitted that I'd like to model in the show.

'Then you should have said, you eejit,' said TJ. 'We're not mind-readers. We thought you might enjoy the evening off to watch the show without having to worry about anything. We do appreciate what you've done and thought a night off would be what you wanted.'

'Oh.' That hadn't occurred to me. I'd thought they were keeping me out because they thought I was getting too big for my boots.

'And what about William Lewis?' she asked. 'Sure he's not bothering you? Is he coming to the dance?'

I'd kept to my vow and hadn't told the girls that I'd totally blown it with William. I still felt such a fool about blabbing Eleanor's secret request to him and didn't want to share it with anyone.

'Probably not,' I said. 'I think he'll be with his sister.'

'So what's happening?' asked TJ. 'Why haven't you met up?'

I shrugged. 'Um . . . his sister is his priority at the moment. I think that they're very close. Before he went to Spain, he told me that she often wants him with her when she's low because he doesn't get all emotional. He said that his parents, his mum in particular, finds it hard not to show her feelings when Eleanor is bad and seeing her mum upset freaks Eleanor out. I guess he manages to act more normal which is why Eleanor always asks him to be with her. He can go and stay over at the hospice so that at least she has company.'

'Yeah,' said TJ. 'A familiar face. I can understand that. Meeting them has made me really understand what the hospice is about. I mean, it must be scary going through what she's going through on her own. There must be times when she thinks, why me? And it must be very lonely as no one can have your treatment for you but at least, if people can stay over, there's someone there.'

'Yeah.'

'Like if one of us was ill,' said TJ. 'Or one of our family, I'd so want to have a friendly face in there with me and in most hospitals, it's an hour at visiting time and then you're on your own.'

I nodded. She'd reminded me what all our efforts were about. What had I been thinking, seeking credit for what we'd been doing? I felt mean and selfish. Sometimes I really hate myself. Like, why couldn't I be selfless and nice like Mother Theresa was? Everything I did was wrong or for the wrong reasons. Everything I said was wrong or came out the wrong way. Sudden tears pricked my eyes at the same time as Lucy and Izzie reappeared at the table.

'Hey, what is it?' asked Lucy as she slid next to TJ.

'I am mean and selfish,' I said.

'No, you're not,' she said. 'You're amazing. We all think that you're amazing. In fact, we were just saying that at the bus stop which is why we came back in. You are one of life's doers. You make things happen.'

'Yeah,' said Izzie as she slid in next to me and put her arm round me. 'And we should have told you. You're right. If it wasn't for you, most of what's been happening lately wouldn't have happened.'

'Yeah, you're like . . . a warrior queen,' said TJ. 'Boudicca, Queen of the Icini leading the troops.'

'Yeah. All hail, Queen Nesta of the Cappuccini . . .' Lucy started.

By now, tears were flooding down my cheeks. 'Oh noooo dooooon't . . . Sorry, sorry,' I sobbed as I scrabbled in my pocket for a tissue. 'Please don't . . .'

Izzie began to sing. 'Oh, darling Nesta, we think you're so top, you get people going and now we can't stop . . .'

And then I began to laugh and then I didn't know if I was laughing or crying.

'What?' asked Lucy, looking around in bewilderment. 'Why's she crying? Why are you crying, Nesta? Don't cry. I hate seeing you cry. We were trying to tell you that we do appreciate your efforts, we really do.'

'Thanks but . . . I . . . just . . . before . . . I . . . oh never mind . . .' I blustered. I was crying because it felt like a dam had burst and I couldn't stop the tears coming and I was laughing because there they were, my mates giving me praise and credit and I suddenly realised that I didn't actually want it. I really, *really* didn't.

> Friends listen to what you say.
> Best friends listen to what you don't say.

Chapter 15

Sorry

'It's show time, folks,' said Tony as he poked his head around my door, then came into my room. He looked as if he'd stepped out of a limo at the Oscars in a black suit, white shirt and bow tie. 'Hey, Mum's gone to bring the car round to take us to the hall. Why aren't you ready?'

'I am,' I said and got up to squeeze past him into the hall.

'Excuse me,' he said as he looked at me in my jeans and T-shirt with disapproval, 'but where's the bling? The fab dress? Come on Nesta. This is your night. It's what you've been working for.'

'But it's *not* my night,' I said. 'Don't say that. I'll come and help set up and then I'm coming home.'

'Oh, for heaven's sake,' sighed Tony. 'One boy gives you the silent treatment and you become a recluse. Come on, Nesta, get over it.'

'Boy? What boy? No. It's not that. And he hasn't given me the silent treatment, not exactly. You don't understand . . .'

'No, I don't but I do know that he hasn't called here this week and you've been going round with a long face. Come on, Nesta. A chance to dress up and strut your stuff and you choose to wear your jeans? Are you hoping that a fairy godmother is going to turn up and wave a wand?'

'No. I'm just not in the mood, that's all.'

'Suit yourself,' said Tony. 'But I can tell you now that the girls aren't going to like it.'

'Don't care,' I said.

I didn't. I just wanted to get the night over with and then get back home. I'd been feeling lousy since my last fatal call with William and I'd tried to phone him since, but he wouldn't speak to me. I'd thought a lot about things since the last meeting in Banner's when the girls went out of their way to make me feel appreciated. I hadn't said anything to them at the time but their praise and kind comments had exactly the opposite effect.

I had realised that on top of being a big mouth that I was also a great big-headed show-off. Always wanting to be the centre of attention. Always wanting recognition. I hated myself. I'd got it all wrong. Wanting to help for all the wrong reasons. So that it would reflect well on me. And now I wanted to be quiet. I'd begun to wish I'd never got involved with charity work. I'd had nothing but trouble since I started it. In future, I would keep my head down, give anonymous donations and stay out of the limelight.

Mum dropped Tony and me at the hall and went off to get changed herself, collect Dad and come back later.

Everyone who was involved was there early and like Tony

were dressed to the nines ready for the activities to begin. The doors were due to open at seven, the fashion show was to start at eight and then it would be time for the band and the disco. It was a hive of activity with everyone dashing about and bumping into each other as they went about their various tasks: Ben and the band members setting up the sound system; Lucy in a room at the back putting the clothes for the show on rails in the order they were to be shown; Izzie organising a dressing area of sorts with make-up and hair brushes laid out. Lal and his mates setting out chairs around the main hall. Tony and his mate Stu had put fairy lights round the hall porch and laid out a red carpet from the car park to the entrance so that it would look like an awards' night in Hollywood. Steve was ready with his camera to take shots of people as they arrived. And TJ was set up to collect tickets at the front door. In every part of the hall, there was an air of anticipation and excitement. Except for me.

'Hey, Nesta,' said Lucy. 'You brought your outfit to change into?'

'Er, not exactly. Er . . . later. Hey. You look great.'

She did. They all did. It was bling city because everyone had taken the Diamond Destiny theme seriously and turned up dripping jewels in fab chokers and tiaras and earrings. Lucy was wearing a gorgeous silver grey sleeveless sheath dress that she'd found on a stall selling vintage clothes in Portobello Road. Very 1920s' elegant. It was made from the finest silk, cut on the bias and probably only Lucy would have been able to get into it as it was so tiny. It was as if it was made for her. Round her neck she had a wide diamanté choker and her hair was up at the back like a real movie star. Tony looked as if he was going to pass out when he saw her as she really did look Class A. Izzie was wearing one of her old favourites: a long black velvet dress and like Lucy, she also had a diamante choker round her neck. With her hair loose and over her shoulders and wearing a deep red lipstick, she looked like the ultimate glam Goth rock chick. And TJ had let Lucy dress her. She looked absolutely stunning in black trousers and a top that Lucy had made for her and diamante earrings. The top was a purple Basque with a zip down the front and no straps. She looked incredibly sophisticated and sexy. All the boys were ogling her chest as if their eyes were glued to it and after a while, she decided that it was too embarrassing and went and put her fleece on until the dancing started later.

Seeing them all looking so glamorous made me feel that I was missing out as usually I like nothing better than to dress up. But the feeling only lasted a minute. What was the point when the only boy that I was interested in wasn't even speaking to me?

Even Miss Watkins had made an effort and was wearing a long royal blue dress and a tiara. Sadly the shapeless dress resembled a tent and the tiara kept slipping over one of her eyes but at least she'd got into the spirit of things which was more than I had done.

At seven-thirty, she called me over from where I was helping Lucy run through the order of the clothes.

'Nesta, Star Axford's here,' she said. 'You're going to look after her aren't you?'

I looked over at Lucy. 'Oh, we didn't decide? Um . . . who should do it?'

'You go for it,' called Lucy. 'We're all busy.'

I raced out to the front to greet Star who was chatting to TJ at the ticket table and she gave me a big smile when she saw me.

'Hey you,' she said. 'We meet again.'

'Yes. And thank you so much for coming. It's totally brilliant of you.'

'So where do you want me?'

'We haven't got a proper dressing room so everyone's piled into a cloakroom area at the back but I can show you to the caretaker's room next door to that if you want some peace and quiet for a while.'

'Lead the way,' she said, then handed me a large Chanel carrier bag. 'And I brought some cast-offs with me as I'd like to donate something as well as my time. A few clothes for the show. In fact, we look about the same size so maybe you could model them.'

'Wow, thanks,' I said. 'I'll give them to my friend Lucy as she's in charge of that side of things but I . . . I'm not modelling tonight. I . . . I'm helping organise things and I'm not staying.'

'Oh, shame,' said Star as she followed me across the hall. 'I'd have thought you'd have been perfect.'

Once inside the small office, I showed her a few things we had put out ready for her. Water. A bowl of fruit. A box of tissues.

'Sorry we don't have much,' I said as I poured her some water. 'We weren't sure what you'd like. Um. Shall I organise someone to go and get you some champagne?'

She took the water and sat behind the desk. 'I don't drink if I'm doing a show so this is fine. Thanks.'

'So what's it like being a model?' I asked. 'I mean, really like?'

Star smiled. 'You'd be surprised. Some places don't offer you anything, not even a glass of water, not even a place to change. So it's mixed. There are good days and bad days, like most jobs. There's a lot of waiting around in strange places. It's not all bright lights and glamour. There's a lot of schlepping around, waiting at airports – all of that but in the main, I love it.'

'Your agent said that you do loads of these types of events . . .'

'Not exactly,' she said. 'Depends on my schedule. I do some.'

'Why?'

Star shrugged. 'I guess it's because . . . I don't know, it's hard to explain. I . . . I know I'm in a privileged position. I want to give something back. And this is one way. Simple as that. Why did you get involved?'

'Because I'm a show-off and I want everyone to think I'm great,' I said.

Star almost spat her water out as she burst out laughing.

'It's true. First I got involved to impress some boy but also because I'm a freaking great show off and want everyone to think I'm a fab kind person who cares about others. Nesta Williams. Miss Do Goody Two Shoes. But I'm a fake. I'm rubbish and my motives are purely selfish.'

. Star laughed again. 'Well, at least you're honest.'

'Honest about being a mess.'

Star put her hand on my shoulder. 'Hey, don't be so hard on yourself, Nesta. You shouldn't worry about your intentions too much. You're doing *something* and that's better than nothing. I'm sure loads of people get involved for all sorts of reasons. Yeah, some to impress others. Others so that they don't feel guilty about what they've got. Sometimes I think that's part of the reason I do it. Because I feel guilty that I have so much. In the end though, I reckon it's all about balance. Enjoy your life but remember to give something back. That's all. Don't think about it too much. Keep it simple.'

'Yeah. Maybe.' Simple for her, I thought.

'So. Who's this boy you wanted to impress?' asked Star.

'His name is William and I really like him . . .'

Star was so easy to talk to that I found myself telling her the whole story right up to how he thought I was only bothering with him because his sister had asked me to.

'. . . and that's not exactly true,' I finished. 'I'd have wanted to see him even if she hadn't asked me.'

'So tell him that,' said Star.

I shook my head. 'Nah. He said he didn't need me feeling sorry for him. He couldn't have been clearer.'

'Do you have his number?'

I nodded.

'So call him,' said Star. 'Give him a chance. Give *yourself* a chance.'

'But I have and he won't pick up . . .'

'Allow for time, Nesta. He may have calmed down by now.'

I shook my head. 'Doubt it and anyway, it's all my fault and I'm probably getting what I deserve.'

Star shook her head. 'People say things they don't mean all

the time in the heat of the moment. People make mistakes. Don't let that stop you trying to make it right again.'

'It's too late,' I said. 'I heard his tone of voice . . . Brrrrr. It was c–c–cold.'

'Coward,' said Star. 'I've got a sister your age. Lia. She was really into this guy and thought that he had been messing about behind her back so she wouldn't speak to him. Actually he hadn't but she didn't know that at the time. Thing is, he didn't give up when she wouldn't take his calls. He kept trying and trying until she gave in.'

'And then what happened?'

'They got back together. Both realised they were being stupid and were miserable without each other. So *call* him.'

'But I *have* . . .'

'So call him again. I dare you. Remember the saying, fortune favours the brave. Don't let fear of rejection stop you. Anyway, what have you got to lose?'

That was true. What did I have to lose? Nothing.

As it got closer to the time for the show, I showed Star where Lucy and the models were getting ready then went out into the car park to call William.

I took a deep breath, punched in his number and waited. I could feel my heart thumping in my chest as I listened to the phone ring. Part of me didn't want him to be there as I was scared that he'd give me an earful. And part of me wanted him to pick up and tell me that it was all OK and had all been a huge misunderstanding and that he couldn't stop thinking about me and that I haunted his dreams. Or something like that.

A few moments later, he picked up.

'Ah . . . ah . . .' I stuttered. Oh God, I thought. I've done a TJ and gone blank. Wargh! This doesn't happen to me.

'Hello. *Hello*?' said William. 'Is there anybody there?'

'Ah . . . Yes. Um. Hi, William. This is Nesta.'

'Oh you . . .'

'Don't hang up! And before you say anything,' I began, and then talked as fast as I could. 'I want to say I'm sorry, actually no I'm not. I haven't got anything to be sorry for . . .'

'You've phoned to say that you're sorry but you're not?'

'Yeah. No. Um. See it's like this. I . . . yes, Eleanor did ask me to cheer you up but . . . actually even if she hadn't asked me to, I would have wanted to. Actually no. That's not right. Not cheer you up. That's not what I wanted to do at all.'

'Nesta. What are you on about? Sorry. Not sorry. Cheer me up. Not cheer me up. What?'

'Yeah. No. Not cheer you up. You said you don't need it and I agree. I mean I don't think that you look miserable, so why would you need cheering up? Actually no, that's probably wrong. You probably do some of the time as your situation must be very hard sometimes with your sister and you probably don't show it being a boy and they don't like to show their feelings sometimes . . . oh . . . what I'm trying to say is. . . oh Dunking Doughnuts! Can we start again? I . . . I like you. I would like to see you again and would have liked to see you even if Eleanor hadn't said anything.'

There was a silence at the other end.

'So?' I prompted.

'So,' William finally said. 'Me too.'

'Me too what?'

'Me too, I would have wanted to see you but I was well peeved with Eleanor for sticking her oar in. I don't need her to do that.'

'I know. I have an older brother who always thinks he knows what's best for me. It can be very annoying but I think Eleanor was only trying to help.'

'Well, it didn't, did it?'

'No. But maybe . . . maybe it's not too late.'

'Maybe. And actually, I guess I did fly off the handle a bit. I tend to do that sometimes, react and shoot my mouth off.'

'What sign are you?' I asked.

'Aries,' he said. 'Why?'

'You sound a bit like me. I'm Leo with Aries rising.'

'What does that mean? Rising?'

'Um, you'd have to ask Izzie as she's our resident astrologer. But anyone with Aries in their chart tends to leap before they look kind of thing. As you said, shoot-their-mouth-off types of people.'

'Sounds familiar,' said William.

'So. You know tonight's the Diamond Destiny Dance?'

'Yeah.'

'Will you come?'

'Sure,' said William.

'Sure? Oh. OK. Brilliant.'

I heard William laugh at the other end. 'I was coming anyway,' he said.

'You were?'

'Yeah. Olivia got me tickets ages ago. Just you be thankful you have only one brother. I have two sisters, both of whom think they know what's best for me. And I wanted to see you in person. Find out if there was anything else that Eleanor asked you to do.'

'Nope, nothing else. So you're coming. Excellent,' I said.

'Yep. See you later then.'

As I turned to go back in, I was struck by how magical the hall looked with fairy lights twinkling around the door. It was a lovely warm evening. Cars were drawing up and people getting out. Cameras were flashing. Music was beginning to pound from inside.

Suddenly I got the feeling that it was going to be a great night.

Fortune favours the brave.

Diamond Destiny Dance

'Hey Nesta, get over here,' called Lucy when I got back into the hall. 'Where have you been?'

'In the car park. Why? What's the matter?'

'Nothing. Not a problem. Just Star gave us these gorgeous clothes to model and no one back here can fit into them. I think they'd be perfect on you, though. Come and try. And hurry. We're due to start in five minutes.'

Gorgeous clothes? Understatement, I thought as I tried on one of the dresses. A white Armani evening dress with tiny straps. It was so elegant and fitted like a glove. I felt a million dollars in it. Next was a gorgeous floaty chiffon dress by Stella McCartney. Then a sophisticated Calvin Klein black dress slashed at the shoulder.

'You'll be the belle of the ball,' said Star as she got changed next to me.

'I can't believe you're getting rid of these,' I said.

Star shrugged. 'I have loads at home and quite honestly, when am I going to wear them all? Shopping at Sainsbury's? I don't think so.'

'Places, girls,' called Lucy as the music started up and Izzie signalled that everyone was in their seats and the show about to begin.

It was such a blast. Like a series of fantasies come true. Following Star out onto the catwalk. The flash of cameras. Mum and Dad cheering like mad. Boys ogling me. Classmates watching and clapping when I appeared. Izzie and TJ grinning like idiots out front. Lucy grinning like an idiot from backstage. And at the very back of the hall, a really gorgeous boy with collar length hair watching with quiet admiration. William. When I looked over at him, he smiled his killer watt smile and gave me the thumbs up.

It was all over so fast. Up and down the catwalk. In and out of clothes. Back out. More flashes from cameras in the audience. (Mainly my dad who beamed with pride every time I stepped out.)

After the fashion show, while all the models got changed, Izzie and TJ got up and did this hysterical double act where they auctioned off the clothes and items from the charity shop. It sounded like a riot from backstage – we could hear them really getting into the part of barrow boys.

'All wight, everyone,' said Izzie in her best Cockney accent. 'So what am I bid for this 'ere novel. It's a first edition. Probably worf loadsa money.'

People started bidding from the audience and soon the sale was up and running with bidders trying to outbid each other for the fun of it.

'Come on, you tight lot,' called TJ. 'What am I bid for this stunning skirt?'

'How about if you're in it?' called a dark-haired boy from the back of the hall.

I went to stand with Lucy at the edge of the stage behind Izzie and TJ and looked round for William. 'Hey look, Lucy,' I said. 'Eyes left. Cute boy alert. Just your type, he looks a bit like Tony.'

'Oh yeah,' said Lucy. 'No. Not *quite* as gorgeous as Tony but not bad.'

I patted her on the head. 'Poor thing,' I said. 'My brother clearly has you under some strange spell and all we can hope is that one day, you'll awaken and see sense.'

'Hey, I think that boy who called out must be Star's brother, Ollie,' Lucy continued. 'See, he's with Zac Axford, over there to the left, talking to my dad.' She pointed at a man who was standing at the back of the hall talking to Mr Lovering. He looked like a rock and roller. He was in his forties or fifties with straggly dark hair and dressed in jeans and a leather jacket. 'Dad didn't waste much time getting talking to him. Star told me that he was coming and when I told Dad, he almost passed out with excitement. He has every one of his albums.'

'Hhmm,' I said as I watched Ollie banter with TJ over the skirt. 'Methinks that yonder Ollie fancies our TJ.'

Lucy glanced back at Ollie and nodded. 'Methinks you is

right,' she said. 'Good. TJ could do with a bit of buff boy attention.'

After the auction, it was time for the music and King Noz soon got the place rocking. I looked around for William in the hope that he'd ask me to dance but couldn't see him anywhere. Izzie did a number with the band and when she'd finished, Lucy's dad got up to join them as well. As he got to the stage, I saw that Zac Axford had followed him over and was saying something. Mr Lovering then beckoned Ben who went over to join them and nodded in recognition at Zac. Ben suddenly beamed, got up and handed Zac a guitar. Next thing we knew, Lucy's dad was up there with Zac Axford and both of them were playing with the band. It was incredible. The crowd went mad, dancing and stomping like there was no tomorrow. I didn't think it could get any better until I felt two hands slip round my waist from behind.

I turned to see that it was William. I was about to say something but he just pulled me back so that I was leaning against him, his hands still round my waist. The sensation of being so close to him made me feel as if I'd turned to liquid. I didn't want the moment to end. It felt so perfect, watching the band like a regular couple. It was only when they began to play a ballad and the pace slowed down that he pulled me to the edge of the crowd.

'I just want to say sorry for my big mouth again . . .' I started.

He leaned over, put a finger against my lips then pulled me to him and gave me a long-deep-to-the-tip-of-my-toes-and-back-again snog. Heavenly, heavenly, heaven.

At the end of the night, when everyone had gone, TJ, Lucy, Izzie and the Dopey Doreens piled into the caretaker's office. Miss Watkins made us tea and we sat around like a bunch of old businessmen to count the takings. I felt brilliant. William had left with Olivia but not before promising to call me in the morning. The future was looking bright.

'Four thousand five hundred,' said TJ who was doing the accounts. 'Cheque for fifty, excellent. Five pounds, ten pounds. Hey, it's looking good . . .'

And so she went on, five thousand. Six. The takings were good, but it didn't look as if we would make our target. Nowhere near. I couldn't help feeling disappointed and wished that there was more that I could have done.

Suddenly TJ's face registered shock. 'Ohmigod, ohmi*god*,' she said as she held up one cheque.

'What? What is it?' asked Miss Watkins.

TJ was speechless as she handed over the cheque. Miss Watkins glanced down at it and she too looked surprised.

Her face lit up. 'Ohmigod,' she said.

'*Whaaaaat*?' I asked.

Miss Watkins beamed. 'Our celebrity guest left us a little donation,' she said and she turned the cheque around so that we could all see. It was signed by Zac Axford and it was for the sum of forty-five *thousand* pounds.

Later, when everything was locked up, I went to sit with TJ, Izzie and Lucy on the wall in the car park while we waited for Lucy's dad to come back and taxi us all home.

'That was totally top,' said TJ as she moved over to make room for me between her and Lucy. 'And did you see the faces of the Dopey Doreens when Miss Watkins held that cheque up?'

'Yeah,' said Izzie. 'We showed them but they were cool in the end, weren't they? At least they had grace to say well done to everyone.'

'But you don't seem so thrilled, Nesta,' said Lucy. 'We *did* it. So what's the matter?'

I looked back at the hall. Only hours before, it had been so full of life, lights on, music blasting out of it. And now it was dark, silent, empty. I looked up at the sky. It was a clear night and up there in the heavens, the stars were twinkling down on us. I felt so small and insignificant.

'I *am* thrilled,' I said. 'Really. It's a great result. Just . . . now it's all over I can't help but think so what? So we raised the money. Big deal. A drop in the ocean. There's still so much pain the world.'

'Hey, Nesta's gone all deep on us,' teased Izzie. 'Usually it's you telling us to lighten up.'

'Yeah. Don't be sad, Nesta,' said Lucy. 'Not tonight. It's been a great night. It couldn't have gone better and you and William . . .'

'But that's just it. William. I really like him. And we're going to see each other. We have a future but I can't help thinking what about Eleanor? What kind of future has she got? What has she got to look forward to?'

The others fell quiet and I could see that I'd put a real dampener on their good mood.

'Sorry, guys,' I said. 'Can't help it. I feel sad. And small and helpless.'

Lucy put her arm through mine. 'I think we have to remember what Mrs Owen said. That day at the jumble sale, remember? Be happy. Do what you can, while you can. Be happy. Enjoy life. All aspects.'

'Yeah,' said Izzie as she linked arms with Lucy. 'Who knows how long we've all got? Any of us. It would be great if our birth certificate came like Mum's credit cards. You know, showing the date of issue *and* the date of expiry. Then we'd know. But we don't. Thing is to make the most of it while we're here and we're healthy.'

'Yeah,' said TJ as she linked my other arm. 'And while we've got each other.'

I felt my eyes fill up with tears. I was so lucky to have such great friends. It must be so hard for William knowing that he was going to lose his sister. I couldn't bear the thought of losing Izzie or TJ or Lucy or any of my family. But for the time being, here we were. My mates. On a wall in a car park in East Finchley under the stars. Who knows what life had in store for any of us. But one thing I did know and that was that summer was around the corner. I was going to do my best to appreciate every single second of it.

Mates, Dates & Sizzling Summers

Cathy Hopkins

Mates, Dates & Sizzling Summers

PICCADILLY PRESS • LONDON

This book is for my dad, Wilf Hopkins (aka Billy Hopkins) whose short stay in hospital the year before last inspired many of the scenes in this book. Not the part about TJ's dad being a grumpy old wrinkly. Er . . . not those, course not. Thanks, as always, to Brenda Gardner, Melissa Patey and all the fab team at Piccadilly. And thanks to Steve Lovering for his constant support and help with all aspects of the book.

Chapter 1

Post-Party

'I tell you, that boy was smitten,' said Izzie as she kicked her shoes off and flopped down on my bed. 'S.M.I.T. Smitten.'

I stood in front of the mirror that hung on the back of my bedroom door and frowned at my reflection. 'Nah. He couldn't be. I mean, look at me. Pale face, spot threatening to erupt on my forehead, bags under my eyes . . . No, this is not a look that smits, smites, or whatever the word is. And a boy like Ollie Axford would never fancy me. Not if he knew me properly. No, it was that top you made me wear, Lucy — I felt like I was walking about in my underwear! Every boy in the place was staring at me . . . or rather at my chest.'

Nesta laughed as she reached into her jeans' pocket to pull out some lip-gloss. 'Not to mention all the dads,' she said as she sprawled next to Izzie and began to apply the strawberry-scented lip-gloss.

'It was soooo embarrassing,' I said. 'Never again.'

Lucy took a pillow off the bed and made herself comfortable on the floor next to my dog, Mojo. 'You looked fab,' she said as she tickled Mojo's ears. 'It showed off your shape, that's all. You should wear things like that more often instead of those tracksuits that you hide away in.'

'I don't hide away in them. They're comfortable.'

Nesta pulled a face and put her gloss away. 'And dead boring. You always amaze me, TJ. You've got gorgeous brown eyes, a mouth most actresses would kill for and great legs. You can look five-star if you want – like you did last night with your hair loose down your back and a bit of make-up on – but most of the time, your hair's scraped back and you slob around in tracksuits like that shapeless grey *thing* you're wearing today.'

'They're cosy and easy to wear,' I retaliated.

'They're passionkillers,' she said. 'If you got it, flaunt it, I say. And you got it, girl.'

You're the ones who've got it, girls, I thought as I looked at the three of them lounging around my room and looking like an ad in a teen mag. Nesta's tall and skinny with long black hair, coffee-coloured skin and fab, high cheek bones; even today when she's only wearing jeans and a T-shirt she still looks stunning. Lucy and Izzie are attractive too but in different ways. Lucy is the smallest of the four of us with short blond hair and Izzie is tall with chestnut-coloured hair, cut in layers down to her shoulders and she's got a gorgeous curvy figure. Boys always look at them wherever we go and I think they're the best-looking bunch at our school. I'm still amazed that they adopted me into their group last year after my best mate, Hannah, went off to live in South Africa.

Izzie pushed her tummy out over her jeans. 'Yeah. If I had a body like yours, TJ, I think I *would* walk around in my underwear all day with a sign in front saying, *Look at me, I look so fab, look at my flat stomach, look at my legs* . . . la la lahhh . . .'

'You're mad, Izzie Foster,' I said. 'But thank God Mum and Dad weren't there last night. Dad would have had a heart attack!'

It was Sunday, the day after the charity ball that we'd been planning for weeks – all through April – and the girls were round at my house for the post-party gossip.

'It feels strange that it's over after all the work that we've put in,' said Izzie, sighing. 'Bit of an anticlimax. All those weeks of putting up posters, selling tickets, organising the music, the fashion show, trying not to panic when it looked like no one was going to show up . . .'

'Worth it in the end though, hey?' I asked. 'I still can hardly believe that we not only met our fundraising target but surpassed it.'

It had been a great night. Nesta had managed to talk a top model called Star Axford into taking part in the fashion show. Her dad is Zac Axford (the famous rock and roller) and, to everyone's amazement, *he'd* turned up to the show, along with his son Ollie. I noticed Ollie the moment he walked in (tall, dark and buff) and he noticed me (or rather my boobs). We both did a double take and then laughed. After the fashion show he'd asked me to dance, and when he left he'd taken my number.

Lucy is our fashion expert and, as I hadn't found a special outfit, she had dressed me for the occasion. I'd been complaining that I had no waist to speak of so she had risen to the challenge and made me a special corset top designed to give an hourglass figure. It was low at the front and laced up tight at the back and yes, it did give me a waist, but it also gave me the most enormous cleavage. My eyes almost popped out of my head (and my boobs out of the top!) when I saw myself in the mirror at the hall where we got changed.

'The effect of cleavage on boys is funny,' said Nesta. 'Like if you show the tiniest bit, they can't help but stare. It's like an eyeball magnet.'

'The tiniest bit is all you get in my case,' said Lucy. 'And actually, you're right. Boys even stare at *my* chest these days.'

'But seriously,' I said, 'I reckon that's the last we've seen of Ollie Axford.'

'I wouldn't be so sure,' said Nesta. 'I saw the way he looked at you. I bet he calls and asks you out.'

'Nah. He was just passing through,' I said. 'And anyway, he looks like a player. You know the type. Too much of a naughty twinkle in his eye to be trusted. And I bet he likes fun girls. He'd soon get bored with me when he realised how straight and sensible I am.'

'You're not straight and sensible,' said Nesta, 'least not all the time.'

'I am,' I said. 'I'm boring.'

'I used to think that you were,' Nesta started, then Lucy thumped her. '*Ow!* Well, I did! Before we hung out, I used to think you were *really* boring, but you're just one of these people who's quiet in the beginning and it takes a while to get to know. Then when you do, you realise they are not boring in the slightest.'

'Steve liked you when he got to know you,' said Lucy. 'Still does I reckon.'

'No. He hardly speaks to me when I see him,' I said.

'Doesn't mean he doesn't still like you,' said Lucy. 'He keeps his feelings hidden.'

I sighed and joined Nesta and Izzie on the bed. 'Boys are so difficult,' I said. 'My whole love life so far has been a disaster.'

It had, too. My first date was with a boy called Scott who was full of himself and tasted of onions when he kissed me. So much for my first snog. *Blargh*. One to remember? I don't think so.

My second boyfriend was Steve. Great friend more than a great passion. We went out for a short while when I was in Year Nine and I felt safe with him. I could be myself and talk to him easily about anything. (With some boys, I go stupid and start talking alien-speak – that's if I get any words out at all.) I hope that we can be friends again one day as I miss our long chats.

After him was Luke . . . not exactly a boyfriend as he was actually seeing Nesta at the time I met him. I fell for him big time – thought he was my soulmate and that he felt the same. He told me that it was over between him and Nesta so I finished with Steve, and then I found out that Luke was lying and I got majorly confused about how I felt about him. When I was with him, I felt like all the clichés in love songs came true and the world was a happier place. Not that I was happier, though. No. He totally did my head in, but I haven't felt what I felt with him since. Just a glance from him and I used to feel like I was a marshmallow melting. As a kisser, he rated eleven out of ten. Even thinking about kissing him still makes my toes curl up. There was something really special there, but . . . it was a mess. Such a mess. I couldn't trust him and I almost lost Nesta as a friend. I still feel sad that things didn't work out differently.

So, disastrous love life? Yes, I'd say so.

And now Ollie Axford. Very cute and he looks bright, like he's got a brain. But would he be another heartbreaker? I don't think I could bear to go through what I went through with Luke again.

'Not all boys are difficult,' said Nesta, picking up on my thoughts. 'They're not all like Luke.'

Lucy squeezed Nesta's foot. 'Nesta's in lu-hurve.'

Nesta smiled. 'It's true. I am. William Lewis, I loooooove yooooooou. It's amazing.'

'William,' said Izzie, thoughtfully. 'Do you realise that if you married him, and he took your surname, then he'd be William Williams?'

'Yes, but I'm not going to marry him. And even if I did, why would he take my surname?'

Lucy rolled her eyes. 'I can't believe that you're talking about marriage when you've only just started going out with him. And you're only fifteen.'

'Sixteen in August,' said Nesta. 'But I agree. I want to have had lots of boyfriends before I finally settle down, and that's if I ever do. I might just go from one boy to another, gathering experience, and then I'll write my memoirs.'

'Memoirs of a slu-urt,' said Lucy, teasing.

Nesta threw a pillow at her. 'You're the slut — stringing my poor brother along the way you do . . .'

We all laughed. Lucy had an ongoing off-on relationship with Tony, Nesta's brother, but we all knew that it wasn't a case of Lucy stringing him along. She really liked him. And he really liked her. He'll be off to university in September though, so depending on which one he gets into, they might not see much of each other because of the distance – which explains why Lucy doesn't want to get too involved. Bit too late for that though, if you ask me. You only have to see them together to see how besotted they both are.

'What about you, Izzie?' said Lucy. 'See anyone you fancied last night?'

'Zac Axford,' said Izzie wistfully. 'I love that jaded-rock-star look.'

'That's because he is a jaded rock star,' said Nesta. 'He must be in his forties at least.'

'And married,' I pointed out.

'A girl can dream, can't she?' said Izzie. 'But apart from him, nope. With my luck with boys lately, anyone would think that I'm destined to be an old maid.'

Lucy leaned back, took Izzie's hand and looked at her palm. 'I see many boys. Many lovers. In fact, you are ze slut around here and although you try to keep quiet about the fact, we all know it and recommend that you behave yourself. In fact, you should be locked up until you are thirty-five.'

Izzie pulled her hand away. 'Pff. Leave the fortune-telling to me, O mystically challenged one.'

Usually it's Izzie who does all the fortune-telling stuff. She has Tarot cards, crystals and often does our horoscopes for the coming months. Sometimes she even tries out simple spells.

'Let's forget boys for a while,' I said. 'We're here for a purpose. At last, at *laaaaaaast*, Mum has said that I can join the new century and redecorate my room. Don't think Dad's too keen, but then he is stuck in the dark ages.'

'Is he here?' asked Nesta.

I shook my head. 'No, thank God,' I said. 'So we can make as much noise as we like without old misery appearing.'

The girls have been wary of my father ever since he told us off for having a pillow fight the first time they came over. They call him Scary Dad as he can be really intimidating when he wants to be.

'Don't be mean,' said Lucy. 'He's your dad. He can't be that bad.'

'You don't have to live with him,' I said. 'So. Room. What do you think?'

Nesta leaped up from the bed, stepped over Mojo who had fallen asleep on the floor and fetched a carrier bag of things that she'd brought with her.

'Here. Mum gave us loads of mags to look at,' she said as she spread copies of interior design magazines on the bed.

'And I brought my feng shui book,' said Izzie. 'So that the room has the right feel in the end, as well as looking good.'

'Any ideas so far, TJ?' asked Lucy.

'Anything will be an improvement on this,' I said, as I looked around. My room is dull with a capital D. Ancient leafy wall-paper on the walls and a faded cream candlewick bedspread on the bed. When I first became mates with Lucy, Nesta and Izzie and saw their fab bedrooms, I was embarrassed to let them see how old-fashioned our house is. And not just the house, but my parents too. They're a lot older than most people's. In fact, when Nesta first saw them, they were out in the garden and she thought that they were my grandparents. Dad is almost in his seventies and Mum's just turned sixty. I call them the wrinklies. I think it was a shock when Mum realised that she was having me. I think they thought they'd had their family with Marie (who's twenty-seven) and Paul (who's twenty-three), and they had a merry old middle-age to look forward to. Then, surprise! Along I came. What they were doing having sex at their age heaven knows. I don't like to think about it, but they clearly did. And they should have known better than to have an unexpected baby, seeing as both of them are doctors. Dad's a hospital consultant and Mum is a GP. It just goes to show that getting pregnant unexpectedly can happen to anyone, and at any age.

Anyway, neither of them have ever been bothered by décor or having the latest sofa or TV. As long as it all works, Mum always says. Both of them have only just come to terms with e-mail and neither will have a mobile phone. Mum likes to garden in her spare time and Dad likes to read or play golf. So they're not Mr and Mrs Groovacious. Unlike Nesta's parents, for instance. They're both so good-looking and cool. Her dad makes films and TV dramas. Her mum is a newsreader on cable. Lucy's dad runs the health shop in Muswell Hill, but he also plays jazz and teaches the guitar. And her mum is great. She's a counsellor and looks like a children's TV presenter — wearing bright colours that don't quite match. Izzie's parents are straighter. Her mum is an accountant in the City and so is her stepdad. Her real dad is more of a wild card, though — he lectures in English at the university in town and is a great laugh. I like him a lot. We have long conversations about books and he often sends me something to read via Izzie.

'I want colour,' I said and got up to find a book from my desk in the corner. 'This place is soooo bland. I got this book on the Far East out of the library. I love the colours they use over there. Reds, oranges, ochres . . . This side of the house. doesn't get much sun so I thought those colours would work better than blues or greens.'

'You could do the room black and white to match Mojo,' said Nesta as Mojo snored in his sleep. 'It's very in to decorate a room to match your pet.'

'Says who?' asked Lucy. 'Some mad journalist who's having a laugh? No. You're right, TJ. Warm colours would be best in here. Make it look cosy. And we could go to Camden Lock and get you an Indian bedspread. Loads of stalls there are selling Eastern stuff at the moment.'

'Yeah,' said Izzie. 'And lanterns. Maybe a little statue of Buddha or the goddess Kali. You could make it look really exotic in here.'

'It's a bedroom, not a temple,' said Nesta. 'She wants some nice cushions, some girlie nick-nacks . . .'

'And some gorgeous fabric at the windows,' said Lucy. 'I used sari material in my room. That would work in here, too. If you go down to Brick Lane they have the most sumptuous colours there: reds threaded with gold, purple with silver edgings. It's going to look great in here.'

'Hey, I haven't got that much money,' I said. 'Mum and Dad don't really believe in spending more than is necessary.'

'Don't worry,' said Lucy. 'There are always ways round it. Markets, ends of rolls, shopping at sale times. We'll make it work within your budget.'

'Which way is west?' asked Izzie, as she got up and pulled a book out of her bag and started flicking through the pages.

I pointed out of the left windowpane. 'That, way, I guess – the sun goes down over there, over the lime trees at the bottom of the garden. How does this feng shui thing work?'

'There are different areas representing different aspects of your life in each room of a property,' Izzie explained. 'An area for career, health, creativity, wealth, relationships and so on. You need a compass and a feng shui book to work out where they fall in each room as it depends on whether a room faces north, south, east or west. And the effect of that can make an area either positive or negative.'

It sounded incredibly complicated to me. I didn't understand a word of it, but didn't like to say as Izzie is so enthusiastic about these sorts of things. 'Er . . . OK. And then what?' I asked.

'Well, for instance, if you have a wealth area in a negative zone where you keep all your savings, accounts, etc. you'd probably find that they didn't do too well. But if you moved them to another room where the wealth area was in a positive space, then they'd probably multiply.'

'Hmm, cool,' I said. 'So what about this room? What's where?'

Izzie consulted her book again. 'Which way does it face again?'

'North,' I said. 'That's why it doesn't get as much light as the front rooms.'

'OK. Good,' said Izzie, flicking the pages and looking around the room. 'Your bed's in a positive creativity place so that's good. You probably have some great ideas when you're falling asleep, yeah?'

I nodded.

And then Izzie let out a soft groan. 'Ohmigod,' she said, as she pointed under my desk. 'Is that where you always keep your bin?'

I nodded again.

'Move it immediately,' she said. 'It's in the relationship area of your life.'

'So why would having the bin there be a problem?'

'It's in a negative zone, so it's like you're putting all your rubbish into your relationships or all your relationships turn to rubbish. It's no wonder things went so weird with Luke. I should have come over and done this for you ages ago! And I would never write any letters to boys you like or take calls from over here,' she said, going to my desk. She began to pull on the desk until it had moved a few feet. 'Here. If we move it over here by the window it will be in a positive career area, plus you'll be able to see outside when you work.'

I picked up the bin. 'And where shall I put this?'

Izzie pointed under the desk. 'You can put that in the career area as well,' she said. 'Just keep the relationship area empty if you can, and don't put a mirror there as it will reflect the negativity.' Izzie looked pleased with herself. 'I think you might find that your relationships take a turn for the better now we've done that.'

Yeah right, I thought. I didn't really believe it myself but I knew that Izzie did, and I didn't want to hurt her feelings.

About two seconds later, the phone rang.

A moment later, Mum called up the stairs. 'TJ, it's for you. Pick up your extension.'

I picked up the phone.

'Hi,' said a male voice. 'Is that TJ Watts?'

'Speaking.'

'Ollie Axford here.'

Handy Hints for Decorating Your Bedroom

TJ: Do your research: get books and magazines on interior design to give you ideas and colour schemes. Try out paint sample pots on the wall to see how the colour looks at different times of the day, and in natural and artificial light.

Nesta: Budget. Work out how much you have to spend and save some money for one super duper eye-catching piece, like a jewelled mirror or fab velvet cushion.

Izzie: Rule number one in feng shui is clear out the clutter, so get rid of old books, clothes and magazines in order to make way for new ones! Don't forget to make sure that your room smells wonderful. Scented candles and sprays can be used for this. Orange blossom is my current fave.

Lucy: Think carefully about your colour scheme, remembering that light colours can open up a room and make it look more airy, whereas dark colours can close it in and make it look smaller but cosier. Gorgeous fabrics can be draped at windows or made into cushions for that finishing touch.

Colour Ideas

Cool Colours: blue and green.

Warm Colours: red, orange and yellow.

Minimal: white, or shades of white.

Bright: vivid pink, lime, yellow, orange and turquoise.

Fairy Tale: pastel colours, like pink, pale blue, lilac, lavender and turquoise.

Romantic: shades of pink and red.

Exotic: spice colours, such as shades of red, all shades of yellow, honey gold and orange.

Stark: black and white.

Chapter 2

The People Who Live in My Head

'So did he ask you out?' asked Lucy.

I laughed. 'You mean you weren't eavesdropping?'

'As if,' said Nesta. 'No. We respect your privacy. Besides, we couldn't hear through the door when we tried. So did he ask you out?'

'He asked if I could meet him on Wednesday night . . .'

Nesta punched the air. 'Result! Excellent. What will you wear?'

'Well, er . . . I told him I couldn't.'

'Couldn't? Why not?' asked Nesta.

'I want to go up to the bookshop in Muswell Hill. Leila Ferrin is talking. She's one of my favourite authors . . .'

'Let me get this straight. You're going to miss a date with a buff boy because you want to go and hear an author talk?' she asked. 'Er, why?'

'Because I love her books and, as you know, I want to be a

writer and . . . oh, a million reasons. I've been looking forward to it for weeks.'

'Good for you,' said Izzie, then turned to Nesta. 'There is more to life than boys, you know, and you should take a leaf out of TJ's book. Don't drop everything because a boy you fancy comes along. Sometimes they like it when a girl is independent and doesn't just fall at their feet.'

Lucy started laughing. 'A leaf out of TJ's book! Good phrase, seeing as she wants to be a writer!'

Nesta looked peeved. 'I *haven't* fallen at William's feet,' she said. 'You know I haven't. I've played it pretty cool with him. But there's a time to be cool and a time to say, "Hello, sailor, mine's a Diet Coke". And anyway, since when have you been the boy expert round here? That's *my* job!'

It was true. Boy expert was Nesta's post, and usually she was spot-on with advice.

'Exactly,' said Izzie and bowed. 'And you have taught us well, O master. Pity thou canst not follow thy own advice.'

Nesta thumped Izzie over the head with a pillow. 'I am sooooo misunderstood,' she said.

'Did he suggest another time?' asked Lucy.

I shook my head. 'No. Well, actually I probably didn't give him the option. I said that I had friends round so couldn't talk for long. Do you think I've I blown it? I have, haven't I? I've just blown it.'

Nesta shook her head. 'No. If he's interested he will be in touch. That's always the rule. It may take a while, but you'll hear from him again. And actually it might work in your favour that you said no.'

'How?'

'Shows you're not desperate,' said Nesta. 'Most boys hate desperate. So without meaning to, you have played hard to get. Miss Über-Cool. He will probably now see you as a challenge to be conquered. Be prepared to hear from him again.'

'Really?' I said. 'Cool.' I felt chuffed. I thought I couldn't play hard to get if I tried, but there I'd gone and done it without even knowing.

'Anyway, we have work of our own to do in the boy department,' said Nesta. 'Got to go and put our bins in the right place. Come on, Izzie, and bring that fong bong shu book with you.'

'Feng shui,' she said.

'Whatever,' said Nesta. 'I can't risk things going wrong with William, and if it means turning to hocus-pocus, just call me Tabuga the Teenage Witch.'

'Feng shui isn't witchcraft,' said Izzie. 'It's about working with the elements to create harmony . . .'

'Sounds like witchcraft to me,' said Nesta, as she gathered up her bag and headed for the door.

After the girls had gone, I got the bus to Homebase and spent my pocket money on little pots of paint samples of all the spice colours that I'd imagined my room in. When I got back, I had a great time painting squares all over the walls. It was amazing because when the paint dried, the colours looked nothing like the shades on the paint chart. They changed colour again as the sun went down and the light faded in my room.

I looked over at the bin in its new position. Funny that Ollie called as soon as we'd moved it. But if my relationship hopes were going to come true as Izzie had promised, then shouldn't it have been Luke who called, not Ollie?

On Wednesday evening, Mum dropped me at the bookshop and told me to call her when the talk had finished to arrange a lift home, as sometimes these events can go on well after the advertised time. A crowd was already inside milling about, chatting and drinking the wine that was left on a table in the centre of the shop. I helped myself to an orange juice, then went to find a seat in the area at the back of the shop where chairs had been set out in front of the bookshelves. Already most of the good places had been taken, and jackets put on chairs for friends that were late. I should have come earlier, I thought. I should have known a writer as popular as Leila would draw a crowd.

'Hey,' said a voice behind me. 'I was looking for you.'

I turned round and found myself looking into a pair of cornflower-blue eyes. Cute face, too, with a wide smile and a dimple on his chin

It was Ollie Axford. He grabbed my elbow and ushered me to the second row.

'I got here early and nabbed us a good spot,' he said as he pointed to two chairs, one with a jacket on it and the other with a copy of Leila's latest book. We squeezed past people who were already sitting and took our seats.

'But . . . nihwee . . . uh . . . how . . . what are you doing here?' I asked, as inwardly I told myself to calm down. The last thing I wanted was to turn into Noola, my alien alter ego in front of him.

'Come to listen to Leila Ferrin, like you.'

'But . . . how did you know where she was on?'

'You said she was giving a talk on Wednesday night. I bought her book. Called her publisher. They told me where she was talking. Easy.'

'But you didn't mention that you liked her when we spoke on Sunday.'

Ollie grinned and flicked a lock of dark hair out of his eyes. 'No. But I do like one of her readers.'

I felt myself blush – he didn't take his eyes off me when he said this. A moment later, the man who ran the bookshop called for attention and, when the room fell silent, he introduced Leila Ferrin.

I'd seen photos of her on her book covers, but she looked different in the flesh. Older and with salt and pepper hair, but prettier. She was probably in her late fifties or early sixties, with grey-blue eyes. She put on a pair of glasses and scanned the room, taking everyone in.

Once everyone was settled, she spoke for about fifteen minutes about how she got started as a writer, and then did a reading from her latest book, *The People Who Live In My Head*. It was so brilliant I'd read it in three nights. It was about a woman who went on a self-awareness-type course and did an exercise where she had to write down her sub-personalities and give them all names – all the different people she was in different situations. I thought it was a great idea because it's true – our behaviour does change depending on where we are and who we're with and we almost become like different people. In Leila's book, one of the sub-personalities tries to take over and suppress the others and, in the end, all her alter egos gang up on her and then they go into therapy together. Some parts of it were very funny and made me laugh out loud, and other parts made me think. I knew all about sub-personalities because of Noola, the inner alien girl that lives in my head and makes an appearance whenever a cute boy is around. It can be so embarrassing as I start to talk gibberish or alienese.

After the reading, Leila asked the audience if anyone had any questions. I had loads, but felt shy to put my hand up as even just thinking about asking a question made my heart beat faster. Plus Ollie was sitting next to me. I didn't want to make a fool of myself by saying the wrong thing or going blank.

Ollie, on the other hand, wasn't at all shy. His hand shot straight up. 'Were the sub-personalities in your book made up or were they actually yours?'

Leila smiled and raised an eyebrow. 'Well, I'd be giving away a lot if I admitted that they were all mine, wouldn't I? And people might think I was crazy and a half.'

'I wouldn't,' said Ollie. 'I think we all have lots of different sides to us.'

Leila smiled again. 'OK, then let's just say that the characters in the book aren't that far removed from the ones that actually do live in my head.'

Ollie had broken the ice with his question and, after that, loads of people put their hands up asking different things: where she got her inspiration from, how long it took her to write a book, what was she working on next and so on. In the end, she didn't have time to answer all the questions people had, and urged those who hadn't had a chance to speak to her to get in touch through her website.

Excellent, I thought, as I jotted down the website address in the notebook I'd brought. I'd have no problem e-mailing her my question, asking for her top tip for wannabe writers.

After the talk, Ollie and I walked out to the pavement to discover that it had started raining whilst we were inside listening to Leila. Ollie looked over at the café next to the bookshop. 'Got time for a coffee?' he asked. 'My treat.'

I nodded. I could hardly say no after the effort he'd made to see me. I felt flattered that he'd gone to the trouble of not only tracking down where I was going to be, but also doing some homework and buying Leila's book. No boy had ever spent that much time on my behalf before.

'So . . . did you actually read the book?' I asked after we had found a table in the café and put in our orders.

Ollie smiled. 'I do like reading. I read a lot, but it's always good to get a recommendation for a new writer – well, new to me if you know what I mean. You sounded such a fan of Leila's when you spoke about her on the phone. And yes, I did read and enjoy her book.'

The next half an hour flew by as we talked about books, our families, school, our mates and our goals. His life was so different to mine. He was a boarder at a private school in Kensington and his parents live in what sounds like an amazing place down in Cornwall, in a mansion with acres of land. They even have a housekeeper.

'It sounds soooo glamorous,' I said. 'Your dad a rock star and your sister a model and your mum an ex-model. Mine are so boring. Both of them are doctors and their idea of a fun time is listening to Radio Four on a Sunday and pottering in the garden.'

Ollie smiled. 'That's not too far removed from what my mum

and dad like to do. We live a pretty quiet life down there apart from the odd party. Mum loves to throw parties. You should come down sometime, we have loads of spare rooms. You met Star at the do last week, but you could meet my other sister, Lia. She's only a year younger than you.'

Your family are *so* different from mine, I thought. I couldn't imagine ever inviting Ollie to stay with us. For one thing the spare rooms are full of junk and, for another, my Scary Dad doesn't even like my girl friends being over, never mind a boy.

I told Ollie that I wanted to be a writer when I left school and he told me that he was still undecided but might study drama and go into acting. He was so easy to be with, charming and interested in me. Not at all how I'd imagined him when I first met him. I'd thought he might be full of himself, the way some really good-looking boys are.

'So . . .' said Ollie as he paid the bill when we'd finished our drinks. 'You want to be a writer. Have you written down your SPs?'

'SPs?'

'Sub-personalities.'

I laughed. 'Might have done.'

'I did,' he said. 'In the cab on the way up here.' He pulled a piece of paper out of his jacket pocket. 'Want to look?'

'How many are there?'

'Eight,' he said, and began to read his list. '"Son", because I'm one person with my parents. "Friend", because I'm definitely different with my mates to how I am with Mum and Dad. "Casanova" . . ."'

'Casanova?'

'Yeah, my sister Lia calls me that. Casanova with the girls. She's only teasing . . .'

'So why does she call you that? Are you a Casanova?'

'Me. Nah. OK, maybe a little. I like girls' company, that's all. I like talking with them. Boys can be pretty stupid sometimes, and you can have a good conversation with most girls. No crime in that, eh?'

No, I thought. No crime, but I hoped that he wanted more than just a conversation with me.

'OK, so that's three,' I said.

'And then there's "Sports Jock", in fact that personality would be called Jock, then there's my studious side . . .'

'Has he got a name yet?'

'No.'

'Call him Nigel.'

'OK,' said Ollie. 'Nigel the nerd.'

'And call the Casanova one Max. I always think that's such a suave name and no doubt your Casanova sub-personality is very suave.'

Ollie frowned. 'OK, or maybe just plain Casanova and then there's no confusion. But . . . hhhmm. I might be giving away too much of myself here. Letting you know all my secrets. Come on, then. What about you? Tell me some of yours before I tell you any more of mine.'

'OK. I also have about eight so far. "Obedient Daughter". My mum and dad are pretty strict so I guess I'm a bit of a goodie-two-shoes type when I'm at home, you know, to keep the peace . . .'

'What's her name?'

'Just that: Goody Two Shoes. It used to be on my e-mail address.'

'Used to be? What is it now?'

'Er . . . oh, I can't remember.' I felt embarrassed to tell him in case he thought I was a bighead.

'Oh, come on. Mine is superstud@fastmail.org.'

I laughed. 'OK. My mates made me change it. So now it's Babe With Brains.'

Ollie gave me a long look. 'Suits you,' he said.

I felt myself getting hot around the back of my neck. It was very unsettling when he looked at me like that. Made my stomach lurch, but not in an unpleasant way.

'With my mates, I reckon I'm just TJ,' I continued. 'I think I'm the most myself with them . . . Um, but I play football and can be a demon on the pitch if I want to be. I'm also arm-wrestling champion. So there's her, the sporty one, Awesome-Arm Annie. Who else? There's the bookworm part of me who reads a lot, but she's probably the same as Goody Two Shoes.'

'What about with boys? Are you the female equivalent of Casanova?'

I burst out laughing. '*Me?* Oh no. No *way*. I turn into Noola the alien girl if ever I see a boy I fancy. My brain turns to mush and I talk gibberish.'

He laughed. 'Noola, huh?'

I couldn't believe that I'd told him about Noola and it was only the second time we'd met. I always thought people would think I was mad, but then Ollie had read Leila's book *and* come up with a whole crowd of his own personalities. If I was mad, so was he.

Ollie stuck out his bottom lip and pouted. 'So that means you don't fancy me. You're talking to me pretty normally.' He reached out and put his hand over mine. 'Noola, Noola don't you like me?'

I laughed. 'Niwingee, blerggghhhh, ehweh . . . See, that's what she sounds like. Like an alien on helium. Nihih. Ug.'

Ollie grinned. 'She *likes* me. Noola likes me. Thank God! So who else is in there?'

I decided not to tell him about the next one I'd put on my list. I called her Lola. She's the girl who came out when I was with Luke de Biasi. Passionate. Romantic. I didn't want to tell Ollie about her in case he asked when I'd discovered her.

'I can't tell you all of them,' I said. 'As then you would know everything about me and so I'd have to kill you, and that would be a shame seeing as we've only just met.'

Ollie laughed. 'I'm glad I came tonight. It's been good seeing you again.'

'Nihih. Ug,' I said, and he grinned even more.

'Noola's back,' he said.

When we left the café, it was still drizzling so we ducked into a shop entrance where I called Mum on my mobile and Ollie called a cab to take him back to his school. As we waited, I wondered if he would try to kiss me or not.

I didn't have to wonder for long.

I was looking in the shop window at the display of shoes when he put his arms round my waist and then turned me to face him. Then he pulled me close and nuzzled into my neck.

'Your hair smells nice,' he murmured. 'Clean. Like apples.'

'Unuh . . . apple shampoo.'

Then he nibbled on my ear lobe. It felt delicious. He turned my face up to his and gave me a kiss. Not a long one, but not short either. It was nice, gentle. He pulled away and I opened my eyes to look at him. He pulled me close again and this time gave me a deeper kiss. I felt my toes curl up and then had a sudden panic. What if Mum drove up and saw us? She'd have a fit if she caught me snogging my face off in the middle of Muswell Hill.

I pulled back. 'Er . . . Mum . . . er, be here . . .'

'No prob,' he said, and reached down and held my hand. 'And hello Goody Two Shoes. Nice to meet you. Can't have Mum catch you mid-snog. And on a school night too!'

I laughed. He was right. Goody Two Shoes had taken over. I hoped he didn't think I was acting childishly or anything. But he was still holding my hand so maybe he didn't mind too much.

'So which of your sub-personalities kissed me?' I asked.

'All of them. They all fancy you!'

I laughed. 'Kissed by eight guys all at the same time. Now that has to be a record. But hey, I don't know all of them yet.'

'Next time,' he said. 'That is, can we do this again?'

'Sure,' I said. I remembered what Nesta had said about there being a time to be cool and a time to say, "Hello sailor, mine's a Diet Coke". This wasn't the time to be cool.

'Maybe Saturday?' asked Ollie.

'Oh. Can't. I'm going to be decorating . . .' I started to say then began to laugh, 'but please don't feel that you have to read a book about interior design and come along and help.'

He laughed too. 'But that's just what I had in mind. I like surprising girls.'

Hmm, I thought. He likes surprising girls. Does that mean that he does this sort of thing a lot?

Just at that moment, his cab drew up and honked.

'I'll call you Saturday,' he said. 'And maybe we can find some more characters lurking within.'

'Deal,' I said, although secretly I thought no way was I telling him about all the people that live in my head. I'd never see him again if I revealed how mad I really am.

Amazing, I thought, as I watched him drive off in the taxi. A date with Ollie Axford. Me. And I've been kissed by him. And all his sub-personalities. It had been a great evening and we'd had a real laugh. He could probably have anyone, I thought. I wonder what on earth he sees in me.

TJ's Sub-personalities (SPs)

Goody Two Shoes: good girl, does her homework, is punctual, sensible and polite.

Awesome-Arm Annie, the Female Wrestler: football and arm-wrestling champion, a fighter, tomboy, swears like a trooper and will take anyone on.

Noola the Alien: the brainless dribbler I become when I meet cute boys – but she's appearing less often.

Lola: likes all the girlie stuff, perfume, a bit of make-up and boys. Loves Luke de Biasi.

Alice (after Alice in Wonderland): endlessly curious, likes to read about other people's lives and experiences in books, also likes to write, to go to galleries and exhibitions and experience everything that life can offer.

Beryl the Bag Lady: I like to be her on the weekend and slob around in old tracksuits with no make-up. Nesta has a fit if I become Beryl when she's around. Probably not one to mention to Ollie as I know that she's not my most attractive self.

Cassandra, the Prophetess of Doom: miserable old cow who lives at the back of my head. Always moaning – you'll never make it as a writer, you're not good enough, no boy will ever fancy you, you're too boring, you haven't got what it takes, loser. (I'd like to shoot Cassandra, but seeing as she is part of me, that's probably not a very good idea.)

Minnie the Mouse: very timid, hates confrontation and will run away and hide rather than face up to an argument or a difficult situation.

Sometimes one of the sub-personalities is more predominant, and sometimes they all talk at the same time. And debate things. And argue. It can get very tiresome having so many people living in my head.

Chapter 3

Kiss Rating

'Out of ten?' asked Nesta the next morning after I'd told the girls about my unexpected evening with Ollie. Of course they wanted all the details right down to how he rated as a kisser.

'Nine and a half,' I replied as we hurried along the corridor into school assembly with a swarm of other chattering girls. 'It was lovely but . . .'

'But what?' asked Izzie. 'Onion breath? Mouth too closed? Too open? Tongue like a wet fish? Teeth like piano keys?'

'Errghh, Izzie,' said Lucy. 'Who have you been kissing lately?'

'No one,' she groaned. 'That's why I can't remember a good kiss.'

'It wasn't like any of that,' I said. 'I don't know. It was lovely, but . . . it was as if he'd read how to do it right, you know? Or like he'd had a lot of practice. It was nice, though. I'm not complaining.'

'I know what you mean,' said Nesta. 'I've been kissed by boys like that. Little bit textbook. Like kissing by numbers. What you really want is someone to be so overwhelmed by their attraction to you they just seize you and go for it but without suffocating you or banging noses . . .'

'You mean like William did that day he kissed you for the first time?' asked Lucy. 'We all saw you. It was *très passionata*.'

'*Très* is French and *passionata* is Italian,' said Izzie, in an attempt to copy our language teacher's posh voice. 'At least, I think it is, so you are mixing your languages, young lady.'

'So?' said Lucy. 'It shows that I am multilingual.'

'Yeah, but I don't think you're meant to speak them all in the same sentence,' said Izzie.

'Says who?' said Lucy. 'Anyway, I like to be different.'

Très passionata. Muchos fabos. That was how Luke kissed me and I kissed him back on the one and only time that we snogged, I thought, though I didn't say that to the girls. I didn't want to let on how much I still thought about him. Kissing him had been like melting into a huge vat of marshmallow and chocolate. Perfect. Perfect.

We took our places in our class line-up in the hall and everyone fell silent as Mrs Allen, our headmistress, stood up and began the announcements. Shame we don't do lessons on the art of snogging – it would be very useful, I thought, as Mrs Allen droned on, and I imagined a new timetable: art, history and snog technique. Preferably being taught by members of our favourite boy band, brought in especially for the day. Now that would be an education.

'So can you take me to Homebase?' I asked Mum when I got

in from school. She was in the kitchen, stirring a pan of soup on the stove. The aroma of onions and garlic filled the air.

She shook her head. 'I've got to go back to the surgery after I've done this,' she said as she indicated the soup. 'Dr Plewes has some virus thing so I said I'd do her evening shift for her. Can't it wait until tomorrow after school?'

'Got a meeting for the mag,' I said. (I work as editor for our school magazine, *For Real*, along with Emma Ford from Year Eleven.)

'Saturday morning?'

'That's when I was hoping to start. See, Nesta, Lucy and Izzie have promised that they would come over first thing and I said that I'd have the paint by then. And I've got footie practice in the afternoon. What's Dad doing? Is he home yet?'

Mum jerked her chin towards the living room. 'He's having a snooze,' she said. 'Wasn't feeling too great when he got in. Might be a touch of hayfever at this time of year. I've had a lot of people coming in complaining of it and it can make some people feel quite poorly. He doesn't feel like much supper, so I thought I'd do something light like chicken soup.'

I went through to where Dad was sitting in his armchair with his eyes closed, listening to some piano concerto on a classical music station on the radio.

I went over to him and put my hand on his arm. 'Hey Dad ...'

'Umph ...' he started as he awoke. 'Wha ...?'

'Can you take me to Homebase?'

He rubbed his eyes wearily and glanced at his watch. 'What, now? No. I don't think so.' And he settled into his chair, laid his head back and closed his eyes again.

'Ohhh, Dad, pleeeease . . .'

'Go away. I'm sleeping.'

'But Dad . . . I really need to go now and Mum can't take me and it will only take us half an hour and I won't be able to carry it all on the bus. I know exactly the paint I want and Mum did promise I could do my room and you won't have to do any of the painting because my mates are all going to do that. All you have to do is take me to Homebase and then you can come back and lie in that chair all night and I'll make you a cup of tea and I won't bother you for another moment. I promise.'

Dad opened his eyes and frowned at me. 'God, what a nuisance you are. Like a bee buzzing around in a closed room. Can't a man get even five minutes rest in his own home?'

'Course he can,' I said. 'Only later.' Dad's not as bad-tempered as he sometimes sounds. He likes to stomp about and huff and puff, but underneath it all he's a softie.

He got up and stretched. 'Come on, then. You've woken me up now. Let's get it over with.'

Mum came into the room behind us. 'Are you sure you're all right, Richard?' she asked. 'You're looking a little grey still. How's the head?'

'Well, I was all right,' he said, 'until this nuisance woke me up with her one of her endless demands.'

Mum went over to Dad and put her hand on his forehead. 'I don't know. I think you should maybe go to bed. TJ's paint can wait for another time.'

'Ohhhhhhhhh Muuuuuuuuuuum . . .' I began. 'He said he would . . .'

Dad threw his hands in the air. 'See what I mean? No rest. I'll go to bed when we get back. That's if she's not got another list of things that have to be done right away.'

I grinned up at him. 'Nope. Just the paint. Thanks, Dad. You're a star.'

'I'll wait here and you go and get what you want,' said Dad, and he took a seat in a quiet corner opposite the checkout. Mum had been right, he didn't look too bright, and for a moment I felt my conscience twinge about dragging him out.

'Won't be a mo,' I said. I knew exactly the colours I wanted: Indian sunset, which was a mustard yellow, and Brick Lane, which was a lovely brick red. I'd seen the colour combination in the *Beautiful Homes* magazine that Nesta had brought round and thought it looked fantastic. I'd tried the sample pots of both of them and in all lights, morning and evening, the patches I'd painted looked warm and rich. Once I'd got all my nick-nacks and Indian artefacts in, the overall look was going to be amazing.

I picked out the paints that I needed and took them back to Dad. He got out his wallet and handed me a twenty pound note. 'You go and pay,' he said. 'I'll wait for you here.'

'Oh . . . Um. It's a bit more than that,' I said.

'How much?' said Dad, rooting round in his pocket. 'I've got some spare change in here somewhere.'

I took the seat next to him for a moment. 'Dad, this isn't any old paint. It's made by a company who specialise in recreating colours from old buildings and dynasties in the past. They're designed to have depth on the walls and capture the changing light.'

Dad snorted with laughter. 'Oh, for heaven's sake, TJ, you sound like an advert. Don't be so gullible. I'd have thought you'd have known better than to fall for tosh like that. Depth. Dynasties. Rubbish. Paint is paint. Designer paint? Whatever next?' He pointed at a stand displaying a special offer on huge tubs of white emulsion. 'Look over there. Get some of that. A lick of that will brighten your room and you'll have money to spare.'

'But, Dad, you don't understand. I'm going for a particular look . . .'

Dad rolled his eyes. 'And what, pray, is that?'

'Eastern. All the spice colours that they use in places like India, Thailand . . .'

'And what would you want to paint your room in spice colours for? Because you've been taken in by some silly promotion that says that this is the next best thing, the trend, the fashion . . .'

Oh here we go, I thought, lecture time. Dad likes nothing better than to get on his high horse sometimes and let everyone know exactly what he thinks about the state of the world.

'I'd have thought a girl with your intelligence would have seen through all of that. Nope. Plain white. Can't go wrong with it. And it's cheap.'

I sighed. 'Look, Dad, I haven't been taken in by anything and I don't want my room to look all white and clinical like a hospital ward. And it's not really designer paint, well, not exactly. You're just out of touch with what it all costs. Interiors and gardens are what people are into these days. Making their home space the best they can. And I've done my homework. I've been experimenting with sample pots and the colours I've chosen really do look good. You'll see. But if you really think it's all too expensive then I'll pay you back half out of my next few weeks' pocket money.'

Dad wasn't really listening. 'Waste of money . . .' he grunted.

I had to make him understand.

'No, Dad, it's not a waste of money. This is really important to me. You don't realise sometimes how embarrassing it is when people come over to our house. It's like . . . so last century . . .'

Wrong thing to say.

'If you are spending time with people who judge a person by such trivialities as what colour their bedroom is, then I pity you, Theresa Watts.'

'No. They're not like that. Don't judge them. You don't understand. Oh . . . sometimes I wish . . . I wish I had a different father. One who understood or at least *tried* to!'

'Theresa!' said Dad. 'Don't you speak to me like that. You'll be sent straight to your room when we get back and no seeing those friends of yours for a week.'

But it was as if a dam had burst inside of me and I couldn't stop the torrent that came out. I felt like he was treating me like an eight-year-old. 'But it's true. And you're so unwelcoming. I hate having mates over when you're in. I can't enjoy it for fear that you're going to blast through the door at any moment and make me look like an idiot by turfing them out, or telling them to keep the noise down like we're a bunch of kids. Ever wondered why my mates don't hang out much at our house and we always go somewhere else? It's because of *you* . . .' I suddenly got a feeling that I might have gone too far. I glanced up at him.

He didn't look angry. Even worse. He looked disappointed. Or tired. He got out a twenty pound note and a ten pound note and waved them at me, then got up wearily. 'Here. Go on. Take it. I can't be bothered arguing. You go and pay. Take the car keys and I'll meet you at the car. I've just remembered a few things I need to get while I'm here. Light bulbs . . .'

I took the money and the keys, went to the till and paid for my purchases. Even with the amount he'd given me, I had to add what I had left of my pocket money to meet the cost. I felt cross with Dad. He can be such a stick in the mud sometimes. Cantankerous old bugger, I thought, as I put the paint in a bag and went out to the car. I was wrong at home earlier when I'd thought that he has a soft centre. He hasn't. He's just gone rotten inside.

Once I'd slammed the boot shut on the paint, sat down in the passenger seat and taken some deep breaths, I calmed down. Oops, I thought. Might have pushed my luck a bit there. I'm usually Goody Two Shoes with Dad. It's the easiest way to be, but some other sub-personality had escaped and had her say. One with a very big mouth! I'll have to think about giving her a name . . . Nesta. I laughed to myself, as she's usually the one out of all of us who speaks before she thinks. I could call my inner-loud mouth Nesta mark two.

As I sat waiting in the car, I began to feel guilty about my outburst. Dad's not so bad, really. Just a bit grumpy sometimes. Maybe I am too. Like father, like daughter. I decided that I would apologise when he got back to the car and make him a special tea tray with the ginger biscuits he likes when we got home.

Dad seemed to be taking ages, so I listened to the car radio for a while then continued concocting an apology in my head. After a while, my mobile rang.

'Hello,' said a male voice.

'Hello,' I said.

'Who am I talking to?'

I recognised the voice as Ollie's. 'I'm not sure,' I said. 'I think I've just met a new character in my head. A very stroppy one.'

'What's her name?'

'Nest . . . no . . . I'll call her Susie the strop queen, I think. Yeah. That fits. Who am I talking to?'

'Er . . . Jock,' he replied. 'I've just finished a squash match so I guess it's my sporty persona that's predominant. Hey, do you think that if Jock had a surname, it would be Strap?'

'Good one,' I said. 'I used to collect mad names and the books they'd written, like Chest Complaints by Ivor Tickliecoff. That sort of thing. Drink Problems by Imorf Mihead. Run to the Loo by Willie Makeit.'

Ollie cracked up laughing. 'Hey, did you e-mail Leila your question?'

'Yes, but she hasn't answered yet.'

'Where are you? I can hear traffic in the background. Sirens.'

'Yeah,' I said as the sirens got louder and an ambulance whizzed past. 'I'm in the carpark at Homebase, waiting for Dad.'

'Sounds like you're in the middle of Piccadilly Circus.'

I turned to see what was going on and saw that the ambulance had stopped at the entrance. Men had got out of the back and were rushing into the store with a stretcher. 'Guess someone's taken ill,' I said. 'It's like ER and they're going in.'

'You said your dad is a doctor, didn't you?' asked Ollie.

'Yeah.'

'So maybe he's in there doing mouth to mouth and that thumping the chest thing they do . . .'

'Yeah. Knowing Dad, he'll be supervising everybody. I'd better go and haul him out or we'll be here all night. Look, I'll call you later, hey?'

'Oh . . . OK.'

I cut Ollie off as I'd suddenly had a strange feeling that something was wrong. I got out of the car and ran back into the store to find Dad. To the right of the till, I could see the ambulance men bent over someone on a stretcher, giving them oxygen. I glanced at the people around. No sign of Dad. Maybe he hadn't got involved after all.

I ran up and down a few aisles to see where he'd got to. Light bulbs, he'd said, but there was no sign of him in the electrical department. A cold shiver ran down my spine.

Oh God, I thought, as I raced back to the front of the store. The paramedics were rushing to get someone into the ambulance. They looked very worried.

I chased after them to see who was on the stretcher, but the man carrying the rear part of it blocked my view.

I could see the patient's shoes clear enough, though.

Expensive looking.

Black brogues.

Dad's.

Chapter 4

Dear God, This is TJ

Waiting for Mum to arrive at the hospital.

Waiting for the doctors to tell me something. Anything.

Waiting. Waiting. Waiting as people in white coats rushed in and out of the room where they'd taken Dad. A young doctor introduced himself as Dr Miller and asked me to wait outside. He directed me to a corner where there were four rows of orange plastic chairs.

I didn't like the smell of the place, a mix between disinfectant and boiled vegetables. Not nice. I sat there for a while and tried to distract myself by looking through one of last year's magazines that were in a well worn pile on the window ledge, but I couldn't concentrate. The words seemed to swim in front of me. I wanted to phone my mates but I knew that mobiles aren't allowed to be used in hospitals, and I didn't want to go outside in case Mum arrived or Dr Miller came out. I thought about texting, but I wasn't sure if that was allowed either and didn't want to risk it. It would be too awful if I used my phone and it interfered with someone's life support machine and they died as a result and then I'd be responsible for killing *two* people in here. I could have used the public phone at the end of the corridor, but I hadn't got any change left. I'd spent it all on that stupid paint. All thoughts of decorating my room seemed a million miles away now. Irrelevant. A stupid idea. If it wasn't for me pushing Dad to take me to Homebase, this might not have happened. Who would want a gorgeous bedroom and no dad? Oh God, I hope he's OK, I thought for the hundredth time. I soooo wish I hadn't said all those terrible things to him.

I remembered a poem that we did in school that starts: *Time is too slow for those that wait*. Tell me about it, I thought, as I got up and paced the corridor. I can't stay here, I'm going mad, I decided, and set off for the escalator and down to the entrance on the ground floor to look for Mum.

An assortment of people flowed in and out the automatic doors. All ages. A bald man on crutches, a teenage girl with a broken arm, a pregnant lady, lots of old people. Outside, I could see people on the grass verge opposite having a sneaky fag and catching the last rays of sun. Inside, people were making enquiries at the information desk, and buying flowers, chocolates, books or magazines at the shop at the back. In and out, in and out people went. It felt unreal. Like a dream. Or nightmare. So many with an urgent look on their face, like me, concerned about a loved one. In a hurry to get somewhere. But where was Mum? Surely she should have been here by now, I thought as I checked my watch. Oh God, please don't let anything have happened to her, too. Maybe I'd missed her and she was going up in the lift when I was going down the escalator.

I raced back up to the first floor, back to the rows of chairs where I'd been told to wait, but she wasn't there. Just empty seats.

Back down the corridor.

Back down the escalator.

My jaw felt so tight. I cursed the fact that Mum didn't have a mobile. No need, they both said. What do we need those newfangled things for, they'd asked. For times like *this,* I thought.

Back to the entrance.

An ambulance flew by and pulled up in the emergency bay. More people coming and going.

Where was Mum?

I was about to call Izzie when at last I saw Mum hurrying across the forecourt. Her face was drawn and anxious. I waved when I saw her and ran out to join her.

She gave me a brief hug as we both walked back inside. 'Oh, TJ. Where is he? A and E?'

I motioned towards the escalator. 'They rushed him through upstairs. First floor. What did they tell you when they called?'

'They didn't really tell me a lot over the phone. Just to get here as quickly as I could,' she said, as we stepped on to the escalator. 'It took me forever to get here, and then the parking – it's a disgrace. I've been driving round and round, and in the end I just had to leave it. Probably get clamped. What's been happening?'

'They haven't told me anything – although when we got here, I think I heard one of them say that he might have had a stroke. What does that mean exactly? Will he be all right?'

Mum took a quick intake of breath. 'I don't know, TJ. Not until I've spoken with the doctors.'

We reached the top of the escalator and stepped off on to the first floor.

'This way,' I said, and led Mum back to where I had been waiting. I showed her the row of chairs. 'They asked me to wait here.'

Mum looked around. It was clear she had no intention of sitting down and waiting. 'Which room is he in?' she asked.

I pointed to the room along the corridor. 'In there. But they wouldn't let me in.'

'You stay here,' she said. 'I'll find out what's happening.'

I sank down on to one of the chairs while Mum charged along the corridor and knocked on the door I'd pointed out to her.

The door opened a crack. I heard hushed voices – Mum's raised – then she disappeared inside.

Once again, I was on my own. Waiting, waiting, waiting.

My imagination went into an overdrive of scary scenarios: the doctors coming out and saying it was all over, nothing they could do. A funeral, Marie, Paul, Mum and I in black. A headstone saying R. Watts. Mum sleeping alone in their big, wide bed, their wardrobe of clothes, his side empty . . .

Stop it, I told myself, *stop* it, stop it. I could hardly breathe. He'll be all right. He's my dad. He's always all right.

To stop myself thinking black thoughts, I got up and went into the Ladies by the escalator. I felt like crying and I felt like kicking something, both at the same time. Angry, mad, sad. I kicked the tiled wall by the sink.

'Owwwwww!' I cried, as bone met tile. It felt like I'd broken my toe.

I went and sat in a cubicle, reached for a tissue but no tears would come. I felt so alone and helpless and never more in need of my friends. Should I go outside and call Izzie, Lucy or Nesta, I asked myself. What could they say? What would I tell them? Plus, I didn't want to wander too far in case Mum came out again. I still felt numb with disbelief that this could be happening. For the millionth squillionth time that evening, I played over in my head the argument I'd had with Dad in Homebase. Why had I said such terrible things? That I wished I had a different father. That I hated having my mates over when he was home. Awful things. I must have really hurt him. I hoped he knew I didn't mean it. I wish I could tell Mum what I'd said and she could pat my hand and say, Oh TJ, you didn't mean that, like she'd done a thousand times when I'd been letting off steam about him after he'd been grumpy. But he'd never had a stroke before. Was what I'd said the last straw for him? Was I to blame? I so wished I could talk to someone about it, one of my mates or Marie or Paul, but I didn't know if I could bear to see or hear their reaction when I told them what I'd said. They'd try and cover it, but inside they'd be thinking, What a mean girl. All the things I was thinking myself.

I felt so ashamed. If people knew what I was really like, I thought, they'd hate me. Hannah would have understood. I thought about going outside and texting her, but decided against it until I had a clearer idea of what was happening. I didn't want to freak her out. I still missed her. We often used to have a moan about our dads as hers was a headmaster and very strict with her. Funnily enough, though, she'd always got on with my dad and could say cheeky things to him that I'd never have got away with in a million years. But that was Hannah. She was so totally bonkers that everybody loved her, even my dad.

I got up, went over to the window and looked out at the evening sky.

How could it all have happened so quickly? One moment you're shopping for paint, and the next your whole life might be altered for ever. My chest tightened with fear.

'Dear God, this is TJ. If you're up there, please, *please* let my dad live. Please don't let what I said to him be the last words between us,' I said to the sky.

Why am I talking to the sky? I wondered. Why would God be up there? They've sent rockets up far enough and they've never come back with any evidence of anything along those lines. There's a sun and stars up there, other solar systems too, but no God and angels. And even if there was, how was he going to hear me from such a long way away. I decided to give it another go anyway.

'Oh God. *Are* you there? *Is* anybody listening?'

If there is anyone out there, I thought, why should he listen to *me*? I'm in a hospital full of sick people and probably all their relatives and friends are praying, at this very moment, leaning out of the windows in the toilets dotted around the hospital on every floor. Please God help us, please God help my dad, my mum, my sister, daughter, son, brother, friend. Over and over again. But people get sick. And die. So if there is a God, why should he, she or it help *me*? Horrible me with the mean tongue. I wished Izzie was here. She thinks a lot about God and life and death and stuff. She might know who to pray to and what to say. If anyone had a hotline to anybody up there, it would be Iz.

I blew my nose and decided to go down and out into the forecourt to call her or Nesta or Lucy, but just as I stepped back into the corridor, I saw Mum come out of Dad's room and look round for me. Her face was as white as the walls and as I raced down to join her, a thought flashed through my mind that Dad must have been mad to have suggested that I paint my room at home that colour. Such a reminder of illness and hospitals and doctors and worry. I'd have thought he'd have wanted to get away from it and flood his life outside with the brightest colours imaginable.

'How is he?' I asked.

Mum sat down heavily on one of the plastic chairs. She looked worn out. 'They've confirmed that he's had a stroke,' she said. 'They're doing tests.'

'What does having a stroke mean, exactly? Will he get better?'

'TJ, stop asking that. We don't know,' snapped Mum, then took a deep breath. 'No one knows at this stage. It depends how bad it was. Some people make full recoveries. Others don't. It's too early to tell, really.' She reached out and put her hand over mine. 'One thing we do know, though, and that is he's a tough old bird.'

'Worst case scenario,' I said. This was a term I'd heard Mum use when talking to Dad about her patients. I knew she'd understand what I wanted to know.

'Worst case? Hopefully it won't come to worst case. Your father's been an active man . . .'

'Mum, I want to know. Nothing could be worse than what I've been sitting here imagining.'

'I don't want to alarm you, TJ. It's too early to say anything for certain.' She patted my knee. 'One of us ought to give Marie and Paul an update. They'll be worried as I let them know that Dad had been brought here before I left home. I'll go and call them, then I'm going back in with your dad for a while. Why don't you go and get both of us something to drink from that shop downstairs while I go and make the calls? I'm parched.'

I stood up and my legs felt wobbly, like someone had taken the bones out. I made myself take a deep breath. I have to keep it together, I thought, for Mum and for Dad. 'OK. And Dad? Would he like anything? Shall I get him a cup of tea?'

Mum's eyes misted over and she took my hand again. 'Not at the moment, love. He's not quite up to cups of tea yet. Maybe later.'

Seeing Mum's eyes fill with tears made my eyes water, too. Up until then, I'd felt too numb. Not sure of what was going on. But seeing Mum's reaction, I now knew.

It was really serious.

And it was all my fault.

> *Time is too slow for those who wait,*
> *Too swift for those who fear,*
> *Too long for those who grieve,*
> *Too short for those who rejoice,*
> *But for those who love, time is eternity.*

Henry Van Dyke (1852 –1933)

Chapter 5

Guru Schmuru

'Don't ask me,' groaned Izzie, as we walked out arm in arm to the playground at lunch the following day. 'I don't know . . .'

'But you're always reading books about God and different religions and meditating . . .' I said as we took up our positions on a bench, ready to take advantage of the early summer sun that we'd been having lately.

'That's because I'm looking for answers. And I'm looking for answers because I don't have any,' said Izzie.

Tell me about it, I thought. I had so many questions, and it felt weird to be at school when I knew that Dad was in the hospital and still in a serious condition. I wanted to be there with him. I was desperate to know that he was all right and then, when it was appropriate, to apologise for the awful things that I had said. I'd called Izzie, Lucy and Nesta when I'd got home and we'd talked for ages on the phone about what had happened. I told them everything and not one of them made me feel bad about what I'd said. All of them said over and over again that it wasn't my fault. Izzie even offered to come over and sleep at my house, but I told her not to as it was so late. I didn't sleep a wink – I kept thinking about Dad and felt exhausted when it was time to get up and go to school. Marie and Paul were at the hospital as they'd both driven through the night when they'd heard the news (Marie from Devon and Paul from Bristol), but Mum had insisted that I went to school and tried to carry on as normal. Normal. Hah! I couldn't concentrate on anything. I felt like my brain was full of bubbles and my stomach full of knots.

Lucy, Izzie and Nesta did their best to comfort me, waiting at the gates for me with hugs and sympathy. I could feel them watching me every minute through morning classes, but even their kindness couldn't take away the fear and shame I felt inside.

'Do you want anything?' asked Nesta. 'Drink? Sandwich? Naked boy to dance in front of you to take your mind off things?'

The image of a naked boy prancing about the playground being chased by Miss Watkins did make me laugh for a moment but I shook my head.

'No thanks. I'm off naked boys this week. Maybe next week. You can bring in a coach-load of them then.'

'Sure,' said Nesta, squeezing my arm, then reaching into her bag and getting out her tiny lip-gloss tin. 'Here. Use this. You don't want your lips to get dry in the sun. And let me know if you change your mind about the dancing boys.'

I took the lip-gloss and lifted the lid. The familiar scent of Nesta's strawberry gloss was strangely reassuring. I applied a little then passed it on to Izzie. 'I will. To tell you the truth, I'm off boys, period. Ollie phoned me yesterday and then texted later after I got back from the hospital, but I don't even feel like talking to him at the moment.'

'I wish there was something we could do to help,' said Nesta. 'I hate seeing you like this.'

'You can help. You can tell me if there's a God or not,' I said.

Nesta laughed. 'Ah,' she said. 'You might have got me stumped there.'

Lucy got her sunglasses out of her bag, put them on and tilted her head up towards the sun. 'Of course there's a God,' she said. 'Has to be. It's obvious.'

'How?' I asked.

Lucy held up her hands. 'Just look around you. Where did it all come from if there isn't a God?'

'Big bang,' I said. 'Universe expanding. Evolution.'

Lucy shook her head. 'Nah. There has to be an intelligent being behind it all. There are too many fab things to look at. Birds. Fish. Animals. Flowers. That's the proof for me. In the same way that you can't have a painting without a painter, you can't have this creation without a creator.'

'OK, but where?' I asked.

Lucy laughed. 'You mean like his address? I don't know. Although when I was a kid I used to write to God and post my letters in the postbox.'

'Me too,' said Izzie. 'And I always used to put on airmail stickers. I imagined God up in the sky somewhere.'

'Yeah. Why is that?' I asked. 'Why do we talk to the sky?'

Izzie shrugged.

'I used to write to Santa Claus,' I said. 'And address the letters to the North Pole.'

'And then put them by the chimney,' said Lucy. 'We all did.'

Up until then, Nesta had been munching on a peanut butter sandwich and listening. She swallowed her last bite. 'OK, Lucy,' she said. 'I can understand your no creation without a creator bit, yeah, but it's not all beautiful is it? It's not all flowers and birds. Like if God created it *all*, why is there so much pain and war . . .'

'God didn't make that,' said Lucy. 'The human race did. It's not God who makes bombs and guns, it's people.'

'But according to your theory, creator behind creation, etc., then the creator made everything down here. So God made the human race too, yeah?' said Nesta.

Lucy nodded.

'If that's the case,' Nesta continued, 'then he must have known that some humans would have a nasty streak. If your God is so top, Lucy, what about snakes and crocodiles and oh . . . all the things in creation that are horrible . . . If God made them too then he's got a nasty streak.' She batted away a wasp that was flying around near her head. 'And wasps! Explain them! Horrible things.'

'And is God a he, she or it? Which, Lucy?' asked Izzie.

Lucy pushed her glasses down along her nose and peered at us. '*Stop* ganging up on me,' she said. '*I'm* not an expert. I just believe that there is something, that's all, and it makes me feel good to pray sometimes. I can't explain it, but *don't* give *me* a hard time over it. And in answer to your question, Iz, God's a she. Haven't you seen those T-shirts with the slogan, *When God made man, she was only joking*? Makes sense to me.'

'Haven't your books told you *anything*, Iz?' I asked.

Izzie shrugged her shoulders. 'Some say that God isn't so much like the clichéd, white-bearded old bloke, but more like a force or energy . . .'

'Yeah,' said Nesta. 'Makes more sense. Like in *Star Wars* . . . may the Force be with you . . .'

'But we don't know where it is or why it is . . .' I said. 'Freaky when you think about it.'

Nesta got out her sunglasses and laid her head back like Lucy. 'Phew, it's hot!' she said, gesturing at the sky. 'Listen guys, the sun is shining, the sky is blue, we have each other. My philosophy is just get on with life and have a good time while you can. You could drive yourself mad questioning it all.'

'I can't help it,' said Izzie. 'I really want to know why we're here and what for and where we go when we die and where we were before we were born.'

'Just accept that you have a pea brain,' said Nesta. 'Some things are just tooooo darn big for you to understand.'

Izzie playfully thumped her arm. 'Me? A pea brain? Cheek. You're right, though. Looking for answers can drive you mad. The number of times I've asked teachers and my parents. No one's told me anything for sure.'

'Where do people go when they die, Izzie?' I asked.

'Devon,' said Izzie, giggling. 'Remember I told you about that little boy at my stepsister's wedding? He said that prayer. Our Father, who art in heaven . . . only he said Devon. If only it was that easy and you got his address and phone number in the telephone directory, like, Doctor: 142 Baronsmere Road; Plumber: 56 High Street; God: 28 Paradise Close, Devon.'

'I reckon the only way to find out what happens when you die,' said Nesta, 'is to die and find out.'

'There are books on the afterlife,' said Izzie, 'and loads of stuff on the Internet about people who have had near death experiences. Most of them said it was wonderful and took away their fear ...'

'Yeah, but how do we know it wasn't a dream or wishful thinking?' asked Nesta. 'And all that stuff that's in books, most of it's speculation. We don't *really* know, do we? You know what I think it must be like, dying?'

'What?' I asked.

'Like going to the airport and knowing full well that you're going on a journey, only no luggage allowed. No make-up, no mags or mobile phones. And you don't know the destination.'

'Really, *really* freaky,' I said with a shudder.

'Might be, might not be,' said Nesta. 'Thing is, though, we don't know. None of us. But what we do know is this: here we are *now*. We're mates. Life is OK — most of the time, anyway.' She smiled sympathetically at me. 'So as I said before, stop freaking yourself out thinking about how it might be and enjoy what is.'

'Wow,' said Izzie. 'That is so Zen, Nesta. You know, you're quite wise in your own stupid way.'

Nesta grinned. 'Ta. Just called me Guru Schmuru.'

I looked around at the three of them. Maybe mates are proof that there's some good in the world, I thought. Never mind angels or airy fairy stuff you can't see. I've got the real thing with Izzie, Lucy and Nesta.

'And I don't think it does any harm to pray now and again,' said Lucy. 'In case anyone *is* listening.'

Izzie put her hand on mine. 'You're thinking about all this because of your dad, aren't you?' she asked.

I nodded. 'Sort of. Does make you think, doesn't it? You know, when something like this happens.'

'What did your mum say when you rang at break?' asked Nesta.

'She said he's stable but he's still not able to talk or move much. Mum says he knows she's there, though. She told him to blink if he understood what she was saying, and he blinked five times.'

'He'll be OK,' said Nesta. 'He's Scary Dad. He won't go down without a fight.'

I wished I could be as sure as she sounded. And I wished that I could believe that there was a God who listened the way that Lucy believed. I decided to put my uncertainty aside and pray anyway. I had nothing to lose, so each night I prayed that Dad would recover fully, that I'd get a chance to apologise and that he'd be able to come home soon. I wasn't sure if anyone or anything was listening, but somehow it made me feel better to talk through my thoughts, hopes and fears out loud.

Every day we visited the hospital and each day there wasn't much change. I was allowed in to see Dad, but I wasn't sure he even knew that I was there, even though he did blink in reply when I asked questions. Most of the time he looked like he was asleep, and it was horrible seeing him strapped to all sorts of machines. I so wanted to apologise to him, but wasn't sure he would hear me.

There was talk of a convalescent home.

Talk of physiotherapists.

Talk of wonder drugs.

But nobody really knew how things were going to develop. It was awful seeing Mum around the house. She was so quiet and looked so strained, and I realised how dependent Dad and she were on each other. I was reliant on my mates and hadn't even known them that long. Dad had been Mum's companion for almost forty years, and without him grumping about the place she seemed lost and didn't know what to do with herself.

She went into work as normal, saying that there was no point in her sitting around moping and that she still had her own patients to see. Marie fussed about cleaning, cooking and insisting that we all ate properly to keep our strength up. I think it gave her something to do, although the endless scones and quiches she made inevitably got binned as no one had much appetite. Paul mainly occupied himself by lying on the sofa watching hours of daytime telly. Mum would normally have told him 'to get off his backside and do something useful' but she didn't tell him off once. She didn't say anything about Mojo sleeping on the end of my bed every night either. Even he seemed to have picked up on the fact that something was wrong and was being especially attentive to me.

The atmosphere in the house was so subdued that I was grateful that the girls insisted that I spent time at their houses whenever I wasn't at school or the hospital. They were my strawberry-scented guardian angels, always on hand at break and lunch with chocolate, lip-gloss, magazines and chat to try and take my mind off things. They seemed to understand that I wasn't in the mood for talking a lot so we'd just hang out, reading magazines or soaking up the sun.

Ollie e-mailed but I didn't feel like answering. He also texted a couple of times. I let him know that Dad was ill so he didn't think that I was rude not replying, but when he texted back again I sent a message that I'd be in touch properly when things were better. In my experience, boys upset the balance and my balance was upset enough as it was at the moment.

Five days after Dad had been in the hospital, Mum got a call saying that he was showing signs of coming round fully. We raced to the hospital and there he was sitting up a little and looking very grumpy. He was still weak, but he could clearly see and he could definitely hear and talk and feel.

I'd never felt so relieved in my life.

'We'll have him back up and about in no time,' said Dr Miller. 'He's doing well.'

'Hrumph,' groaned Dad. 'Call this doing well? Your eyesight needs testing, man.'

After that his recovery was swift, and it wasn't long before Dad was back in his Scary Dad persona: ordering the nurses around, telling the doctors what to do, moaning about the food, being woken up too early, the noise, the hard bed, lumpy pillows and the man in the room next door who was snoring.

I was so happy to hear him and grinned every time he opened his mouth to complain. It meant Dad was back. He was getting better.

'A change of lifestyle,' said Dr Rolland, one of Dad's doctor friends who was over one evening for a visit. 'That's what you need, Richard. Take a break.'

'I will, I will,' said Dad. 'Just get me out of this place.'

'All in good time,' said Dr Rolland. 'Just a couple more days, but don't even think of getting back to your normal routine. Time off is what you need.'

Dad pulled a face and, for a moment, looked like a naughty schoolboy, but he nodded. 'Don't worry,' he said. 'I'm not an idiot.'

'Didn't say you were,' said Dr Rolland, 'but if you don't take heed of what your body's telling you, you will be.'

As a further sign that Dad was recovering, Marie and Paul went back to their respective homes. The night after they'd gone, I finally got some time alone with him.

'Um . . . Dad?'

'Yes?'

'About . . . well . . . about what happened . . . you know . . . at Homebase?'

Dad nodded.

'Yes. But before that, I . . . I said some awful things and I want you to know . . .' I felt a lump come into my throat and I didn't think I was going to be able to get the words out. 'I . . . I want you to know that I'm truly sorry and I didn't mean what I said and I do love . . .'

Dad put his hand over mine. 'Forgotten, TJ,' he said. 'We all say things in the heat of the moment, but you and I know what we really feel about each other, don't we?'

Tears pricked my eyes and Dad looked at me with such tenderness.

'Hey, hey,' he said and squeezed my hand. 'No need for the waterworks.'

I leaned over the bed and rested my head on his chest. 'I'm *so* glad you didn't die, Dad.'

'Me too, TJ,' he said softly. 'Me too.'

When God made man, she was only joking.

Chapter 6

Sweaty Betty

'Where are you off to?' asked Mum, the Thursday evening after we'd got back from the hospital. It was exactly one week since Dad had collapsed, but it felt like a lifetime.

'For a run,' I said, as I laced up my trainers and headed for the front door.

Mum gave me a quizzical look. 'But you're wearing make-up.'

'Never know who you might bump into,' I said, and waved. 'Back soon.'

I took off down our road and jogged over towards Cherry Tree Woods. I felt the need to work off some of the pent-up feelings and energy after the rollercoaster week with Dad. There was a light rain, but the evening was warm and it felt good to be out in the fresh, fragrant air after so many evenings cooped up in the hospital room with its airless, claustrophobic atmosphere. All the front gardens were beginning to flower –

pink montana and roses of every variety tumbled over porches, and pergolas, yellow laburnum and lilac trees dripped flowers over fences, while rhododendrons and azaleas budded in corners. I knew all the names because Mum'd taught me them when we used to go for walks when I was little.

I got to the park and, after once round, still felt I could go further so I ran towards Highgate and down to the Archway Road. As far as Biasi's, then I'd turn back, I thought. Biasi's was the restaurant owned by Luke's parents. He worked in there sometimes and, as I ran towards it and it came into view, I had an idea. I'd get a takeaway for Dad for his lunch tomorrow. Mum could take it in for him. He loved good Italian food and had complained non-stop about the hospital food since he'd been in there. I could go into Biasi's and get him something. I had a ten pound note in my pocket so it should be enough. He'd love it. I slowed my speed down so that when I arrived there, if by any chance Luke was working, I wouldn't look like a pink sweaty Betty.

There were only a few customers at tables when I pushed the door open and made my way over to the bar area, where a middle-aged man was talking to Mrs Biasi. She looked as glamorous as ever, in a low-cut red top showing off her ample cleavage. I didn't expect that she'd remember me as I'd only been in there once with Nesta and the others. It didn't matter. She seemed to treat everyone like they were her long lost friend.

'Eat, enjoy,' she was saying to the man as she handed him a takeaway carton. 'And come back soon, it's always good to see you, and bring that lovely wife of yours.'

I waited until she had finished, then took a step forward.

'Er . . . I wonder if you can help me. I want to order some food for my dad. He's in hospital so I thought my mum could take it to him for lunch tomorrow . . .'

Mrs Biasi's expression became concerned. 'Oh, your papa's not good, so sad,' she said.

'He'll be OK, I think. Just he hates the hospital food . . .'

'Understandable,' said Mrs Biasi, and she made a face like she had a bad smell under her nose. 'It not good.'

'So something light and fresh, I thought.'

'You good girl. You think right. We fix him something very nice in the kitchen. I have just the thing for him. You wait here. Eat olives,' she said as she thrust a bowl towards me then disappeared into the back. I popped an olive into my mouth. It was delicious. Then I looked around for Luke. There was no sign of him; only one Italian-looking girl serving the waiting customers. It felt strange to be on Luke's territory: exciting in one way as I knew that he might walk in at any moment, and scary in another as I wasn't sure how I'd react. Or how he would. It had been months since I'd seen him and the sharpness of his features had begun to dim in my mind. Was he really as gorgeous as I remembered? Would I feel the same about him? Now that I had met Ollie, I wanted to know if those feelings for Luke were still there.

Mrs Biasi came back about ten minutes later and handed me a bag that smelled of herbs and garlic. 'Your father will enjoy this,' she said. 'Made with fresh pesto and sundried tomatoes. Very good. My own recipe. Now you make sure you come back if he'd like some more. Good food and sleep, that's what he needs. Tell him to rest. Not get up too soon.'

I had to laugh. She had never met him and here she was saying what he needed. I paid her for the food and was about to leave when I found myself turning back.

'Er . . . I . . . is Luke around?'

Mrs Biasi gave me a penetrating look. 'Luke? Ah. You're a friend of Luke's?'

'Er . . . sort of . . .' No need to explain that actually we weren't friends, I thought, or that I was Nesta's friend and had almost stolen her boyfriend. No need for details.

'He's at class tonight,' she said. 'Acting class.'

'Oh, right. Yes,' I said. 'Sorry. Thank you.'

'What's your name? Shall I tell him you called?'

I could feel myself blushing. I started to back away. 'Oh. No. Thanks. I'll come again.'

Mrs Biasi looked amused. I bet she'd seen a hundred bashful girls come in and ask for her son over the years.

'OK. Right. Bye then,' I said and left as fast as I could.

I felt disappointed as I walked up the street. Deflated. And I felt tired and no longer in the mood for running home. I crossed the road and went to stand at the bus stop where, luckily, I didn't have to wait long as already I could see a bus lumbering up the hill. It drew up at the stop and the doors opened. I stood aside to let the passengers off. Out of the corner of my eye I saw a tall guy get off and head down the hill then swing back.

'TJ? TJ Watts?'

I glanced up and my heart almost stopped.

It was Luke.

'Oh. Ah . . .' I said as I stood frozen to the spot.

'You getting on or going to stop there all day?' called the bus driver when everyone was aboard.

'Er . . . I . . .'

Luke pulled me into a bear hug. 'She'll catch a later bus,' he said.

'Ohmigod!' said Izzie later that night. 'And then what happened? Eyes met. Stomachs lurched. Arms touched. I can hardly take the suspense. Then what?'

I'd called Izzie immediately after getting home. It wasn't that I didn't want to tell Lucy or Nesta about seeing Luke, it was just that Izzie had been so supportive of me through the whole painful saga with him before Christmas. I knew that she'd listen without jumping to conclusions or judging me in any way. Even though I loved all three of my mates, I sometimes felt that Izzie understood me best.

'We went and had a coffee in a café up the other end of the road to Biasi's. He seemed sooo pleased to see me . . .'

'Coffee? *Coffee?* Didn't he sweep you away to some romantic little spot and confess his undying love to you?'

'No. We went to a burger joint.'

'*Burger* joint? Pff. He's got to work on his romantic locations, TJ.'

'But it was romantic. Anywhere he is feels romantic.'

'Ah. So you still feel the same about him?'

'Yep. Stronger than ever.' Seeing Luke again had been amazing and he was twice as gorgeous as I remembered. Tall with shoulder-length hair, chiselled jaw, wide mouth. With his looks, he was classic Hollywood material. 'I really do, Iz. And seeing him again has only made me more sure that there's something special between us. He has this effect on me that is totally amazing. Like time stands still, like the world is a happy place . . .'

'Eewww. Totally vomitous.' Izzie laughed at the other end of the other end of the phone. 'But I always knew you had it bad for this guy. Did you snog him?'

'No. I wanted to. Boy, did I want to. *Boy*, did I want to. But no. I haven't forgotten how he was two-timing Nesta and I, and God knows who else.'

'So what did you do?'

'We talked.'

'Talked?'

'Yeah. He asked how my writing was going. I asked about his acting classes. Then we talked about our dads. Remember his dad is like mine in that he's way strict. He was actually lovely about Dad, really sympathetic. And he held my hand all the time and stroked my hair. And he was so pleased to see me. He said . . . he said that he'd thought about me a lot and wished that things could have been different and that he was sorry he blew it.'

'Amazing how you just bumped into him like that,' said Izzie. 'Where was it?'

'Well . . . er . . . down near the Archway Road.'

'Isn't that near where his parents' restaurant is?'

'Is it? Oh . . . um yes, it is, isn't it?'

Izzie laughed. 'And you just *happened* to be passing.'

'Yes, actually. It wasn't planned.'

'Yeeaah. Right. Sounds to me that you're in denial about Luke, and I don't mean the river in Egypt.'

'No really, Iz. OK. So I do still fancy him. Yes, the chemistry is very strong, but I hadn't planned to go in and see him . . .'

'Not consciously. But it sounds like your unconscious knew exactly which way it was thinking.'

'So what do I do?'

'I don't know. Do you want to see him again?'

'Yes.'

'But what about Ollie?'

'What about Ollie?' I asked.

'Ollie Axford? Last seen in Muswell Hill snogging your face off. Aren't you going out with him?'

That shut me up for a moment. I hadn't even thought about Ollie.

'TJ, TJ, are you still there?' asked Izzie, as I took a few moments to wonder if I *should* be considering Ollie Axford. The image of him nibbling my ear up in Muswell Hill flashed through my mind. Hmmm. He is cute and fun to be with and now that Dad's getting better maybe I should reply properly to his texts and e-mails.

'Yeah, I'm still here. Thinking about Ollie. It's not exactly as if I'm going out with him. Oh God, I don't know. I like him too. But we're just getting to know each other, really. He's great company but it's not like we're in a relationship.'

'Are you going to see Luke again?'

'He did say that he'd like to and I told him that I'd think about it. It would be OK, wouldn't it? It wouldn't be like I was two-timing either of them.'

Izzie was silent at the other end of the phone.

'Izzie . . . are you still there?'

'Yeah.'

'So what are you thinking?'

'I'm thinking, my dear TJ, that you sound just how Luke must have sounded when he talked about you and Nesta. Liked both of you, etc, etc. Very tempting to see both of you, etc, etc.'

'But I wouldn't do that. He was *dating* Nesta and he told lies,' I said. 'I've been on the other end of that and I know how it feels.'

'So you'll be telling Ollie about Luke then will you? And Luke about Ollie?'

'Yeah. Of course, if it comes up. Oh, I don't know. I like both of them. Why does it have to be like this? Boys, huh? They're like buses. You wait for ages, no sign of any and then along come two. Do I *have* to choose?'

'Some time,' said Izzie.

'But I can't. And it would be mad to tell either of them about the other when it's such early days. They'd be like, er, what's your problem? We're not even dating regularly. Can't I just see both of them and then decide?'

'Yeah. You could,' said Izzie, then she was silent again.

'Holy crapoley,' I said. 'I'm a love rat!'

> Denial is not a river in Egypt.

Chapter 7

Destiny?

In the end, I decided it wasn't Ollie or Luke that I needed to talk to. I discussed it some more with Izzie and we both agreed that there was someone far more important to tell.

'Hey, Nesta, can I have a word?' I asked when I saw her come through the school gates the next morning. Luckily she was on her own. Izzie and Lucy had already gone in as they wanted to go to the cloakroom before assembly.

'Looks serious. Are you OK? Is your dad OK?'

I nodded. 'He's going to be fine. No, it's . . .'

Now that she was standing in front of me, I felt nervous. Luke had almost broken us up as friends and now here I was about to ask her permission to see him again. No. I couldn't do it. 'Er . . . tell you what, Nesta. It doesn't matter. Temporary loss of insanity. Forget it.'

'Wow. It really is serious. Come on. You can trust me.'

'I know. And that's exactly why I . . . um . . . have changed my mind.'

Nesta began to mock-strangle me. 'Then I vill have to kill you. I hate it when someone begins to say something then holds back on me. My imagination goes into overdrive.'

'Sorry. I hate that too, but really, it doesn't matter.'

Nesta's expression grew concerned. 'It's about William, isn't it? You've seen him with another girl? You know something about him that you don't want me to know . . .'

'Nooooooooo. No. Course not. It's not about William. OK. It's . . . it's about Luke.'

'Luke?'

'Yes. I saw him when I was out jogging and we went for a coffee and . . .'

'You're still crazy about him?'

I nodded.

'How does he feel?'

'Sorry. Said he was sorry. But pleased to see me and . . . look, I'm sorry too, Nesta, but I still really like him a lot. And I think he'd like to see me again but I'd never ever, ever do it if it made you unhappy for an instant, because our friendship is a million times more important than he is.'

'Only a million, huh?'

'Squillion.'

Nesta was thoughtful for a moment, then she nodded to herself as if she'd made up her mind about something. 'Go for it,' she said. 'I mean it. Go for it. He was always yours. I always kind of knew that, and if he'd met you before me then there wouldn't have been the mix up. Besides, I have William now. It would be mean of me to pull a strop for no good reason.'

'You sure?'

She made a sign of the cross over me. 'Go in peace. You have my blessing.'

I laughed. 'Sure? Double sure?'

'Triple,' she said, as she linked arms with me and we walked into school. 'Hey, but what about the gorgeous Ollie Axford? Shame to see him go to waste.'

I grimaced. 'Well, see here's the thing: I like Ollie too, and at this stage, to be honest, I'm still not exactly sure about Luke. I just wanted to check out how you felt first, because if you didn't want me to see him again, then I wouldn't. Not for a second. So that was number one on the to-do list. Next is to check out the Luke situation. Is he involved at the mo, because if he is, then no way am I getting caught up with him.'

Nesta laughed. 'Wow, you sound organised!'

'Just . . . I don't want to get hurt again, you know . . . after last time . . .'

Nesta nodded. 'Course. And I don't blame you. But I can check the Luke situation. Don't forget, William knows him.'

'Oh. OK. If you don't mind, but, er . . . Nesta, will you do it . . . you know . . . subtly?'

Nesta looked horrified that I could ask such a thing, but she has got a big mouth sometimes.

'How else?' she said.

'Well, I wouldn't want it to get back to Luke that I'd been asking about him or anything, especially as nothing may happen.'

Nesta tapped the side of her nose. 'Trust me.'

'And I'm going to check out Ollie. For all I know, he may have a whole harem of girls. If he's available and really is interested in me then I'll decide between them.'

'Cool,' said Nesta. 'Sounds like a plan. And I'm sure it will become clear who is the real contender.'

'You think?'

'Yeah. Like if it's meant to be, it's meant to be. As our Iz always says, fate or destiny will make it clear.'

Later that day, another man came back into my life.

When I got back from school, Mum was arguing with him in the hallway.

'Go to your bed this instant!' she commanded.

Dad rolled his eyes to the ceiling then beckoned me over to him. 'Oh, for heaven's sake, give me a break,' he said to Mum as we hugged each other. 'I'm fine. I'm going to work on the computer and that's not strenuous, it's just sitting. Hello, daughter.'

'Hi, Dad,' I said. It felt great to see him back on familiar ground again, harrumphing around like he normally did. 'I got Mum's message that you'd be back this afternoon so I got some DVDs on the way home for you. You could lie on the sofa and watch them.'

'I could,' said Dad. 'I *could*, but I have some calls to make. Better things to do than lie about watching DVDs!'

'Everything's taken care of both here and at work,' said Mum. 'You can relax. I've taken a week's leave to look after you and Dr Miller said you *have* to take it easy. You know you should.'

'I will. All in good time,' said Dad. 'But first there are things to do. There's a pile of mail for one thing, plus I'm expecting Dr Rollands. He wanted to pop in to see me at the hospital again, so I told him that they were letting me out and to come here.'

Mum sighed but I started to laugh. Whether at home or at the hospital, Dad proved to be a difficult patient who wouldn't do as he was told.

'And TJ,' he said when he spotted me laughing. 'Go and make me a cheese sandwich, will you? With tomatoes. And plenty of mayonnaise. It's been hours since I had that lunch you sent me, which was delicious by the way.'

'Cheese? Mayo? Richard,' said Mum, 'we have to look at your diet. All that fat is not good for someone with your condition.'

Dad rolled his eyes.

'Lucy's dad runs the health shop in Muswell Hill,' I said. 'He says you are what you eat and I've heard him says loads of times that people can change their health by changing their diet. I've seen loads of tip sheets in there to help various conditions. Would you like me to pick one up for you?'

'I would not. I know all about that stuff. I'd rather have a cheese sandwich and die happy than eat brown rice and lentils and be miserable,' said Dad. 'Oh, come on. I'm just out of hospital. I've been dreaming of a decent sandwich. And excuse me, but *who* is the doctor round here? I know what's good for me and what's not.'

This time, both Mum and I sighed. You couldn't tell Dad anything as he always thought he knew best even though Mum was a doctor too.

At that moment, the doorbell rang.

I opened it to find that it was Dad's friend, Dr Rollands.

'What are you doing out of bed, man?' he said when he saw Dad in the hallway.

Dad threw up his hands in exasperation. 'Can a man get no peace in his own home?' he exclaimed, then stomped into the living room.

Dr Rollands then proceeded to have a discussion with Mum about Dad and his condition, his progress and so on.

It was funny because, unseen by them, I could see Dad was listening from behind the door.

' . . . Hmmm, yes, I can see that,' said Dr Rollands. 'Must be difficult. But then he always was stubborn. What he needs is to get away. Somewhere quiet with no distractions. Complete rest and recuperation.'

'OHHH for heaven's sake,' said Dad coming out from his hiding place. 'I'm fine. Get away? Are you mad? Travel is one of the most stressful things on the planet. Delays. Traffic. All the yobs you have to mix with to get where you going. Strange beds to sleep in. No, forget it. I'm staying here. And if no one is going to make me that cheese sandwich, I'll do it myself!'

Dr Rollands put his hand on Dad's back and ushered him into the living room where he made him sit down. He then produced an envelope from his briefcase. 'Ah, now that's where you're wrong,' he said as he pulled a number of photos out of the envelope. 'Take a look at these.'

I went over to Dad's chair and looked over his shoulder. Inside the envelope there were photographs of an idyllic detached pink cottage in a garden full of flowers.

'Cornwall,' said Dr Rollands. 'You couldn't find a more peaceful spot if you tried.'

'Yes. Lovely. So?' Dad asked.

'So. It's mine and I'm offering it to you and your family,' said Dr Rollands. 'It's been our second home for years and we were down there every summer while the boys were growing up, but now they've flown the coup. We won't be using it this year; in fact, we seem to be spending more and more time in France. The place is yours if you want it as a place to go and recuperate for a week or so.'

Mum took the photos and had a look. 'We do love that part of the world, don't we, Richard? And Marie will be close by in Devon. In fact, we even thought of moving down there last year, didn't we?'

'But you're not going to?' I asked, as a sudden panic hit me. 'You knocked that idea on the head, right?'

Dad nodded. 'Don't worry, TJ. No. We decided we'd miss London too much, but . . .' he took the photos and had another look. 'It does seem tempting. What's it like inside? Water? Heating? All mod cons? I can't be doing with any of these go-back-to-nature-type trips away.'

'Do me a favour,' said Dr Rollands. 'There's a computer there with Internet. The cottage even has cable. All the sports channels. And the movies.'

After Dr Rollands had left, while I made Dad his sandwich, Mum and Dad had a chat. For once they seemed to be in agreement.

Mum got on the phone fast to make arrangements. She didn't want to waste any time. The plan was that she and Dad would drive down there on Sunday so that Dad could begin his recuperation as soon as possible. My brother Paul would come up to stay with me in the interim and then we'd drive down to join them a week later for half-term. And she also called Lucy's dad to ask him to pop in with the diet sheet.

'He may be a top surgeon,' she said to me after she'd put the phone down, 'but nutrition is not always top of the agenda with any of them. It's never too late to learn some good new habits.'

'Could be fab,' said Izzie, when I told her the plan later on the phone. 'But you'll be away for a week leaving me alone with the love-bubble couples. Lucy and Tony. Nesta and William. And Izzie and Izzie. I'll be a billy loner. What am I going to do without you?'

'We can text, and apparently there's a computer there so we can e-mail.'

'In that case,' said Izzie, 'I'm going to do something that I've been meaning to do for ages: set up a private chat room for the four of us so we can all talk while you're away without it costing a fortune.'

'Excellent idea,' I said.

'I'll do it next week so it's ready for half-term. So . . . a week up here with Luke with no parents to cramp your style? Hmmm. Could be interesting.'

'Maybe it's meant to be, hey?' I said, hopefully.

'Ah, but with whom? It's worked out perfectly for you to spend the half-term down in Cornwall with your other lover.'

'What other lover? I don't know anyone down there . . .'

'Er, come on, stupoid. Get your brain in gear. Where do the Axfords live?'

'Oh my God! Yes. Cornwall. I'd forgotten that the Axfords have a house down there. Because Ollie is at school in

Kensington, I think of him as a Londoner. But it's bound to be miles away from where we'll be. Cornwall is an enormous place.'

'Hold on, I've got the copy of *Vogue* with the article on Star Axford in it – Lucy left it here last week,' said Izzie. 'I think it even mentioned where the house was.'

The phone went quiet for a while.

'Iz. *Iz,* are you still there?'

A moment later, she came back on the phone. 'Rame Peninsula,' she said. 'Where's the house you'll be staying?'

'Not sure. Just a mo.'

I ran out into the hall and called down the stairs. 'Hey, Mum. Where in Cornwall is Dr Rolland's house?'

'The Rame Peninsula, dear,' she called back.

'Ohmigod!' I said, as I went back to the phone.

'I know,' said Izzie. 'I heard. It's destiny.'

E-mail: **Outbox (1)**

To: <u>hannahnutter@fastmail.com</u>

From: <u>babewithbrains@psnet.co.uk</u>

Date: 21st May

Subject: God

Hey Hannahlulu,

Sorree it's bin so long.

A million things have been happening this end.

Dad was ill but he's better now, thank God. Talking of which or who, have you any idea if there is one? A God, that is. And if there is, have you got his address as no one over here seems to have it and it's not in the Yellow Pages cos I've looked. A phone number, website or e-mail address would do. An official www.god.com would be a gas, wouldn't it? We could just go to a site and leave a message for him? As in, Dear God, heeeeelp. Why am I here? Where have I come from? What happens after you die? Why did you create wasps?

Lucy says there has to be a God cos of all the beautiful things in nature.

Nesta says we all have pea brains and it's too big a question for us to grasp the answer, so we should just get on and enjoy life.

Izzie's still looking.

And I don't know.

U wouldn't believe what else is happening. Not one boy but two in the running. Ollie Axford. His dad is a famous rock and roller. Ollie is mucho cute. And the other boy is Luke. Remember him? Cause of big trouble last Christmas. I thought he was my soulmate. Still do, maybe. Don't know what's going to happen though as it's early days . . . watch this space.

Stay in touch.

Luv and stuff
TJ.

Chapter 8

Liberation

'Byeee. Have a great time.' I called as Mum waved from the driving seat.

Dad waved from the back of the car, where he was sitting like royalty, propped up with pillows and blankets.

Mum started the engine and off they went.

When the car disappeared round the corner of our road, Paul and I turned and went into the house. It felt so quiet after the flurry of activity in the last few days. Mum had done endless shopping trips so that cupboards and the freezer were stuffed with quick and easy meals. Mr Lovering had been over with boxes of health foods. Dad had patiently sat and listened to what he had to say about 'you are what you eat,' then pulled faces at the bags of oats and lentils when he'd gone. For a wrinkly, Dad could act really childishly sometimes, but I think he liked Mr Lovering as I heard them laughing about something. Probably the time he caught Lucy bouncing on my bed wearing a bra on her head. And then of course there was the packing. And repacking. Mum was unsure what to take as, with it being only May, the weather could turn colder again. In the end, she packed things for all seasons, and it had been good to see her back to her normal self, smiling and singing as she went about the house organising everything and everyone.

'So just us, kid,' said Paul as I closed the front door.

'Yep,' I said. 'Quiet, isn't it?'

'Yep,' said Paul. He went into the sitting room, scanned the CDs then put one in and turned the volume up.

Rock music blasted out so loud that it made the room vibrate. We both began to play air guitar and throw our heads around like mad heavy metal stars. A look that Paul had down well as with his long hair and denims, he does look like a scruffy musician.

Two seconds later, there was a loud knock on the window. We both looked up to see Mum's angry face.

'Oops,' said Paul and motioned for me to turn the music down.

As the house grew silent again, we both raced into the hall and Paul opened the door.

'What on *earth* is going on?' demanded Mum. 'I've been gone less than five minutes and you're acting like teenagers.'

I didn't think that now was the time to say, 'Er, actually I *am* a teenager'.

Paul shifted about on his feet like a naughty ten-year-old. 'Sorry . . . Just . . .'

'I don't know,' said Mum. 'Maybe this wasn't such a good idea, I mean you're barely out of your teens yourself, Paul. Can I trust you?'

'We were just being silly,' he said. 'And I'd say that twenty-three is well out of my teens, not barely. We'll be fine. Don't worry. I'll make sure she's in bed by ten every night and let her take mind-expanding drugs only on Fridays. I'll only allow boys up into her room on the weekend and absolutely no vodka unless she's got friends round.'

Mum slapped his arm lightly. 'Good job I know you're joking,' she said, 'although that's not funny at all.'

'So why've you come back?' Paul asked.

Mum spotted a bag in the hall. 'Forgot our supplies for the journey. Now, TJ, I know you're a sensible girl so I expect you to behave. And Paul, I want you to take this responsibility seriously. No staying out late on school nights. Early to bed . . .'

'Mum, we've been through all this,' said Paul and ushered her back to the door. 'Go. Enjoy. We'll both be fine.'

We stood at the door and waved them off for a second time.

As soon as we saw the car disappear around the corner of our road again, Paul dashed back into the sitting room, turned the CD back on full blast and came back into the hall where we both giggled at each other and resumed our air guitar playing.

Paul can be a real laugh, although Mum and Dad don't exactly appreciate that side of him at the moment. They had such high hopes for him when he got top As in his A-levels. They thought that he'd follow in the family footsteps and go to medical school. He did for a year, but wasn't happy so he dropped out and went travelling to India, Morocco and Ethiopia. He's been back in England for a few months now and still isn't sure what he wants to do. For the time being he's freelancing as a painter and decorator in Bristol, and Mum and Dad (especially Dad) aren't happy about it at all. They want him to get a 'proper' job. Paul insists that being a decorator is as proper as it gets, but he knows what they mean. He told me that he still doesn't have a clue what he wants to do so, until then, he's painting to earn a bit of dosh and pass the time.

Luckily Mum didn't come back a second time, and after our spate of guitar playing I went up to get ready for football practice. While I was changing, Ollie Axford called.

'Got a spare ticket for the Cirque Du Soleil,' he said. 'Ever seen them?'

'No. Are they like a proper circus?'

'Better,' he said. 'They're amazing. Beautiful. Hard to describe. You've got to see them. It's like an alien race has landed and come to entertain us.'

'When?'

'Thursday night. Albert Hall. Star was supposed to come with me, but she's had a last-minute booking for a job in Milan. So you up for it? Might mean a bit of a late night. I know your Goody Two Shoes sub-personality won't be able to come as it's a school night, but maybe one of the others could. Tell your mum I'll put her in a cab.'

I felt flattered that Ollie had not only remembered about my sub-personalities but also their names. 'Hold on, I'll ask,' I said and raced down to ask Paul.

'No problem,' he said. 'Cirque Du Soleil are brill. You have to see them.'

Great, I thought, as I went back to the phone. Life without the wrinklies was going to be fun.

The next few days were brilliant. Liberating. Paul let me stay up late. We ate what we wanted when we wanted. Coco Pops for supper and cold pizza for breakfast. We played more loud music. And, best of all, Izzie, Nesta and Lucy came over to my house on Sunday afternoon after Mum and Dad had left and then every night after school. Partly to just hang out in a parent-free zone and partly to get stuck into painting my bedroom. I hadn't even given the decorating a thought while Dad was in hospital and would have put it on hold even longer if he hadn't insisted that I go ahead with it and no arguing! I said I would be happy to take the paint back to Homebase and have the room white, but he wouldn't hear of it. He said that I had to take advantage of Paul's skills before he went back to Bristol and that I decorate in the colours that I wanted, no expense spared.

Paul was 'site manager' and did the ceiling and most of the difficult work while I was out at school, but us girls did some of the woodwork. By the time Tuesday evening came, most of it had been done and the room looked transformed from a drab interior to a fresh but cosy room.

'Tomorrow evening after school we'll do Camden,' said Lucy as she surveyed our work. 'Look for nick-nacks.'

'And then we'll have some time for beautification,' said Izzie. 'Please. My skin and nails need some attention.'

'And I need to start getting ready for my date with Ollie,' I said.

Nesta laughed. 'I thought I was bad. Your date is on Thursday. Are you saying you need a whole twenty-four hours to get ready?'

'Yep,' I said. 'I need all the time and help I can get.'

'What about Luke?' asked Izzie. 'Is he out of the picture now?'

I looked at Nesta, who tapped her nose. 'I just have to do a little detective work on Monsieur Luke. Sorry, TJ, I haven't had a chance to get William on his own and I don't want to ask him on the phone in case Luke is sitting right there with him. I should see him on Thursday and will deliver my report as soon as poss on Friday morning.'

'And I'll date the divine Ollie Axford for an evening,' I said, 'and deliver my report back and then you can all help me decide.'

'Sounds good to me,' said Lucy. 'Although it's your decision in the end.'

'I know,' I said. After what happened last time with Luke with everything feeling so secret and underhand, this time I wanted to let everyone know what was happening at all stages so that there could be no weird feelings. 'And hey, let's have the beauty session here. We can play music and run around with our face packs on without worrying that Tony or your brothers are going to see us.'

'Cool,' said Izzie. 'Though what about Paul?'

'Oh, he'll want to join in, probably,' I replied. 'He's always nicking my moisturiser.'

And so it was settled. It felt good to be able to have my friends over without worrying about upsetting Dad or making too much noise. Life was just getting better and better and there was still the date with Ollie to come.

The week seemed to fly by and, before I knew it, it was Thursday evening. I got the Tube down to Kensington High Street then walked along to the Albert Hall. I wasn't sure how long it would take so I'd set off in plenty of time. The last thing I wanted was to be late. I ended up being half an hour early and, not wanting to seem too keen, I went over to the park opposite and sat on a bench to pass the time. It was a warm evening for May and it seemed like half of London was in the park enjoying the weather and the other half were swarming about the Albert Hall, ready to go in and watch Cirque Du Soleil.

I said I'd meet Ollie at seven-fifteen, so at ten past seven, I got up, crossed the road and looked for him amongst the crowd of people outside and flowing into the reception area. He was standing on the steps by the entry and waved when he saw me.

'Hey,' he said as he kissed my cheek and handed me a carton of juice. 'There you are. You look great. I got here early so went and got us something to drink.'

'Yunuh . . .' I started, then laughed as I knew that he knew that I was talking alien-speak.

'Cool,' he said. 'That's Noola, isn't it? She's the one who comes through when you fancy someone?'

'Uh . . .' I nodded, then felt myself blush furiously. What was the matter with me this evening? I'd managed to be totally normal with him last time we'd met, but seeing him again was having a strange effect on me. He seemed to get better-looking each time I saw him, even though by the look of his black jacket and loosened black and yellow striped tie, he was still in his school uniform.

'Sorry I didn't have time to change,' he said as if reading my thoughts. 'Had a drama rehearsal that went on a bit late.'

'It's OK. Your uniform suits you. So what play are you doing?'

'*Romeo and Juliet*. I've got the lead so I couldn't miss the rehearsal. I had to fly to get here. Didn't think I was going to make it but I ended up being early. I often do that – I hate being late for people.'

'Me too,' I said. 'So the lead, huh? Juliet? I bet you look gorgeous as a girl. Who's playing Romeo?'

'Oh, ha ha. *I'm* Romeo . . .'

'I knew that,' I said. 'Just joshing.'

As he took my hand and led me through the mass of people arriving and eager to get inside, Luke flashed into my mind. Funny how both he and Ollie were interested in acting.

'Shall we go and find our seats?' asked Ollie.

The effect of his hand in mine made my brain go blank. 'Yuhnuh. I mean *yes* . . .' I blustered, as inwardly I told myself to chill.

Inside the air was buzzing with anticipation as people took their seats, chatted, stood up for late-comers, got out glasses, turned off mobile phones and generally settled themselves for the show.

'This place is stunning,' I said as we took our seats in the vast red and gold circular hall.

'How's your dad?' whispered Ollie as the lights dimmed.

'Really good,' I whispered back. 'He and Mum have gone down to a country cottage to recuperate. Actually, it might be near you. It's on the Rame Peninsula.'

'You're kidding! Where? What's the address?'

'Um. Rose Harbour Cottage, I think. It's in a private bay . . .'

'I know it,' said Ollie. 'Pink?''

'Yeah.'

'It's near where I go walking when I'm down there. So . . . this is all a bit fast, isn't it? So who's looking after you?'

'Paul,' I said. 'My brother. We've been having a real laugh.'

I wasn't sure whether it was the lighting in the hall or my imagination, but Ollie's eyes seem to glint with interest. 'Oh, really?'

I nodded. 'Paul's driving us down this Saturday to join Mum and Dad.'

Ollie grinned. 'This is sooo cool. And I'm going on Sunday. Fantastic. I can show you around.'

He tucked his hand through my arm, slipped his hand into mine and squeezed it. Our second date. And now the promise of half-term. Did this mean we were becoming an item? I wondered. Item as in boyfriend/girlfriend? For a moment I felt panic as I wasn't sure if I was ready. I still had Luke to check out before I committed myself to one boy. Oh God, oh God, I thought, I am worse than most boys. I have commitment phobia.

I didn't have a chance to give it much more thought as soon I got totally caught up in the show. It was breathtaking. A mix of dance, opera, rock music and acrobatics, with the most fabulous costumes and stunning light effects. It was like being transported to a dream world, as Ollie had said, of beautiful aliens who could do things with their bodies that made my eyes water just to look at them. We watched tightrope dancers, clowns, trapeze artists, jugglers, stiltwalkers, contortionists – probably about forty of them in all – who performed to the accompaniment of musicians. Each performer seemed to have taken their particular art and perfected it. I watched spellbound and, for a while, even forgot that I was sitting next to Ollie.

When we got outside after the show, Ollie made his way on to the pavement. He seemed to be looking for someone.

'I prebooked a car,' he said. 'Seemed the best option as we'd never get a cab here at this time of night.'

I had to admit that it seemed like he'd made the right decision as already I could see a queue of people waiting for taxis and only one in sight. Paul had acted the worried parent when I left and made sure I had twenty-five pounds for my taxi fare home. It was really sweet of him as I know he'd given it to me out of his own money and he didn't have much at the moment.

'Ah, there he is,' said Ollie as he spotted a driver, complete with chauffeur's cap, leaning against the bonnet of a white limo a short distance away. 'Come on.'

He waved at the chauffeur, took my arm and ushered me towards the car that was waiting about a hundred yards up the road.

'But . . .' I started. I only had the money that Paul had given me in my purse. No way could I afford to pay the fare for a car like the one waiting for us. 'It's OK, Ollie. I'll get the Tube.'

'On your own at this time of night? No way.'

'I can call my brother to meet me at the station.'

Ollie shook his head. 'It's my duty to see you home and I will.'

'I . . . I . . . Ollie, I can't afford a car like that.'

Ollie stopped, turned and looked at me. 'What kind of cheapskate boys have you been going out with, TJ? Like, no way would I ask you to pay. I'm paying. Actually no, my dad's paying. He has an account with the company. Mum and Dad always use these cars while they're in London and he lets me use one whenever I need. Dad likes these cars because they allow him to be private – they have those tinted windows where the passengers can see out but no one can see in.'

'If you're sure . . .'

'No biggie, come on,' he said and waved. 'Hey, Peter.'

The chauffeur waved back. 'Mr Axford,' he said, and opened the door to the back seat. Ollie turned, grinned and raised an eyebrow at me as if he found it all amusing.

A moment later I was sitting on plush leather seats being chauffeured through the streets of London. I felt like a princess.

'Do you want to go and eat somewhere?' asked Ollie. 'My treat?'

'Oh. No thanks. That is, thanks for asking but I ate before I came out and . . .'

Ollie smiled and patted my knee. 'School night and SP Goody Two Shoes is out?'

'Maybe. A bit,' I replied feeling like a twelve-year-old. Get a grip, I told myself. I so wished I had a grown-up sophisticated type of alter ego because I could certainly use her at the moment. Maybe I'd act the part anyway. That's what Nesta told me she does when she feels out of her depth. She picks a character from a movie and pretends that she's her. I'd pretend that I was Lady Penelope out of Thunderbirds.

'Drink?' asked Ollie, as he opened a mini-bar in front of us.

I nodded and put on a posh voice. 'Yar, please. Champagne. Vintage. Oh, and I'll have some caviar while you're at it, my man.'

Ollie pulled a half bottle of champagne out and held it up. 'Think this is vintage, not sure we have any caviar though.'

'Oh! I was only joking . . .'

'You can have some if you want. I'm going to,' said Ollie, popping the cork. He leant forward again and found two glasses, poured the champagne and handed one to me.

'Oh. Thanks,' I said, as I took the glass and debated whether to have some or not. Stop being such a baby, I told myself. I'd never had champagne before and, as I sipped it, I felt little bubbles go up the back of my nose. It was nice, like pop. I decided not to tell Ollie that I hadn't had champagne before as I didn't want him to think that I was immature.

Ollie leaned forward again, flicked a switch and some sultry music began to play through speakers behind us.

'Hmmm, cool music,' I said.

'Yeah. Dad always requests it so they always have the CD when there's an Axford booking.

'Yeah. It's good.'

'To us,' said Ollie, and clinked his glass with mine.

'To us,' I replied, thinking I knew exactly which of Ollie's sub-personalities was present at the moment. Casanova. He was *sooo* smooth.

I sat back and looked out of the window as the car glided through the dark streets of the city. It felt so sophisticated and I couldn't wait to tell Lucy, Izzie and Nesta about it in the morning.

As the car cruised up towards North London, I began to wonder why we hadn't stopped off at Ollie's school.

'Didn't you say your school was in Kensington?' I asked. 'That's just down the road from the Albert Hall. I thought we'd be dropping you off.'

He nodded. 'Just seeing you home safely first.'

'Oh, you don't need to do that,' I said. 'I'll be fine.'

Ollie stuck his bottom lip out. 'Don't you want me here?'

'Oh. No. *No*. It's not that. I didn't want to put you out.'

Ollie leaned over and brushed my lips with his, sending a tingly sensation up and down my spine. 'You're not putting me out,' he said, then he put down his glass and moved in closer.

We spent the rest of the journey snogging our faces off and I don't know whether it was the champagne, the soulful music, the buzz of riding in the back of a limo or Ollie, but it felt faaaanbubblytastic.

Before I knew it, we were cruising down our road. I hoped that some of the neighbours were up so that they could see the car and watch me getting out of it. I could just imagine their tongues wagging the next day. Thank God Mum and Dad were away as they would have had a fit.

'What number is it again?' asked Ollie.

'Number eseven.'

'Seven?' asked Ollie.

'Elesen,' I said.

Ollie laughed. 'I think you're a bit piddled, TJ Watts,' he said.

'Nah,' I said. 'I don't drink. Elesen. Eleven.'

Ollie laughed again. 'I think I'd better see you in.'

That woke me up. 'Oh. No! Be OK.'

The house was in a mess as, although Paul and I had meant to clear up, we'd kept putting it off. There were takeaway cartons in the kitchen and we hadn't done the washing-up since last night. And I hadn't moved back into my room yet after the decorating so all my stuff was all over the upstairs hall. No. Ollie coming in was not an option. I snuggled into him to distract him from the idea. 'One more song?'

Ollie leaned forward, opened the partition to the front and said something to the driver. Then he closed the partition, turned the music up and leaned back with me again.

Once again, we started kissing. It was nice. Very nice. Snuggly, cosy. Everything seemed to be merging together, the music, the smell of leather, the sensation of Ollie's lips on mine. I could really get to like this lifestyle, I thought, as I ran my fingers through Ollie's hair.

Ollie sighed and pulled me closer and then . . . was it my imagination or was his hand creeping up my inner thigh? No. It was on my knee. That's OK. No. No. It was definitely creeping up. Ohmigod, I thought. This is it. What do I do? This is what Lucy's been on about with Tony. Wandering hands. Or maybe not. No. Ollie's hand left my leg and came up to my waist. More kissing. Phew. He must have changed his mind about trying anything. Must remember to soak the paint brushes in turps before we leave for Cornwall. (Cripes! Where did that come from?) Oh no, Ollie had gone back to my knee and, oh no, his hand was moving up again. It was so weird because it partly made me feel tingly and partly made me go rigid with panic, like, what was he going to do next and how should I react? Whatever, I knew that I didn't want him to do any more than he was already doing. I put my hand over his and moved it up to my waist. Big mistake. It gave him *totally* the wrong idea. He cupped my right breast in his hand, gently squeezed and let out a groan.

'Oh, TJ . . .'

Oh jumping Jonahs, I thought, as I moved his hand down again. Back up it went. My head began to clear fast. I am so not ready for this, I thought. It's only our second date. He'll think I'm so easy if I let him carry on. And yet if I stop him, will he think I'm a baby? But he did pay for the tickets for the circus and organise the car home. But no. No. This doesn't feel right. I don't owe him anything just because he paid for everything. No. I don't want to do this.

I pushed him away.

'Wha . . .?'

'Stop it,' I said, and slid over to get out of the car.

'But I thought you wanted to . . .'

'Well, you thought wrong.'

I opened the car door and leaned down to pick up my bag.

'TJ. TJ. Don't go. I'm sorry. I thought you wanted to.'

I got out, slammed the car door shut and ran into the house.

I felt so confused. Had I given off signals that I'd wanted to go further? If I had, they weren't intentional. Had I led him on or was he just trying it on? I fumbled with my key at the door. I desperately wanted to get inside. I wasn't ready to be sophisticated. I wasn't ready to deal with boys' fumblings and being grown up. I didn't know how to be.

All I wanted was Mojo and to get under my duvet and hide.

E-mail: **Inbox (1)**

To: <u>babewithbrains@psnet.co.uk</u>

From: <u>hannahnutter@fastmail.com</u>

Date: 25th May

Subject: Oh my God!

Darlingus TJ

Gordie Lobachops! How vunderba to hear from you.

And karambo!!! Ollie Axford as in Zac Axford's son. F . . . f . . . fab fabarooney. I looked him up on the Internet. He's like mega!!! Dad Axford, that is. There were loads of sites about him and a pic of the family. So glam. Two sisters and Ollie wollie dingle dangle doodle all the way. He looks sooooo cute. Don't be a picky poo person, make sure you pick the right one.

Let me know how it goes and all and all cor blimey love a duck! You can text me as well as e-mail, yuno.

Life over here in sunshine land is happy dappy. Love life okee dokee, new boy from down under at school. We call him Bruce but his name is Dan. Cute as pie and I have offered to show him around. Hahahahahaha.

Miss my mates over there in Englandy land.

Toodleoo.

Hannahharmonicus

PS: Give luvie dovie smackeroo kisses to Scary Dad and tell him that he's still my pin-up! Glad he's OK.

PPS: Will get back to you on the God front! I'll see if anyone over here knows anything . . . You never know.

Chapter 9

Luke

'Has he called since?' asked Nesta after I'd filled them in on the latest in the break at school on Friday morning.

'Twice,' I said. 'And left a text saying sorry, sorry. I haven't answered his calls or the text. I don't know what to say. See, it wasn't just the groping. It was how it made me feel. Really mixed up. Like a hundred thoughts were going through my mind all at the same time and I thought, God, I hope it's not like this the first time I have sex. You know, that I'm focusing on the experience but also wondering if I've given in too soon, wondering if he thinks I'm a kid, am I any good at it, not to mention thinking about paintbrushes.'

'Paintbrushes?' asked Lucy.

'Yeah. Out of the blue, mid-kiss, I suddenly remembered I hadn't put the paintbrushes in to soak. I mean, how unromantic is that?'

At that moment Miss Watkins came out of the classroom and saw us propped up against the wall in the corridor. 'Outside, you girls. It's a lovely day. Go and get some fresh air.'

'I've had that,' said Izzie as we all pushed ourselves up and headed for the playground. 'Like you're kissing someone and part of your mind is thinking that you need to make a phone call or something.'

'I think you only get that when it's boring,' said Nesta. 'If it's the right person then all that matters is the sensation of being with them . . .'

'Oh, I don't know,' said Lucy. 'It can depend on the mood that you're in. Like with Tony and I, sometimes it's magic and other times, I think about other stuff. I think it gets like that when you've been with someone a while. The passion fades and paintbrushes or phone calls or whatever can take over sometimes.'

'Well, all I know is that what had started out as a great evening went flat,' I said.

Izzie linked arms with me as we reached the playground and headed for our favourite bench in the far corner. 'Hey,' she said. 'Don't worry. Most boys have octopus arms and hands. Lucy gets it all the time, don't you?'

'Yeah. But that's just it,' I said. 'She's been going with Tony for *ages*. Over a year on and off . . .'

'And on and off and on and off,' said Izzie, laughing.

'And he's been behaving lately,' said Lucy.

'But this was only my *second* date with Ollie. *First* date if you don't count meeting in the bookshop. I mean, who does he think I am? Do you think I have a sign on my head that says, *Hello boys, I'm easy*?'

Nesta grinned and looked at my chest. 'Er . . . Not on your head, dearie.'

Lucy linked my other arm. 'Maybe it *was* that top that I made you for the Diamond Destiny dance. He can't stop thinking about your jelubis . . .' She put her hands over her boobs and made a jiggling motion and we all cracked up.

'Yes,' said Izzie. 'He'll be sending you postcards for the rest of your life. From Peru, from India, from Scunthorpe. Oh TJ. T . . . T T T . . . J. I just caaaan't stop thinking about your magnificent jelubis.'

'You looked very nice in that outfit,' said Nesta. 'Don't let some stupid boy who's got the hots stop you dressing like a hottie . . .'

'Well, some boys might say I was asking for it,' I said.

'Well, they need a sock in the face,' said Nesta. 'It gets me so mad that sometimes a girl can't wear something pretty without some twerp thinking that the only reason she's doing it is because she wants some oik to ogle her or grope her. As if. Listen, TJ, don't worry and don't start dressing down again. You, *we* in fact, need to learn how to handle these sorts of situations and if it doesn't feel right, then learn to say, Oi you, noooo. And without feeling bad about it or guilty or obligated or worried that they might think you're a lesbian. Ollie was trying his luck, that's all. It's not your fault. Cute though he is, I had him figured for a player from the start.'

'But I think he does genuinely like you,' said Izzie. 'You said no to him but he's called since and apologised. That has to mean something.'

'Yeah,' said Lucy. 'He must like you.'

'Did you ask him about other girls?' asked Izzie.

'No. I meant to. We didn't get round to it.'

'Too busy playing backseat wrestling,' said Nesta. 'But talking of other girls, I have done my homework *à la* Luke situation and, according to William, Luke hasn't been out with anyone since before Christmas.'

'Christmas?' said Lucy. 'Veeeery interesting. Isn't that when you both broke up with him?'

'Yep. I think he's still interested in you, TJ,' she said. 'So does William.'

'Er . . . Actually he called a couple of times last night and left a message when I was out. Asked if I'd meet him for an hour this evening in the café at Jackson's Lane. Said he has something to say.'

'Are you going to go?' asked Lucy.

I nodded. 'I already called and left a message. I got his voicemail but I said I would.'

Izzie rolled her eyes. 'Some girls have all the luck. Not one buff boy after you but two. Hey, give us one if one's going spare.'

'Oh, but you can have either one if you want. You know . . .'

Izzie punched my arm. 'I don't fancy either of them. You know that. Not that I don't appreciate that they are both cute, just they're not my type. I'm not worried, though. I looked up the progressions in my horoscope last night and it said that I'd have to wait until later in the summer before love comes my way.'

'What are progressions?' asked Lucy.

'The progress of your birth chart,' Izzie replied. 'Like what's coming up next.'

'Did you look up ours?' asked Nesta.

Izzie nodded. 'Lucy's is steady at the moment. Which we all know. Things with Tony going nicely.'

'We agreed no complications while he does his A-levels, and they're coming up next month,' said Lucy. 'He's studying like mad. No two-timing. No wandering hands on his side and no dumping him on my side. He needs to focus. And then . . . we'll see. If he gets into Oxford, and I'm sure he will, I have to let go.'

Izzie was looking at Lucy with a soft expression when she said this. A cross between sadness and concern, and I thought, hmmmm, Izzie has read something else in Lucy's horoscope that she's not saying. I hope it's not going to be painful when Tony goes but then goodbyes are always hard.

'What about mine?' asked Nesta.

Izzie's face brightened. 'Fun, fun, fun. No worries there, Nesta. Venus is brilliantly aspected in your chart at the moment.'

'And, er . . . mine?' I asked.

'Ah . . .' said Izzie. 'Yes. Um . . . interesting times ahead for you, TJ. Venus is square to Saturn, which means some major life lessons are to be learned about love and stuff.'

'Major life lessons? Woopeedoop,' I said unenthusiastically. 'Sounds like fun. Not.'

I arrived to meet Luke at Jackson's Lane fifteen minutes late. Everything had conspired against me. After realising that I'd drunk alcohol when I was out with Ollie, Paul had had a personality change and given me the third degree about where I was going and who with and what time I'd be back. Honestly, not even a full week and he'd turned into Scary Dad. I finally got away after he demanded that I keep my mobile on and that I was back at a reasonable hour. I tried pleading with him that it was Friday and now half-term, so no school in the morning, but he kept on about how we had to close up the house tomorrow and pack and be on the road for Cornwall by midday. I don't think he likes responsibility very much.

And then there was a delay on the Tube. Signal failure at Whetstone, so I ended up half walking, half jogging. I hadn't wanted to do that as the weather had turned cloudy and was threatening rain – there was one thing damp weather did to my hair and that was turn it frizzy . . . and I wanted to look good when I saw Luke.

Unfortunately he was already there when I arrived, so I didn't even get the chance to go to the Ladies and reapply my lip-gloss or comb out the tangles in my hair.

'Hi,' I said as I sat down opposite him at the table he had taken in the café area. 'Sorry I'm late. I . . .'

'Hey,' he said and leaned over and took one of my hands in both of his. 'You look gorgeous. I'm *so* glad you came. I was beginning to wonder if you were going to show.'

'I said I would. So. You said you had something to say?'

Luke sat back with a serious expression on his face. 'Wow. Right. Yeah. Straight to the point. OK. Yes. I do have something to say.' He leaned forward, took my hands again and looked deeply into my eyes. I felt my chest tighten as a familiar feeling hit the pit of my stomach. There was no denying it. There was some very powerful chemistry between Luke and me. 'OK. I'm just going to come out with it, TJ. I know I blew it last time . . . with you and Nesta and not telling Nesta that it was over when I should have. I've been cursing myself ever since. I know we have something special. You feel it, don't you?'

'I . . .' I did feel it, but I wasn't sure if I wanted to expose myself so readily. I'd got so hurt last time. 'I know that there's something but, well, it was awful. I almost lost Nesta as a mate and I really value her. All those girls in fact.'

'I know and I'm really sorry . . .'

Suddenly all the feelings for him that I'd made myself bury threatened to come to the surface. I mustn't let them, I thought as I took a deep breath. I still don't know if I can trust him. But as I looked into his face. I wanted to trust him. He looked so earnest and sincere. Not the face of someone who would lie and cheat.

'Listen, Luke, you have no idea what I went through. How I felt. Because yes, I did feel that we had something special and I thought you felt it too and that's why I trusted you and . . . well . . . you betrayed that trust. I wish for just two minutes you could have been in my shoes and known how it felt . . .'

'I know. I know. My fault. Stupid. It's because I don't want to hurt anyone, but in the end I hurt everyone, including myself. But what I wanted to say was . . . I've learned my lesson. Could we . . . do you think you could give me a second chance?'

'But why now? It's been months since we've seen each other.'

'Well, you made it very clear at the time that I wasn't welcome in your life. But I haven't stopped thinking about you, honestly I haven't, and I just about thought I'd got you out of my mind. And then there you were at the bus stop last week and I realised that all the same old feelings were still there. I couldn't kid myself that I was over you.'

Me too, I thought. As he continued to look at me, I felt like leaning forward and kissing him. He was like a magnet, pulling, pulling . . . I made myself resist. I wanted to be completely certain that he was on the level this time. No secrets. No complications. I couldn't bear to get so hurt again.

'I . . . I . . . It's half-term now . . .'

'I know and there's so many things I want to do and places I'd love to take you. There's a great exhibition . . . Oh. I . . . I was just assuming that you're not with anyone at the moment, but of course, you might be. Sorry. Is there? Have you got a boyfriend at the moment?'

For a moment, I considered telling him about Ollie, but what was there to tell? He wasn't my boyfriend, and after the fiasco in the limo the other night, even though he'd apologised, I wasn't sure if I wanted to see him again.

'No. No one at the moment, but we're going down to Cornwall tomorrow for half-term. Mum and Dad are already there. How about I think about what you've said while I'm away?'

Luke looked disappointed but he nodded. 'OK. Sure. It's your call.'

I squeezed his hand and he smiled.

'No secrets?' I asked. 'No acting weird? No complications? If we do get back together, I'd want everything out in the open.'

'Absolutely,' he said and looked more hopeful. 'I promise.'

I looked around. The café and bar were beginning to fill up with people who had come for the evening's performance in the theatre at the back of the centre. 'How about a walk?'

Luke looked at his watch. 'Sure. A quick one. I'm on shift at the restaurant tonight. They're short-staffed so Dad hauled me in.'

'OK. So walk me home. My brother Paul, who is usually Mr

Liberal, has suddenly assumed the role of Mr Strict, so he'll be very happy if I get back a bit earlier.'

'Sure,' said Luke.

On the walk home he took my hand and we talked easily about general things. It was as if he respected the fact that I needed time to think and he wasn't going to push anything by making the conversation too personal. As we walked up Archway Road, I couldn't help but think how different my journey home this evening was compared to the night before. I felt like I was in my world, on my territory and being with Luke felt completely natural. Last night had felt as if I had been transported to another planet, with the theatre, the limo, the mini-bar and Mr Ollie 'Suave' Axford. I smiled to myself when a white limo like the one I'd ridden in cruised past. Already it was like something that had happened in another lifetime.

When we reached my road and front gate, Luke glanced at his watch again. 'Better get going to the restaurant or Dad'll kill me,' he said.

'OK. So I'll call when we're back.'

'Or while you're down there. It would be great to hear from you whenever. Whenever you're ready, TJ.'

And then he pulled me to him and held me, and it felt like he'd wanted to do it for a long time. I pulled back and turned my face up to his so that he knew that I was feeling the same and he leaned down and kissed me. Tiny sparks of electricity shot through me. It was exactly how I remembered. Marshmallow and chocolate melting . . . melting . . . No reminders to soak paintbrushes. No inner voices arguing with each other.

Only outer voices! It was Luke who pulled back first and looked around.

'TJ!' repeated Paul from the front door.

'TJ!' called Ollie from the open door of the white limo that had just drawn up outside our house. 'And this is?'

Luke looked at me and then at Paul and then at Ollie.

Ollie looked at me then at Luke then at Paul.

Paul looked at Ollie then Luke and then me.

I looked at the open front door and, like a coward, ran for it.

E-mail: **Inbox (1)**
To: babewithbrains@psnet.co.uk
From: leilaferrin@fastmail.com
Date: 26th May
Subject: Top Tip

Hi TJ,
My top tip for writing is: Never give up. Persevere through rejection and tough times and it will pay off in the end – a tip which I apply to my life as well as my writing.
Hope this finds you well, and good luck with it all.

Leila Ferrin.

Chapter 10

Relationship Rollercoaster

The long drive down to Cornwall was a blessing. It gave me time to think. And Paul time to tease me like mad. He thought Ollie turning up just when I was mid-snog with Luke was hysterical.

'If you could have seen your face,' he said, as we drove down the A303. 'It was a picture.'

'Well, I'm glad someone found it entertaining,' I said.

After I'd taken refuge inside last night, Paul said that neither Luke nor Ollie had hung about for long. Apparently Ollie had got out of the car (carrying a bunch of flowers, no less) and gone to speak to Luke. Paul couldn't hear exactly what was said, but Ollie soon got back in the car and Luke stormed off down the road.

Later that evening, when I'd calmed down and my breathing had gone back to normal, I'd picked up my e-mails. There was one from Leila Ferrin saying persevere through the bad times. I thought I should apply that philosophy to Luke so I tried to phone him at the restaurant. Whoever picked up the phone said he was working and couldn't talk. It could have been his dad, it could have been one of the other waiters acting on Luke's instructions not to take calls. I felt really bad about my reaction earlier. I had just panicked. My Minnie the Mouse sub-persona had taken over and taken the coward's way out. And then I'd regretted it. I'm not a coward. Not normally. I just didn't know what to do or say. Later in the evening, I tried Luke's mobile. It was switched off. And I tried again a few times this morning before we left but still no luck. I thought about texting him, but changed my mind as I wanted to talk to him in person.

As we drove along, I texted Izzie, Nesta, Lucy and Hannah to bring them up to date, then gazed out of the window at the passing fields and rolling hills that told us we were out of London. The weather had cleared since last night and it looked like it was going to be a gloriously hot day. As I stared up at the blue sky, I replayed the earlier part of the evening with Luke over and over again in my mind. Luke and I did have something amazing. I really wanted to make it work and, even though the end of the evening had turned out disastrously, in one way it proved to me how these sorts of things could happen. It made me think that I had judged Luke too harshly in the past. I believed now that he hadn't meant to hurt me and he hadn't meant to hurt Nesta. It was just a case of bad timing, just as it had been with Ollie showing up around the same time that Luke came back into my life. If I had met Ollie just after Christmas we could have gone out, broken up, gone out and broken up several times over by now. All those months I didn't have any boyfriends, then, as luck would have it, I meet Ollie a week before I bump into Luke again. Bad, *bad* timing, but I would explain to Luke that he was the one I wanted to be with. I wasn't two-timing him. Hopefully he'd understand. If anyone *should* understand, it was him.

I hadn't called Ollie yet even though he'd tried again to call me this morning. I was still working out what I wanted to say. I had his number down in Cornwall so I knew that I could call him and apologise there. I was going to tell him that I hadn't purposely kept anything back from him about Luke because up until that evening there was nothing going on. And then I'd explain that Luke and I were (hopefully) going to get back together. I hoped that Ollie and I could be friends and that he'd understand and not think that I was a scheming, conniving love rat.

After cruising down the A303 for about an hour, Paul turned off the road into a service station. 'Got to get some petrol,' he said. 'So if you need the Ladies, now is the time and, while you're there, get some chocolate supplies.'

As Paul filled the car up, I went and got a few things from the shop inside, then got Mojo out of the back of the car and went and sat on a grassy verge outside the café area where I dialled Luke's mobile. This time, he picked up.

'Oh Luke, hi! It's TJ.'

'Yes. I know who it is,' he said. His voice sounded cold.

'About last night . . .'

'Yes. You made your point. Quite a set-up.'

'Set-up? What do you mean?'

'Earlier. When we were at Jackson's Lane, you said you'd love for me to feel what it was like to be hurt the way that you were. To be two-timed. Well, mission accomplished. Well done. I wouldn't have thought revenge was exactly your style, but I guess I had it coming.'

'No . . . Luke, it wasn't like that.'

'No? What about when I asked if you were with anyone at the moment. You said you weren't. So who was the guy in the limo, then? You don't need to tell me. I asked him and he told me that you'd been dating.'

'No, but we're not . . .'

'Look, I'm not stupid, TJ. Go on, go ahead. Say *all* the stuff that I said to you. It's not serious with him, etc, etc. You're the one I want, etc., etc. Go on, get your own back. I hope you're enjoying it.'

'No, Luke, listen please . . . About Ollie . . .'

'No, you listen. OK, I walked right into it. I got what I deserved. I said I was sorry, but you got me anyway. So now we're equal. I don't want to play games, TJ. And contrary to what you might think, I did really care about you.'

'But . . .'

He didn't give me a chance to say anything. 'Stick with your rich boyfriend,' he said. 'Maybe he doesn't mind girls who play head games.'

And then he hung up!

I felt like I'd been punched in the stomach. So much for perseverance paying off. I felt so mad I wanted to kick something.

'Arrrghhhhhh,' I cried.

Mojo, who was always eager to join in whatever I was doing let out a loud howl. '*Awooohhhh.*'

'Exactly, Mojo,' I said. 'Ablooming*wooooooooh.*'

'You all right, love?' asked a middle-aged lady who was going into the service station.

'Oh yes, fine,' I said. 'Just stubbed my toe.'

She gave me a strange look and carried on her way.

'Hey, TJ, come on,' called Paul from the car. 'Best get going if we're to be there for supper.'

For the next couple of hours we drove along listening to the radio, each of us locked in our thoughts and private worlds. I didn't want to discuss my feelings with Paul because I was stunned at Luke's reaction. It was totally unreasonable. He'd thought the worst possible thing about me. Not only that I was seeing someone else, but that I would flaunt it in front of him for revenge. As if! Well, that killed any romantic notion that he somehow knew the real me. I would *never* do anything so calculated, and if he thought I could then he could stuff it. I wasn't into playing games. And he hadn't even given me a chance to explain my side of the story. Pfff. There was no hope for us as a couple. If a boy wasn't even prepared to listen, then what chance did we have? None.

As we drove further down south, the countryside began to open up and became greener. Paul and I began to chat more and for a while it took my thoughts off boys and what complications they caused. We drove on through Exeter, down past Plymouth, across the Saltash Bridge and on to one of the B-roads leading to the Rame Peninsula.

'Not much longer,' said Paul as we drove down a road with

high hedgerows on both sides. 'In fact, we've done good time. Four and a half hours. We should be there before five.'

He turned a corner and suddenly we were out in the open again and could see where we were.

'Wow!' I gasped when I saw the panoramic view in front of us.

'Woweekazowee,' said Paul, and pulled the car over so that we could take it all in.

The countryside in front of us was spectacular. A perfect scene. A perfect day with not a cloud in the blue, blue sky. To our right and ahead as far as the eye could see, was the ocean – glistening silver blue in the late afternoon light. Miles and miles of it along an unspoilt coastline that stretched out in front of us until, in the far distance, it reached a part of the landscape that jutted out into the sea. To our left were rolling hills, valleys and fields of green and honey colours.

'This is absolutely stunning,' I said. 'It's like a painting.'

Paul consulted his map then pointed out to the sea. 'That's Whitsand Bay along there, and that hill with the little church on top in the far distance is probably Rame Head.'

'Fanbloomingtabulous,' I said.

'Exactly,' said Paul as he started up the car again.

We drove on down through winding lanes, through a small village called Millbrook, and once we were through it, we found the landmarks that Mum had told us to look out for. Left at the school at the top of the hill, two miles through woodland, two big rock boulders after the turn off to Anderton, and then take a left on a road with an orchard on your left and a field with horses on your right.

We carried on down the sandy lane as instructed, took a left at the bottom and then found ourselves in a private bay.

It was beautiful. A quiet inlet of water with one boat bobbing about in the low tide. The only sound was the water lapping gently. On the land in front was Rose Harbour Cottage and there, in a deckchair on the lawn leading down to the bay, was Dad. It looked like he was asleep as he had his Panama hat over his face. He looked the picture of perfect peace.

Mum came running out when she heard the car. She looked much more rested than when they left last week and so pleased to see us. She took our bags from the boot and ushered us inside the cottage.

'It used to be a coaching inn,' said Mum as she gave us the tour and led us through the forty-foot, low-beamed living room and into a vast open kitchen with a little conservatory off to the right. The whole place smelled of woodsmoke, as if hundreds of log fires had been burned there. 'And I think this part was built later.'

Upstairs on two floors were four spacious bedrooms, each with double windows, a window seat and a view of the ocean. There were two large bathrooms and, at the back in an outhouse, there was a snooker room, complete with table. There was a garden with a pond and barbecue area at the side, as well as the lawn at the front. Fabulous, I thought. I could see that we were going to have a great week here.

After tea and sandwiches, I went up to my room on the first floor to unpack. As I was putting things away in the pine wardrobe, my mobile rang. For a moment my stomach turned over as I thought it might be Luke calling to apologise or talk things over.

'Hi,' said Ollie's voice.

'Oh. Hi,' I said. 'I'm glad you called. I wanted to talk to you. Er . . . About last night. I want to explain.'

'No, me first. I want to explain about what happened in the limo on the way back from the circus the other night. I'm sorry I pushed things along too fast. That's why I was there waiting for you last night. I'm really sorry. I got carried away and . . . well, sorry.'

'You're sorry? Oh right. Yes, of course, the limo!' I said. I'd been so busy thinking about what I was going to say to him about running away last night and about Luke that I'd completely forgotten about the groping incident. 'It's cool. Apology accepted.'

'Really?'

'Yes. Forgiven. Forgotten.'

'Wow, TJ, you really are something. Excellent.'

'And I wanted to say that I'm sorry too. You know . . . for diving inside last night when I saw you. Sorry.'

Ollie laughed. 'That guy didn't seem too happy to see me either,' he said. 'Who was he?'

'Luke. No. I guess he wasn't too happy.'

'And Luke is?'

'Old boyfriend. Unfinished business.'

'Still unfinished?'

'Nope, I think we've pretty well got that one wrapped up now.'

'Fab, so we can hang out,' said Ollie. 'And I promise no more funny stuff. You on your way down to Cornwall?'

'No. I'm here already.'

'Excellent. I'll be down tomorrow, so see you at your cottage?'

'Yeah. Sure,' I said. Why not? I thought. Luke has just blown me out. Why shouldn't I see Ollie? 'And . . . you're not mad or anything about last night?'

'Nope,' said Ollie. 'It's not as if we were married or anything. We're young, we're free, we're single! And a girl like you, I expect competition.'

Hah! I thought. If only you knew my track record (or lack of it).

'Yes, it really is difficult some days,' I said. 'I have to fight the boys off.'

'Me too. Or girls that is in my case.' Ollie laughed. 'It's hard being as drop-dead gorgeous and desirable as I am.'

I laughed, but I hoped he was joking.

'OK, so we're cool,' I said.

'Yep. We're cool,' said Ollie.

Wow, I thought as I clicked my phone shut. Relationships really are a rollercoaster. On-off, on-off, up-down, up-down. But did I make a mistake saying I'd see him? No. Why shouldn't I? Luke had just made his feelings very clear, and if he wasn't prepared to talk *and* listen, what could I do? I wasn't going to spend the week pining over him. I'd spent too many weeks doing that when I could have been having a life. I'm a free agent. No ties. No commitments, and I have two choices. Sit down here and mope about Luke, who may never want to see me again. Or go out and have some fun with a guy who is great company.

I knew which option I was going to take.

Texts to TJ from the girls about the
Luke/Ollie situation:

GIVE OLLIE ANOTHER GO. *Lucy*

FIND A NEW BOY, BET THERE ARE LOADS DOWN THERE. *Nesta*

DON'T GIVE UP ON LUKE. THINK HE OVERREACTED COS LIKES U V. MUCH. KEEP AN OPEN MIND. AND DON'T FORGET OUR MSN CHAT ROOM! *Izzie*

THANKS A LOT, GUYS. NOW I AM REALLY CONFUSED! *TJ*

Chapter 11

Half-term Hols

'So what's it like?' asked Izzie when I called her on Monday evening.

'Amazing,' I replied. '*Le Anglaisie* paradise. I love it down here. You've got to come down some time.'

'How's your dad?'

'Good. He looks a lot better. He's not venturing too far from the cottage, but he's happy enough just hanging out in the front garden or watching one of the old movies we found in the TV cabinet. The cottage looks right out on the water and is so peaceful. What have you guys been up to? I sooo wish you were all here. I miss you like mad.'

'Oh, same old, same old,' Izzie replied. 'I wish I was with you too. Nesta and William are inseparable. They went to Hampton Court today with Lucy and Tony and they did invite me along, but no way was I going to go and be the sad singleton. Can you imagine a day out watching those guys fawning over each other? No thanks. Vomitous.'

'I thought Tony was revising for his exams?'

'Yeah, he is most of the time so Lucy will be around tomorrow and later in the week. I don't mind that much. I've got loads to do. I went over to see Ben and the boys from the band today. We went over some new material. Have you seen Ollie?'

'Yes. Today. Paul went back to Bristol last night as he's got a decorating job, so Mum and Dad are really pleased that I know someone down here who can show me around. That way, they can relax and be close to the house and not worry about me getting bored. It's been amazingly hot down here. Everyone says it's like August weather. We've been to some fabtastic places already and I've taken a ton of photos to show you.'

'And is Ollie Wollie behaving?'

'Not a wandering hand in sight.'

'Cool. Keep me updated and don't forget our MSN! I've set it up and I'm the only one who's been in it so far! I've spoken to Lucy and Nesta and we've agreed that for the rest of the half-term we'll go in there at precisely six o'clock every day for a proper catch-up. Be there or be square.'

'Will do.'

After I'd hung up, I checked in with Izzie in the chat room but we'd already said most of what we wanted on the phone so I didn't stay on too long. I did promise that I'd send her some pics though so I went through the ones I'd taken on Mum's digital camera.

Ollie had shown up after breakfast this morning in a bright turquoise Beetle car and, after I'd introduced him to Mum and

Dad, he told me that I was going to be a tourist for the week and he was going to be my guide. He drove me all over the peninsula to give me an overview and it was totally amazing. On one side were the twin villages of Kingsand and Cawsand. They were small fishing villages with cobbled backstreets and a maze of pretty-coloured cottages painted in pink, yellow and blue. There was one road that wound its way through the villages and it was so narrow that there was barely enough room for one car. I loved it. In each village there was a bay that was easy to get to so there were lots of families with kids splashing in the water and enjoying the unseasonably hot weather.

On the other side of the peninsula was Whitsand Bay, where Paul and I had stopped on Saturday afternoon. Ollie took me to a café called the View, which was on top of the cliff up there. It was so named because the outlook from the picnic tables at the front was stunning: just ocean and sky as far as the eye could see. It was completely different to the other side of the penninsula as it was more rugged and unspoiled and people could only get down the cliff side to the beach via a narrow, dusty path through boulders and shrubs.

After Whitsand Bay, we drove down to a place called Cremyl where there was a pub and a foot ferry that took people over to Plymouth. Near there were acres of parkland spread out on a slope overlooking Plymouth, and at the top of a hill stood a grand old house called Mount Edgecumbe that was open to the public.

Ollie was the perfect gentleman all day. Held my hand. Kissed my cheek. No funny business at all, and I began to wonder if I'd imagined the octopus incident in the limo up in London.

The biggest revelation, however, was when he took me to see

his house. I thought it would be like one of the houses in Kingsand village, only maybe a little bigger. Hah! More like a palace. He lives in a place called Barton Hall and you have to drive through huge wrought iron gates and up a long lane past trees to get there and, when you do, wow! It's not big, it's enormous! Like a posh old hotel. It has several reception rooms, a library, loads of bedrooms (I lost count), tennis courts, a swimming pool and his dad has a studio down by a lake at the back. The whole place was decorated beautifully — every room like a page out of one of Nesta's mum's interior magazines, with lovely antiques and huge vases full of gorgeous flowers.

His dad was up in London, but I met his mum, who is blonde and beautiful, and I saw pictures of his sister Lia, who is a year younger than me. Like her mum, she is also very pretty. I hoped I'd get to meet her later on in the week as when we were up at the house she was out somewhere with her boyfriend, Squidge. Ollie told me that Lia had changed from a school in London to a local one because she loved the area so much and wanted to be at home. I asked why he hadn't done the same, but he said that he liked being in London too much and would miss his mates.

I also met the family pets: Max and Molly, two gorgeous red setters, Ug, the Vietnamese pot-bellied pig, and the latest addition, Fish, the ginger kitten. Ollie told me that Fish followed Max and Molly everywhere and thought that he was a red setter too. I thought it must be very confusing for poor Fish, not only thinking he was a dog but having to answer to the name Fish!

'You have very strange pets,' I said.

'Thank you,' said Ollie.

'Why did you call your poor cat Fish?'

'Not my idea. Squidge's mate Mac named him. Apparently he used to have a cat called Rover.'

'Yeah,' I said. 'Kind of follows.'

'All Lia's mates are mad,' said Ollie.

I thought they sounded like fun. It made me realise that I was missing mine even though it had only been three days since I last saw them, which is why I'd called Izzie for a long natter.

Tuesday 6 p.m.

TJ: Hi guys. S'me. Been exploring with Ollie at old house called Mount Edgecumbe today. Fab. So many interesting paintings and antiques to look at.

Izzie: Blarrgghh. Sounds v. boring. Heard from Luke?

TJ: Nope. Sad that he and I aren't on speaking terms, because exploring old houses and imagining who'd lived there and what they were like is one of his favourite things, too. I made myself put him out of my mind, though. I was there with Ollie and had to stop comparing them.

Izzie: Yep. I agree. Love the one you're with. Which in my case is no one. Boo hoo.

Nesta: How's the snog scale with O?

Izzie: And any spare decent boys down there in case I ever go there?

TJ: O kissed me properly before he dropped me off at the cottage. I can tell that he's making a big effort to hold back and not be pushy. Still not sure what I feel about him, though.

Nesta: Look on it all as good practice. It's good for your confidence to flirt and spend time with boys who aren't the great love of your life, as you learn something from everyone.

TJ: What u all be up to?

Lucy: Hanging out with Tony. Movies. Mooching.

Nesta: Hanging out with William. Movies. Mooching.

Izzie: God help me. Come home, TJ. All is forgiven.

Wednesday 6 p.m.

Nesta: Hi guys. How are you all?

Lucy: Fabola.

Izzie: Been down Camden with Lucy. What you bin up 2, TJ?

TJ: O and I got the foot ferry over to Plymouth today. Cool harbour there. Also an aquarium but there was a huge queue for that so we just mooched about the shops and sat about outside cafés, drinking Cokes and watching the boats and the world go by. Felt like holiday time. Sun shining. O is great company. Wonder why I think about grumpy old Luke when a boy like Ollie is interested in me. I'm starting to like him more and more.

Nesta: Be careful. I still think that boy is a player!

Lucy: Don't worry, TJ. You're not stupid. Enjoy. It's fab weather up here. Hot, hot, hot.

TJ: Here too. Lovely jubbly.

Thursday 6 pm.

TJ: Oh God. Iz, Luce, Nesta are you there?

Izzie: Only me. Lucy and Nesta out with the boys somewhere. Tell me all.

TJ: I think that Ollie has put a spell on me as I can't stop thinking about him and Luke is beginning to fade into the distance. I even turned my mobile off as I'd been keeping it on all day in case Luke rang, but as the week has gone on, I don't know if I care. I realised that I don't even know Luke that well. We haven't actually spent much time together talking, not the way that Ollie and I have in the last few days. All I know about Luke is that he's into history, wants to be an actor, has a strict dad and . . .

Izzie: When he looks into your eyes, your stomach lurches and when he kisses you, you turn to jelly. You might have forgotten but I haven't.

TJ: Yeah, but even the memory of that is beginning to fade. Ollie is taking over.

Izzie: Hhhmmm.

TJ: What's that supposed to mean?

Izzie: Means . . . hhmmm.

TJ: That's no help!

Izzie: Sorry. Feeling sleepy. It's sooo hoooot up here . . . Look TJ, don't worry. You don't have to make up your mind today. You can decide later. For now, just enjoy being down there.

On Friday morning, Ollie drove us along the Whitsand coastline then out towards Liskard.

'Where are we going?' I asked.

'Surprise,' he said.

After about five minutes, he turned off the main road and the car bumped up a dusty lane to a car park area under some trees.

We got out and walked towards what looked like a small zoo.

'Owl sanctuary,' said Ollie, grinning. 'It's one of my favourite places.'

It soon became one of mine too. We paid three pounds each to a man in a little shed and then set off into the sanctuary.

There were large cages on either side of a walkway and inside each one were different species of owls staring out at us. Barn owls, tawny owls, snowy owls, Siberian Eagle owls. All sorts, all sizes. They were so funny. All of them had beautiful feathers, sharp beaks and some had the most vivid, wide orange or yellow eyes, but what made me laugh about them was their expressions. Some of them looked sooooo haughty, others looked sooooo cross and others looked stoned out of their heads and like they were having such a hard time keeping their heavy-lidded eyes open that they were going to fall asleep and drop off their perch at any moment.

'That one looks like our PSHE teacher, Miss Watkins, when she's not pleased with our homework,' I said, as a tawny owl regarded me with utter disdain. It blinked its eyes and turned its head away as if it was so bored looking at me it could no longer bear it.

'I know,' said Ollie. 'They're hysterical, aren't they? I think owls must be my favourite bird.'

'A while back,' said the keeper, who had come out of his shed and was walking along behind us, 'everyone wanted one. It was after the Harry Potter books came out. He's got one, hasn't he?'

'A snowy owl,' I said.

'That's it,' said the keeper. 'Anyway, parents were calling from all over the country. Oo, my Nigel has got to have a snowy owl for Christmas. Oo, my Arabella has to have one for her birthday. Not from me, I told 'em. See, I know what's involved looking after an owl. They're not toys. A lot of kids that got 'em from other places soon lost interest after a few weeks, and who was supposed to feed and look after the poor thing then, eh? We've had a few brought here that were abandoned after some spoiled kid had 'ad enough and realised that owls don't like to be cuddled.'

Ollie looked sheepish for a moment. 'I wanted one when I was eight,' he whispered when the keeper had moved on. 'Dad wouldn't let me have one, though, as I think he knew that they take some looking after. At the time I was so upset as I imagined that the owl would fly to my school in London with post from my mum and dad, but that's only in the books and movies, isn't it?'

'Guess so,' I said. 'I read the books when I was eight, too. I wanted a dragon and even phoned a load of pet shops to see if anyone had them. I thought they were real.'

At the end of our visit, the keeper brought out four baby owls and put them in my hands. They were so gorgeous, like little balls of fluff, and Ollie took a picture of them. He went totally soppy over them and held them for ages. Luke was so wrong about Ollie, I thought, as I watched him stroke the baby owls. Calling him 'my rich boyfriend' as if he showed off about it or something. He wasn't like that at all. So yes, he lived in a fab place, but he wasn't all swanky about it. In fact, when we got back in the car, he told me that what impresses him most in the whole world are natural things like animals or birds or fish. As we drove away, I got the feeling that I'd just met another of Ollie's sub-personalities. A gentle one with a great love of nature.

After the sanctuary, we drove back towards Whitsand where, after a short distance, Ollie turned off the main road again.

'Where to this time?' I asked. 'Another surprise?'

'Lunch,' he said and pointed down to the right.

'Wow. Now that looks like it's straight out of Harry Potter,' I said as a grey stone castle, complete with turrets, came into view.

'Whitsand Bay Hotel,' he said. 'I thought we could get a bite there and then go down to the beach.'

I nodded. 'Sounds great.' I felt so happy. I was falling in love with the area. And after seeing how sweet Ollie was with the owls, I was falling in love with him.

Already I was having fantasies about owning a cottage down here when I was older. I could come down to write or paint. Of course, all my friends would be here too with their various partners and kids and dogs, cats, goats and chickens, and we'd sit and watch the sunrises and sunsets and laugh and live happily ever after.

The inside of the hotel reeked of history, with oak-panelled walls, old paintings, parquet flooring and huge floor-to-ceiling windows overlooking a garden planted with shrubs and palm plants on terraces that led down to the sea.

Ollie ordered cheese and tomato sandwiches and Cokes from the bar then found us a table outside as the sun was shining brightly and we didn't want to miss a moment of it. I sat back in my chair and closed my eyes to soak up the rays.

'This place has to be as close to heaven as you could find,' I said after the waiter had brought us our sandwiches. 'Not too busy or touristy. The most divine views. I don't know. There's something about the place. I feel so happy here. Peaceful.'

Ollie nodded. 'That's what Mum and Dad say. That's why they moved here. And Lia. She loves it too.'

'I can see why,' I said, and pulled my phone out. When I turned it on, it bleeped that I had a message waiting.

'Oh, leave it,' said Ollie. 'Whatever it is, it can probably wait. I'm going back to London this evening so we have to make the most of our last few hours here together.'

I smiled back at him. 'Yeah. Later,' I said, and put the phone away. I had promised that I'd let Mum know what time I'd be back, but it felt like nothing mattered. The sun was shining. The sea in front of us was twinkling with silver sparkles. The world felt at peace.

After we'd eaten our lunch, we went for a walk on the beach in front of the hotel. We held hands and paddled in the sea and then lay on our backs in the sand for a while and talked and cuddled. I turned to look at Ollie's handsome face and traced his profile with my index finger.

'I feel very happy,' I said.

He caught my finger with his lips and kissed it. 'Me too, TJ Watts. I think you are one of the coolest girls I have ever met.'

And then he leaned over and kissed me on the lips.

When Ollie kissed me this time, it felt real. Like he meant it. And for me there was no more thinking about his technique or paintbrushes or phone calls I had to make later. I felt totally in the present and only aware of the sensation of his lips on mine.

Around four, Ollie dropped me back at the cottage as he had to go and catch the train back to London. Plus I had promised that I'd go for a walk with Dad and Mojo before supper.

After a goodbye snogathon in the car and promises to see

each other in London, I got out and pretty much skipped down the lane to Rose Harbour. It had been the best day ever and I was feeling really good about being with Ollie. I haven't felt this happy in ages, I thought, as I went to open the front door.

It wouldn't open.

I tried again but the door was locked.

I knocked but no answer.

I peered through the window, but couldn't see any sign of Mum or Dad. Only Mojo at the window, barking his objection at being left inside. Where could they be, I wondered? Maybe Mum had left the key for me in our secret hiding place under the pot of geraniums and then gone into the village for supplies, but then why hadn't they taken Mojo? Maybe Marie had come over from Devon and taken them off somewhere? But no, she wouldn't have. I'd spoken to her on Monday night and I knew she had to work and make up for the time she had off when she was up in London after Dad's stroke.

I found the key and let myself in to the cottage. Then I got my phone out and switched it on to see if Mum had left a message on my voicemail.

She had.

Three.

'TJ. Your dad's not good. I'm taking him to the hospital in case he's had another stroke. Keep your phone switched on so that I can get in touch if there's any news. I'll call as soon as I can.'

'TJ. Oh God, where are you? Why haven't you got your phone on?'

'TJ. I'm at the hospital now. The doctors are doing what they can. Here's the number of the ward. 01752 33546, ward 14. Call when you get this message.

Suddenly the day felt cold. My happy mood disappeared like water down a drain.

Chapter 12

All Mates Together

Mum wouldn't hear of me going to the hospital.

'There's nothing you can do. I'll call as soon as there are any developments.'

'But . . . what happened? Is he going to be all right?'

'Too early to tell, love. Are you still with your friend Ollie?'

'No. He's gone.'

'Then take Mojo out for a walk, take your phone with you and this time keep it switched on.'

'But what exactly happened?'

'He . . . Oh . . . got to go, the doctor's come out. I'll call later.'

She hung up. I felt like I'd been punched in the stomach. I stared out of the window at the sea for a while. Hell, I thought. Heaven and hell. All in one day. I didn't know what to do with myself. I felt numb. I didn't want to eat. Didn't want to drink. I flicked on the TV but couldn't concentrate. I checked my watch. Four-thirty. Too early for MSN. I thought about phoning the girls up in London, but if I left a message then they might phone back when Mum was trying to get through. Best to leave the line free. And anyway, what could they say? Or do? Nothing. And I couldn't call Hannah in South Africa. It would cost a fortune.

'Come on,' I said to Mojo. 'Let's go for a run.'

Mojo wagged his tail in agreement. He clearly thought it was an excellent idea.

I stuffed my phone into my back pocket and ran down to Cremyl, through the Italian gardens at Mount Edgecumbe, and then followed the footpath through the woods and along the coast. It felt good to run. It took my mind off the dark thoughts that were threatening to take over. SP Cassandra, prophetess of doom, had taken over. I could hear her moaning on in the back of my head. *Woe, woe* . . . Get lost, you creep, I told her. Dad's going to be all right. I know he is. He's going to be all right.

Mojo ran ahead of me and then back to make sure I was keeping up and then off he'd charge ahead again as we panted our way through the woods and over towards Kingsand. Once there, I ran down through the back lanes of the village and then on to the main street through into Cawsand. It was as if I couldn't stop. The pound pound pound of my feet on the ground was stomping out bad thoughts. I ran down into the square at Cawsand then turned left on the beach area, and there at last I stopped to catch my breath. The beach was occupied by a few families still enjoying the late afternoon sun, so I scanned the area to try and find a quiet spot where I could be alone. Over to the left, there were several moored boats and behind there was an area where the beach looked stony. No one was sitting there. I made my way over and sat down on the gravel behind a large boulder.

Once I knew that I was hidden from the rest of the beach by a boat, I let the tears flow. Mojo looked at me with alarm and put his paws up on my shoulders and tried to lick my face.

I buried my face in my arms and sobbed. I hate this feeling, I thought, hate it hate it hate it. Not nice. Please, please God, let Dad be all right. The scare a few weeks ago was bad enough, but I thought he was getting better. Was this how it was going to be now that he was getting older? Scare after scare? Or was this it? The end? And Mum's getting older. When would Mum die? Oh God. She was going to die sometime, too. On and on I sobbed. I didn't want them to die. I didn't want anyone I knew to die.

'Hey,' said a voice up to my right. 'Are you OK? At least, I can see you're *not* OK, but is there anything I can do? Anyone I get for you?'

I looked up and saw that a girl, about my age, with short dark hair, was standing by one of the boats and staring down at me. She had a sweet, pixie face, was very pretty and dressed in denim shorts and a pink T-shirt with a silver glitter star on it.

I wiped my nose and my eyes. 'Oh God. No. Sorry. I . . . I didn't think anyone would come over here. I . . . I thought I was safe.'

The girl came and sat down next to me. 'You are safe here. I'll go away if you want but . . . I can stay too if you like.'

'Sorry . . .' was all I could say as another wave of tears rose up inside of me. 'I . . . don't . . . seem . . . to . . . be . . . hic . . . able to stop crying.'

The girl put her hand on my arm. 'Hey. Don't be sorry. Sometimes it's good to have a good cry. I'll let you into a secret. That's how I know about this place. It's my place to come and cry.'

'Yours? But why?'

The girl shrugged. 'Oh . . . few reasons. I used to come here when I was little with my family.' She pointed at the families playing a distance away on the sandier side of the beach. 'That was us. Happy families. Mum died when I was nine. So I come here partly to remember her and the times we had here when she was alive and partly to blub my head off when I want to. Don't laugh, but I like it best when it's really stormy, like *really* throwing it down and I can sit here and cry and watch the ocean and the rain and feel like the whole world is crying with me. It's very therapeutic.'

'Yeah. Sounds it.'

'So what's the matter?'

I took a deep breath and let the last sob subside. 'My dad's not well. He's at the hospital and I'm scared . . . he's . . . going . . . to die . . .' The tears started again.

'Hey, hey,' said the girl. 'I understand. You don't have to give me details if you don't want. I know what it's like. Like you're raw inside.'

'Yeah,' I sniffed. 'Raw and numb at the same time, and . . . I feel like every part of me is being stretched too far and it . . . it . . . sob . . . hurts.'

The girl put her arm round me and gave me a hug. 'We all know that people die,' she said. 'But no one's ever ready for it.'

'Yeah,' I sniffed again. Poor girl. Her mum actually had died and that only made it seem more possible that Dad might. I could feel I was going to start blubbing again.

'Want me to leave?' asked the girl.

'No. Not unless you have somewhere to go.'

'Nope. Nothing urgent. I mean, my dad could probably find me a million things to do if he wanted which is actually why I'm hiding down here. He runs the shop up in village. Have you been there?'

I shook my head. 'No, but my mum probably has, I think. Um . . . I'm TJ by the way. Least, my friends call me that.'

'Cool name,' said the girl. 'My friends call me Cat. Cat Kennedy. Short for Catherine.'

'Suits you,' I said. 'You look a bit like a cat.'

Cat smiled. She seemed nice. Easy going. I was just about to say something else when my phone rang. I quickly answered it.

It was Mum.

'TJ, love?'

'Yes. How is he?'

'He's doing fine. Indigestion,' said Mum. 'So false alarm.'

'Oh, thank God,' I said. 'So it wasn't another stroke?'

'No, it wasn't. But it's a warning, I think. He really does have to change his diet and keep off the rich food he likes so much.'

'Are you still at the hospital?'

'Yes. The doctors are doing a few more tests to be on the safe side, and of course your father is driving them all mad by telling them what to do and not letting them get on with their jobs, but . . . I guess that's a good sign.'

'Are they going to let him home?'

'We'll be back in an hour or so.'

I beamed at Cat as I clicked my phone shut and let out a deep breath.

'Good news?' she asked.

'He's going to be OK. Oh, God. I must look a right mess. God. I'm so sorry, crying all over you. And nicking your secret place.'

'You're welcome to it,' she said. 'I'm really pleased your dad's going to be OK.'

'Yeah. Mum said that they'll be home in a hour or so.'

'That's great,' said Cat. 'So, I haven't seen you down here before. Where are you from?'

'London. North London. We're staying at Rose Harbour Cottage . . .'

Cat nodded. 'I know it. Oh. So your mum and dad are the doctors?' Then she laughed. 'Sorry. Everyone knows everyone's business down here. Especially when your dad runs the local shop.'

'That's us,' I said. 'I've fallen in love with the place. I want all my mates to come down in the summer if they can as I think Dad wants to rent the cottage where we're staying again. Hey, seeing as you're local, you don't happen to know a good B and B do you? Somewhere my mates could stay in case my brother and sister happen to be visiting the cottage and hogging the spare rooms.'

'Yeah. I know just the place,' said Cat. 'My mate Mac's mum runs one. Actually it's his gran's house. It's a lovely place. Loads of space. Great views. She was really glad when they came down. His gran, that is. I think she was finding the place too big for just her. Anyway, Mac's mum has great taste. She's done the rooms out beautifully. Mac used to live in London, then his parents got divorced and he moved down here with his mum . . . anyway, long story. He didn't like it at first, wanted to be back in London all the time, but he likes it now. Actually he's in London for half-term visiting his dad. God, I'm rambling, aren't I? Sorry. You asked if I knew a good B and B. Yes. Mac's. Wouldn't mind staying there myself. I'll give you the number, and mine too if you like.'

'Thanks. That would be brill.'

'You could check it out before you go back if you want. It's not far from Rose Cottage. God. Mac would *love* it if a bunch of London girls came down and stayed there. He's always going on that there's a lack of girls down here. He used to go out with my mate Becca for a while but they broke up. Still friends, though. But yes, if you and your mates came down, Mac would think he'd died and gone to heaven.'

'What are the boys like here? Are there any decent ones? See, my mate Izzie is single at the moment and her horoscope said that she'd find love in the summer.'

Cat laughed. 'Really? Hey. Maybe she'll get it together with Mac. And then we can all be friends. But apart from him, local boys? Well, there's a few. Mac's cute. Not my type . . .'

'What's your type, then?' I asked. After the intensity of the last hour, it felt good to be chatting about boys and normal stuff like I did back home with Izzie, Lucy and Nesta.

'Mine? Hmmmm. I have to admit I do like good-looking boys. I know in the end it doesn't matter, as it's whether they're good company or not that's important, but I am a sucker for a handsome face.'

I laughed. 'I know what you mean.'

'They can be trouble, though,' said Cat. 'Especially the ones who know that they're good-looking. They can mess you around.'

'Tell me about it.' I really liked this girl. She was so easy to talk to. 'Sounds like you're speaking from experience.'

'I guess I am. Like, there's this guy I have an on-off thing with. He's so cute. Like sooooo cute. But good company, too. He's dead bright. But I never know where I am with him. In fact, I've got a feeling that he's seeing someone else at the moment and not telling me about it.'

'Really?'

'Yeah. It's funny because I met him here, too. Right here last summer. This very spot. He came over and chatted me up. I liked him straight away. And now well, we see each other when he's down from school, but this half-term I've only seen him twice and it's like he's distracted so I don't know . . . I feel like something's going on. I think he's two-timing me but then, because he's at school up in London and I'm down here, it's not as if we've made each other promises to be faithful, etc, etc. No point. I know what he's like. His sister warned me that he was a Casanova. It's just I thought that down here, well, you know . . . I thought down here that he was mine.'

Alarm bells had begun to rung when she said this boy came down from school in London. And was a Casanova.

'Why don't you ask him?' I asked.

'No way. That would really scare him off if I came over all possessive. I mean, I know this boy and he's got severe commitment phobia.'

'Er . . . what's his name?'

'Ollie,' said Cat. 'Ollie Axford. He's one of the Axford family. His dad is Zac Axford. Ever heard of him?'

I felt myself wince inside. Outside, I nodded. 'Rock star.'

'That's him. Really nice bloke, though. I've met him. I know his whole family, in fact. Lia, his sister, is one of my best mates. She goes out with Squidge, who was my boyfriend when I was younger, but we broke up and now we're all mates. All mates together. Me, Lia, Becca, Squidge and Mac. Hey TJ . . . Are you OK? You look like you're going to cry again.'

'No,' I said. Bugger bugger bugger, I was thinking. I meet this great girl. I know we could be friends, but how do I tell her that actually *I'm* the one who's seeing her boyfriend. I'm the one that he's two-timing her with. And as for Ollie Axford. I think I may have to kill him.

E-mail: **Inbox (2)**

To: <u>babewithbrains@psnet.co.uk</u>

From: <u>hannahnutter@fastmail.com</u>

Date: 29th May

Subject: Ollie!

My fruity little fruit fly.

Sorry it's been a while, left my phone at Bruce's so only just just seen your last text.

Excooth me? You were being groped in back of car by Ollie Wollie? Er . . . excoooooooth meeeeee? You can't just leave it there. Details darlingus, details. Calling TJ Watts, calling TJ Watts, what on earth are you getting up to over there in Slutville? E-mail back tutto pronto.

Hannahlulu

E-mail: **Inbox (2)**

To: <u>babewithbrains@psnet.co.uk</u>

From: <u>hannahnutter@fastmail.com</u>

Date: 31st May

Subject: *Ou est tu?*

Oi you! *C'est moi, le grand poo.*

Hasta la banana baby. Why have I bin cast so cruelly from your life?

Missing person alert. Where is u gone to my lovely? Oh I

know! Mi forgeti. Tis the half termius and you wos going down to Cornwallus. Oh well. Don't eat too many Cornish pasties . . .

Barbecue happening at Bruce's, so got to go and do scoffie gobs.

Luvvie duvvie wotsits, spik spok soon.
Hannahlulu

PS: Bin thinking about the big quessie. The Big Boss. God. Think the lovely Lucy is right about no creation without un creator. Got to be something or someone over the rainbow and all. And I think that probably like all artists/creators, he/she/it would probably like it if people appreciated his/her/its work. So Nesta is right, too.

Get on and enjoy it. Get down and boogie, baby. There's so much great stuff going on to see, to hear, to feel, taste and touch so let's get on and groove like a groovemeister and dig it, wasps and all. Olé.

PPS: I asked Bruce about God and he said that he is the Chosen One. Sad innit how all boys think that they are God.

PPPS: My mate Confucius, he say he who knows the way is wey hey hey.

XXXXX Squillion love things, and may your flobablobs be mighty!!

Chapter 13

Cowardy Custard

That evening, after meeting Cat, I didn't even bother trying MSN. Nor did I feel like answering Hannah's e-mails when I checked on the cottage computer. I needed to hear Izzie's voice.

'So why didn't you tell her?' asked Izzie after I'd told her what had happened.

'Don't know. Panic. I froze. I just couldn't do it, Izzie. She'd been so nice to me about Dad and I didn't want her to think that I am a ratfink boyfriend stealer. I can't believe it's happening again. Last year with Luke and Nesta, and now with Cat and Ollie. She'd have hated me if I'd told her.'

'But it wasn't your fault, TJ,' said Izzie. 'You weren't to know that he had a girlfriend down there . . .'

'And God only knows how many up in London. No wonder he was so cool when he saw me snogging Luke before I came down here. Remember he said, "Oh well, it's not as though we're married". I've been such an idiot. Naïve is my middle name. He even told me that one of his sub-personalities was called Casanova, so it's not as if he didn't let me know what he was like. I'm soooo stupid. I should have asked him if he was involved with anyone. It's just that things felt so good between us that I presumed . . . well . . . I presumed that we were an item. Sadly, Cat thought that too.'

'*Not* your fault, TJ. And you mustn't beat yourself up about it. You really mustn't.'

'Stupid and a coward. Cowardy cowardy custard. That's me. A Minnie the Mouse. Part of me didn't tell her that I knew Ollie because I'm a coward and I knew that we're coming back to London on Saturday, and if I don't come down here again I will never have to see her.'

'But all week you've been saying that you wanted us all to come down in the summer? You, me, Lucy and Nesta hanging out down there.'

'Changed my mind,' I said. 'There must be other parts of Cornwall. I'm never coming here again.'

'But you love it down there, you told me.'

'I know. I do. But what about Ollie and Cat . . .?'

'Oh, TJ,' said Izzie. 'If you stay away from a place you like then you really are a coward. And to avoid Cat, a girl who you *like*? You're mad. I bet you she'd understand if you explained it all to her. And what about Ollie? Are you going to see him again?'

'He can take a running jump as far as I'm concerned. He's already texted me to say that he's on his way back up to London and is looking forward to seeing me up there. I haven't replied, though.'

'But as you said yourself, he told you he was a Casanova so he didn't exactly lie to you. He just didn't tell you the whole truth. You can't spend your whole life running away from people or avoiding them because you're afraid of confrontation or what they might think of you.'

'I know,' I groaned. 'Just . . . honestly, Iz, I'm feeling really disillusioned at the moment. Boys. I'm through with all of them. You can't trust any of them. I am going to stay single for the rest of my life. In fact, I will probably become a nun.'

I could hear Izzie laughing at the other end of the phone. 'Ah, so you won't want to know about Luke, then?'

'Luke? What about Luke?'

'Well, if you're through with boys and never want to hang out with one ever again, there's really no point in me telling you.'

'Izzie?'

'Yes, TJ?'

I couldn't see Izzie's face, but I knew she had an almighty great smirk on it. 'If you don't tell me what you know about Luke, Izzie Foster, I will have to . . . have to go and throw myself off the nearest cliff.'

'Ah, but then you'll *never* find out what I have to say . . .'

'IZZIEEEEEEE!'

'OK. OK. Luke has been asking about you.'

'Asking you?'

'No. Not me. Nesta. Well, not Nesta exactly, but Nesta through William. William told Nesta that Luke asked him to find out everything that he could about you and Ollie. And she said that Luke told William that he's really hung up about you and thinks he might have blown it by overreacting last time he saw you. He also made William promise not to tell Nesta any of this, but she knew that he knew something and threatened to dump him if he didn't spill, so he told her everything . . .'

'Wow,' I said. 'That was really good of her because she likes William a *lot*.'

'Yeah, but she knew that he'd give in. He's lucky that she didn't go to Plan B, which was to give him a Chinese burn if he didn't talk. She has her methods, does our Nesta, and isn't one to give up. Anyway, William made Nesta promise not to tell any of us. Ha ha. As if. She was straight on the phone. I think she tried to phone you too, but it was engaged.'

'I was probably talking to Mum,' I said. And then thought, oh no, Luke asking about Ollie? Even though I love Nesta dearly, God only knows what she told William with her big mouth.

'What exactly did Nesta say?'

'She says she didn't tell him anything except that you had only met Ollie recently and it was early days, and she didn't know if you were even going to see him again as you weren't sure if he was your type.'

'Really? Hey, good for her. That's not bad. It leaves it open.'

'Yeah,' said Izzie.

'Cool,' I said.

'Yeah, cool,' said Izzie. 'Sounds to me like you and Luke have some unfinished business.'

'Very possibly,' I said as I thought about our last kiss. Second kiss, actually. Our first kiss last year in our living room in London was disturbed by my parents coming home, and our second kiss was disturbed halfway through by Ollie and Paul. So Luke and I definitely had unfinished business. Of the snogging type.

'Izzie?'

'Yes, TJ?'

'Do you think I am a slut?'

'Definitely.'

'No, really.'

'Yes, really,' said Izzie, but I could hear her laughing. 'Why would you think that?'

'Well, only this lunchtime there was me thinking that Ollie was maybe The One, and last week when I saw Luke I thought he was *definitely* The One. And now that I know that Ollie likes to play the field, I don't think he could possibly be The One for me because I don't think that I could handle feeling strongly about someone and knowing that they were seeing someone else as well. I couldn't do the open relationship thing. I think I'd get too jealous. But he and Luke have shown me that I can feel for more than one person at the same time. I have. I did. I do. Ollie and Luke. It's different with both of them, least I feel different things. Both nice. So does that actually make me the love rat? And not them? I think I'm very confused.'

Izzie was really laughing now. 'Yeah, really confused. Er . . . can you run that by me again?'

'Run what?'

'All that you just said.'

'Oh God no,' I said. 'I can't even remember what I said.'

'Confused,' said Izzie. 'You.'

'Yes. I think that was about the gist of it.'

'Don't worry,' said Izzie. 'Love can be very confusing. It will get clearer. Give it time.'

Izzie is so wise, I thought. 'OK,' I said. 'How long?'

'Oh . . . about three or four . . . hundred years.'

'Thanks a bunch.'

'You're welcome,' said Izzie, and then she started sniggering again.

'Well, I'm glad you find my love life so amusing.'

'Don't worry so much,' said Izzie. 'All you need to do is be true to yourself and honest with everyone else.'

'Right,' I said. Easier said than done, I thought. Be true to myself? Which one of my selves? There are so many people living in my head. All with voices. And all with feelings. And those feelings keep changing every five minutes. I think I am well and truly and completely and utterly bonkers.

'And if you're not true to yourself,' said Izzie, 'the universe will conspire to make you. Least that's what I think. If you try and run away from what you fear then something will happen to make you face your fears. So there. Iz the Oracle has spoken.'

Izzie was always coming out with stuff like that. I think that she may be bonkers too. That is probably why we are such good friends.

'I hear and obey, O wise one,' I said.

On Saturday morning, as Mum packed up our things ready for our return to London, Dad and I took Mojo for a final walk in the woods.

'I want to talk to you about something important,' said Dad as we set off through the fields that led down to Cremyl.

My heart almost stopped – he looked so grave when he said this. Immediately Cassandra, prophetess of doom, raised her head ready to hear the worst as my imagination went into overdrive. Ohgooooood, said her gloomy voice, he's going to tell you that he hasn't long to live. Woe oh woe oh blooming woe.

Dad put his hand on my shoulder. 'Hey, no need to look so worried.'

'So what is it?'

Dad looked around and gestured at the landscape with his right hand. 'This place. It is wonderful, isn't it?'

Oh no, I thought. I know what's coming. He wants to live here. Last year he and Mum were on about moving to Devon, leaving London. Oh God. I'm not ready to move.

'Er . . . yes. Lovely. Very nice, but . . .'

'Don't worry, TJ, we're not going to leave London. Not yet. Your mother's not ready to retire yet and I'm not ready to leave London forever. I still love living there. No. But maybe there's a compromise that everyone will be happy with. Dr Rollands phoned last night with a proposition that your mum and I are considering carefully, and of course we want to know what you think as well. He's buying a place in France and needs to make some capital, so he's putting Rose Harbour Cottage on the market. He wanted to know if we were interested. What your mother and I thought was that we could have it as a holiday home. I need to slow down a bit, take note of the warning signals my body's been giving me lately, so we thought I'd go part time at the hospital. We'd spend most of the year in London, but summer and the odd weekend down here. Best of both worlds. What do you think?'

'Yes . . . Best of both worlds,' I said.

Izzie was right, I thought, as we walked on and chatted about the cottage. I can't object to something that will be so good for Mum and Dad because I'm a coward. I can't run away from what I fear. If we're going to be down here for summers and the odd weekend, there were two people I was bound to bump into from time to time and I'd have to sort things out with them sooner or later.

Ollie and Cat.

Gulp.

Be true to yourself and honest with everyone else.
Mystic Iz

Chapter 14

Coming Clean

I answered Hannah's e-mails the moment I got home from Cornwall, and put her in the picture. Then it was out the door and off to see Lucy, Nesta and Izzie. I didn't even unpack. It was straight round to Nesta's, where we'd all arranged to meet for a proper catch-up.

Nesta was dying to show the photos she'd taken on her digicam. 'So you can see exactly what I've been up to,' she said.

'You'd be a rubbish travel journalist,' I said as I scrolled through. 'All of these are close-ups of William. None of them show the location.'

Nesta laughed. 'He was the most interesting part of the landscape. Come on, then, show us yours.'

I got my camera out and showed them my pics of the Rame Peninsula, although I'd already e-mailed some of them through from the computer down at the cottage. All of the girls were up for going there in the summer.

'I've asked Mum and Dad already,' said Lucy. 'And they're into the idea as they spent their honeymoon down there and want to go back. Steve and Lal like the idea too.'

'I think Mum and Angus want to go to some château in France this summer, so I don't know if I can come with you,' said Izzie.

'There is room at the cottage,' I said. 'You could come with us and then your mum wouldn't need to worry.'

'Good plan, Batgirl,' said Izzie. 'And then Mum and Angus can go and do their Frenchie thing *sans* teen. She'd probably love that. What about you, Nesta?'

Nesta sighed and draped herself on her bed. 'I don't know if I could bear to be apart from William for too long, and Mum and Dad have been talking about going to Italy for a while so I'll let you know. If William has to go away with his family then of course I'll be down some time.'

'Excellent,' I said. 'I just know you're all going to love it.'

'So what are you going to do about Ollie?' asked Lucy.

'And Cat?' asked Izzie.

'And Luke?' asked Nesta.

'Who?' I asked.

Nesta gave Izzie and Lucy the nod and they grabbed pillows from Nesta's bed and began to beat me with them. I tried my best to grab one and fight back, but I didn't stand a chance.

'Hey, not fair, three against one,' I groaned, as they wrestled me to the floor and Lucy sat on my back.

'We've been giving your situation a lot of consideration while you've been away,' she said, 'and we, the council, have decided that you need to come clean with all of them. Cat, Luke and Ollie.'

'I will. I was going to. Honest.'

'When?' said Izzie.

'Oh . . . some time this week.'

'Do you have their numbers on you?' asked Nesta.

I nodded.

'So do it now,' said Nesta.

'Now? No. I . . . have to think about it. What to say and all that.'

Lucy shook her head. 'The more you think about it, the more scary it will seem. Do it now. Remember my mum's saying, don't put off until tomorrow what you can do today.'

'I can't. You're all here. I can't do it while you're all listening in. You'll make me laugh.'

'Promise we won't,' said Nesta. 'But which one are you going to go for? Ollie or Luke.'

'Luke,' I said. It felt weird coming out with it like that to Nesta, seeing as he was her boyfriend first. I was still worried that it might all turn sour again. 'I . . . I think he wants to be with me. Just me. And so does Ollie, in a way, but not just me – I'd be one on a list and I can't do that.'

'Good,' said Nesta, 'because you're worth more than that. You deserve someone who wants you and you alone. I think it's disrespectful to you to put you on a list, like you're not special enough. And you are. And I think Luke knows it.'

'Yeah,' said Lucy. 'I think he knows he blew it with you before.'

'Yeah,' said Nesta, 'you have to tell him how you feel now. And Ollie, too. I think through all of this you've been putting them first. How they feel. What they want. Your feelings matter too, TJ. What you want.'

Nesta is so top, I thought. It was so kind of her to say what she just did and not hold any grudges about what happened in the beginning with Luke and I.

'So what are you going to say to Luke?' asked Izzie.

'Oh, I don't know. It wasn't just my fault that things went wrong . . . I don't know. I'll see how it comes out. I will try and tell him how I feel. Oh Godd*ddd*. Do I have to do it now?'

The thought of talking to Luke filled me with dread. What if what I wanted to say came out all wrong? What if we misunderstood each other again? I couldn't bear it.

Nesta stood up. 'Izzie, Lucy – in the kitchen. TJ,' she said, and then pointed to the phone on her bedside cabinet. 'Phone, and you're not allowed out until you've done them all. Luke. Cat. Ollie.'

'God, you're bossy!' I said.

Nesta grinned. 'Thanks.'

Lucy got off my back. 'She's right, though. Get it over with.'

Izzie got up and gave me the thumbs up.

And off they went.

I stared at the phone for a few moments, then got my notepad out of my bag. Who to call first?

I checked the numbers, then dialled.

Mrs Biasi's voice on their answering machine told me that no one was home. I tried Luke's mobile. It was on voicemail.

I dialled the next number.

'Hello,' said a young boy's voice a moment later.

'Er, is Cat there please?'

'CAAATTTTTTTTTTT,' the boy yelled at the other end. He was so loud he almost shattered my eardrum.

I heard footsteps. 'Hello?'

I took a deep breath and launched in.

'Hi Cat, it's me, TJ, the girl you met on the beach and I'm sorry that I didn't tell you at the time but I am the girl that Ollie was seeing behind your back but please can we be friends? I didn't know that he had a girlfriend down there and if I had known I wouldn't have gone out with him because I don't like boys who are two-timers. I don't two-time people . . . and I don't want you to think that I'm a boyfriend stealer because I'm not. I genuinely didn't know about you.'

There was a silence at the other end.

'Cat. Are you there? Say something.'

'Oh, sorry,' said Cat. 'My stupid brother was at the door trying to listen in so I had to shoo him away. Yeah, you were saying about Ollie. Yeah. I thought there was someone else, so it's good to know that I'm not crazy and imagining things. And yeah, I knew what he was like. He never said that we were an item as in girlfriend and boyfriend. It was always understood that we'd hang out in a casual way. So . . . are you going to see him again?'

'Don't think so. Not on his terms. I'll be totally honest. I was starting to like him a lot but I don't think I could continue if I knew that he was seeing other girls as well. It would do my head in.'

Cat laughed. 'Tell me about it. Have you told him you met me?'

'Not yet. I haven't spoken to him since I got back. But I will tell him. You bet I will.'

Cat laughed again. 'Hah. I'd love to be a fly on the wall when you speak to him! Listen, TJ, I'm cool. You do what you have to. I have no expectations of Ollie Axford, and to be totally honest with you back, I was thinking of calling it a day with him anyway. Same reason as you. He does my head in. It was fun for a while, but we weren't really going anywhere. I think he's one of those boys who likes a challenge, you know? He's not ready to have a proper relationship, and I am. I want more and I know that I'll never get it from him.'

'That's exactly how I feel. We deserve more than to be a number amongst many in his little black book.'

'Yeah. Right on, TJ. Us girls rule, yeah?'

'Yeah. But Cat, listen, my mates are really into coming down in the summer so I hope that we can meet up again. I hope that we can all be friends.'

'Yeah, sure,' said Cat. 'I'd like that. And now that you've called I *know* that we could be friends. That you're an honest person. To be doubly, trebly honest, after I'd met you, I saw my mates down here, you know, Becca and Ollie's sister, Lia. I said I'd met this great girl on the beach called TJ and Lia went pale. I asked why and if she knew you or something and, well, Lia can't lie to save her life and she told me that she thought Ollie had been seeing someone called TJ. So I did know it was you in the end. But I'm really glad you called and told me yourself.'

'I should have done it on the beach but . . . sometimes I panic and I was scared you'd hate me.'

'Nah,' said Cat. 'I wouldn't have hated you, although I have to admit I was a bit jealous when I found out. OK, a lot jealous, but then again it showed me what being involved with Ollie would always be like. I don't want to get in too deep with him if it's forever going to throw up that kind of emotion. I want to move on from that and find some guy who adores me and only me and doesn't need to see other people. Know what I mean?'

'Exactly,' I said. 'I can't do the casual thing either. You know, it's funny. Ollie told me all about Lia and I really wanted to meet her, but she was never there when we went up to the house. Now I know why. I guess he didn't want us to meet because he knew she was a mate of yours.'

'Probably. So listen, I've got to go . . . My dad's doing supper and it smells like he's burned something as usual. Stay in touch and see you in the summer, hey?'

'Will do,' I said. 'And good luck finding the right guy.'

'You too, TJ.'

We swapped e-mail addresses and promised to stay in touch. I felt so much better when I put down the phone. I'd been dreading the call, but Cat was cool about the whole situation. And talking to her had made it much clearer what I felt about Ollie. I did like him, but she was right – a relationship with him could never go anywhere. He was a player, and involvement with him would always be a rollercoaster of emotions. Not for me, I thought, as I dialled Luke's mobile again.

It was still on voicemail. I didn't leave a message.

I was about to dial Ollie's number, but then I thought, no, I'd text him. Cool. Calm. Collected.

HI OLY. BK IN LNDN. MET CAT IN CRNWL. CU L8R.

I was about to send it when I thought, no, I'm being a coward again. I can do this. My feelings matter too, and I need to express them. I need to come clean with him and talk to him in person.

I deleted my message and dialled his mobile.

'Hello, stranger,' he said.

'Er, hi, yeah. It's TJ.'

Ollie laughed. 'I know that. I know your voice. Plus your number came up on my mobile. So when did you get back?'

'Earlier. Listen, Ollie, I need to ask you something.'

'Shoot.'

'Er . . . do you have a girlfriend down in Cornwall?'

He was silent for a moment. 'Why do you ask?'

'Oh just . . . well, we never talked about stuff like that. For all I know you may be engaged or have been with someone for ages.'

Ollie laughed again. 'Actually, I'm married with four kids, but I didn't want to tell you in case it put you off.'

'Seriously, Ollie. I need to know.'

'Right. OK. Serious. Do I have a girlfriend in Cornwall? Yes. I have a few girls who are friends in Cornwall. And a few more up here.'

'You know what I mean. *Girlfriend* girlfriend.'

'You mean as in exclusive?'

'Yes.'

'No.'

'OK, so who's Cat then?'

'Ah. Now I'm beginning to get the picture . . .'

'So am I. We met on the beach in Cawsand and . . . well, put it this way, put two and two together.'

'Cat's a mate,' said Ollie. 'A good mate. We never said we wouldn't see anyone else.'

'I know. She told me that.'

'So what's the problem?'

'Well, what about us?' I asked. 'Are we just mates?'

I could hear Ollie sigh at the other end of the phone. Tough, I thought. I know boys hate conversations like this, but I didn't care. I wanted to know what he had to say.

'What about us? I don't know, TJ. We're having a good time, aren't we? Hanging out.'

'Yes.'

'And I told you that I really liked you. I meant it. I think you're really cool. What else do you want?'

I had to think for a moment. What did I want from Ollie? Commitment? To be his one and only? And he to be mine? I wasn't sure. All I knew was that I didn't want to be one of many.

'Actually, I don't want anything,' I said. 'At least, not anything you can give at the present time, I don't think. It's cool. It really is. I just wanted to know where we stood. Where I stood. So thanks. Thanks for being honest.'

'Anytime. So now you're back, want to get together next week?'

'Er . . . probably not,' I said. 'I'll be honest, too. I can't do the let's hang out and see where it goes type of thing. You were beginning to be more than a mate to me, and if you don't feel the same way then I can't see the point of us hanging out. It would do my head in. So sorry, no can do.'

'Oh,' said Ollie. He sounded surprised. 'But . . .'

'Later,' I said. 'I really enjoyed the time we spent together.'

'Me too. But . . .' Ollie stuttered.

'Later, hey.'

And then I hung up. It felt great to have said what I wanted to and not to worry about what he did or didn't think. Nesta was right. My feelings mattered too, and my main feeling was that I wanted a guy who wanted me and me alone.

Phew, I thought as I put the phone back. Done. Dusted.

Almost.

I got up to go and find the others in the kitchen, but when I got there, it was empty. The French doors leading to Nesta's garden were open and I could hear voices.

I followed the sound of the voices and found Izzie, Lucy, Nesta and William standing by the gate that led to the road. They all looked very shifty.

'Ah, TJ. Er . . . finished?' asked Nesta.

'Almost,' I said. 'Hi, William.'

William shuffled about on his feet as if he was uncomfortable about something. 'Er . . . hi,' he said. 'Er . . .'

'Yes. Right,' said Nesta. 'We're just going down the shop to get some . . . milk.'

'Yes. Milk,' said Izzie and opened the gate.

What was going on? I wondered. Everyone was acting very strangely.

'I'll come with you,' said Lucy as she went to join Izzie. 'Later, TJ.'

'But I'll come too,' I said.

'No!' said Nesta. 'You stay here. In case . . . er, we're expecting a delivery. Can you stay and open the door?'

'But where's your mum and dad? And Tony?'

'All out,' said Nesta as she hauled William out of the back gate. 'Go, TJ. Back inside. Go. Inside. Go. Answer door.'

'But . . . hey, can't one of you stay with me?' I called after them.

Izzie shrugged. 'We've got to get a *lot* of milk,' she said, then sniggered and disappeared behind the hedge besides the gate.

And then I heard them all laughing.

What on earth were they up to?

After they'd gone, I went back into the flat and went to sit in the living room. I was flicking through a magazine when I heard the front doorbell go.

Ah, the mysterious delivery, I thought, as I got up to answer.

I went into the hall and opened the door.

It wasn't a delivery.

It was Luke.

Don't put off until tomorrow what you can do today.

Chapter 15

Summer Sizzler

'I think Dad might have had a personality transplant the last time he was in the hospital,' I said as I watched Dad in the garden. He was wearing a Homer Simpson apron and was busy cooking sausages (vegetarian soya!) and chicken legs on the barbecue. 'Either that or he's been taken over by aliens.'

'Well, he looks the same,' said Izzie, 'but you're right, there is something different, and I don't just mean the apron.'

'He's smiling,' said Lucy. 'That's what it is.'

'Yeah,' said Nesta. 'And at us, too. It's worrying, isn't it?'

We'd been back in London a week, and Dad had been acting peculiarly from the moment we got home.

On Monday while I was at school, he'd gone out with Mum and bought a barbecue and two mobile phones.

'His and hers,' he said with a grin as he held the phones up to show me. 'Latest technology. Man in the shop says it does everything. I can text on it, speak into it. I think it even turns into a helicopter if I can only work out how to use it.'

'And the barbecue?' I asked. 'You always disapproved of them. Excuse to undercook meat and make a lot of noise that annoys the neighbours you always said.'

'I'm a new man,' said Dad. 'Life is short. Seize the day and all that, that's my new philosophy. So this Saturday, invite all your friends. Lucy and Nesta and Izzie. And their parents. And be sure to ask that nice Mr Lovering who owns the health shop. See if he can come with his wife. Yes. We'll have a party.'

It was then that I knew something was seriously wrong. Dad didn't do barbecues. He didn't do parties. If by any chance he had to attend a social gathering, he'd put himself in a corner from where he would scowl and be grumpy and growl at people.

But buying the barbecue and phones was only the start of his new persona.

On Tuesday, after talking to his solicitor, he put in an offer on Rose Harbour cottage. 'Looks like it's in the bag,' he said when I got home from school. 'We have us a holiday home. I'll put on the kettle and we can celebrate. Oh ha ha, I'll put on the kettle, bet it won't suit me.'

Mum and I exchanged anxious looks. Dad making jokes? Even making bad ones was a novelty for him.

On Wednesday, I returned home wondering what he'd have bought that day while I was out. I wasn't disappointed. He'd got us cable TV.

'Seventy channels plus all the film channels,' he said.

'But Dad, you always said that people have better things to do with their time than sit about watching TV,' I said.

'Changed my mind,' he said, grinning. 'Now that I'm going to be relaxing a bit more, I can catch up with all the movies I've missed over the years. And I'm going to get myself one of those comfy footstools so that I can put my feet up while I'm doing it.'

Thursday and Friday were even stranger. I found him with his nose in recipe books preparing for Saturday. Dad had never so much as boiled an egg before and now, today, he was out there being King of the Barbecue, with a big smile on his face, handing out drinks, cooking fish and meat and discussing how to marinate a courgette with Lucy's dad.

Miracles will never cease.

Everybody came. Lucy's mum and dad. Her brothers, Steve and Lal. Nesta's mum and dad. Tony. Izzie's mum and her stepfather Angus. And William. And Luke.

When I'd found him standing on the doorstep at Nesta's last week, I soon realised that I'd been set up. To begin with it had felt awkward and neither of us seemed to know what to say. It was Luke who'd plunged in first.

'I'm so sorry about the other week,' he said. 'You must have thought I was a total jerk.'

'Not really,' I said. 'I . . . well . . . OK, I did. You didn't let me explain. See, Ollie . . . I only met him a short time ago. We weren't even seriously dating or anything. I . . .'

'I know. I jumped to all the wrong conclusions. I'm so sorry. I thought you'd set me up . . .'

'What, like Nesta did to both of us just now?'

Luke smiled. 'Yeah. Er . . . hope you don't mind. I asked her to let me know when you were back. I've been thinking about you all week and . . .'

He was looking at me with such tenderness, I felt myself starting to melt.

'I wouldn't have set you up to hurt you,' I said. 'I'm not like that.'

'I know. I should have known. I . . .'

I took a step towards him. I couldn't help it. Whenever he was in close proximity he was like a magnet, and I was helpless to resist. 'One question, Luke,' I said as we stood so close I could see how black and dilated his pupils were.

'Sure. Anything.'

'Is there anyone else in your life at the moment. I mean, any other girls?'

'No. Same question to you. Is there in your life?'

I was about to say, no, no girls in my life either, but it didn't feel like the time for jokes. It felt too intense. Serious. I shook my head.

Luke sighed with relief and smiled. 'Good,' he said, 'because I think we got off to a bad start. Me being with Nesta and even before that a whole load of different girls. But I knew there was something special as soon as I met you. I'd really like to spend more time with you, TJ. Get to know you better. That is, if you'd like to.'

I couldn't bear it any longer. I put my arms around his neck and kissed him.

A few seconds later, I heard the sound of cheering. Izzie, Lucy, Nesta and William were all standing at the front gate grinning like idiots. I don't believe it, I thought. Will we *ever* get a chance to snog without being interrupted?

We did.

Monday after school.

Tuesday after school.

Wednesday after Luke's shift at the restaurant.

Thursday before Luke went off to his acting class.

Friday before we both went off to catch up on homework.

And today he came to the barbecue and met Mum and Dad and just about everyone else I know. This time we're out in the open. A couple. No secrets.

As we sat around the garden, our plates piled high with burgers and salads and baked potatoes, I looked around me. The sun was shining down. The forecast was that it was going to continue and we were in for a sizzling summer. Lucy with Tony, Nesta with William. Luke chatting away to Izzie. Everyone seemed to be smiling. This is one of those precious moments, I thought. I'm with the people I love. Everyone is well. Who knows what the future holds for any of us? All we can be sure of is that everything changes. Life never stays still. Up and down we go. People come and go into our lives. Boys come and go into our lives.

I noticed Lucy looking at me quizzically.

'What are you thinking, TJ?' she asked.

'Oh you know, just that everything changes . . .'

'Some things,' she said, and put her hand on the table. 'But some things stay the same. Like us guys. Mates forever.'

I put my hand over hers. 'Mates forever,' I said.

Izzie put her hand over mine.

And Nesta put hers over Izzie's.

I looked up at the sky. I don't know much about what's out there or where it all came from or why. And I still don't know if there's anyone like a God up there after space or in some heaven looking down. But I do know that here, where I am, planet earth, this three-dimensional wonderland, life can be good sometimes. So my philosophy is going to be Hannah's philosophy. Dad's new philosophy. To seize the day. Appreciate. Enjoy life. To experience it all to the best of my ability, and maybe the big questions will get answered along the way. Maybe. Maybe not. In the meantime, there's the rest of the summer to look forward to. A holiday in Cornwall. I've got a great family and the best bunch of mates ever. I must always remember to let them know that's what I think while we are all here. And not just on days like this.

I looked down at the table.

Four hands. Four friends. Forever.

E-mail: **Inbox (1)**
To: <u>babewithbrains@psnet.co.uk</u>
From: <u>grooviechick@firstmail.com</u>
Date: 10th June
Subject: Summer

Hey TJ,
Spoke to Mac. Told him all about you. There are rooms free at his mum's place in July and August, so we're all set for your visit down here. The long-range weather is for hot and hotter. Hope you're still planning to come. My mates can't wait to meet yours, and Mac is already having fantasies about Izzie. Tee hee.

Cat
XXX

It may be the end of the Mates, Dates series, but Lucy, Nesta, Izzie and TJ are starting to appear in Cathy Hopkins's other series TRUTH, DARE, KISS OR PROMISE!

LOVE LOTTERY sees the Mates, Dates characters take a trip to the Rame Peninsula where one of them gets a most unusual welcome! The London crowd soon discover that they have a lot in common with the Cornish gang and Becca in particular finds that her new friends can help her through a turbulent time in her life.

And in the very last TRUTH, DARE, KISS OR PROMISE book – ALL MATES TOGETHER – Lucy, Nesta, Izzie and TJ spend a few weeks in the summer with Cat and her friends Lia, Mac, Squidge and Becca. Romance is definitely on the cards!

The complete

Mates, Dates

The MATES, DATES series

1. Mates, Dates and Inflatable Bras
2. Mates, Dates and Cosmic Kisses
3. Mates, Dates and Portobello Princesses
4. Mates, Dates and Sleepover Secrets
5. Mates, Dates and Sole Survivors
6. Mates, Dates and Mad Mistakes
7. Mates, Dates and Pulling Power
8. Mates, Dates and Tempting Trouble
9. Mates, Dates and Great Escapes
10. Mates, Dates and Chocolate Cheats
11. Mates, Dates and Diamond Destiny
12. Mates, Dates and Sizzling Summers

Companion Books:
Mates, Dates The Secret Story
Mates, Dates Guide to Life
Mates, Dates and You
Mates, Dates Journal
Mates, Dates and Flirting
Mates, Dates and Saving the Planet

What would you do if you had to tell the complete **truth** for a day? Would you **dare** enter a national singing competition? Could you cope with what happens when you **kiss** the school heart-throb? Could you **promise** to be faithful, whatever form temptation takes?

Becca, Cat, Lia, Squidge and Mac all enjoy playing the *Truth, Dare, Kiss or Promise* game to liven up their lives – but they can never predict where it's going to lead them!

The TRUTH, DARE, KISS, PROMISE series

www.cathyhopkins.com

Like this book?

Become a mate today!

Join **CATHY'S CLUB** and be the first to get the lowdown on the LATEST NEWS, BOOKS and FAB COMPETITIONS straight to your mobile and e-mail.

PLUS there's a FREE MOBILE WALLPAPER when you sign up! What are you waiting for?

Simply text MATE plus your date of birth (ddmmyyyy) to 60022 now! Or go to www.cathyhopkins.com and sign up online.

Once you've signed up keep your eyes peeled for exclusive chapter previews, cool downloads, freebies and heaps more fun stuff all coming your way.

☆

www.piccadillypress.co.uk

☆ The latest news on forthcoming books

☆ Chapter previews

☆ Author biographies

☆ Fun quizzes

☆ Reader reviews

☆ Competitions and fab prizes

☆ Book features and cool downloads

☆ And much, much more . . .

Log on and check it out!

Piccadilly Press